John Francis H. Claiborne

Life and Correspondence

of John A. Quitman - Vol. 2

John Francis H. Claiborne

Life and Correspondence
of John A. Quitman - Vol. 2

ISBN/EAN: 9783337399900

Printed in Europe, USA, Canada, Australia, Japan

Cover: Foto ©Andreas Hilbeck / pixelio.de

More available books at **www.hansebooks.com**

LIFE AND CORRESPONDENCE

OF

JOHN A. QUITMAN,

MAJOR-GENERAL, U.S.A., AND GOVERNOR OF THE STATE OF
MISSISSIPPI.

BY

J. F. H. CLAIBORNE.

IN TWO VOLUMES.

VOL. II.

NEW YORK:
HARPER & BROTHERS, PUBLISHERS,
FRANKLIN SQUARE.
1860.

Entered, according to Act of Congress, in the year one thousand eight hundred and sixty, by

HARPER & BROTHERS,

In the Clerk's Office of the District Court of the Southern District of New York.

CONTENTS OF VOL. II.

CHAPTER XVII.

CHAPTER XVIII.

CHAPTER XIX.

CHAPTER XX.

APPENDIX.

LIFE AND CORRESPONDENCE

OF

JOHN A. QUITMAN.

CHAPTER XIV.

Visits Washington.—Plan for the Occupation of Mexico.—Opposition to Southern Expansion the Motive for the Peace.—Applies for his Brevet.—His Opinion of the Regular Army.—Quitman and the Vice-presidency.—Gen. Butler.—Presentation of a Sword.—Nominated for Governor.—Election.—Inaugural.—Political Movements in Mississippi.—Union of Parties.—Judge Sharkey.—Conventions. —The Adjustment or Omnibus Bill.—President Taylor.—Secret Call upon the President.—His Inflexibility.—Civil War imminent. —Views of Gov. Quitman.—Gov. Seabrook.—Position of South Carolina. — Gen. Henderson, of Texas. — Letter to Hon. John J. M'Rae.—Convenes the Legislature. — His Message. — Action of that Body.

On his arrival at Washington Gen. Quitman urged upon the President and secretary of war the permanent military occupation of Mexico, and showed that it might be held without expense to the United States, and with but temporary opposition from the Mexican people.

"how shall we occupy mexico?

"To occupy the whole country in detail would be liable to several objections.

"It would require a great increase of force and much expense.

"Such occupation would be likely to offend and irritate the people, and thus provoke hostilities which might be avoided.

"It would demoralize the army, and, by dispersing it, render impracticable those regulations necessary for its subordination and good discipline.

"For the same reasons it would endanger the safety of the smaller detachments.

"I am of opinion that we should occupy only a limited number of positions in the vital parts of the country, to be selected principally with a view to revenue, consulting at the same time the security of the posts, which includes the preservation of communication between them.

"The most palpable sources of revenue are,

"Duties on imports.

"Imposts on the assaying, coining, and export of the precious metals.

"Direct taxes.

"To realize to the fullest extent the first, we should occupy positions commanding the internal trade of the great sea-ports. The city of Mexico bears this relation to Vera Cruz; San Luis Potosi to Tampico; Orizaba and Tehuacan to Alvarado. These cities should be held, and an open communication preserved to their respective ports.

"To command the revenue from the mines, the cities of Zacatecas, Guanaxuato, and Queretaro should be occupied.

"Zacatecas, San Luis Potosi, Zula, and Tampico, constituting a military line, would require 8000 men, distributed as follows:

"Zacatecas and San Luis, 2500 each; Zula and Tampico, 1000 each; and 1000 movable.

"Guanaxuato and Queretaro, on line in communication with Mexico, 2500 each.

"Mexico, Puebla, Perote, Jalapa, Puente National, and Vera Cruz, 13,000, distributed as follows:

"Mexico, 5000; Puebla, 2500; Perote, 800; Jalapa, 1200; Puente National, 500; Vera Cruz, 1000; movable, 2000. Total, 13,000.

"Orizaba and Tehuacan, 2000.

"The whole number of troops required under this disposition of the forces would be 28,000 men.

"The occupation of a line from Zacatecas to Tampico would render it unnecessary to hold Monterey and Saltillo, or to keep open the communication between those points and the Rio Grande.

"The above estimate does not include any forces required for the Rio Grande or Pacific frontier."

These views were plausible, popular, and demonstrative; but two causes operated to defeat their adoption. First, the jealousy of Southern expansion common to all parties in the non-slaveholding states — a jealousy the most absurd on the part of a manufacturing and commercial people. Secondly, it had become apparent that the acquisition of territory would be followed by a demand for the exclusion of slavery therefrom; and although it was obvious that, in the course of events, a contest upon that demand was inevitable, and that it should be met at once, nevertheless, many Southern statesmen concluded that it "was better to bear the ills we have than fly to those we know not of." This jealousy and these apprehensions, encouraged by the constitutional timidity of President Polk, who was then cherishing the hope of a re-election, soon brought the war to a close, and we surrendered a conquest more glorious, more available for great national purposes, and more important to the commerce of the world than any that has been won since the days of imperial Rome.

Quitman had gone to Washington with expanded views, which are farther revealed in the extracts that follow from a letter to his former aid, Lieut. Lovell:

"Upon opening my budget to the President he immediately condemned the whole course of Gen. Scott in refusing to give me a full division, so long as I was on duty with him, and promised me for the future it should be corrected. He went so far as to say that I might select such position in the army, consistent with my rank, as I might choose. I immediately expressed my preference for the command of the Army of Occupapation (Gen. Taylor's district), if I might be permitted to establish my head-quarters at San Luis Potosi. *This he promised*, if, by the passage of the Ten Regiment Bill, that force could be strengthened by the addition of another brigade. I remained awaiting the result until the news of Trist's treaty, first received by private intelligence, and soon afterward officially communicated, put a stop to the bill. I, of course, remained to witness the fate of the treaty in the Senate. At first it seemed to be unfavorably regarded by the Democrats, but gradually gained strength, and was ratified. Quite confident in my own mind that the inducements held out to the half-starved Mexicans of securing $15,000,000, and the possession of their capital, and their sources of revenue, will assure the acceptance of the treaty as modified by the Senate, I applied for leave to return home, and there await the course of events."

His Position at home and future Views.

"I am now safely stowed in my own arm-chair in my library, quite certain that my next important movement will be to resign my sword and resume the occupations of peaceful life. I shall be well content here in my quiet nook to moor my bark. The gales of popular favor have, however, blown so strong upon me, I do not know but I may be compelled to launch out upon the tempestuous ocean of politics. If I must incur the hazard of a storm, give me a wide sea and a flowing sail. I would rather go down gloriously, engulfed by a mountain wave on the great deep, than be swamped in the surf of the sea-shore. My receptions every where have been enthusiastic in the extreme. No description reaches the reality. These manifestations are embarrassing, and I avoid them whenever it is possible. I have declined over one hundred invitations to public dinners and ceremonies."

Refutes the Charge that he was hostile to the regular Service.

"I have always received these public attentions as a tribute of respect for the gallant American army which has shed such lustre upon our arms. This reminds me that Lieut. Wilcox, whom I met in Baltimore, informed me that there was a report in circulation about Twiggs's head-quarters, Vera Cruz, that, in a speech at Charleston, I declared that I had joined the army for the express purpose of showing that volunteers were superior to regulars, and that events had proved the truth of my position. I have since learned that something of this kind is reported in the Charleston papers. I have never seen it, or I should deem it worthy of contradiction. Such a sentiment was never uttered by me. I would not state what I do not believe. In speaking of the army and its deeds I have never dissimulated, always ascribing its successes in part to the skill and gallantry of its commanders, in part to the military science diffused by the national military school, and in part to the general effects of our free institutions. A speech delivered in the open air, amid the tumult of an immense crowd, may be easily misinterpreted; but I feel seriously concerned that any officer of the army would do me the injustice to attribute such a sentiment to me."

Not in Mr. Polk's Confidence.

"You are long since informed of the course which the War Department has thought fit to pursue in relation to the difficulties between some of the generals. Though Shields and myself were at Washington when the information came, we were not consulted. At the request of Lieut. Col. Duncan I suggested the propriety of having his trial ordered in the United States, but could not ascertain the views of the President. I have never even seen the list of brevets, or been in any way consulted in respect to them. While the President treated me with politeness (of course), I did not possess his confidence. Just as I was leaving the secretary of war apologized for not having shown me the list of brevets, but requested me to write to him should I find any omissions.

From their great want of official candor and trust, I have troubled them with few applications."

In relation to his own case, the neglect of which subjected him to just mortification, he had addressed the secretary of war as follows:

(*Unofficial.*)   "U. S. Hotel, Washington, June 4th, 1848.

"SIR,—My departure in the morning to attend the Court of Inquiry at Frederick compels me to say in writing what I would have preferred saying in person. Both you and the President have declared that you consider me entitled to the usual mark of merit for services at Monterey. Why have I not received it? While the President doubted his authority to confer brevets on officers appointed to command the volunteers, the question might be satisfactorily answered. But since he has solved his doubts by conferring brevets on officers similarly conditioned, there is no apparent cause for the delay; and the inference will be either that I am unworthy of the distinction, or that justice is withheld from me. The omission being unexplained, he or I must suffer in history. Most likely my reputation will have to suffer his apparent judgment against my merits, though only three days ago, in the presence of the Hon. R. J. Walker, he acknowledged my right, and declared he would confer with you on the subject. I have been silent while there appeared to be a reason for the omission. I now claim it of you to present the case to the President. I submit to you whether, considering all that has occurred, and the alleged causes for which brevets have been conferred, there will not be upon my conduct at Monterey an implied censure; to repel which, and to protect my reputation hereafter, I shall be obliged to collect and preserve the evidence of the officers of the army present in those actions, that the facts of history may not be perverted.

"Whatever may be done in this case I desire may be done promptly, and before the end of the war, which now seems very near."

On the 7th of Sept. following he received his commis-

sion as brevet major general for distinguished services
at Monterey—a distinction he was pre-eminently entitled
to, but which, it is probable, he would not have received
but for his own firm assertion of his rights.

Gen. Quitman to John O. Knox, of Virginia.

"Washington, March 8th, 1848.

"I scarcely know how to reply to your friendly and
very complimentary remarks in relation to myself and
the presidency. I will, however, address you frankly,
regretting that my time will not permit me to do so
fully. You do not mistake my opinion upon the great
political questions particularly connected with Southern
interests, and which, I firmly believe, if rightly understood, would be regarded as equally the interests of the
whole Union. I am thoroughly a free-trade man, believing that capital, industry, enterprise, and intellect
should be left as free as the air we breathe. Our country may not be ripe for that just and righteous mode of
raising revenue necessary for defraying the current expenditures by an equal tax on all descriptions of property; but while customs are resorted to, trade and commerce should not be burdened for any other purpose
than mere necessary revenue on a scale of frugal expenditure.

"From the time that the idea was first suggested in
Congress by a state-rights member from Virginia, I have
ever been the warm advocate of the independent treasury, specie provision and all. As early as 1831, while a
member of the convention to revise the Constitution of
Mississippi, I introduced a proposition to separate, then
and forever, the government and the banks. I proposed
that the Legislature should be absolutely prohibited from
borrowing money, or pledging the faith of the state for
banking purposes. With these principles of public policy, I am, of course, utterly opposed to a national bank,
even were it authorized by the Constitution.

"In relation to the war with Mexico, it was undoubtedly the duty of the President, in the absence of any specific legislation, to occupy and protect the territory of the
State of Texas. She had established, in the exercise of

her sovereign power, the western bank of the Rio Grande as her frontier; and the President, in my opinion, would have been liable to impeachment had he failed to exert his military power to defend and protect it. Our troops were attacked within our territory, and thus a state of war ensued. Being brought about by the act of Mexico, and accepted by our national authorities, it should be prosecuted with the energy and vigor worthy of a great nation until the enemy shall propose satisfactory terms. If Mexico refuses to offer suitable terms or to submit, we should prosecute the war even to the conquest of her whole territory. I am unable to perceive the very great evils to arise from adding to our confederacy one of the most beautiful and productive countries on the face of the earth, abounding in agricultural and mineral wealth, and possessing withal the power of taxing the commerce of the world by the junction of two oceans. If we can not make peace on the proper terms, I would occupy with a sufficient force the vital parts of Mexico, principally with a view to revenue, and extract from it, by a proper system of taxation, enough to defray all the expenses of occupation. Finally, if peace should not be made, I would organize the country into civil departments, with a view to its permanent annexation.

"These are bold views, but I am persuaded they are practicable. The subject is one upon which volumes might be written, but my time forbids, and I only fear that my attempt at brevity will render me unintelligible."

In the National Democratic Convention that assembled this year in Baltimore Quitman was strongly pressed for the vice-presidency. He had more personal strength and popularity in that body than any other man in nomination, but was defeated mainly by one of those combinations that seem to be unavoidable in bodies thus organized, with so many conflicting sections and claims to reconcile. He attributed his defeat in part to citizens of his own state, and has left an elaborate memorandum of the whole affair. It is useless, however, to revive a controversy when most of the parties are in the grave.

In a letter to his friend, Capt. John B. Nevitt, of Natchez, he thus refers to the subject:

"Washington, June 9th, 1848.

"Having given my testimony before the Court of Inquiry, I am now here attending to some official business demanded by my approaching retirement from the army. You will have heard of the nominations of the Baltimore Convention. I heartily approve of them. Gen. Butler had higher claims and merits than I for the vice-presidency, and I was not disappointed. He is every inch a man, and I hope the Democracy of Mississippi will sustain him with all their energies. I have but to regret what I learn from many sources, that —— was very busy in his efforts to prejudice the delegates against me, reiterating the old falsehood that I had been a Whig, and that my name would weaken the ticket in Mississippi; —— was also active against me. I feel complimented by the vote I received; and I am told, had not this nomination been mixed up with the presidency, I should have been nominated. Taylor and Fillmore have just been nominated by the Whigs: we must be prepared for them."

To Gen. Shields.

"Monmouth, Sept. 9th, 1848.

"MY DEAR SIR,—I perceive from the papers that you are still attracting public attention. I learn, too, from my correspondents that there is little doubt that, in spite of the hostility of some high functionaries at Washington, you will be returned to the Senate from Illinois. I give you my hand upon your prompt rejection of the honor of exile, which our cool and calculating friend the President was disposed to confer on you. It would be a very convenient thing if our President possessed the power of sending, '*nolus volus*,' as Gen. Taylor would say, every popular man across the Rocky Mountains. I hope to see you in the Senate. In the trying times that are before us, I, as well as all your friends in the South, believe you would be as true to us and to the Union as is your excellent friend Douglas.

"I am doing all I can for Cass and Butler, and think they will overrun Mr. Polk's majorities. Since my return from Washington I have been quietly engaged in reducing to system the chaos of my neglected affairs. I shall soon glide out of the memory of the public, but shall not be forgotten, I hope, by my personal friends."

From General Butler.

"Carrollton, Ky., Oct. 22d, 1848.

"My dear General,—I had the gratification of receiving your kind and welcome letter, written on the anniversary of the battle of Monterey, a day that will never be forgotten by either of us, and well deserves to be remembered by our country. * * * * * * Kentucky has presented me a splendid sword for my conduct in that battle. I accepted it, not for myself alone, but as an honor conferred equally upon the officers and soldiers of my gallant division, in the name of those who fell and those who conquered at Monterey. And believe me when I say that, of all that noble band, there is not one for whom I entertain so high a regard as for him who led my second brigade to victory.

"When I reached Washington, immediately after my first return from Mexico, I was mortified and vexed to find that justice had not been done to the volunteers, and rank injustice to your immediate command. The old slander that there was no enemy in Fort Teneria when you stormed it was in busy circulation. I promptly put down the calumny and demanded for you a brevet. Congress was not in session, and the President did not think he had the power to confer a brevet until the meeting of the next Congress. (*Why had he not done it before?*) He moreover doubted his power to confer brevets upon the new appointments. In a few days, however, he did me the honor to consult me as to the appointments of the major generals for the command of the additional forces of the regular army, and I placed your name at the head. I am happy to believe that my recommendation prevailed. For this you owe me no thanks. I performed an act of simple justice.

"It has been a source of regret to me that our friends in the Baltimore Convention placed us in a position where we might be considered as rival candidates for office. Had we been present it would not have been done. Judging by myself, it did not require your letter to assure me that this state of things could produce no change in our kindly relations."

On the 2d of December the citizens of Natchez and the adjacent country assembled to witness the presentation of the sword voted to Quitman by Congress for his conduct at Monterey.* It was presented by James S. Johnston, Esq., of Jefferson County, in behalf of the President of the United States. After a brilliant summary of his military career, the eloquent speaker concluded as follows:

"To a magnanimous mind like yours, general, the consciousness of having done your duty, and your whole

---

*   *General Quitman's Swords.*

1. *Sword presented by Congress.*—Heavily embossed gold scabbard, the hilt set with two large jewels, one in the head and one on the guard, and ornamented with reliefs representing the storming of Monterey, and a group of American arms wound round with a scroll, on which are these words: " Storming of Monterey, 21st, 22d, and 23d Sept., 1846." On the scabbard: " Presented by the President of the United States, agreeable to a resolution of Congress, to Brig. Gen. John A. Quitman, in testimony of the high sense entertained by Congress of his gallantry and good conduct in the storming of Monterey. Resolution approved March 2d, 1847."

2. *Sword presented by the Citizens of Natchez and Adams County.*—Gold scabbard, the hilt of alternate rows of gold and pearl, studded with buttons of gold; on the top an eagle's head of solid gold, crowned with a large jewel; the eyes jewels. On the guard a group of arms and banners, in the midst of which sparkles a brilliant, illuminating the inscription: "Presented to Maj. Gen. John A. Quitman by his fellow-citizens of Adams County and the City of Natchez, as a meed due to his gallantry at the storming of Monterey, the battles of Chapultepec, and Garita de Belen, in which he gloriously sustained his own character, the character of his state, and of his country."

3. *Sword presented by Citizens of Charleston.*—Hilt and scabbard of gold, with devices of the Palmetto richly chased on scabbard and guard, with this inscription: "Presented to Gen. Quitman by the German and United German Fusileer Companies of Charleston, South Carolina."

4. *Sword worn by General Q. in the War with Mexico ; made by F. W. Widman, Philadelphia.*—The scabbard of brass, with armorial devices; hilt mother-of-pearl wound with a gold cord, and surmounted with a knight's head, crest, and helmet, and vizor down. The form of the hilt is a Maltese cross. This sword is bronzed with the smoke of battle, and on the blade are the traces and stains of blood.

duty, to your country, in the hour of her trial and danger, is alone and of itself an all-sufficient reward. The *patriot* claims no equivalent, demands no satisfaction, to compensate him for the sacrifices and sufferings he endures in his country's defense. But, sir, while a grateful and approving government proffers to you no *reward* for your patriotic devotion, the public authorities have rightly respected the popular will, and fitly reflected the national sense and appreciation of your eminent services, by voting to you, as a *compliment,* this superb and elegant sword.

"In their name, therefore, and on their behalf, as deputed thereto, I now present you this beautiful and apposite token of the nation's gratitude. In receiving from me, as their humble organ, this delicate and sacred trust, you have already given the best and surest pledge, by your deeds, that you will never suffer the slightest stain of dishonor to tarnish the unsullied surface of its pure and polished blade, and that you will ever be ready to wear it, and, if need be, to flesh it, in defense of the nation's rights, whenever foreign aggression is to be repelled or an insolent enemy chastised.

"Accept it, then, general, as the gift of the American people ; and, like the giant's sword, which the ancients kept suspended in the sacred temple, only to be drawn down and used in times of public danger, so, sir, may this fine commemorative weapon never be unsheathed by you for use, except to punish your country's foes, or to avenge your country's wrongs."

In reply, General Quitman said:

"SIR,—I accept the elegant weapon you have been charged by the President to deliver to me with emotions of the profoundest gratitude. Were it but an oaken staff, instead of this superb and splendid sword, as a testimonial of the nation's approbation of my poor and unworthy services, it would possess a priceless value in my eyes.

"In the complimentary remarks with which you have thought proper to accompany its delivery, you have done me no more than justice by declaring that I embarked in the war from the sole patriotic motive of serving my country in what I conscientiously believed to have been a just and righteous struggle for the protection of her sacred rights.

"In hastening to her defense, I felt like one of the champions in the old mode of deciding disputes by wager of battle, ready and willing to appeal to the God of battles for the justice of our cause. It was my fortune to lead to battle and to victory the brave sons of Tennessee and Mississippi, and it is to their invincible bravery that I am indebted for all the honors my country has bestowed upon me. To them, and not to me, is due this flattering testimonial of national approval. In their name, therefore, and on their account, I am proud to accept this elegant sword as a tribute of their country's gratitude to them.

"Be pleased, sir, to convey to the President my kind acknowledgments for the very obliging and gratifying manner in which he has executed the flattering intentions of Congress toward me, and say farther to him, if you please, that he could have transmitted this handsome token to me in no way that would have been more welcome or acceptable to me than through the hands of one between whom and myself, for so many years, have subsisted mutual relations of the most cordial and intimate friendship."

The following letter was written to one of a numerous tribe in the South, an adventurer who, by practicing small courtesies and making pretexts for a gossiping correspondence with distinguished men, contrived to recommend himself to their favor, and to impress those around him with a grand idea of his influence in high quarters. He was a New Englander, and a Whig; but not being appreciated by that party, he jumped upon the Texas annexation hobby, opened a correspondence with R. J. Walker and other of its leading advocates, and obtained the ear of President Tyler, by whom he was appointed surveyor of the port of New Orleans, much to the chagrin and astonishment of the citizens, to whom he was an entire stranger. He was retained in office by President Polk. His letters, when compared, show that he was a mere political Dalgetty, who watched the rise or wane of individuals and the fluctuations of party, and regulated his friendship and his principles accordingly.

To David Hayden.

"Monmouth, July 12th, 1849.

"Your letter of the 6th inst. has been received. I was not aware before that Major Grayson had been so neglected by President Polk. No officer under Gen. Scott contributed more to our success in Mexico by his admirable administration of the commissariat. He was no less prominent for his gallantry, energy, and courtesy. He was always ready for any emergency. I will address the President on this matter. *I have, however, no influence.* My staff, and several of my most worthy and deserving friends in the army, have been treated *with marked neglect.* I have been unable to effect any thing in several cases in which I had, with no other interest than that which a strong sense of justice occasioned, applied to the President. This, however, shall not deter me from trying to serve Major G.

"You have better hopes of Gen. Taylor than I have. In my opinion, his leading measures will be Whig, ultra Whig. The old fogies of that party will not readily break with him if he consents to rob the South by a high and partial tariff, and to squander the public treasure by a brilliant system of national improvements. They will allow him to indulge some 'no party fancies' in small matters, and control all the leading measures of his administration."

In 1849 Quitman was nominated by spontaneous meetings of the people, and afterward by the State Democratic Convention, as a candidate for governor. Many of his best friends were averse to this movement, some because they doubted his capacity for administration; others who, anticipating for him a national position, did not desire to have him complicated with impending issues pregnant with strife and acrimony. His opponent, Hon. Luke Lea, made a vigorous canvass, relying chiefly on what he considered the political inconsistencies and errors of the nominee. The result was the election of Quitman by a majority of some 10,000 votes. On the 10th of January, 1850, he was sworn into office, and delivered his inaugural address. It is a brief but lucid exposition of his theory of the relations between the federal and state governments, and may be put forth as the creed of the party whose acknowledged leader he became after the death of Mr. Calhoun.*

* *Inaugural Address of Governor John A. Quitman, delivered before both houses of the Mississippi Legislature, January 10th, 1850.*

The Constitution of the state, to secure individual fidelity in the execution of public trusts, prescribes that every officer, before entering upon his duties, shall take an oath faithfully to discharge the duties of his office. Elected by the people of this state to be their chief executive magistrate, I now come before you, senators, representatives, and fellow-citizens, publicly, in the presence of the guardians of the commonwealth, to take upon myself the solemn obligation which the Constitution enjoins upon me.

I shall enter upon the discharge of my official duties with a firm determination to assume no powers refused, and to shun no responsibilities required by the Constitution and laws, and to spare no effort, by a faithful performance of my duty, to deserve the high confidence which the generous people of this state have reposed in me.

Among a free people, addresses from a public servant to his constituents should be frank and without disguise. When his opinions may affect the public welfare, they should not be concealed. I feel it my duty, therefore, in this first official address to the sovereign people of Mississippi, briefly to express my opinions upon some of the prominent questions which now appear to occupy the public mind. They will furnish the best indication of the course of policy I shall study to pursue in my official action upon all subjects.

In our union of sovereign states, there are few questions, however they may appear strictly federal, which do not sometimes demand the consideration of the respective states of the confederacy.

The members of our national union consist of equal co-ordinate sovereignties, whose interest, for good or for evil, may be affected by the federal government. They are not only entitled to exercise a watchful care over its proceedings, but when the Constitution, or the reserved rights of the states, or the people are threatened, upon the state governments especially devolves the duty of taking proper measures to defend the one and protect the other. National questions are, therefore, necessarily a part of state politics.

My views of the original structure of our government, and my interpretation of the Constitution, are strictly democratic. Regarding

In this inaugural he referred to the progress of anti-slavery sentiment in the Eastern States, and the neces-

the federal Constitution as a compact between independent political communities, acting in their character as sovereigns, it follows that the government erected by it is one of delegated powers. Over all political powers not delegated the states retained an absolute and exclusive control, with all the rights and powers necessary to maintain and preserve their sovereignty. Over these they are as supreme as if the Constitution had never been adopted. Various causes, among them national glory—because it feeds our self-esteem—are continually operating to incline the public mind toward centralism and consolidation. This is the tendency of our government; and, as our country grows in wealth, power, and importance, the contrast between the state and federal governments will become wider, and increase the danger. A frequent recurrence to the history and character of our federal system is, therefore, essential to the preservation of the state governments. In my opinion, a little jealousy on the part of state officers is commendable. The assumption of power by the federal government has already more than once produced convulsions which have shaken the strong pillars of our political temple; the failure to exercise a doubtful power has never caused alarm. The danger is from assumption, not inactivity. Construing the federal government as one of limited delegated powers, I deny its right to supervise the manufactures or the agriculture of the country, or to take under its charge and control the highways and the harbors of our broad land.

If such power be not delegated, it is a fraud upon the Constitution to attempt these objects indirectly under color of the power granted "to lay and collect duties and imposts," "to establish post-offices and post-roads," or "to regulate commerce."

I am opposed to the establishment of a United States Bank, or to the conversion of the national treasury, by ingenious modifications, into any other similar fiscal agent. The plan of collecting and disbursing the revenue by the simple machinery of the independent treasury, seems to me best suited to the simplicity of our republican institutions, and best calculated to preserve honesty and purity in the administration of the public finances. I have thought fit to allude to these questions, because they are again agitated.

Connected with our federal relations is another subject of deep and vital interest to us, in common with a large portion of our sister states of the Union, a question which, in the last few years, has assumed a momentous and startling aspect.

One half of the sovereign states of this glorious confederacy, in the exercise of the undoubted right of self-government, have chosen to retain, as a part of their elementary social system, the institution of the domestic slavery of an inferior race. This institution is entwined in our political system, and can not be separated from it without destruction to our social fabric. It has existed here since the cavaliers of Jamestown and the Puritans of Plymouth Rock first built their pilgrim fires upon the shores of America. It was recognized in the formation of the federal Constitution, and to its existence among us, as sity of timely action on the part of the South. The course of events in that quarter had already attracted

much as to any other single cause, is attributable the rapid advance of our country in its career of prosperity, greatness, and wealth.

That Supreme Being, whose all-seeing eye looks down upon the nations of the earth, has beheld and tolerated its existence among us for more than two centuries, and has poured out upon us the choicest blessings of his providence.

We do not regard it as an evil; on the contrary, we think that our prosperity, our happiness, our very political existence, is inseparably connected with it. We have a right to it above and under the Constitution of the United States. We can not give up that right. We *will* not yield it. We have a right to the quiet enjoyment of our slave property. We can not and will no longer permit that right to be disturbed. It is of those essential rights which can not be yielded up without dishonor and self-degradation. None who believe that we have inherited the free spirit of our fathers can doubt our determination, at all hazards, to maintain these positions so essential to our security.

The statesmen in the non-slaveholding states who attempt to trample upon our rights, either mistake the intelligence and spirit of the southern people, or knowingly hazard the integrity of the Union. They should know that the South is now aroused to the magnitude of the danger. We are no longer permitted to doubt that a systematic and deliberate crusade against our sacred rights is now in progress, and has assumed a character which requires us to act.

Distinguished northern statesmen have not only avowed their determination to exclude the slave interest from the protection of the Constitution, but to use all the powers which, by a broad construction of that instrument, they can assume to effect its ultimate extermination.

Some of the non-slaveholding states have, by resolutions of their Legislatures, re-echoed these pernicious doctrines, and many of them, in palpable violation of their constitutional compact, have enacted laws effectually to prevent the reclamation of fugitive slaves.

These insulting and offensive measures have not been confined to individuals or to the state governments. The halls of Congress, where northern and southern men should meet as brethren, have become the theatre of this war upon slavery. Already has the attempt been made, as is threatened to be renewed, I fear with prospects of ultimate success, to exclude the slaveholding states from an equal participation in the common territory of the states—to confine the slaveholder and the slave for all time to come to the states in which the institution now exists—to abolish negro slavery in the federal district, and to suppress the internal slave-trade between the states.

These measures, not only threatened, but actually introduced in Congress, too plainly speak the deliberate intention of their instigators to wage a war of extermination against our most valued rights. Whether they originate in fanaticism, affected philanthropy, or calculations of political power, they can have no other object than the ultimate the attention of the people of Mississippi. On the 7th of May, 1849, an imposing meeting, consisting of distin-

destruction of our domestic institutions, or the dissolution of the Union. The advocates of these destructive measures seek to perpetrate wrongs to which the people of Mississippi, of all parties, recently assembled in convention, have solemnly declared that they can not and will not submit. They cherish the Union constituted by the wisdom of our fathers; they will defend the Constitution, which established and alone maintains that Union, but they have no love or veneration for any other union than that which is written and defined in the Constitution. They are not to be deceived and robbed of their constitutional rights by men who, uttering hollow professions of attachment to the Union, are deliberately severing the ties that bind us together. Should this glorious Union perish, let the indignant patriot heap curses upon the traitors who, by destroying the compromises of the Constitution,-sapped the foundations of

"The realm,
The last and the noblest of time."

I may have dwelt too long upon this subject, but I regard it as the great, the absorbing question of the day; one which must now be met deliberately, calmly, and boldly. The South has long submitted to grievous wrongs. Dishonor, degradation, and ruin await her if she submits farther. The people of Mississippi have taken their stand, and, I doubt not, their representatives will maintain it, by providing means to meet every probable contingency. I here pledge myself firmly to execute their will to the extent of my constitutional powers.

We live, fellow-citizens, in a progressive age, marked by some of the boldest improvements in the sciences, and the most remarkable discoveries and inventions in the arts. It is the part of the political power of the state to apply these improvements to the increase of the wealth, and the promotion of the happiness of the people. If we can not reach perfection, we may approach it. The struggle, at least, is worthy the highest exertion of the human intellect. The immense resources of our yet infant state are not fully developed. A wide field for internal improvements is still open. A system of common-school education, suited to the character and condition of our country, may be established. Our jurisprudence and judicial systems are open to great reforms. The abuses of petty corporations may be corrected. Our military establishment may be rendered more efficient. Some wise and efficient provision, based upon the consent of the people, gradually to extinguish the public debt, may be matured. The revenue system may be made more equal and just, and the burden of self-government be thus alleviated. All these objects are worthy the consideration of the best talents of a state which has taken the lead among her sister states in great constitutional reforms.

With sentiments of the deepest gratitude to my fellow-citizens for the confidence reposed in me; with sincere distrust in my abilities, yet with a proud consciousness of the elevated station to which I have been chosen, as the chief magistrate of a state distinguished for the talents of her statesmen in council, and the intrepid gallantry of her guished citizens of both parties, had been held in the Capitol, Governor Matthews in the chair. They were addressed at great length by Chief-justice Sharkey, and, at his instance, the people of the respective counties were invited to send delegates to a convention on the first Monday in October, to consist of an equal number of Whigs and Democrats. In pursuance of this recommendation primary meetings were held, and, on the day designated, the convention assembled. It was composed of the most prominent men in the state, of both political organizations. Chief-justice Sharkey, long the acknowledged head of the Whig party, was chosen president by acclamation, and, on taking the chair, pronounced, with great solemnity, a carefully prepared exposition of our constitutional rights and the encroachments upon them. He concluded by reducing his argument to two interrogatories: " *The great and serious inquiry is, shall we submit to farther degradation, or shall we seek redress ? If the latter, how is it to be obtained ?*"

To ponder on these grave questions, the convention immediately adjourned. When it assembled next day, the chief justice, on taking the chair, again addressed it in amplification of his positions. These elaborate addresses, emanating from the chief of the judiciary and the leader of the Conservatives, declaimed with an official pomp and stateliness of manner that gave them the force of an oracle, at once convinced and captivated the convention. A committee of twenty, a large majority of them ultra state-rights men, was appointed by President Sharkey, who promptly presented a report (embodying the views of the chair), and a series of resolutions covering the entire controversy between the slaveholding and non-slaveholding states, asserting our rights

sons in war, I am now ready, in this presence, and before Almighty God, to take my solemn oath of office.

in the territories; recommending the Legislature to pass laws to encourage the carrying of slaves into the territories; urging the appointment of delegates to a Southern convention at Nashville to deliberate over the aggressions on our rights; and appealing to the Legislature to authorize the governor to issue his proclamation, and issue writs of election for a general convention of the people of the state, upon the passage, by Congress, of the Wilmot Proviso, or any law abolishing slavery in the District of Columbia or prohibiting the slave-trade between the states.

Chief-justice Sharkey was appointed to lead the delegation to Nashville, and, by acclamation, the same distinguished gentleman was placed at the head of the committee to address the people of the Southern States. His colleagues on this committee were A. Hutchinson, George Winchester, C. R. Clifton, W. R. Hill, John J. Guion, and E. C. Wilkinson, a brilliant galaxy of lawyers, five of whom had been upon the bench, and the majority of them what were then called state-rights or Calhoun Whigs. The address is one of the strongest papers that the unhappy controversy of the times gave birth to. It explains the theory of the Constitution; the exact relations of the federal and state governments; the origin and constitutional recognition and guarantees for negro slavery; the attacks made upon it; the danger of submission; the remedies to be applied; and concludes with an appeal to the people of the Southern States to appoint delegates to a general Southern Convention on the first Monday in June, 1850.

What is called the Compromise or Adjustment *projét* was then pending in the Senate of the United States, reported by Mr. Clay from a committee of thirteen. It provided, 1st. For the admission of California *as a state.* 2d. Territorial governments for Utah and New Mexico.

3d. For the settlement of boundaries between Texas and New Mexico. 4th. Amendments to the Fugitive Slave Bill. 5th. A bill to abolish the Slave Trade in the District of Columbia.

1. The *California Bill* excluded the South, with its slave property, from a domain acquired by our national arms, after the South had paid $60,000,000, and the non-slaveholding states but $30,000,000 of the $90,000,000 of war debt which the acquisition of California had cost. It prevented the enhanced value of at least 50 per centum upon the slave property of the South by debarring their access to the mines, which, upon the $1,200,000,000 at which the slaves at the South have been valued, would have given an aggregate increase of $600,000,000. The immutable equality of the states is a fundamental principle of the Constitution, and the California Bill, in giving the North the exclusive dominion and domain over the whole country, and forever depriving the South of both, making her pay at the same time two thirds of the cost, wholly destroyed the constitutional equality between the free and the slave states. It admitted California into the family of states, in violation of every precedent, of a solemn compact, and upon principles pregnant with danger to the Union, and even to social order.

2. *The Texas Boundary Bill.* The treaty made by Santa Anna, President of Mexico, with Gen. Sam. Houston, fixed the Rio Grande, from its mouth to its source, as the western boundary of Texas. It is true he was a prisoner at the time, though no duress or compulsion had been employed. The same treaty was signed and approved by his general-in-chief at the head of the retreating Mexican army, and Mexico ratified it by accepting the provisions it contained in her favor, viz., the release of her chief magistrate, her vanquished army, and the spoils of war. This ratification bound Mexico, but,

with proverbial treachery, she afterward broke her faith, and held on to New Mexico *east* of the Rio Grande. In her compact of annexation to the American Union Texas insisted upon the Rio Grande as her legal bound-ary, and the claim was acknowledged by our own government, and its reclamation from Mexico was one of the inducements on the part of Texas for annexation. The war with Mexico ensued; the invasion of Texas territory was the pretext; the United States drove the Mexican army and authority from New Mexico, and, of course, turned it over to the jurisdiction of Texas, whose title was just as valid as her title to any other portion of her territory. She proceeded to organize it into counties and judicial districts. But the Free-soilers of the North, finding that New Mexico was about to become a slave state, clamored against the title, resisted the jurisdiction of Texas, abetted and sustained by all the federal functionaries in New Mexico, civil and military, and President Taylor, embracing their opinions, threatened to support them against Texas with the army of the United States. Not content with this, they demanded from Texas 70,000 square miles of undisputed slave territory to add to New Mexico; and for this the bill proposed to pay her $10,000,000, of which, in reality, the South paid $6,500,000, and the North only $3,500,000, through the unequal taxation which results from collecting weekly the whole revenue through the customs.

3. *The Fugitive Slave Bill* professed fairly on its face, but was defective in two important particulars. 1st. In making no provision for the restitution to the South of the $30,000,000 of which she had been plundered through the 100,000 slaves abducted from her in the course of the last forty years. 2d. In not binding the marshal's sureties to the payment of the fine it imposes, which could not be done without a renewal of their bonds which was not provided in the bill.

4. The bill for the *Territorial Government of Utah and New Mexico* was passed upon the plea that the Mexican law interdicted slavery, and that a practical Wilmot Proviso was already in force there, and it was useless to urge upon the dominant majority that the Mexican law had been superseded by the American Constitution, which recognizes no Wilmot Proviso, and no exclusion of slave property from the territories of the United States.

5. *The abolition of the Slave Trade in the District of Columbia.* Only two years before, the conservative commonwealth of Virginia, by solemn legislative resolve, had classed this as among the measures whose passage she would "resist at every hazard, and to the last extremity." Most of the Southern States had spoken with equal emphasis the same language. The whole South insisted that Congress had no power to legislate on the subject at all, and that the abolition of slavery in the district would involve a breach of faith and of the Constitution likewise. How can it be pretended that the Constitution authorizes a discrimination against slave property, when the only discrimination it makes is in favor of slave property, giving it a special importance and protection, which it withdraws from all other property; such as a federal representation to three fifths of the slaves, exempting two fifths of them from federal taxation, and giving it protection even in the free states by requiring the rendition of fugitive slaves. But under the bill in question, while the citizens of the free states were not disturbed in their privilege of taking into the district any species of their property for sale, the citizens of the Southern States were expressly debarred from introducing their slaves, their most valuable property, under penalty of seizure and confiscation. When the Constitution provided that "the citizens of each state shall be enti-

tled to all the privileges and immunities of citizens in the several states," did it mean that they should not have equal privileges in the district and in the territories, the common property of the Union? If it did, the doctrine of the constitutional equality of the states is a fiction and an absurdity.

When the fifth amendment of the Constitution was imposing specific restraints upon the powers of Congress, it provided, "Nor shall private property be taken for public use without just compensation," by imposing confiscation and emancipation as a penalty for bringing slave property into the district. The law of confiscation is substantially a decree for public use, and yet this bill expressly stipulated that the owner shall receive no compensation. When the Constitution provided that " excessive bail shall not be required nor excessive fines imposed," did it mean that a fine confiscating the whole property or thing to which the penalty referred would not be excessive? If so, expunge the amendment. It carries a lie upon its face.

The avowed object of this bill was to get rid of the public slave-markets at the seat of the federal government. It is a fact, however, that but one existed at the time, and that one in a secluded place. Slavery itself was rapidly disappearing, having been reduced since 1840 from 4694 to 650, by "underground railroads" and felonious abductions. While the bill was under discussion, Mr. Pearce, of Maryland, succeeded in ingrafting upon it an amendment providing for the protection of slave property owned in the district and the punishment of the felons. But it was subsequently stricken out, on the express ground that it would endanger the passage of the bill, as though Congress would sooner aid the felons in their work of emancipation, by confiscating the slaves brought into the district by honest citizens, than punish scoundrels for abducting them out of it. The bill affirms the power and policy of checking slavery in the district, virtually the power to abolish it there, and was but the predecessor, as we have since seen, of more serious and unfortunate encroachments on our rights.

It is not intended by this analysis to assail those who regarded the adjustment as the only means of saving the republic. Those most prominent in its support had long been illustrious in the public service. They, doubtless, foresaw that the slavery question involved more than one great problem which must one day be solved. But as the boldest tremble on the verge of eternity, and shrink from the dark abyss beyond which all is uncertain, so they were willing to postpone for posterity this dread solution. Not one of them but would have shed his blood freely for his country, and now they clung to this compromise as the mariner clings to the last plank in the surging seas. Let those who feel themselves infallible sit in inexorable judgment on the motives of their fellows, and condemn Clay, Benton, Webster, and Cass, the leading advocates of the plan of reconciliation. Such judgment is not for me. Had these four men pronounced the words " No compromise," war would most probably have ensued—fratricidal war! And who knows but that the God of vengeance and of righteousness would have stamped upon us the brand of Cain, and sent us to wander over the earth vagabonds among the nations ?

A large portion of the Southern people, however, perceived in the proposed measures an aggravation of their grievances, and it must be conceded that their apprehension was just.

While these bills, styled at the time the " *Omnibus*," were pending, and the public mind, in the South especially, in a state of great excitement, Gen. Zachary Taylor occupied the executive chair. Wholly unknown as a statesman, with but a limited education, ignorant of the structure and theory of our government, he had been elected by an overwhelming majority upon the fame of his military exploits, and upon the popular belief that so firm and tried a soldier would make a wise and impartial chief magistrate. His brief but disastrous administration, which (upon the authority of Mr. Webster) brought us to the verge of civil war, exhibited an incapacity in striking contrast with his brilliant campaigns a few years before. The circumstances attending his nomination and election had left no real cordiality between him and Mr. Clay and Mr. Webster, the great leaders of the opposition; and he found himself dependent for advice chiefly upon the young and ambitious, the mercenaries in pursuit of plunder, or the more crafty statesmen of the North, who built their hopes of power on a mischievous sectionalism. Mr. Seward, a senator from New York, whose sagacity never fails to second his great abilities, became the chief adviser of the President. Under this influence he urged the immediate admission of California; he disapproved the adjustment scheme; he favored the Wilmot Proviso; he 'rejected the claim of Texas upon any portion of New Mexico as wholly worthless, and expressed his determination to try the issue by force of arms. In a few months it became apparent that the Southern Whigs could no longer support him. On the 1st of July, 1850, a secret meeting of the Whig members of Congress from the Southern States was held at Washington, and it was determined, before coming to an open rupture, to appoint a committee to remonstrate with the President. Mr. C. M. Conrad, of Louisiana, Mr. Humphrey Marshall, of Kentucky, and Mr. Toombs, of Georgia, were appointed. They called on him separately, and informed him that his Southern friends would be driven into opposition if he persisted in his demand for the admission of California and New Mexico as states, and in his menacing attitude toward Texas. He refused to yield an inch. He insisted on the right of California to come in at once, and declared that, as soon as the Constitution of New Mexico reached him, he would recommend her admission likewise; and he scouted the title of Texas to any portion of New Mexico. He remarked that he was in a position that would compel him to sacrifice one wing of his party, and that he ought not to be expected to give up 84 men from the North for 29 men from the South, these being the proportions into which the Northern and Southern members of Congress of the Taylor party were then divided. Those who knew the constitutional obstinacy of the President—persuaded that he was acting, as he always acted, under honest convictions of duty—had no longer any hope. It was known, likewise, that while he was meditating an order to Col. Monroe, then in command at Santa Fé, to repel by arms any attempt of Texas to exercise jurisdiction in New Mexico, Mr. Crawford, of Georgia, secretary of war, appalled by the collision certain to ensue, after urging every argument against it, frankly stated that he could not sign such an order. The President coolly remarked that he would sign it himself. This was the condition of things when the sudden death of the President devolved the executive functions on Vice-president Fillmore. He adopted the views of Messrs. Clay, Cass, and Webster, as to the adjustment measures, but adhered to the attitude of his predecessor in relation to the military occupation of New Mexico, and the exclusion of the claims of Texas.

Such was the general posture of affairs when Quitman held the office of governor. For years, as may be seen by his correspondence, he had anticipated them with a morbid anxiety and with prophetic forecast. He knew that one weak point of our system is the tendency to consolidation or federalism, and the gradual conversion of a limited into a splendid government, to be controlled first by corruption and ultimately by the sword. He believed, likewise, that there was another evil of still greater magnitude, the tendency of mankind to abuse regulated liberty, to trample upon law and precedent, to set up moral conviction as paramount to the Constitution, and to substitute the sovereignty of the mob—or, as some prefer to call it, the higher law of conscience—for the sovereignty of the law. This had been the bane of the republics of antiquity, and our own country, yet in its youth, had furnished examples; and he now saw, in the movements in California and New Mexico, the realization of evils more demoralizing, more tyrannical and exacting than the monarchies of the Old World, and more to be dreaded than the imperial rescripts.

With such views, honestly entertained, and regarding his new relation to the state as that of an officer intrusted with the safety of a beleaguered fortress and of those who were sheltered behind its defenses, is it matter of surprise that he should have entered with all his strength into the controversy, and favored the most energetic measures of resistance? The Mississippi senators and representatives in Congress had warned him of the unconstitutional legislation then about to receive the sanction of Congress and the President—the admission of California, to the exclusion of the rights of Southern slaveholders—an exclusion which the several conventions of the people of the state had solemnly pledged themselves never to submit to.* He beheld, at the same

---

*   "Washington, January 21st, 1850.

"*His Excellency John A. Quitman, Governor, etc. :*

"SIR,—We, the senators and representatives in Congress from Mississippi, feel it incumbent upon us to advise you, and, through you, our

moment, a conflict of jurisdiction and of title between the State of Texas and the United States, and the federal authorities preparing to maintain their claim by force of arms, with the view, as he believed, to exclude the South from New Mexico, to abolitionize the northern and Rio Grande frontiers of Texas, and to circumscribe and repress the natural expansion of slaveholding communities. From all portions of Mississippi, and from other states, and by men of all parties, he was appealed to " to put his house in order" for the defense of Southern rights. Hundreds of influential citizens, whose letters now lie under inspection (some of the most distinguished of whom in Mississippi afterward made open war upon him, or timidly recoiled from their positions), reminded Gov. Quitman that palliatives and remonstrances would no longer answer, and called for the adoption of decisive measures.

"For the first time," he writes to a friend, "in the common constituents, that we have a well-defined opinion that California will be admitted as a state of this Union the present session of Congress. The President earnestly recommended it, and we can not be mistaken in supposing that a majority of both houses of Congress will be found to vote for it. Our individual positions have undergone no change. We regard the proposition to admit California as a state, under all the circumstances of her application, as an attempt to adopt the Wilmot Proviso in another form. But separated as we are from our constituents, and having no convenient means of consulting them as to their views on the face of this perplexing question, we desire through you to submit the single fact to the people and to the Legislature, that California will most likely obtain admission into the Union with her constitutional prohibition of slavery, and we beg leave to add that we shall be greatly pleased to have such expression of opinion by the Legislature, the governor, and, if practicable, by the people, as shall clearly indicate the course which Mississippi shall deem it her duty to pursue in this new emergency.

"Very respectfully, your obedient servants,

(Signed),   "JEFF. DAVIS,

        "H. S. FOOTE,

        "J. THOMPSON,

        "W. S. FEATHERSTON,

        "WM. M'WILLIE,

        "A. G. BROWN."

history of our country, the North is dominant in the federal government. We are now at their mercy, politically speaking. They will pass the California Bill, the Texas Bill, the New Mexico Bill, the Bill to abolish slave-trading in the District of Columbia, and others. When these are enacted, will they stop? You might as well expect a band of robbers who have plundered a house to leave the money-chest untouched."

His correspondence at that period explains the views that influenced him, and the feeling that pervaded the South.

Gov. Seabrook, of South Carolina, to Gov. Quitman.
"Pendleton, S. C., Sept. 20th, 1850.

"DEAR SIR,—The aggravating circumstances under which California will come into the Union, and the certain determination of Congress, the executor of its will, practically to change the form of our government, demand of the slaveholding states prompt and effective resistance. They now occupy a position of degradation and inequality. Submission will constitute them forever mere dependencies of a great central head.

"In the assurance that Georgia will shortly be summoned by her executive to meet in convention, may I ask whether Mississippi is prepared to assemble her Legislature, or adopt any other scheme to second that commonwealth in her noble effort to preserve unimpaired the Union of '87?

"As there are satisfactory reasons why South Carolina should move cautiously in this matter, I need only assure your excellency that, as soon as the governors of two or more states shall, by proclamation, assemble their respective Legislatures, or furnish some other evidence on the part of the states they represent, of determined resistance, in disregard of consequences, I shall, in that event, consider it my duty, unless the nearness of the regular session prevent, to call together the representatives of the people, with a view to their adoption of measures that will, so far as it affects this state, effectually arrest the career of an interested and despotic majority."

In his reply to this letter, dated Jackson, Sept. 29th, Governor Quitman informs Governor Seabrook that upon the passage of the California Bill, and the bill in relation to slavery in the District of Columbia, he had deemed it his duty to issue his proclamation convening the Legislature on the 18th of November, and thus continues:

"Without having fully digested a programme of the measures which I shall recommend to the Legislature, it may be of service to you to know that I propose the call of a regular convention to take into consideration our federal relations, with full powers to annul the federal compact, establish new relations with other states, and adapt our organic law to such new relations, etc., etc.

"Having no hope of an effectual remedy for existing and prospective evils but in separation from the Northern States, my views of state action will look to secession."

From Gov. Seabrook.

"Charleston, Oct. 23d, 1850.

"I have the pleasure to acknowledge the receipt of your letter of the 29th ult., which, from its tone, has given me the assurance that Mississippi will be the banner state in the noble contest in which the South has been forced to engage. If the result prove this, my belief, to be true, and your gallant commonwealth adopt the decisive course suggested by you, I scarcely need say to your excellency that South Carolina will be found by her side. On this subject permit me to remark, that on no great political question have the people of this state ever been so united as on the necessity of resisting, in disregard of consequences, the rapid encroachments by the federal government on the compromises and guarantees of the Constitution. Having lately completed a military tour through every district, where a large proportion of the population are non-slaveholders, I did not meet with one man who was not favorable to the only certain remedy—secession. The general desire seemed to be to exhaust the scheme of joint action before an independent step should be taken by South Carolina; farther, that by no precipitate movement on her part ought the impression to be made abroad that she was anxious to occupy a position in the van. Whether true or false, the belief here is, I may say, universal, that the great cause would receive, perhaps, a fatal blow should this state attempt to take the lead. Under this conviction, and in consequence of the nearness of the constitutional time of meeting, I, with the assent of the people, have declined to convene the Legislature. My published reasons are contained in a letter to a friend, a copy of which is inclosed. Let me, however, reiterate the asssurance that South Carolina is prepared to second Mississippi, or any other state, in any and every effort to arrest the career of a corrupt and despotic majority. She is ready and anxious for an immediate separation from a Union whose aim is the prostration of our political edifice. May I hope that Mississippi will begin the patriotic work, and allow the Palmetto banner the privilege of a place in her ranks?

"The desire of our public men is, that the Nashville Convention, the Georgia Convention, or the Legislature of Mississippi, should recommend the call of a Southern congress, to be composed of delegates elected by state conventions, either, as the weaker measure, for the purpose of consultation, their decision to be ratified by conventions of the states represented, or to be direct. The first course will produce delay, and may enable Congress and the politicians of the North so to shape their policy as to create the impression among the unreflecting and timid in the South that every cause of danger to our institutions had been removed. A Southern congress, with full authority on the part of the states represented to secede from the Union forthwith, or to submit to the supreme authorities of the country propositions for a new bargain between the states, by which equality among the members of the confederacy and the protection of Southern property shall, in future, be put beyond the possibility of hazard—either of these measures (we prefer the former, because, in the event of a conflict, we shall have a government actually in operation), emanating from the Nashville Convention, or any Southern state except South Carolina, for reasons already hinted, will go far to, if it do not entirely accomplish the great object it is so desirable to effect."

From the same to the same.

"Columbia, December 17th, 1850.

"Yesterday I ceased to be governor. My successor is Gen. Means, who defeated Col. Pickens, whose opposition to Mr. Calhoun a few years ago has never been forgotten by the people.

"Your letter of the 2d instant has afforded me great satisfaction, and inspirited a few confidential friends to whom it was my duty to show it. It was all important for us to know that there was one state at least on whose co-operation we might confidently rely. In the two branches of the Legislature now in session there is but one man in favor of ultimate submission. Even he, however, advocates the policy of a Southern congress. Your letter, discreetly used, has enabled me to suspend the scheme of many prominent men of publicly avowing that in one year, if unaided by some other state at that time, South Carolina would withdraw from the confederacy. On some points there are two parties: one, in favor of following, and not taking the lead from Mississippi; the other, urging the necessity of designating the time and place for the meeting of a Southern congress. The former is in favor of a convention of the people of the state to nominate delegates to that body; the latter is of opinion that these should be chosen by the Legislature, and the people in their primary meetings. It is probable that a compromise between the parties will take place to-day. On Saturday the Senate determined, by a vote of 37 to 6, to call a convention of the people of the state to consider our federal relations, and to elect delegates to a Southern congress, the election to take place on the 2d Monday in October, and the convention to assemble the 1st Monday in December. Should this bill meet the approbation of the House, which I think improbable in its present form, the honor of naming the time and place for the convocation of the Southern congress will devolve on your gallant state. I candidly confess to you that I am advocating the plan of an early meeting of our state convention, or immediate action of the Legislature, in order to suggest the 1st Monday in December next for the time, and Montgomery, Alabama, as the place of meeting of the congress. Should it assemble in 1852, the presidential question will perhaps absorb all others. With a view, too, to divide the South, both Congress and the Northern States will abstain for a season from their encroachments.   *   *   *   *   *   *

"I am rejoiced to state that the House, by a vote of 109 to 12, resolved to suggest to our Southern sister states the propriety of meeting in congress at Montgomery on the 2d of January, 1852. To consider the acts of that body, a convention of the people of this state is proposed for the fourth Monday of February, 1852. For arming the state, $350,000 has been put at the disposal of the governor. That the Senate will concur I have no doubt. Had I convened the Legislature two or three weeks before the regular meeting, such was the excited state of the public mind at that time, I am convinced South Carolina would not now have been a member of the Union. The people are very far ahead of their leaders, and can with difficulty be restrained. The speeches of influential men in the Legislature, and the belief that Mississippi and other states are preparing their moral and, if necessary, physical power to support the equality and sovereignty of the states, have had the salutary effect of checking the course of the impetuous and unreflecting. I shall be happy to know that the time and place of the proposed congress will be agreeable to Mississippi. If our movement be seconded by her, I have good reasons for the belief that Alabama, Florida, and Arkansas will soon follow the patriotic example. Your whole course in reference to federal relations has met with the decided approbation of the people of this state, and especially of her public men. The only reason why South Carolina has deemed it advisable to designate the time of the meeting of the Southern congress is the conviction that, had it been left to your state, an earlier time than April or May, 1852, could not have been named. The states now have a year's notice."

There were other elements of disaffection abroad during this eventful period that operated on the mind of Governor Quitman, and braced him up to the contemplation of decided measures. The Texas claim on what is called New Mexico, and the menacing attitude of the federal government, had enlisted the sympathies of the South. A collision between the two claimants, one drop of blood shed by the troops of the United States, would have set the country in a blaze. As far back as July he had received the following letter from General J. Pinckney Henderson, a distinguished soldier of Texas, who died, in 1859, a senator from that state:

"San Augustine, July 22d, 1850.

"Your excellency will doubtless have seen, ere this reaches you, that Texas is about to come to drawn daggers with the general government at Santa Fé. Had President Taylor lived until our troops reached there a collision would have been unavoidable. His successor may be more cautious, and, inasmuch as the United States has surrendered all civil jurisdiction to the Mexicans, Indians, and Abolitionists, who have presumed to establish a government within the territory of Texas, the President may, perhaps, leave the settlement of the question of jurisdiction to them and us. Should he, however, order the United States troops that are stationed in that quarter to resist our attempt to enforce our jurisdiction, I ask you to tell me candidly, how far is Mississippi prepared to redeem the pledge made by her members in the Nashville Convention? Will she stand firmly by us in the contest? Governor Bell has convoked our Legislature, and calls for 1000 volunteers. He must send more —not less than 2000 at first; and, should the United States interfere, we shall need our whole strength and the aid of our friends. The people in this section and throughout the state are indignant and resolved. Our Legislature, I presume, will appeal to the Southern States. From Mississippi we expect efficient aid. It is useless for me to enter into details to show how we are wronged. You know our rights, and you have seen the national executive trampling them under foot, and holding over our heads the sword of power. I am now leaving for Philadelphia, where my wife and little daughters are spending the summer. I wish to bring them out of the enemy's country before this war begins; for war it must be, unless President Fillmore backs out from the position of his predecessor, or unless, by some base and mercenary combination, our rights are trafficked away by a sale or surrender."

Governor Quitman to General Henderson.

"Jackson, August 18th, 1850.

"The course of policy which the new administration means to pursue is now developed by the message of Mr. Fillmore and the letter of Mr. Webster. They are ominous, and evince a determination to have a trial of strength. Be it so. If we must have an issue, the present is the best occasion, because, in my opinion, it will produce a perfect concert of action on the part of the South. But will Texas stand firm? Will she accept the bribe, magnificent as it is, which the federal government is tendering to her? Will she sell her sovereignty? Will she be a party to an arrangement that will convert a large portion of her territory into free soil? Will she consent to plant upon her own border, and in proximity with her domestic institutions, a magazine of combustibles? Will she, at any price, surrender a portion of her sovereignty, and especially under duress, which she is well able to resist? I hope not. Her title is indisputable. Will we—will the Southern States—seeing Texas contending for rights vital to us all, not make common cause with her? Certainly they will. I shall not be wanting in the prompt and firm discharge of my duty on the occasion. So soon as I shall be satisfied that a collision of arms is probable I will convene the Legislature on the shortest possible notice, and urge it to adopt efficient measures to aid our sister state in the maintenance of her sovereignty against federal usurpation. I can not doubt that the other Southern States will adopt similar measures. My arm was once exerted for Texas in the early stages of her struggle, and now, when she is menaced with a far greater evil than Mexican invasion, I am always ready to strike in her defense.

"All we wait for now is her response to Pearce's bill, which I regard as worse than Mr. Fillmore's bayonets, because it is no better than a bribe."

He soon after issued the following

PROCLAMATION.

Whereas the people of Mississippi have repeatedly, in public meetings, in popular conventions, and by legislative resolves, claimed and asserted their equality of right with the other states of this Union in and to the free use and enjoyment of the territory belonging in common to these United States, and have frequently and publicly declared their fixed determination, at all hazards, to maintain these rights, so essential to their freedom and equality.

And whereas, by recent acts of Congress, the people of Mississippi, in common with the citizens of all the slaveholding states, have been virtually excluded from their just rights in the greater portion, if not all, of the vast and rich territories acquired from Mexico in the late war; and thus, by unjust and insulting discriminations, the advantages and benefits of the federal Union have been denied to them.

And whereas the abolition, by Congress, of the slave-trade in the District of Columbia, and other acts of the federal government, done and threatened, leave no reasonable hope that the aggressions upon the rights of the people of the slaveholding states will cease until, by direct or indirect means, their domestic institutions are overthrown.

Now, therefore, That the proper authorities of the state may be enabled to take into consideration the alarming state of our public affairs, and, if possible, avert the evils which impend over us, that the state may be placed in an attitude to assert her sovereignty, and that the means may be provided to meet any and every emergency which may happen,

I, *John A. Quitman,* Governor of the State of Mississippi, exercising the powers in me vested by the Constitution, do hereby convene the Legislature of this state, and do appoint *Monday, the eighteenth day of November* next, for the meeting of both houses of the Legislature, at the capital, in Jackson, the seat of government of this state.

His letter to the Hon. John J. M'Rae fully explains the views that induced this special call.

Governor Quitman to Hon. J. J. McRae.

"Jackson, September 28th, 1850.

"MY DEAR SIR,—It would have been more satisfactory to me could I have advised with you before convening the Legislature, but, after the contingencies had happened, I was desirous of acting promptly, that our noble state, which had taken the initiative in measures of resistance to the contemplated outrages, should not be suspected of backing out, now that these aggressions have been consummated. I would have been faithless to the position in which the people have placed me had I hesitated, in the emergency, to afford the people of the state an opportunity of invoking the action of the sovereign power to determine upon the mode and measure of redress. I could not do otherwise. I have ever held that the admission of California, under the circumstances, was equivalent to the passage of the Wilmot Proviso, and means were placed under my control by the Legislature to meet the expenses of a convocation of that body in case of the passage of a law to abolish the slave-trade in the District of Columbia, to say nothing of other measures which, I solemnly believe, have effectually destroyed the Union as our fathers made it. Now it is highly important that the Southern party, both in the agitations of these questions before the people and in the action of the Legislature, should move in concert. Unless we pull at the same rope we will fail, and failure would plunge the country into irretrievable ruin. Unless measures to check the federal government be devised we will ever remain a mere dependency on the North. I have not acted without first looking to the ground before me, and I take the privilege of communicating to you, in confidence, thus early, a hasty programme of our future movements. It is still undigested, as I wish the full benefit of the views of all the true men of our state, especially of those in position.

"First, then, I believe there is no effectual remedy for the evils before us but secession. If any other measure short of it can be shown to promise a radical cure of the evils, I am willing to adopt it.

"My idea is that the Legislature should call a convention of delegates elected by the people, fully empowered

to take into consideration our federal relations, and to
change or annul them, to adapt our organic law to such
new relations as they might establish, to provide for
making compacts with other states, etc., etc., and that
in the mean while an effective military system be established, and patrol duties most rigidly enforced. My message should glance at all these measures.

"Now, my dear sir, on all these subjects I wish the
benefit of your suggestions and advice as early as possible.

"I shall ask, in like manner, the free opinion of Col.
Davis, Thompson, Brown, Barton, Stewart and other
friends. With the benefit of such suggestions as they
and you furnish, either a committee should be appointed
to meet here and frame a plan of operations, or you all
must intrust that to my discretion, so that we may act
together.

"Whatever plan shall be thus determined on, should
be fully sustained by every Southern man. I am ready
to pledge to it my time, my labor, my fortune, and my
life.

"In the mean time, every patriot should leave no point
untouched where his influence can be exerted. Cheer on
the faithful, strengthen the weak, disarm the submissionists with instructions; send the fiery cross through the
land, and summon every gallant son of Mississippi to the
rescue. Hold meetings and challenge the submissionists
to discussion, and agitate the question every where.

"My proposed movement is not antagonistical, but in
harmony with the Nashville Convention. I have not
much confidence in its efficacy beyond presenting a plan
of joint action for the states. We, therefore, call into
exercise the state powers to receive it. I do not believe
Judge Sharkey will give notice of its reassembling; he
is opposed to it. If that convention shall meet, our
Legislature will meet on the following week: we can
then communicate daily by telegraph. At the same
time the Georgia Convention will be in session; the
Legislature of South Carolina also, and probably Alabama.

"We will take care to have confidential reporters at
each point.

"I hope that we will teach the impudent conspirators, North and South, who are attempting to stifle truth, reason, justice, and patriotism by the firing of cannon, the ringing of bells, and vociferous cheering, that we have not so far lost our senses as not to know the difference between a loaf of bread and a stone.

"With the exception of the merchants, the traders, the brokers, the millionaires, and their dependents, the people are with us.

"Resistance to wrong and insult, at all hazards, and to the last extremity.

"P.S.—The people of the eastern counties should not fear a secession. Its effects would be to build up their sea-ports and establish connections with the interior.

"Last week a wealthy capitalist dined with me: he has some $50,000 to invest, which he would put into stock of the Eastern Railroad but for the danger which impends over our domestic institutions; he speaks of investing it in a free state. Thus already our capital is flowing out of the country. This alone will make our fair land a howling wilderness. Instead of ornamenting and beautifying our houses, building up public and private improvements, covering our pine-hills with vines, and herds, and flocks, the country will sink into decay and poverty. The government now over it is its worst enemy. Can the mind of man conceive worse evils than what must flow from such a state of things?"

When the Legislature assembled, the governor sent in an elaborate message. He thus alludes to the progress of the anti-slavery element:

"This hostility to slavery has now become the all-absorbing, all-controlling element of political action and party movement, both in Congress and throughout the Northern States. Political parties unite, separate, and are modified with reference to it. Political platforms are built upon it. It is the main question in the selection of candidates for all offices. It is the active element of religious, benevolent, charitable, and even literary associations, and the spice which seasons private society. The Constitution of the United States, the rights of the states, the gravest questions of public policy, all are construed and determined with reference to this question of domestic slavery ; and the Congress of the United States, whose powers are limited mainly to the regulation of national and external objects, are now found devoting nearly all their time to subjects of a domestic nature, over which it was never intended that they should exercise jurisdiction."

IIe next points out the injustice done to the South by the recent legislation of Congress, and shows that even the strong barriers of the Constitution have fallen, one by one, before the march of Northern encroachment and fanaticism.

"The limits of a message do not permit me to detail other measures which have justly caused alarm and excitement in the South ; for, however some of our own people may, from anxiety to allay excitement, seek to, excuse these measures, there are few whose breasts are not filled with a dread of the dangers which from these quarters lower in the horizon of the future. Iu my opinion, it would be weak, timid, and disastrous policy to shut our eyes to these dangers ; it is the part of wisdom to meet them. Let us, then, survey our position and that of our opponents.

"There is nothing to encourage the hope that there will be any respite from aggression. Never has hostility to slavery been more distinctly marked or more openly asserted. Shades of difference in opinion may distinguish Northern statesmen, but all unite in stern opposition to the extension of slavery, and in declarations of their fixed determination to confine it to its present limits, and forever to close the public territory against us.

"The North has just triumphed in every claim she has asserted ; and yet, at this moment of our humiliation, their people, less patient than we, are in a blaze of excitement at every attempt to execute the bill to secure the return of fugitive slaves. This plain compliance with one of the clearest injunctions of the Constitution is not only disregarded, but conventions of both political parties, formal meetings of the people, and deliberate addresses of dis-

tinguished men openly take ground that, being against
the public sentiment of the people of the North, it should
not be executed ; and persons of all classes, with a pli-
ancy of conscience which characterizes Abolition philosophy, adapt their moral code and their constitutional duties to their prejudices and their interests.

"Such, then, is the triumphant attitude of anti-slavery.
It now controls the entire government. No questions
arise in which it does not intermingle. And wherever
it exhibits itself it controls all other subjects. Every
great interest in this government is now directed and
managed by it. It has broken and sundered the strong
ties which bound together the religious denominations
North and South. It has even now severed the bonds
which for sixty years have united parties, and in their
place it has sown the seeds of hostility and hatred. It
now stands the stern, unyielding despot, consigning to
the bed of Procrustes every object whose fitness is questioned.

"What is to be the fate of the institution of domestic
slavery under such government? this great interest, with
which the civilization and refinement of man on earth is
connected—upon which so much of the trade and commerce between Europe and America depends—which employs the labor of millions and distributes the comforts
of civilization to so many families—this great social interest, upon which are founded the prosperity, the happiness, and the very existence of the people of fourteen
states of this Union?   What is to be the fate of this institution?   If left to the tender mercies of the federal
government its fate is doomed. With the prejudices of
the age against it, it requires for its kind development a
fostering government over it. It could scarcely subsist
without such protection. How, then, can it exist, much
less flourish and prosper, under a government hostile to
it—a government organized upon principles of hostility
and opposition to the institution? Is it proper? is it
philosophic? is it not absurd to intrust the prosperity,
the protection, and even the existence of a great and
delicate interest to a political power having its origin in
and drawing its vigor from the very element of hostility
to this interest?

"To state the proposition clearly: The government of the United States is now hostile to slavery. It will hereafter be selected with reference to its hostility to this interest and its activity in the use of doing injury. If this great and vital interest, then, remains subject to the government and control of its enemy, *it must perish!* Sooner or later, I repeat, it must perish."

The governor then states that, in view of the dangers that menace the state, its sovereignty, constitutional rights and institutions, he felt called on to convene the Legislature, and proceeds to say:

"To devise and carry into effect the best means of redress for the past, and to obtain certain security for the future, I recommend that a legal convention of the people of the state should be called, with full and ample powers to take into consideration our federal relations, the aggressions which have been committed upon the rights of the Southern States, the dangers which threaten our domestic institutions, and all kindred subjects; and jointly with other states, or separately, to adopt such measures as may best comport with the dignity and safety of the state, and effectually correct the evils complained of. A convention thus assembled, and representing the sovereignty of the state, would, of course, possess plenary powers, uncontrolled by any instructions or restrictions which the Legislature might interpose.

"It might, therefore, be sufficient for me to recommend the passage of proper laws to bring into existence such a convention, leaving the mode and measure of redress entirely to their wisdom when thus assembled. To this high power, representing the majesty of the people, and constituted the proper exponents of their deliberate will, all public authorities and all good citizens would yield cheerful and prompt obedience.

* * * * * * *

"When I reflect upon the pertinacity with which the assaults upon our rights have been for years prosecuted, the evident increase of anti-slavery sentiments at the North, and the excitement there pervading nearly all classes against the law to provide for the extradition of fugitive slaves, I have little hope left that these guarantees, indispensably necessary to our safety, will be yielded by a majority flushed with recent victories and encouraged by apparent divisions among ourselves. Yet, to leave no effort at conciliation untried, and still farther to unite with us those of our own people who still look for a returning sense of justice in the North, let the propositions be distinctly made to the people of the non-slaveholding states to remedy the wrong so far as it may be in the power of Congress to do so, by obtaining from California concessions south of 36° 30' or otherwise, and to consent to such amendments of the federal Constitution as shall hereafter amply secure the rights of the slaveholding states from misconstruction and from farther aggression.

"But, in the event of refusal, I do not hesitate to express my decided opinion that the only effectual remedy to evils which must continue to grow from year to year is to be found in the prompt and peaceable secession of the aggrieved states.

"The probability of the ultimate necessity of a resort to this effective and unquestionable right of sovereign states should be kept in view, whatever measures may be adopted by this state, either alone or in concert with her sister states, to remedy existing evils. In the mean time, and as early as practicable, it is of the highest importance that some common centre of opinion and action should be authoritatively established. This may be effected by the conventions of the several assenting states providing for the organization and subsequent frequent periodical appointment or election of a committee of safety for each state, to consist of a number equal to their senators and representative in Congress. These committees, whose duty it should be periodically to assemble at some central point for the transaction of business, should be invested with adequate powers, absolute or contingent, to act for their respective states upon all questions connected with the preservation and protection of their domestic institutions, and their equal rights as sovereign states. Such a body of men, even if clothed with the authority of but two or three states, would command respect, and secure quiet and peaceable results to their determinations.

"I have thus ventured to present some suggestions, for which I am alone responsible. They may be modified or changed by the result of the Nashville Convention now in session, and the action of the Georgia Convention, which will shortly meet for the purpose of taking the same important question into consideration.

"Under our system of government, happily the right and privilege of determining these grave and momentous questions, involving the honor and safety of the state and the happiness and prosperity of all its citizens, whether rich or poor, slaveholder or non-slaveholder, belongs alone to the people. To them the appeal must be made, and their deliberate voice must control and direct the destiny of the state. I therefore respectfully recommend to the Legislature to provide for an expression of the will of the people by the call of a convention at an early day. In this there will be safety. When the sovereign power shall have spoken, all good citizens, whatever may be their opinions, will acquiesce. All will vie with one another in patriotic zeal to maintain the dignity and authority of the state. Mississippi will then be united, and harmonious counsels, and wise, energetic action will secure her safety.

"The very important and vital character of the questions which are forced upon our consideration has led me to look solely to remedies not merely palliative, but effectual and permanent. There may be some temporary remedial measures within the power of the Legislature. If such can be devised, it will give me great pleasure to co-operate with you in their application."

This Legislature indorsed and reaffirmed the resolutions of the convention of October, 1849, and directed the publication of 75,000 copies of its proceedings. It elected twelve delegates to the Nashville Convention. It denounced the course of President Taylor in respect to California, and declared that its admission ought to be resisted—the mode of resistance and of redress was referred to the Southern Convention; and it pledged the state to sustain the measures of redress which that body should recommend. It promulgated an address to the people setting forth the perils that menaced our institutions, and inviting them to vigilance and action; and it passed resolutions of censure on Senator Foote, and of approval of the course pursued by the other senator and representatives of the state, and it provided by law for a convention of the people of the State of Mississippi to consider the state of public affairs.

Such was, apparently, the public sentiment at that period. The people of Mississippi seemed almost unanimous in their opposition to the measures of the administration, and determined to defend their equality in the Union, or to retire from it by peaceable secession. Had the issue been pressed at the moment when the excitement was at its highest point, an isolated and very serious movement might have occurred, which South Carolina, without doubt, would have promptly responded to. But the majority wisely preferred the co-operation principle, and the Legislature, as we have seen, referred the whole matter to the convention at Nashville.

CHAPTER XV.

Cuba.—General Lopez.—Interview with Mr. Calhoun.—Visits Governor Quitman.—His personal Appearance.—Proposals rejected.—Quitman's Reason therefor.—Fillmore's Proclamation.—Its illegal Character.—Indictment and threatened Arrest of Quitman.—Letter from Hon. Jacob Thompson.—Letters to the United States District Attorney.—Letter from General Henderson.—Governor Quitman resigns.—Patriotism of the Ladies.—Arrested.—Appears in Court in New Orleans.—Is discharged.—Reception by the People. — Legal View of the Case. — Original Letters from La Fayette, Adams, Webster, and Clay.—Lopez sails for Cuba.—Failure of the Expedition, and the Cause.—His Capture and Death.—Capture of Crittenden and Party.—Their Execution.—Atrocities in Havana. —Death to the Americans.—Future Retribution.—The Proclamation and General Concha. — The Liberators vindicated. — Great Britain and France.—Power of Republics.—Our proper Policy.

While these important matters were transpiring, an event occurred that, for a time, concentrated public attention in another quarter. In 1849, General Narcisso Lopez, a native of Venezuela, a veteran soldier of Spain, and long domiciliated in Cuba, visited the United States. On his arrival at Washington Mr. Calhoun called on him, and repeated his visit the next day. Soon afterward General Lopez had another interview with Mr. Calhoun and four distinguished senators in a committee-room of the Capitol. He submitted to them in detail the condition of the island. The people are allowed no share in the administration of affairs even by the expression of opinion ; there is no freedom of speech, of the press, or of occupation. From a population of little more than a million, including the slaves, Spain exacts annually, by an arbitrary system of taxation, and every sort of vexatious excise, a tribute of 24,000,000 of dollars. It employs 20,000 regulars, besides a formidable marine, and a legion of spies and stipendiaries, to watch the movements of individuals and keep the people in subjection. No trade or business can be pursued without first paying for a license; no guest be received, no company entertained, no festival in any private residence, and no removal from one domicil to another, without a formal permission. The productions of the plantation are taxed, most of them ten per cent. on their value; tithes are exacted to the amount of more than a quarter of a million of dollars, yet the inhabitants are obliged to support their places of worship and cemeteries by private subscription. No native is allowed to hold any office, civil, judicial, military, or ecclesiastical; every place of honor, trust, or profit is confided to Spaniards. Cuba has no representative in the Spanish Cortes. She is literally governed by the sword. The captain general is absolute as the Sultan of Turkey, and promulgates any law or regulation which his caprice may dictate. Under his rule the slave-trade—which the British government and his own maintain a mixed commission, and our government and Great Britain, at vast expense, keep squadrons on the coast of Africa, to prevent—is actively carried on; negroes are surreptitiously admitted in great numbers, not to contribute to the prosperity of the Cubans, but because a heavy douceur is paid to the authorities for their admission, and these negroes, and their threatened emancipation, are relied on by the government to intimidate the citizens.

The captain general at that period was General Concha, a field-marshal of Spain, and a thorough absolutist in his political opinions. He had a consultative junta, the members of which were named by himself, and were the creatures of his will. The institutions of charity, of policy, and of finance, the army and the navy, were under his control. In private life bland, courteous, gallant, and magnificent, as supreme chief he crushed, with a hand of iron, every shadow of liberty.

The people of Cuba, in the mean time, were panting for independence, and only waited an opportunity to revolt. The want of arms, the difficulty of concert owing to incessant surveillance, and the hope of intervention or aid, in some way or other, from the United States, had hitherto postponed any serious attempt. But they were ready, feeble and scattered as they were, to make the effort if any assurance of aid could be communicated to them.

This was the sacred mission that brought General Lopez to the United States. His statements made a deep impression on Mr. Calhoun, the most circumspect and conservative statesman of our country. In several interviews with Lopez he expressed himself in favor of the annexation of Cuba to the United States, but as that could not be immediately accomplished, he referred to the assistance that might be lawfully proffered by the American people in the event of an insurrection of the Cubans. He declared, moreover, in such event European intervention need not be apprehended. Both England and France are bound by their own precedents.*

In the spring of 1850 Gen. Lopez waited on Gen. Quitman privately at Jackson. He was received with cordi-

---

* Subsequently Mr. Calhoun, it must be conceded, became more lukewarm on this subject, owing to the increasing gravity of the issue between the North and the South on the slavery question. He feared that the Cuba question, so full of interest and chivalry, would draw the minds of the people from an internal to an external contest. He desired to confine public attention, and the South particularly, to a special issue of vital importance, and, therefore, discouraged all collateral matters. But the same arguments he employed for the acquisition of Texas apply to Cuba, and would have made him the advocate of its annexation.

ality. The general declared that the people were ripe for revolution, and he came in their name to solicit the auxiliaries that the citizens of a great republic should not refuse to their oppressed neighbors. He exhibited confidential communications and credentials from every portion of the island, and letters of encouragement from distinguished sources in the United States. He said that he had no ambition but for the liberation of his country; that he had long been convinced that it needed an infusion of American blood to vitalize its energies; that Cuba once free, and her resources put in motion by an energetic will, the regeneration of Mexico and of the distracted governments to the south of it would follow, and a new empire, the centre of the world's production and commerce, governed by the great principle of unrestrained free trade, would soon be established. He concluded by offering Gov. Quitman, in the name of his compatriots, the leadership of the revolution, and the supreme command if their armies should triumph.

This was the tempting scheme submitted by the Cuban patriot. It made a deep impression. Quitman was ambitious, and these grand ideas of revolution and progress, of changes to be accomplished by liberal principles and energetic rule, were his own. To lead such a movement in aid of an oppressed people, and for the introduction of American civilization and Southern institutions, had been the dream of his life. The battle-field and its glory, the clangor and the charge rose up like a gorgeous pageant to dazzle his imagination. Lopez perceived the impression, and led the conversation to Chapultepec and Belen, and the fame he had acquired, and the enthusiasm with which the Cubans and many of the Mexicans would rally around his standard. He was an eloquent and winning man in conversation. His brow bore the traces of suffering and reflection; his square-built and upright car-

riage, and measured pace, and grizzled mustache denoted
at a glance the veteran soldier; his voice was low and
musical, his manners singularly mild; his eye, small but
lustrous, indicated concentration and enthusiasm; the
prevailing expression of his countenance was firmness
and sincerity. He used no gesticulation, but he stood
before the governor, fixed his eyes upon him, and poured his low voice into his ear. It was the wizard spell
upon a magnetic temperament which was never entirely
broken, not even by the bloody drama that soon ensued,
and the prosecution and calumny that followed like
blood-hounds upon the track.

Quitman long and anxiously reflected. No one disturbed the silence. Lopez slowly paced the apartment,
like a sentinel on guard. The few confidential friends
who had been specially invited to the interview felt the
sorcery of his presence. All hoped that the governor
would accept the offer, and embark in a career so just
and so prodigal of glory. Thousands at a word would
have followed his standard, and with his flashing sword
he would have made

"His name
A light, a landmark, on the cliffs of fame."

It required no ordinary virtue and an iron will to reject a career so brilliant. But Quitman did reject it.
He was influenced simply by the sentiment that pervaded
his whole life—the sentiment of duty and honor. He
acknowledged the justice of the demand of Cuba for
aid; the moment she fired the first gun, and shed the
first blood, as our forefathers did at Lexington, it became
legitimate to go to her assistance, whether authorized by
the government or voluntarily as individuals. He would
resign the office of governor in an hour to accept the responsibilities tendered to him but for the menacing posture of public affairs. Our rights as a sovereign state

C 2

had been encroached on by the federal government; our institutions and domestic tranquillity were threatened; measures of redress were being considered; we had placed ourselves in consultation with our sister states of the South; that consultation might eventuate in redress or collision, and, until the result could be ascertained, the resignation of the chief magistrate, to embark in another service, would be like the desertion of a general on the eve of battle. He could not reconcile it with his notions of honor or obligation.

And thus this high-minded man, for a principle, and from a sense of duty to his state, renounced a career that would have rendered his name illustrious, and, in all probability, secured the independence of Cuba!

He said that, as affairs stood, he could only put his heart in the enterprise and contribute some pecuniary aid. He laid the map of Cuba on the table, which he had long carefully studied, and pointed to the proper field of operations. He insisted on the necessity of having an advance column of 2000 men to maintain a foothold in the island until re-enforcements could go to their relief, and he cautioned General Lopez against the probability of treachery and ambuscade. His last words, uttered with an electric emphasis, were,

> "Who would be free,
> Themselves must strike the blow!"

And thus the two chiefs parted, both in the spirit of self-sacrifice and mutually appreciating each other—the one to watch over the interests of his state; the other, who had renounced wealth, and ease, and courtly presence for the sake of liberty, to pursue his heroic mission, over which the shadow of death even then impended.

Very soon after this memorable interview General Lopez left New Orleans with a detachment of volunteers led by O'Hara, Hawkins, Pickett, Bell, Wheat, and other chivalric spirits, chiefly from Kentucky. They landed at Cardenas without opposition, but were soon attacked by Spanish troops, whom, however, they drove back with considerable loss. Disappointed at the absence of any demonstration in his favor, Lopez re-embarked, intending to make for some other point on the island; but the appearance of the Spanish war steamer Pizarro, which gave chase, compelled him to run into Key West, where civil proceedings were instituted and the volunteers dispersed.* The indefatigable Lopez returned to

* The disasters of this expedition did not affect the popularity of Lopez. The following is taken from the Delta.

" General Lopez in Mississippi.

"On Sunday, 23d instant, General Lopez, accompanied by General Gonzales, Colonel Yznaga, and Mr. T. Gotay, left New Orleans in the steamer Amazon, Capt. Portervino, for Gainesville, Miss. They were escorted by Capt. Ives, late a state senator, A. B. Bacon, Esq., Dr. Gouldin, Cyrus Butler, and other citizens. The trip was altogether an impromptu one, the general having a desire to see the great pine-forests of Mississippi, and the waters of the beautiful river that irrigates the heart of that noble state. As soon as the general reached the boat, Capt. Portervino promptly and warmly tendered its hospitalities and a free passage to him and his suite; and the company sat down to a table bountifully spread with all the luxuries of the season. The Amazon landed at Gainesville at eight o'clock P.M., and, there being many citizens in town for the purpose of celebrating the masonic anniversary next day, as soon as it was known that Gen. Lopez was on board a meeting was held, at which the following proceedings occurred:

"Hon. T. B. Ives being called to the chair, and Dr. J. J. Gaines appointed secretary, the annexed resolutions were unanimously adopted:

"*Resolved,* That the citizens of Gainesville, Miss., have heard with pleasure of the arrival of the patriot, General Lopez, and his brave companions; that we welcome them to the hospitalities of the town, and to a state that appreciates their efforts in the cause of freedom—a state that regards liberty as the highest of earthly boons, and which is ever ready to offer its sons to defend it, and to interpose its sovereignty for their protection.

"*Resolved,* That Col. T. J. Ives, Dr. J. J. Gaines, J. W. Blackman, Benj. F. Leonard, C. F. Folsom, John Graves, S. B. Pierce, James Graves, J. W. Moore, C. F. Frazer, L. A. Folsom, Capt. Bulkley, Col. Bird, and Capt. Jos. Johnson be appointed a committee to wait on Gen. Lopez and welcome him and his friends to Mississippi.

"The committee, attended by a large concourse of citizens, waited on the general, and were introduced by Col. Ives, who delivered the

New Orleans to renew his efforts. In the mean time President Fillmore issued a second and more memorable proclamation, in the following words:

following speech, which was interpreted to the general by Gen. Gonzales:

"'GEN. LOPEZ: In behalf of the citizens of this town and county, and, I may say, of the people of Mississippi, I welcome you and your brave companions here. Your visit is unexpected, or we should have received you with the ceremonies due to your position and your valor. We tender you, sir, and your friends a homely but hearty welcome to a soil consecrated to liberty, where we have homes and sanctuaries for our friends, arms and graves for our enemies.'

"General Lopez replied in the Spanish language at considerable length and with great animation.

"Col. J. F. H. Claiborne being present, was requested to explain the sentiments expressed by the general.

"'He said he found it difficult to give their full emphasis to the expressions of the distinguished gentleman. He desired, in behalf of himself and his gallant companions, to return profound acknowledgments for this generous reception. It touched the sensibilities of their hearts. The most acceptable homage a patriot can receive is the approbation of a free and enlightened people. This spontaneous welcome and just appreciation of his motives and position were indemnities for many misfortunes. Though highly gratified by this manifestation of public feeling, it was no more than might be expected from the citizens of a state whose great staple regulates the commerce of the world—which first, by its Constitution, invested the people with all the attributes of sovereignty, and whose institutions are now the admiration of mankind. Though born in another land, and speaking a different language, he was not ignorant of the history of Mississippi. He knew what she had achieved in 1815 on the plains of Chalmette, where the gallant Hinds, at the head of her dragoons, braved the fire of the whole British line, and became "the pride of one army and the admiration of the other." He remembered the deadly execution of her rifles at the storming of Monterey—the flashing sword of Davis on the field of Buena Vista—her battle-riven banner, when it was planted on the walls of Mexico by the heroic Quitman, now governor of the state. (Tremendous applause.) With these memories of brilliant events, he came from a kindred and friendly state—from noble-hearted Louisiana—to breathe for a few days the pure air of your forests, and to tread a soil consecrated to liberty. He desires to know and to mingle with you, a brother republican, anxious to see and to study your practical exemplifications of free government, and to witness the phenomenon of a whole people, engaged in trade, agriculture, and mechanics, comprehending and practicing the political problems that Europe, with all its philosophy, refinement, and learning, has never been able to solve. Again he thanks you for your hospitality, and for himself and comrades accepts it with pleasure.' (Great applause.)

"The citizens then pressed forward to shake the general by the

" *Whereas* there is reason to believe that a military expedition is about to be fitted out in the United States, with intention to invade the Island of Cuba, a colony of Spain, with which this country is at peace; *and where-as* it is believed that this expedition is instigated and set on foot chiefly by foreigners, who dare to make our shores the scene of their guilty and hostile preparations against a friendly power, and seek, by falsehood and misrepresentation, to seduce our own citizens, especially the young and inconsiderate, into their wicked schemes—an ungrateful return for the benefits conferred upon them by this people, in permitting them to make our country an asylum from oppression, and in flagrant abuse of the hospitality thus extended to them. *And whereas* such expeditions can only be regarded as adventures for plunder and robbery, and must meet the condemnation of the civilized world, while they are derogatory to the character of our states, which declare," etc.

The Cuban patriots, "few but undismayed," were now in arms in the Coscorro Mountains, in the vicinity of Principe, 450 miles from Havana, and combats had occurred at Las Tunas, Nagasa, and at San Miguel, where the brave Aguero de Aguero made a brilliant stroke.

hand, and, amid enthusiastic cheers and the discharge of cannon, he and his suite were conducted by the committee to the apartments prepared for them at Mrs. Nixon's and Mrs. Roberts's. Here they were soon presented to a number of the fair ladies of the country—the mothers, wives, sisters, and daughters of patriotic men. The general and the gallant young friends around him were delighted with this part of the reception, and surrendered themselves unconditionally to the ascendency of bright eyes and sunny smiles. At 12 o'clock M. the next day, an immense crowd from the surrounding country, drawn together by the Probate Court, the masonic celebration, and the rumor of Gen. Lopez's arrival, assembled on the public square. A procession was formed, preceded by a band of music, some one hundred ladies, the pupils of the academy, Gen. Lopez and friends, the masonic brethren, and the Sons of Temperance. Having marched round the public square, and through the principal streets, it entered the Court-house, where an eloquent address was pronounced by the Rev. Mr. Pitts, and then the company adjourned to a sumptuous dinner at Mr. Bradford's. Gen. Lopez and friends were hospitably entertained at Mrs. Roberts's; and, indeed, the houses of all the citizens were thrown open on the occasion, and each vied with the other in civilities to the distinguished guests."

Lopez was anxiously expected, and Quitman, it was believed in Cuba, would head the expedition. Nor was the impression confined to the Cubans. It prevailed generally in the United States. In June the grand jury of the U. S. Circuit Court, N. O., ignorant of their powers, or grossly overrating them, found a bill against John A. Quitman, John Henderson, and others, for setting on foot the invasion of Cuba. A rumor that this proceeding would be followed by his arrest having reached Gov. Quitman, he addressed the Hon. Jacob Thompson, a representative from Mississippi, as follows:

"Jackson, Aug. 15th, 1850.

"I have felt it my duty to ferret out all the information I can procure on the subject of the prosecution against me. It may hereafter form a part of the history of the attempt of the government to "*try · its strength.*" I shall feel honored with being the first subject of the experiment. I may fall in the breach, but if so, I trust that my fate may be a useful lesson to the people. Do I understand you and our excellent friend Johnson to recommend resistance to an arrest? I would like to know by return of mail whether I am thus to understand you. Please to be explicit. I will act upon my own responsibility, but desire the advice of my friends. The only question with me is one of duty. The path it directs, however beset with dangers, I think I have the courage to pursue."

Mr. Thompson replied in a very high-toned letter:

From Hon. Jacob Thompson.

"House of Representatives, Sept. 2d, 1850.

"MY DEAR SIR,—Your favor of the 15th ult. was duly received, and I reply promptly and without hesitancy, but I regret I have not the time to examine the subject thoroughly and in all its bearings, but I give you such views as present themselves on the surface.

"The opinion expressed in my last letter in reference to your standing a trial before the United States Court held in Louisiana, is not only seriously entertained, but definite, clear, satisfactory, and determinate.

" As chief magistrate of the State of Mississippi, you are the sole representative of her sovereignty. The state is responsible for no act, default, or crime (if you please) before any tribunal on earth save and except the great tribunal of public opinion. The very idea of sovereignty carries with it the sequence of impunity in her action and conduct. You, by virtue of the power imposed upon you by the people of the state, are required to maintain and uphold the right and dignity which belong to the government you represent. You are made the commander-in-chief of her forces, to execute her laws and preserve intact her rights and her honor. An injury done to you must be felt by the state, and any interference with you in the discharge of your high official trusts, is an interference with the sovereign and independent prerogative of your government. When the President of the United States commands me to do one act, and the executive of Mississippi commands me to do another thing inconsistent with the first order, I obey the governor of my state. To Mississippi I owe allegiance, and, because she commands me, I owe obedience to the United States. But when she says I owe obedience no longer, right or wrong, come weal or woe, I stand for my legitimate sovereign, and to disobey her behests is, in my conscience, treason.

" The sovereign State of Mississippi has made it your duty to remain at the capital of the state, and to see that the laws are faithfully executed. She has ordained that, for malfeasance or non-feasance in office, you are liable to impeachment. But she has also appointed that this trial shall be under her own supervision, and by her own direction. No provision is made for any authority outside of the state to interrupt the executive in the discharge of his duty. No power is known to our state which can arrest the execution of our laws, or call in question any one of the great departments of the government.

" Now admit that a grand jury, at the instance of the United States, in other and foreign states, could find an indictment against the governor of a state and arrest

him, or the judiciary issue a process for his arrest.   If
they can arrest, they can refuse bail; if they can refuse
bail, they can, without trial, take him away from his duty,
incarcerate him, and, by rendering it impossible for him
to perform his official duties, virtually vacate the office
of governor, and leave the state without a chief executive.
This is an absurdity.   The consequence of the power
claimed annihilates state sovereignty, and soon we may
expect to see governors of states, like Roman satraps,
brought to the capitol in chains, if the power claimed is
tamely submitted to.

"You intimate the possibility that the judge of our
District Court may issue his warrant for your arrest.
The very idea appears to me preposterous, and I do not
believe Judge Gholson or Judge Daniel will be guilty of
such folly.   The theory of our government is based upon
the distinct division of the powers of government into
three independent departments—the executive, the legislative, and the judiciary; each is independent of the
other, and no control can be exerted by the one over the
other.   I take it for an undisputed position that a federal
judge has no higher powers in a state over persons
and officers than the judges of the state; and I can not
believe that for any offense the judiciary of the state
would order the chief magistrate of a state to be arrested as a criminal until he had been first deposed by the
proper authorities.   In this case I shall not believe till
the order is made that any judge of our state will assume
any such power.

"But, in the event that it is done, I think you owe it
to the office you hold, which should never be degraded
in your person—you owe it to yourself to refuse submission to the mandate.

"If, feeling your innocence, you should desire to stand
a trial on the charge made against you, you can not submit to it till you have resigned your station.   Being
guiltless will be a greater reason for your resistance;
and, under the circumstances, no power on earth should
make me resign.   The power is claimed to try the Governor of Mississippi: before I submitted, I would first
vindicate the honor and dignity of my place and position.
The sovereignty of Mississippi should never be tarnished
or degraded in my person.

"The times, too, are out of joint. The doctrine is now preached from high places that the sovereign states are no more than mere petty corporations—mere integral portions of a mighty empire. The tendency of every movement in the central government is to consolidation with unlimited powers. The majority claim the power to construe our Constitution, and they are limited in their construction only by their wishes and their views of policy. When the majority thus act, they hold it treason in any one of the parties to this confederacy to judge for itself, and to resist the action of the majority, however obnoxious and however disastrous. If this tendency of our government is not resisted and arrested, we shall soon have passed through a revolution, and constitutional liberty will be numbered among the things that were. The first effort to degrade the state will be made in your person, and, by all the powers above, I would resist it.

"I have written more than I intended, and what I have said has been said in great haste. But these are my opinions, and you can make such use of them as you please. I hold no opinion on this subject which I would not give to the world.

"Our friend Johnson,* who has just left my room, concurs with me in these views, and desires to be remembered in kindness to you."

Many of the governor's friends advised him not to resign. Some of his friends openly rejoiced in the probability of his arrest, urging him to resist, and thus precipitate a collision between the federal and state authorities, which would, in its sequel, involve the other Southern States. The following address will explain the course that he took in this emergency.

" *To the People of Mississippi.*

"In November, 1849, I was elected, by your free suffrages, governor of this state. My term of office commenced with my inauguration on the 10th of January,

* Senator from Arkansas.

1850. By the provisions of the Constitution, it will expire on the 10th of January, 1852. In the middle of my term of office, and in the active discharge of its duties, I am to-day arrested by the United States Marshal of the Southern District of Mississippi, by virtue of process, originating out of charges exhibited against me in the District Court of the United States for the Eastern District of Louisiana, for an alleged violation of the neutrality law of 1818, by beginning, setting on foot, and furnishing the means for a military expedition against the island of Cuba.

"Under these charges, the marshal is directed to arrest me and remove my person to the city of New Orleans, there to be tried for these alleged offenses.

"Unconscious of having, in any respect, violated the laws of the country, ready at all times to meet any charge that might be exhibited against me, I have only been anxious, in this extraordinary emergency, to follow the path of duty. As a citizen, it was plain and clear I must yield to the law, however oppressive or unjust in my case; but as chief magistrate of a sovereign state, I had also in charge her dignity, her honor, and her sovereignty, which I could not permit to be violated in my person. Resistance by the organized force of the state while the federal administration is in the hands of men who appear to seek some occasion to test the strength of that government, would result in violent contests, much to be dreaded in the present critical condition of the country.

"The whole South, patient as she is under encroachment, might look with some jealousy upon the employment of military force to remove a Southern governor from the jurisdiction of his state, when it had been withheld from her citizens seeking to reclaim a fugitive slave in Massachusetts.

"On the other hand, the arrest and forcible removal from the state of her chief executive magistrate, for an indefinite period of time, would not only be a degradation of her sovereignty, but must occasion incalculable injury and disaster to the interests of the state, by the entire suspension of the executive functions of her government. The Constitution has not contemplated such an event as the forcible abduction of the governor. It has not provided for the performance of his duties by another officer except in the case of a *vacancy*. Such vacancy can not happen while there is a governor, though he be a prisoner to a foreign power. Although he may be absent, and incapable of performing his duties, he is still governor, and no other person can execute his office.

"It follows, therefore, that in such case the state would practically suffer some of the evils of anarchy. The pardoning power would be lost. Officers could not be commissioned or qualified; the great seal of the state could not be used; vacancies in office could not be filled; fugitives from justice could not be reclaimed or surrendered; the public works, the operations of the penitentiary, and all repairs of public buildings must stop for want of legal requisitions to defray the expenses thereof. The sale of state lands, and the location of recent grants, must bè suspended.

"The convention of the people, called at the last session of the Legislature, could not assemble for want of writs of election. In case of the death or resignation of the administrative officers of the state government, these important offices, including the treasury, would be left without the superintendence or care of any authorized person. In fine, the whole government of the state would be in confusion and great inconvenience, and perhaps irreparable injury flow from such a state of things. For all these evils there is but one remedy. That remedy is my resignation.

" I therefore, fellow-citizens, now resign the high trust confided to my hands, with no feeling of personal regret except that I could not serve you better; with no feeling of shame, for I am innocent of the causes which have induced the necessity of this step. On the contrary, although personally I fear no investigation and shun no scrutiny, I have spared no efforts consistent with self-respect to avert this result. So soon as I learned that attempts would be made, under an act of Congress of the last century, to remove me from this state, I formally offered to the proper authorities of the United States any pledge or security to appear in New Orleans and meet the charges against me so soon as my term of office should expire; and I remonstrated against *the indignity* thus about to be offered, not to myself, but to the state, in dragging away from his duties her chief magistrate.

"My proposition was not accepted, and my remonstrance not heeded.

"It is not for me to complain. You are the aggrieved party. My course in this matter meets the approval of some of the most patriotic citizens near me. I sincerely hope, as it was dictated alone by my sense of duty to the state, it may meet the approbation of my fellow-citizens.

"In thus parting from my generous constituents, it would be proper to give them an account of my stewardship during the short but interesting period that I have acted as their public servant, but the official connection between us has been so summarily and unexpectedly severed, that I must defer the grateful task to a future day.

"I have but to add that, during my short but exciting period of service, I have in all things striven to be faithful and true to the rights, the interests, and the honor of the state. For this I have been abused and calumniated by the enemies of the South. Treachery and faithlessness would have secured favor and praise from the same sources.

"Fellow-citizens, I now take my leave of you with gratitude for the generous support you have extended to me, and with cheering confidence that your honor and your interests may be safely confided to the hands of the faithful and able son of Mississippi who, as President of the Senate, succeeds to my place.

"JOHN A. QUITMAN.

"Executive Chamber, Jackson, Monday evening, Feb. 3d, 1851."

Gov. Quitman to H. J. Harris, Esq., U. S. Attorney for the Southern District of Mississippi.

"Executive Department, Jackson, October 2d, 1850.

"SIR,—I avail myself of the first leisure moment to answer your letter of the 28th ult., received several days since. Upon the receipt of the first intimation that I had been indicted in the United States District Court in New Orleans for a participation in the late Cuban affair, my personal inclinations would have induced me promptly to meet the baseless charges that had thus been exhibited against me by the federal government or its agents, and to demand an investigation; but, as those who brought about this prosecution are perfectly aware, my official position as Governor of the State of Mississippi imposes upon me solemn and responsible duties, which do not leave me at liberty to consult my private inclinations, especially when the consequences of my action might result in a suspension of the executive power of a sovereign state to which my primary allegiance is due.

"In the peculiar and unprecedented attitude in which I am placed, my sincere desire is to ascertain the rule of action which should govern me, and to perform my whole duty.

"To enable me to decide correctly, it is my purpose to consult competent legal advisers, and I hope to be enabled within a fortnight to return a definite answer to your inquiry, whether I will give the assurance that I will voluntarily make my appearance in New Orleans and give bail according to law, or whether I shall decline doing so.

"In the mean time I pray you to make known to the attorney who has thought fit to exhibit this indictment against me, that I am ready at all times to give the assurance that I will appear and meet the charges made against me so soon as the termination of my official duties as governor of this state shall leave me the control of my own movements."

Gen. John Henderson to Gov. Quitman.

"New Orleans, Nov. 6th, 1850.

"DEAR SIR,—It is requested by Gen. Lopez's friends here that I should write you with respect to the present state of affairs of the great enterprise in which he is engaged, and in which you have heretofore taken—and I am quite sure do not cease to take—the most lively interest.

"Gen. Lopez is here, actively preparing for another expedition. I am not fully informed in the particular views he now entertains of renewing this enterprise, but, as far as it may be necessary, I presume Mr. L. J. Segur will inform you. Suffice it for *me* to say, it is meditated to get a steamer here; but embark for Cuba from the coast of Georgia, where most of his present armament is preparing. To get the steamer is now the great difficulty. One can be had here for $25,000; and I believe about *half* the funds necessary for the purchase are within reach *here.* But the want of the other half delays the departure. Besides the great desire Gen. Lopez has to haste and complete the redemption of Cuba, he and many of us have a special pride that the *work be progressing* under his command *at the time* he might be *called* for *trial* for the attempt last spring. All concurring testimony from Cuba reports favorably of the present auspices. It is said the people have been *preparing* ever since the affair at Cardenas; that a considerable armament has been procured, and some degree of organization been effected, and much of zeal and hope inspired. And certainly Gen. Lopez indulges the strongest confidence of success.

"I need not tell you how much I desire to see him move again, and it is more useless to tell you also how wholly unable I am to assist him to make this move. With my limited means, I am under the *extremest* burdens from my endeavors on the former occasion. Indeed, I find my cash advances for the first experiment was *over half* of all the cash advanced to the enterprise, and all my present means and energies are exhausted in bringing up arrearages. Yet I still believe in the importance, the morality, and probability of the enterprise; and I believe it is one the South should steadfastly cherish and promote. I *feel* it more specially incumbent on us who have once failed to retrieve our judgments with the country, and to retrieve ourselves from so much of opprobium and reproach as the defeat has cast upon us. For we all know that, could we succeed, we should win all those triumphs which success in such enterprises never fails to command. And would not such triumph be glorious?

"With unabated zeal, therefore, I present the project to your consideration for farther pecuniary assistance, if you can devise the means to render it that assistance. Yet I wish you to believe that I submit it to your own unbiased judgment, and not as pressing it with personal persuasions. I believe you yield equal consideration to the importance of this subject as I do; and, as a Southern question, I do not think, when properly viewed, its magnitude can be overestimated; and I am quite sure the time is near at hand when it must be so appreciated generally throughout the South. Yet, impatient of delay, and perhaps a little sore from the reproach suffered from our recent failure, I have a painful anxiety to see the object attained, and that *now.* Hence this communication."

Governor Quitman to H. J. Harris, U. S. Attorney.

"State of Mississippi, Executive Department, }
Jackson, November 9th, 1850. }

"SIR,—A protracted indisposition has prevented me from giving the additional reply to your letter of the 28th of September, promised in mine of the 2d of October, to which I again refer.

"I had some hopes that the government, in view of all the circumstances, would be disposed to suspend the prosecution against me until the termination of my official services as governor of this state might leave me at liberty to repair to New Orleans and meet the charges against me.

"I am now informed by your note that this proposition is not satisfactory, and I am called on, under threat of arrest and forcible removal from the state, to say whether I will voluntarily make my appearance in New Orleans and give bail according to law, in any reasonable time, etc.

"I again assure you that if I felt at liberty to pursue my personal inclinations I would hasten to meet the charge exhibited against me, and confront my accusers; but, upon full reflection, I have concluded that the highest obligations which can bind my conscience, and the highest duties of allegiance to my state, forbid me from voluntarily placing myself in a position in which I can not comply with the one nor perform the other.

"I therefore respectfully decline making any voluntary pledges for the surrender of my person, except that heretofore proposed of meeting the indictment promptly on the termination of my present office, if the same should be acceptable.

"As an individual charged with a violation of an act

of Congress, and asserting my innocence, I have no favors to ask from the government, but, as a citizen and a public officer, I may be permitted to suggest the entire absence of any necessity for pressing to serious consequences a prosecution which, so far as the public interest is concerned and I am reputed to be connected with it, certainly deserves to be regarded as frivolous, when a short delay will quietly effect all proper objects of the prosecution.

"The government can scarcely hope to involve me seriously in the charges preferred.

"But should it be that the indulgence of some sympathy for the oppressed people of Cuba calls for the infliction of some punishment, it seems to me that the offended laws of the country would be amply vindicated by the eventual punishment of the offender, without deeming it necessary to invade the government of a state, forcibly seize upon her chief magistrate, remove him from the performance of his duties, and actually suspend for a time the executive powers of a sovereign state."

The United States district attorney had a painful duty to discharge. He was the personal and political friend of Governor Quitman, but his instructions were peremptory and pressing. A decision had to be made between resistance or resignation.

A few days before he thus explained his views to the Hon. R. Barnwell Rhett, of South Carolina.

Gov. Quitman to Hon. R. Barnwell Rhett.

"Jackson, Jan. 24th, 1851.

"DEAR SIR,—Indisposition, which I trust is temporary, causes me to use the hand of my private secretary. Before this letter reaches you I shall have resigned the office of governor. Between the alternatives of bringing about a collision of arms between this state and the general government prematurely, and, on the other hand, of permitting the executive department of the state to be suspended for an indefinite period of time, there remained a somewhat middle course for me to pursue consistently with my sense of propriety; that was to lay down my official character before submitting to an arrest. This prosecution has led me to reflect much upon the dangerous powers granted by Congress to the district and circuit courts in certain criminal cases. For instance, the act of 1818, under which I am prosecuted, would, according to the construction placed upon it by the federal court of New Orleans, cover the case of furnishing a dinner, or even the necessaries of life to Gen. Lopez or those who participated with him, if aware at the time of their plan.

"The description of the offense, as in the case of the 'Bloody Bill,' is so vague as to furnish a suitable cloak for the boldest tyranny.

"My purpose, however, was not to criticise these measures, but to suggest to you that it may be a suitable time for a vigorous assault upon the judicial encroachments of the federal courts.

"I favor the entire abolition of both circuit and district courts, or the confining their jurisdiction to the trial of causes connected with the collection of the revenue."

On hearing of his arrest, the Hon. A. G. Brown wrote:

* * * * * "Your resignation and appearance in New Orleans has created a deep sensation here. Your enemies are confounded, and your friends rejoiced at your cause. The Fillmoreans fancied that you would *resist. They hoped you would;* for, in the general excitement growing out of such resistance, they hoped an indignant community would lose sight of the treachery and imbecility of an administration which either will not or can not arrest a fugitive slave in Boston.

"I take this occasion to say that I approve your course with all my heart, and have never doubted that our people will sustain you most triumphantly; and, if they do not, I for one shall confess myself a disbeliever in the ability of the people to govern themselves.

"A highly intelligent and patriotic lady, Mrs. Morse, the wife of the member from Louisiana, desires me to say that if the Southern men refuse to sustain you, the ladies will volunteer in your cause. She says you may rely on the ladies of her state, and I add that they could not have a more worthy leader in any enterprise than Mrs. Morse.

"We expect that fraud and bribery will give you some trouble in New Orleans, as they have already given Gen. Henderson; but we feel a moral conviction that you will come out without even the smell of fire on the hem of your garments.

"You have the hearty good wishes of every true friend of the South."

A patriotic militia general wrote: "If you are in trouble and need assistance fire a cannon, and my brigade will turn out to a man."

The letters he received from every quarter, and from other states, though giving very conflicting advice, manifest the hold he had on the affections of the Southern people, and their anxiety for the regeneration of Cuba.

Sixty of these letters are from ladies of education and position in ten different states, all breathing the noble enthusiasm of the accomplished and estimable daughter of Louisiana, who commissioned the Hon. A. G. Brown to speak for her.

The record will explain what occurred after his arrest.

"THE UNITED STATES *vs.* JOHN A. QUITMAN.

"*Indictment for Violation of the Neutrality Laws of 20th of April, 1818.*"

"The prosecution was commenced by indictment, which was found by the Grand Jury of the United States District Court for the Eastern District of Louisiana, on the 21st day of June, 1850. And on the 26th day of June, 1850, on motion of Logan Hunton, Esq., U. S. Attorney, and under the provisions of the act of 8th of August, 1846, the indictment was remitted to the U. S. Circuit Court for the Eastern District of Louisiana for trial.

"A copy of the indictment certified as required by the statute was presented, and application thereon based was made to Hon. Samuel J. Gholson, Judge of the District

Court of the United States for the Southern District of
Mississippi, for the arrest and removal for trial of John
A. Quitman to the Eastern District of Louisiana. The
writ of arrest was issued by Judge Gholson on the 13th
of January, 1851, after General Quitman (as the writ recites) had been heard by himself and counsel in opposition to the granting of the application. The return of
the marshal on the writ is as follows: 'In obedience to
the commands of the within warrant, I did, on the 3d of
February, 1851, execute the same on John A. Quitman,
in the city of Jackson, State of Miss., and have him now
before the United States Court for the Eastern District
of Louisiana. '

       "'Fielding Davis, Marshal So. Dist. Miss.
"'New Orleans, 7th February, 1851.'

"On same day (7th February, 1851) General Quitman
appeared before the United States Circuit Court, Hon.
Theo. H. M'Caleb presiding alone, and entered into recognizance in the sum of $1000, with H. R. W. Hill* as
his surety, for his future appearance.

"On the 6th of March, 1851, the third trial of General
Henderson having resulted in a mistrial, the jury being
unable to agree upon a verdict, a nolle prosequi was entered on the 7th of March, 1851, upon motion of Logan
Hunton, United States Attorney, as to all the defendants
embraced in the indictment, one of whom was General
Quitman."

Governor Quitman, after his arrest, had endeavored to
evade any sort of demonstration from his friends. Before leaving the seat of government for New Orleans he
had written to Mr. Mellen and Major Elward, of Natchez, to check any manifestation of popular feeling in
his favor. But it was not to be thus stifled by his modesty. The moment he left the court-room in New Orleans the multitude pressed around him. Large numbers attended him to his quarters. Deputations from

* The late Harry Hill, an eminent merchant of New Orleans, and
a man of enlarged views and noble heart.

Mississippi, Alabama, Carolina, and other states, waited upon him. He was serenaded, and forced to appear on his balcony by the acclamations of the people. With one voice they applied to him the vigorous lines of Rogers:

> " Thou hast served, and well, the sacred cause
>   That Hampden, Sydney died for. Thou hast stood,
>   Scorning all thought of self, from first to last,
>   Among the foremost in that glorious field;
>   From first to last; and, ardent as thou art,
>   Held on with equal step as best became
>   A lofty mind, loftiest when most assailed;
>   Never, though galled by many a barbed shaft,
>   By many a bitter taunt from friend and foe,
>   Swerving or shrinking."

Events reproduce themselves. Thirty-six years before, in the same city, the illustrious Jackson left the head of his victorious columns, threw aside his sword, and appeared in court in obedience to the mandate of a federal judge. And now the community beheld in their midst a modest and unpretending man, the hero of Chapultepec, who had proudly and properly refused, as chief magistrate of a sovereign state, to acknowledge any paramount authority, but for the sake of peace, and to manifest his respect for the laws, had resigned his high position, and now appeared to answer a charge of which he was wholly innocent. The incident had in it much of the moral sublime, and was in beautiful concord with the whole character of the man—his love of liberty, his intense feeling of state pride, his fearless pursuit of duty wherever it might lead, and the obedience to law which he always considered the part of a good citizen. The prosecution, as we have seen, was finally abandoned. "The charge," said the Delta, "upon which the federal government insisted that the sovereign State of Mississippi should surrender up her chief executive into the hands of the government, of which that sovereign state is one of the creators, has been abandoned by the representative of the federal authority. But even this voluntary retreat of the government has been adopted in order to cover a still more complete defeat, in the certain, the inevitable acquittal of that gentleman if the matter had ever been brought to trial. And now, what is the position in which this result places the federal government? There were about a dozen persons indicted for being engaged in this Cuba expedition, all of whom were ready for a trial.

"The case of General Henderson has already consumed two months; there is no reason to suppose that the other cases would not have taken as long a time, and thus the better part of two years would have been consumed in the trial of the other parties besides General Quitman. Suppose, however, that these cases took up the rest of the term—and of that there could be no doubt—it is certain that, by placing General Quitman last, his term of office as Governor of Mississippi would have expired before his trial. Now all that the governor asked was that the process against him should be waived, and when the government was ready to proceed with his case he gave his pledge of honor that he would be on the spot to meet the charge. His reason for making the request was, that he did not believe it compatible with the sovereignty of the state which he represented to be detained as a prisoner by another authority. Right or wrong, these were his honest convictions; they are the convictions, too, of a large class of our people, and of some of the most distinguished constitutional lawyers in the country. Such opinions were entitled to some respect.

"It was evident that, in this view of his duty, Governor Quitman had but two alternatives. The one was to resist the process of the federal court, the other was to resign his post as Governor of Mississippi. Due notice was given of the attitude assumed by him. The question then arises, did the nature of the charge against General Quitman, or of the proofs in the possession of the officers of the federal government, justify the government in forcing him to one or the other of these alternatives? The result of the trials gives a satisfactory negative to this query. But, farther, if the charge and proofs were more serious than they are, was not the well-ascertained fact that the other cases could not be got through with in time to reach Governor Quitman's before the expiration of his term of office an ample and satisfactory reason for the acceptance of the governor's proposition?

"There can be no hesitation, in any properly organized mind, in answering this question. Had the government been influenced by any respect for the rights of the states of this confederacy, by any of that comity which exists even between foreign and independent nations, it would have said: 'We will not, even to accommodate our dear friends of Spain, unnecessarily force the Governor of Mississippi into open war with us, or into a resignation of his office. We will not embarrass the affairs of one of the confederacy so unnecessarily. We will wait until we are ready to proceed with the governor's trial.' Such would have been the dictate of magnanimity—of respect for state sovereignty. Such a course, too, would have saved the State of Mississippi from great inconvenience, and the federal officers in this city from the reproaches which are now thickly heaped upon them for the lame and impotent conclusion to which their labors have come. The government has been ignominiously foiled and defeated. General Quitman has not been forced into a position of resistance to the federal authority, so as to afford grounds for an indictment of high treason, as was expected. And as to the triumph in his resignation, it is but a barren one. The gallant people of Mississippi will regard it their sacred duty to restore him to the executive post from which he was so indecorously, unjustly, and improperly dragged, to dance attendance on proceedings got up, it is now avowed, wholly to satisfy the pride of a foreign despotism."

The following telegraphic dispatch to the New Orleans papers indicates the public feeling throughout the country.

"Natchez, March 8th, 11 A.M.

"So great was the joyful excitement in Natchez last night on the termination of the Cuban humbug in your city, that the night was made voiceful with the roar of cannon. Fifteen guns were fired for Quitman, and fifteen for Southern States. Many persons pulled off their stockings for cartridges, and fired several for mankind in general."

The right of the federal authorities to cause the arrest of the chief magistrate of one of the states, and to remove him out of the state for trial before a federal court, for an alleged infraction of the laws of the United States, was much mooted at the time, and drew forth, on both sides, very able and searching discussion. Governor Quitman and his friends contended that no such hostile and despotic power is lodged in the federal government under the Constitution; none such exists, as an incident, either proper or necessary to the maintenance of the Union, or the integrity of the federal government. Having no such power under the Constitution, it can confide none to any of its departments.

The government of the United States is the creature of the states; formed by them in their sovereign capacity, existing for their benefit, and dependent, for its continued existence, upon their will. The supposition is monstrous that a government thus formed possesses an implied power, virtually, to destroy the government of a state. It is manifest that if the federal government, through its judiciary, can deprive a state of its executive, by legal process against the person of its governor, it can, by the same process, issued for the same, or similar cause, deprive the state of its legislative power also. If, on an indictment found in a federal court, the governor of the state can be arrested and forcibly taken from the state, every member of the Legislature, and, indeed, every other state officer, may be dealt with in the like manner, and thus the state, without its will or consent, be deprived of its entire government, and this on an *ex parte* proceeding of a grand jury at Washington, against the governor and the members of the Legislature while in session (whether well founded, or the offspring of an arbitrary malevolence), would result in their immediate arrest and abduction from the state, thus leaving it, in effect, a disorganized community—a state without a government *de facto*, although possessing a government *de jure ;* and, what is worse, without the power of organizing itself again, unless by a recourse to its primitive right of revolution. Is it possible, and do we now learn for the first time the fearful fact, that the states of this Union hold their right of self-preservation by no better tenure than this, and that their political organization may be thus annihilated at any moment that an arbitrary government, through its judiciary department, may choose to exert the portentous power in question—suspending the existence of a state government by arresting the officers to whom the functions of government are for the time intrusted ?

So insolent an assertion of power—one so utterly subversive, not only of a separate state sovereignty, but of all correct ideas of government—has never before been made in this country; and yet such an assertion of power, and to such extent, is directly and necessarily involved in any proposition asserting the legality of the arrest of Governor Quitman.

Are the public men of the South so wanting in foresight and sagacity as not to perceive the application that may be made of this doctrine to the future contingencies likely to be forced upon us? Are they so blind as not to discern the cloven foot of federal despotism imprinted by this stealthy and noiseless step upon the most vital part of the sovereignty of the states—upon the very centre of their being as political communities? Is the federal judiciary so immaculate, and so independent of federal influence, that we are willing to permit this assertion of power by the government of the United States to pass unchallenged? What efficient measure of self-preservation, taken by the South, may demand exemption from the assertion of this portentous right to strike dead the organization of the states by a simple movement of the judicial arm of the federal government?

These are questions that force themselves, with vivid significance, upon the mind of every thinking man in the country who considers this subject in connection with the trying crisis that awaits the South—a crisis written among the decrees of Providence, and which no human power can avert.

The idea that the federal government, or any of its departments, possess this species of jurisdiction over the existence of the state government, is as novel as it is absurd, and ought not to be tolerated for a moment.

There is not a state Constitution in the Union that provides for a vacancy occasioned by the arrest or imprisonment of its governor, at the suit of a foreign jurisdiction. If there is, the provision is a disgrace to the man who wrote and the state that adopted it. No such provision has ever been incorporated among the fundamental laws of any political community or sovereignty on earth, and for the obvious reason that no sovereignty will, for a moment, contemplate its own destruction, or the suspension of its vitality at the will of another. There is, of course, no such provision in the Constitution of Mississippi; no clause providing against the contingency of a capture and forcible abduction of its executive department. Such a concession to any power extraneous to the state would be a grotesque and ridiculous anomaly in the Constitution of a state, such as the wildest devotee to federal supremacy never dreamed of. See, then, the result in Mississippi of the proceeding in question. The Constitution of the state making no provision for filling an official vacancy thus occasioned, if Governor Quitman had not resigned, and had been taken from the state by force, it would have been as completely disorganized during his absence (which the trial or conviction might prolong for years) as if the entire government had been subverted by violence. In the mean time the laws of Mississippi would have been without the means of enforcement, the government itself (or rather the part of it that remained in the state) without the very first element that enters into the being of government, viz., the means of self-preservation. Without its executive power a state (organized as ours is, and all other free states of modern times are) is without the means of maintaining either its organic or municipal law against insurrectionary violence from within, or armed force from without. This power of self-preservation forms the essential idea and basis of a state, and without it the most subtle and profound organization would, of course, be unavailing and delusive, to place the community beyond the condition of primitive and unorganized force.

The question may be asked, has any one who happens to be governor of a state any right to claim exemption from punishment for the violation of the laws of the Union simply because he is governor? Unquestionably it would be better that he should be thus exempt altogether than punish him at the hazard of so great a calamity as the destruction of the government of the state, and of making a concession that prostrates every state government in the Union at the feet of a central despotism. The presence of the governor in his state is essential to its existence as such, and the lesser evil must yield to the greater. Destroy the organization of the state, and no crime can be effectually punished. But there is really nothing in this suggestion, because the exemption is merely pending the office, and does not involve his exemption altogether. If punishable at all, while his official character continues, it could only be by the voluntary consent of the state—a consent which no sovereignty would probably ask another to give.

Can the President of the United States be indicted in a state for an offense committed there, be arrested and brought thence by a state officer, and be tried and imprisoned, or capitally punished, in the state whose law he had offended, pending his official character?

What confusion of ideas grows out of such arbitrary assertions of power in this country! Into what absurd inquiries are we necessarily launched, when we abandon the idea of the sovereignty of the states, and contemplate the Union as a consolidated community?

1851. On the 2d of August a second liberating expedition, notwithstanding the ferocious proclamation of President Fillmore and the vigilance, real or simulated, of the local federal authorities, set out from New Orleans in the Steamship Pampero. The following is a list of the field and staff officers:

General-in-Chief—NARCISO LOPEZ.

Sub-commandant and Chief of the Staff—John Praguy.

Staff Officers.—Captain, Emmich Radrich; Lieutenant, Joseph Lewohl; Lieutenant, Sigis Rekendorf.

Corps of Adjutants.—Colonel, Eugene Brummenthal; Captain, Ludivig Schlesinger; Lieutenant, Ludivig Muller; Dr. Henry A. Fourniquet; Commissary, G. A. Cook.

Staff of the First Regiment.—Colonel, R. L. Downman; Lieutenant Colonel, W. Scott Haynes; Adjutant, George A. Graham; Commissary, Joseph Bell; Adjutant of the Regiment, George Parr.

Company A.—Captain, Robert Ellis; Lieutenant, E. H. M'Donald; Sub-lieutenant, J. L. Labuzan; Sub-lieutenant, R. R. Brelenbridge.

Company B.—Captain, John Johnson; First Lieutenant, James Dunn; Second Lieutenant, J. S. Williams; Third Lieutenant, James O'Reilly.

Company C.—Captain, J. C. Brigham; First Lieutenant, Richard Howden; Second Lieutenant, G. A. Gray; Third Lieutenant, J. D. Baker.

Company D.—Captain, Philip N. Golday; First Lieutenant, David L. Rousseau; Second Lieutenant, John H. Landingham; Third Lieutenant, James V. Howain.

Company E.—Captain, Henry Jackson; First Lieutenant, William Hubble; Second Lieutenant, Thomas A. Simpson; Third Lieutenant, James Craugle.

Company F.—Captain, William Stewart; First Lieutenant, James G. Owens; Second Lieutenant, John G. Bush; Third Lieutenant, Thomas Hudnall.

First Regiment of Artillery.

Staff.—Colonel, William L. Crittenden; Adjutant, R. C. Stanford; Commissary, Felix Huston; Surgeon, Luduvig Hanks.

Company A.—Captain, John A. Kelly; First Lieutenant, T. C. James; Second Lieutenant, James A. Stevens; Third Lieutenant, J. O. Bryce.

Company B.—Captain, James Sanders; First Lieutenant, Philip S. Van Vechten; Second Lieutenant, Beverly E. Hunter; Third Lieutenant, William H. Craft.

Company C.—Captain, Victor Kerr; First Lieutenant, James Brandt; Second Lieutenant, H. T. Vienne.

Cuban Patriots' Regiment.—Captain, Ildefonso Oberto; First Lieutenant, Diego Hernandez; Second Lieutenant, Miguel Lopez; Third Lieutenant, José A. Planos; Fourth Lieutenant, Pedro Lopez.

Hungarian Regiment.—Major, Geo. Bontila; Captain, Ladislaus Palank; Lieutenant, Joseph Csermelyi; Lieutenant, Johan Peteri; Lieutenant, Adalbert Kerakes; Lieutenant, Conrad Eichler.

German Regiment.—Captain, Hugo Schliht; Lieutenant, Paul Michsel Birot; Captain, Pietro Muller; Lieutenant, Giovanni Placosio.

The Pampero steered for Key West. The current opinion was that Lopez would land at Neuvitas, and unite with Aquero and other patriots of Puerto Principe, who had already raised the standard of revolt. It is alleged likewise that he was induced, by intelligence received at Key West through an emissary of the captain general, to abandon this plan. These views were erroneous. Before his departure from New Orleans the point of debarkation had been agreed on: he had determined to make his first movement in the Vuelta Abajo, a mountainous district well known to him, and whose inhabitants, he had been persuaded, were ready to revolt. He knew the hazard of prolonging his voyage on the coast of Cuba, then vigilantly watched by Spanish cruisers; and, by landing at an intermediate point between Havana and Principe, the attention of the Spanish authorities would be directed from the latter until the insurrectionary movement there could be consolidated. And thus, with the self-sacrifice and daring that characterized him through life, he resolved to relieve his friends by drawing upon himself the first fury of the storm. On the 12th of August the expedition landed at Morillos, Bahia Honda, some fifty miles north of Havana; and to encourage his followers with the hope of re-enforcements, and to impress upon them the stern fact that the die was now cast, and that victory or death was the alternative, Lopez ordered the Pampero to return immediately to the United States. As she hoisted her anchor and steamed rapidly out of the bay, the general commenced his march for the interior, leaving Crittenden, with his detachment of about 120 men, to bring up the baggage. At Las Pozas, on the 13th, Lopez was vigorously attacked by the Spanish troops, but drove them back with great slaughter by an impetuous charge, in which Gen. Praguy, chief of his staff, who had distinguished himself in the Hungarian war, was killed. The Spaniards fell back for re-enforcements; the liberators drew off toward the mountains, in the vain hope of being joined by the natives. On the 16th, when encamped in a hacienda formerly owned by Lopez, he was suddenly assailed by a strong body of lancers, supported by a veteran regiment of infantry under Gen. Enna, a Catalonian officer of distinction. They came up gallantly to the attack, but the troops of Lopez rushed headlong upon them with revolvers and bowie-knives, and converted it into a hand-to-hand fight instead of a battle of musketry. In this desperate affair Gen. Enna received a mortal wound. He called to the nearest officer and said, "I am badly wounded; put your horse before me that mine may follow yours and conduct me privately from the field." He then sent for Brigadier Rozales and directed him to continue the fight. The railroad from Havana and the Spanish steamers bringing fresh troops, Lopez was compelled to fall back. He first directed his course to the mountains, afterward toward the coast. For some days he seems to have marched and counter-marched in a circumscribed area, suffering from exposure and hunger, his men cut off in detail, and a Spanish detachment facing him on every road. To fight was out of the question, his arms and powder having become useless, and to escape seemed impossible. At length, on the morning of the 21st, he was surprised by Col. Elizalde, at the head of a strong column of Royalists, and with difficulty escaped. On the evening of the 21st he could only muster 125 men and 20 muskets fit for service. For the last 48 hours they had been without food. Here and there parties of the enemy fell on them, and they were ultimately forced to disperse. Some fled toward the coast; Lopez, with a handful of followers, struck for the mountains, still encouraging them by his enthusiasm, setting them an example by his patience—the dream of liberty still exciting his imagination, and his faith in the fidelity of friends and the triumph of his cause still unsubdued. Not a complaint escaped him. His canteen of wine he divided among his followers, seeing that they needed it more than himself. His last crust he soaked in a cup of water, and gave the bread to a comrade, saying that he could live very well on the water. On the 29th he was betrayed by his guide, and captured and sent in chains to Havana. He was immediately sentenced to die by the garote. On the 1st of September he was conducted to the place of execution: he declared his attachment to liberty, his undying faith in the redemption of his country, and died with the calmness of a martyr. His last words were, "Dear Cuba, adieu!"

Gen. Lopez fell into the very errors against which Quitman had cautioned him. He relied upon the co-operation of the Cubans without estimating the circumstances that restrained them; he had little suspicion of treachery in a cause so sacred; and he had left New Orleans with a force wholly inadequate in point of numbers, consisting chiefly of young men who had been taught to underrate the Spanish soldiery—once the most distinguished in Europe, and every where and at all times constitutionally brave. The weakness of his force, however, was owing to the unexpected rigor of the federal authorities, which had disconcerted his arrangements until the Gulf swarmed with Spanish and American cruisers, in league against the expedition. He was deceived as to the disposition of the Vuelta Abajo, and therefore his point of debarkation was unfortunate, bringing him, as it were, under the very claws of the tiger. His separation from Crittenden was a grave error. The motive for his advance was to strike a blow and win a victory, and thus draw the inhabitants to his standard before the royal troops could be concentrated against him. After his first battle he might have crossed the mountains in safety, and with the prestige of success, but for his reluctance to abandon Crittenden. With the hope of a junction with him he lingered in the vicinity of Las Pozas until it was too late to retreat with safety, and hence the disastrous result. Lopez was probably better fitted for guerrilla or desultory warfare, requiring little more than energy and daring, than for the organization and control of an army of invasion. Both his expeditions manifest a want of generalship. Bravely, however, and to the last, did he fulfill his mission. He accomplished enough to show that, with the co-operation of the Cubans, or without it, but for the intervention of the United States, the liberation of his unhappy country would have been effected.

While Crittenden was yet upon the beach, delayed by the want of transportation, a communication was received from Gen. Lopez directing him to advance to Las Pozas with all possible dispatch. Abandoning much of his material he pushed forward, utterly ignorant of the state of things before him. He had halted for breakfast without the precaution of posting sentinels, when he was fired on by a party of the enemy, who fell back, however, before the impetuous charge of the Americans.

Unfortunately, too little importance was attached to this affair. Satisfied with having so easily driven back what was considered a mere foraging party, when it was, in fact, the advance-guard of a column of the enemy 500 strong, they laid aside their arms and resumed their breakfast, without even taking the precaution to post sentinels. In fifteen minutes they were surprised by a heavy fire immediately in their rear. Crittenden gallantly led the charge, and drove the enemy from his strong position, but the superiority of numbers was overwhelming. After two bold but ineffectual rallies, the Americans were dispersed. Captain Kelly, with a small party, making a circuitous and dangerous march, succeeded in forming a junction with Lopez in time to take part in the battle of the 16th. Crittenden, with some sixty followers, finding it impracticable to advance against the artillery and cavalry of the enemy, now swarming on every road, entered the chapparal, and with great difficulty made their way to the coast, where they seized some small fishing-boats, with the hope of falling in with a neutral vessel that would give them refuge. They were soon captured by a Spanish steamer, and sent in irons to Havana. The captain general forthwith condemned them to be shot. Stripped to the shirt, their hands bound behind their backs, they were carried in front of the castle of Atares, guarded by the Spanish troops, and dogged by the ferocious rabble. The U. S. sloop of war Albany, and the U. S. steamer Vixen were in port, and their officers and crews witnessed the sad procession. The ensign of the republic was flying at the American consulate. One lingering look those heroic young men cast at the flag of their country, and, as the last hope of intervention passed away, the bitterness of death was aggravated by the feeling that they were to die as outlaws when they should have been claimed as citizens. But not even this, nor the exulting shouts of the Spanish rabble, shook the fortitude of the devoted band. Pale as ghosts, attenuated by exposure and fatigue, they fearlessly faced their grim executioners, and calmly surveyed the apparatus of death—the leveled muskets and the file of dead-carts waiting for their remains. No invocation for delay, no cry for mercy, no last promise of treacherous revelation with the hope of pardon, was heard from them during the protracted ordeal. In squads of six they were successively shot down, the officers being reserved for the last. When ordered to his knees, Crittenden replied, "*Americans kneel only to their God.*" They were ordered to reverse their position. "*No,*" said Victor Kerr, "*we look death in the face.*" "*Cowards,*" cried Stanford, "*our friends will avenge us.*"

"*Liberty forever!*" exclaimed Lieutenant James, and his last words mingled with the crash of musketry, and echoed over the sea. The quivering corpses of the fifty lay upon the ground. Before they could be transferred to the dead-carts the rabble rushed forward and trampled upon and mutilated the poor remains, with loud shouts of "Death to the Americans!" Their bloody shirts were borne through the streets, and exhibited in the great Dominica coffee-house. Passengers were arrested by ruffians with bloody hands, and forced, as they said, to "smell American blood." The cry resounded all night through the city, and was caught up by the Spanish outposts, and re-echoed back from the Moro and the frigate Esperanza, "*Death to the Americans of the North.*"*

* *Names of the Martyrs:* Colonel, W. L. Crittenden; Captains, Frederick S. Sewer, Victor Kerr, T. B. Veasey; Lieutenants, James Brandt, J. O. Brice, Thomas C. James; Surgeons, John Fisher, H. A. Fourniquet; Adjutant, R. C. Stanford; Sergeants, J. Whitercns, A. M. Cotchett, Napoleon Collins, G. M. Green, J. Salomon; Privates,

And thus perished those brave men, true representatives of the sympathies, the faith, and the ultimate mission of the republic. They perished as outlaws, but are canonized as martyrs. Their bodies were thrown into a ditch, where their bones now moulder. But one day from their sacred ashes may rise a flame that will put all Cuba in a blaze; and then, perhaps, the world may witness a repetition of a grand drama of the heroic period of Europe. Charles the Bold, Duke of Burgundy, in his war upon the Swiss, ordered the whole garrison of the Grison, eight hundred strong, to be put to the sword. Soon afterward, as though Providence designed to make this atrocity the special subject of its vengeance, the brilliant and glittering army of Burgundy—the most renowned in Europe—was exterminated at Moret by the peasantry of the Alps, and the ducal butcher fled, with the loss of his laurels and his power. His camp was prodigal of the richest spoils of war; the wine, the lace, the embroidery, the jewels and golden armor of the most opulent people in Europe. But these had no attractions for the Helvetian mountaineers. They passed them by to plunder the battle-field of a more terrible spoil. They gathered the skulls of the slain, and built a monument long known as the *charnel-house of Moret*. And there it stood, in its ghastly grandeur, until 1794, when the French of the Cote d'Or, having driven the Austrians from this same battle-field of Moret, pulled·down the structure and restored to the earth the bones

N. H. Fisher, William Chilling, G. A. Cook, S. O. Jones, M. H. Ball, James Bulet, Robert Caldwell, C. C. William Smith, A. Ross, P. Brourke, John Christdes, William II. Holmes, Samuel Mills, Edward Rulman, William B. Little, George W. Arnold, B. J. Wregy, Robert Cantley, John G. Sanka, William Niseman, C. T. Collins, James Stauton, Thos. Harnett, Anselmo Torres Hernandez, Patrick Dillon, Alexander M'Ilcer, Thomas Hearsey, Samuel Reed, John Stubbs, James Ellis, H. T. Vienne, William Hogan, M. Phillips, Charles A. Robinson, James S. Manville.

of the Burgundians! That the republic will one day gather the bones of their fifty sons who perished at Atares, and give them an honorable burial in FREE AND INDEPENDENT CUBA, no impartial student of history can doubt.

An expedition for higher and nobler objects has never been set on foot. Sympathy for the oppressed and love of glory were the main considerations that influenced those who joined it. It was authorized by the precedents of the most enlightened nations. It was organized under the advice of eminent jurisconsults. It was a legitimate aid, sanctioned by public law, to an oppressed people then actually in arms.

The summary proceedings of the captain general, in decreeing the execution of the prisoners without a trial, may be traced to the proclamation of the President of the United States, which had denounced the liberators in advance as plunderers and robbers. To the feeble application of the American consul for delay or mitigation of punishment he replied that he had President Fillmore's authority for considering them as enemies of mankind. He afterward gave a similar explanation to Com. Parker of the U. S. steamer Saranac. The British premier, Lord Palmerston, in a dispatch to the British minister at Washington, dated October 22d, 1851, referred to the fifty victims as "persons whom the United States government itself has denounced as not being entitled to the protection of any government." Mr. Andrew Jackson Donelson (a few years later a candidate for the vice-presidency on the Fillmore ticket) used, on the receipt of the news of the execution, the following language:

"ALL ACCOUNTS AGREE THAT THE AMERICAN CONSUL AT HAVANA DID NOT INTERPOSE TO PREVENT THE HURRIED MASSACRE IN THAT CITY. *It is stated that he ex-*

*cused himself from interfering by Mr. Fillmore's procla-
mation of the 25th of April last—two months and ten
days before the rising in Cuba.* The proclamation states
that 'there is reason to believe that a military expedition is about to be fitted out in the United States,' intended for the invasion of Cuba, etc. The proclamation
then asserts that 'such expeditions can only be·regard-
ed as adventurers for plunder and robbery.' Truly, this
was unnecessary. The administration believed, on the
25th of April, that a military expedition was about to be
fitted out from our shores, and then went on to denounce
the persons who might engage in such expedition as
robbers and plunderers! WE FEEL NO HESITATION IN
SAYING THAT THIS PROCLAMATION EMBOLDENED THE SPAN-
ISH AUTHORITIES TO BUTCHER OUR CITIZENS AS THEY
WOULD HAVE BUTCHERED DUMB BEASTS. WITHOUT THIS
PROCLAMATION THE SPANISH AUTHORITIES WOULD NOT
HAVE DARED TO PURSUE THE COURSE THEY HAVE PUR-
SUED."

It is painful thus to refer to the act of a chief magistrate in whose character there is much to admire and
respect. But in making up the record, this fatal proclamation can not be overlooked. It was based upon imperfect information. It was an official assumption of
facts not proved. It was a sentence without trial. It
pronounced a sentence and indicated a penalty, which,
without the sanction of a court, is wholly inoperative in
this country, but which was eagerly seized on by the
captain general of Cuba. It must ever stand a reproach
to the American government. Posterity will not understand how a republic that owed so much, in its infancy,
to the fleets and armies of other nations, should be the
first to condemn as felonious the instincts of her citizens
in behalf of the oppressed.

The extent of the offense committed by the expedi-
tionists was a misdemeanor as against the statute law
of the United States. It is the duty of the President to

guard against piracies on American commerce, but what has he to do with piracies against other nations? Lopez and his men were not even pirates as against Spain. The sovereignty and eminent domain and jurisdiction of Cuba belong to Spain, but the property of the island, the realty, or the great bulk of it, belongs to the native Cubans. And there is no proof or presumption that they meant to make war on them or their property, but they went, upon the invitation of the Cubans, to make common cause with them, and aid them in the expulsion of the Spanish authority from the island, and to proclaim its independence or bring about its annexation to the United States. Was this piracy? Piracy is defined as "the offense of depredating on the seas without being authorized by any sovereign state, or by commissions from different sovereigns at war with each other." By the statutes of England piracy is defined to be "an offense which consists in the commission of those acts of robbery and depredation upon the high seas which, if committed upon the land, would have amounted to felony there."

Other authorities, such as Waller and Arbuthnot, define piracy to be "the act, practice, or crime of robbing on the high seas; the taking of property from others by open violence, and without authority, on the seas."

Blackstone says, "The crime of piracy, or robbery and depredation upon the high seas, is an offense against the universal law of society; a pirate being, according to Sir Edward Coke, *hostis humani generis.*"

These definitions can not be tortured to apply to Lopez and his men, or to the Pampero, which was not fitted up or designed to make captives on the high seas.

The President had no right to denounce as a capital crime what, at the utmost, can only be construed as a misdemeanor. And the captain general was no more justified, according to the law of nations, in executing our countrymen than the British would have been had they captured and executed Lafayette, Steuben, De Kalb, or Pulaski.*

* In 1825, when Greece was struggling for her liberties, under circumstances very similar to the Cubans when Lopez went to their assistance, the late Felix Huston, then an ardent young man, associated a band of young adventurers with him, and determined to go to her assistance. His plan was to repair to Europe and recruit a sufficient force there among the restless spirits to be found in London and Paris. He went to Washington with some of his comrades and submitted his scheme; and Mr. Clay, Mr. Webster, John Quincy Adams, Mr. Forsyth, and other distinguished men gave him letters of recommendation. Lafayette was then at the capital, the guest of the republic. He entered warmly into the views of the young Kentuckian, and presented him the following letter:

"Washington, 16 Février, 1825.

"La résolution que prend M. Houston d'aller servir la noble cause de la Grèce est bien digne de son caractère et des sentiments qui lui ont valu l'estime et l'amitié de ses concitoiens de Kentucky, et nommément, de notre ami commun M. Clay, président de la chambre des Représentants: c'est à lui qu'il appartient surtout de faire connaître la situation respectable de M. Houston, par lui-même, ses parents, et ses liaisons dans cet état: je demande neanmoins à me joindre, dans une autre langue, à ces témoignages d'estime et d'intérêt, pensant qu'il pourra rencontrer en Europe quelques-uns de mes amis. Ma famille serait trés empressée de le recevoir en France. Je le prie d'accepter ici tous mes vœux: ils se joignent à ceux que je forme dans tout ela ferveur de mon âme, pour la liberté republicaine, et la parfaite independance d'amis comme d'ennemis qui a été si bien meritée par le peuple heroïque donc il va partager les glorieux efforts.

"LAFAYETTE."

"Washington, February 15th, 1825.

"*James Brown, Esq., Envoy Extraordinary and*
    Minister Plenipotentiary, Paris.

"DEAR SIR,—Mr. Felix Huston, the bearer of this letter, is recommended to me by mutual friends as a person of highly respectable character and acquirements. He visits Paris upon purposes of benevolence and public spirit. I beg leave to recommend him to your kind attentions, and am, with great respect,

"Dear sir, your very humble and obedient servant,
"JOHN QUINCY ADAMS."

"I do hereby certify and make known that the bearer hereof, Mr. Felix Huston, is a native and highly respectable citizen of the State of Kentucky, one of the states of the North American Union; that his connections are among the most eminent and highly esteemed in that state; and that he is a member of its bar, and has practiced his profession for some time with great promise of success and attaining

The right of expatriation, with or without arms, singly or in companies, is in this country a constitutional right, exercised openly in the case of Texas by Fannin, Shackleford, and other American patriots, who raised regiments and went to her relief, in disregard of the acts of Congress of 1778 and 1818—acts that disgrace our statute-book, and can never be constitutionally enforced. When we threw off the political yoke of Great Britain, we still remained, to some extent, under the bondage of her opinions and precedents. Many able lawyers maintained that the unwritten common law of England was in force in this country, and Story and Kent insisted that the despotic British doctrine of perpetual allegiance had a federal force in these states, thus precluding the constitutional right of expatriation. Upon this hypothesis the acts of Congress referred to are based. No decision could ever be had on this question in the Supreme Court, and the question remained unsettled until it was settled by Congress in 1837. The recognition by Congress of the independence of the people of Texas, who had so recently and notoriously migrated thither by land and sea, in companies and in battalions, with arms in their hands, for the avowed purpose of fighting the Mexicans and establishing a government of their own, all which was accomplished without let or hindrance, leave or license

eminence. Fired with a laudable zeal for the establishment of Grecian liberty, Mr. Huston has determined to dedicate himself to that noble cause. I have great pleasure in recommending him as a man of honor and gallantry to all good men.   II. CLAY.
"Washington City, 16th Feb., 1825."

"Washington, Feb. 16th, 1825.
"Mr. Felix Huston, a citizen of this republic, is known to me, by the recommendation of persons of intelligence and high character, as a young man of distinguished worth and value. An ardent emulation leads him to Europe, and probably to Greece; and the object of this writing is to commend him to the kindness and regard of those to whom I may happen to be known, if he should meet with any such. I beg to express for him my esteem and good wishes.
"DANIEL WEBSTER."

of the federal authorities; and this act being fully ratified thereafter by the judiciary department, three propositions are established :

1st. That every American citizen has the right *to change his allegiance* and remove to any other country when he thinks proper to do so; and hence, that the feudal and despotic absurdity of " PERPETUAL ALLEGIANCE" has neither domicil nor resting-place within these states.

2d. That *the right of voluntary expatriation* is an inherent and constitutional right, which is imprescriptibly vested in every American citizen, and consequently, that they may migrate singly or in companies, with or without arms, whenever and wherever they please; and ceasing to be accountable to this government for their actions when a marine league from its shores, so long as they abstain from assailment of the rights, properties, and citizens of these states.

3d. That, as an inference from the foregoing propositions, any and every act of Congress heretofore or hereafter made, tending to destroy, abridge, or obstruct the exercise of the citizen's constitutional right of expatriation, are to be deemed, and are, unconstitutional, absolute nullities, and void.

The whole case may be summed up under the following corollaries :

1st. That, the Congress of the United States having declared, in the acts of 1799 and 1818, that the infractions of their provisions would be "*misdemeanors*" only, the prosecution of all offenders, their arrest, trial, and punishment, devolved *exclusively* upon the *judicial* department of the United States, and consequently, the President of the United States had nothing to do with the matter unless specially called upon by the *judiciary* to aid in enforcing its judgment.

VOL. II.—E

2d. Even admitting that the President could have rightfully taken the initiative, and without any judicial process whatever, against Lopez, Downman, Crittenden, and their comrades, *while they remained in the country,* he had no authority whatever to pursue, intercept, or capture them upon the "high seas," and beyond the jurisdiction of the United States, for a simple "*misdemeanor*" against the laws thereof.

3d. That, though the offenses had been committed against the laws of the United States which were actually in force at the time (*which was not the case*), and though the parties had been actually tried, and committed, and convicted of the same (*which was not the case*), the President would not have had any authority whatever for spoliating the term "*misdemeanor,*" which Congress·had used, for the term "PIRACY," which he substituted in its stead; and still less for denouncing the offenders to the civilized world as "PIRATES AND PLUNDERERS."

4th. That, as the acts of Congress of 1799 and 1818 were regarded and dealt with by the executive, Congress, and the judiciary in the case of Texas in 1837, as out of force, they became and were, by virtue thereof, "dead letters," nullities, and obsolete upon the statute-book; and as President Fillmore had no authority to revive them and put them in force, his interference in Cuban affairs was in derogation of the rights of the citizen and of the behests of the Constitution.

5th. That the President of the United States, knowing that Lopez, Downman, Crittenden, and their comrades had committed no breach of any *existing* law of the United States, or certainly none amounting to either a *felony* or a *crime,* and that they meditated neither assault or affray *against the commerce, property, or citizens of the United States,* had nothing to do with any *other* nation or people; but knowing, as he did, just as surely, that no *piratical* motives or aims against the property or lives of the Creoles of Cuba mingled in the enterprise, and that it was solely designed for the overthrow of despotic power, by making common cause with the native Cubans in their struggle for liberty, the President was left without the shadow of an excuse for denouncing them as "PIRATES AND PLUNDERERS."

6th. That the *executive's instructions* to the United States district attorney at New Orleans to prosecute *Henderson, Quitman, Sigur,* and *Lopez,* and his comrades, under the act of 1818, for "MISDEMEANOR, and *not* for PIRACIES," for the "expedition" set on foot against, and the hostile invasion and capture of *Cardenas,* in the island of Cuba, furnish ample and irrefutable proofs that the President did not, nor could have regarded the *second* "expedition" to Cuba (by the same parties and for precisely the same ends and objects as those which had prompted the *first* "expedition" to Cuba) as to any extent more "*piratical*" than the *first;* and hence that, in denouncing Lopez and his comrades as "*pirates and plunderers,*" he disregarded executive knowledge, official duty, and adjudged truth.

7th. That the President's *instructions* to our naval commanders in the Gulf specially and positively ignored the charges of PIRACY imputed by the *proclamation,* for the naval officers were without the shadow of an excuse for meddling with them, except under a law that *they were still American citizens and owed allegiance to the United States;* and if they were, how dared he to hold them up to the civilized world as "*pirates*"—that is, as "*enemies of the human race,*" and, of course, without citizenship or protection any where, and mere Ishmaels, their hands against every man, and every man's hands against them?

8th. That, as the President of the United States thus claimed Crittenden and his comrades as AMERICAN CITIZENS by his instructions through the Navy Department, and, AS SUCH (*for he had nothing to do with them unless he so regarded them*), the right to exercise authority and jurisdiction over them, he can not be justified for standing by with his consul, and ships of war in the harbor of Havana, in merciless indifference, while fifty of his gallant countrymen were butchered in cold blood, and the bodies of the dying and the dead were brutally mutilated, to the lasting shame of our country!

9th. That the murder of these men by the Spanish authorities, without trial, without counsel, without agents, without access to any body, or any possible means of defense, was in flagrant violation of our treaties with Spain, and that it was the duty of the President to interpose his authority to *prevent* it; and *that* failing, to have called Congress together to *punish* the breach of the treaty with Spain (October 27th, 1795), Article 7th, in the following words:

"And it is agreed that the subjects or citizens of each of the contracting parties, their vessels or effects, shall not be liable to any embargo or detention on the part of the other for any MILITARY EXPEDITION, *or other public or private purpose whatever;* and in *all* cases of *seizure,* detention, or arrest for debts or OFFENSES *committed by any citizen or subject of the one party within the jurisdiction of the other, the same shall be made and prosecuted by order and authority of law only. The citizens and subjects of both parties shall be allowed to employ such advocates, solicitors, notaries, agents, and factors* as *they* may judge proper in *all* their affairs, and in all their trials at law in which they may be concerned before the tribunals of the other party; *and such agents shall have free access to be present at the proceedings in such causes, and at the taking of all examinations and evidence which may be exhibited in the said trials.*"

And this 7th ARTICLE was expressly continued in force by the 12th *Article* of our *last* treaty with Spain (that of February 22d, 1819), which provides that—

"The treaty of Limits and Navigation of 1795 remains conformed *in all and each one of its articles*, excepting the 2d, 3d, 4th, 21st, and 22d clause of the 22d Article, which, having been altered by this treaty, or having received their entire execution, are no longer valid."

10th. That the steamer *Pampero*, in her voyage to Cuba, being neither *equipped*, nor *armed*, nor *designed* for hostilities, and wholly impotent for either *assault* or *defense*, but exclusively engaged and used as a *passenger-vessel* between the port of New Orleans and the island of Cuba, committed no other infraction of the laws of the United States through that voyage but the *venial* one of violating the 93d section of the act of March 2d, 1799, *in leaving the port of New Orleans without a clearance from the Custom-house*, thereby subjecting, not the *owner*, nor the *vessel*, nor her *apparel*, *tackle*, or *furniture*, but her *master* (Capt. Lewis), *personally*, to the mere fiscal penalty of $500.

11th. That it is obvious that the steamer Pampero, in neither her objects, equipments, passengers, nor voyage, violated *any* of the provisions of *any* of the sections of the act of April 20th, 1818.

She did not violate the 3d section of that act,

Because—She was not "FITTED OUT AND ARMED" at all, nor was she "TO BE EMPLOYED IN THE SERVICE OF ANY FOREIGN PRINCE OR STATE," etc.; nor was she "TO CRUISE OR COMMIT HOSTILITIES AGAINST THE SUBJECTS, CITIZENS, OR PROPERTY OF ANY FOREIGN PRINCE OR STATE," etc.— all which was *necessary* to complete the offense denounced in this *section*.

She did not violate the 4th section of that act,

Because—Whatever her preparations may have been, they were not made "WITHOUT THE LIMITS OF THE UNITED STATES, nor was she "FITTED OUT AND ARMED" *within it*, nor "*to be employed to cruise or commit hostilities upon the citizens of the United States or their property*," etc.—all which was *necessary* to complete the offense denounced in this section.

She did not violate the 5th section of that act,

Because—On her arrival at the port of New Orleans from the port of New York, she was *not* "IN THE SERVICE OF ANY FOREIGN PRINCE OR STATE," etc.; *because* she had no *armament* on board to be "INCREASED OR AUGMENTED," etc.; *because* she did not "ADD TO THE NUMBER OF HER GUNS, OR CHANGE THOSE ON BOARD OF HER FOR GUNS OF A LARGER CALIBRE" (for she had no guns either to add to or change) ; all which was *necessary* to complete the offense denounced in this section.

She did not violate the 8th section of this act,

Because—The *Pampero* was *not* "FITTED OUT AND ARMED," nor was she an "*armed vessel*" in *foreign* service, whose *armament* was "INCREASED OR AUGMENTED" in the port of New Orleans; nor a vessel in which "any military expedition was begun or set on foot, CONTRARY TO THE PROVISIONS AND PROHIBITIONS OF THIS ACT"— (which the "*provisions and prohibitions*" contained in the sections cited and to be cited, do and will negative) —all which was *necessary* to complete either of the offenses denounced in this section, as *conditions precedent* to any interference with her by the land or naval forces of the United States.

She did not violate the 10th section of this act,

Because—As the *Pampero* was *not* "AN ARMED VESSEL" *sailing out of a port of the United States*, no obligation devolved upon her "owners or consignees" to "enter into a bond to the United States, with sufficient sureties," conditioned that she should not "cruise or commit hostilities against the subjects, citizens, or property of any foreign prince or state," etc., as therein prescribed, which was *necessary* to complete the offense denounced in this section.

She did not violate the 11th section of this act,

Because—Unless the *Pampero* was a "VESSEL MANIFESTLY BUILT FOR WARLIKE PURPOSES" (and she was not), and unless she was "*intended to be employed by her owner or owners to* CRUISE OR COMMIT HOSTILITIES *upon the subjects, citizens, or property of any fereign prince or state*," etc. (and she was not), the collector of the port was not even authorized to "DETAIN" her; *nor then, until the decision of the President be had thereon: nor could he "*DETAIN*" her at all, if her owner or owners should give such bond and security as is named in the* 10*th* SECTION *just before referred to.* And every lawyer of the land at once realizes the absurdity of a *law* of the United States providing that a vessel which had *already* committed a *mis*demeanor (if the *anti-Cubans* are to be relied on) is to give "bond and security"—not to answer for *that* "misdemeanor," but conditioned merely that she should not commit a *future* "misdemeanor" against the laws of the United States.

Now these being the only sections of the act of 1818, or of any other act of Congress, bearing in the *smallest* degree upon or against the movements of the *Pampero*, it is apparent that the President of the United States, in ordering her, her tackle, apparel, and furniture to be *libeled and seized* in a sister state, for *condemnation and forfeiture*, grossly misconceived and transcended his powers.

12th. From all which it results

That, if Lopez, Downman, Crittenden, and their comrades ceased to be citizens of the United States by virtue of their voluntary expatriation from their country, and designed no hostilities against the United States, their citizens or property, the President had no grounds for denouncing them to the civilized world as "*pirates and plunderers.*"

That, if the President claimed jurisdiction over them as *American* citizens (as his instructions to our naval commanders unequivocally imports), far from having an *excuse* for denouncing them as "PIRATES AND PLUNDERERS," it became his imperative *duty*, as an *American magistrate*, to demand and secure to the captives all the privileges vouchsafed them through our *treaties with Spain*, and to have saved·them from those brutal cruelties and shocking desecrations (committed with impunity in the presence of an *American consul and an American ship of war*) which have tarnished with a deep stain the *national escutcheon and the American name!*

That the indiscriminate butchery of Crittenden and his comrades in cold blood, if taken *as captives in war*, was an open affront to every nation of the civilized world, and might lawfully be resented as a departure from all the usages of civilized warfare, and a flagrant breach of the positive provisions of the modern Law of Nations, which, as binding on all, all may enforce; and the king-dom of Spain would have been without the shadow of a defense for this revolting severity, and have been liable to be dealt with as an OUTLAW by the United States, and by all other civilized states, had not *the chief magistrate of the nation from whence they came* put them out of the protection of the *United States and of all other nations* as "PIRATES AND PLUNDERERS," and "ENEMIES OF THE HUMAN RACE."

The case of the Americans in the Lopez expedition is likewise completely covered by Mr. Webster, when secretary of state, in his dispatch to Mr. Fox, the British minister at Washington, after the difficulties on the Canadian frontier :

"Her majesty's government are pleased to speak of those American citizens who took part with persons in Canada engaged in an insurrection against the British government as 'American pirates.'

"The undersigned does not admit the propriety or justice of this designation. If citizens of the United States fitted out, or were engaged in fitting out, a military expedition from the United States, intending to act against the British government in Canada, they were clearly *violating the laws of their own country*, and exposing themselves to the just consequences which might be inflicted on them if taken within the British dominions. But notwithstanding this, they were certainly not pirates, nor does the undersigned think it can advance the purpose of fair and friendly discussion so to denominate them. Their offense, whatever it was, had no analogy to cases of '*piracy*.' Supposing all that is alleged against them to be true, they were taking a part in what they regarded as a civil war, and they were taking part on the side of the 'rebels.' Surely, Great Britain herself has not regarded persons thus engaged as deserving the appellation which her majesty's government bestows upon these citizens of the United States.

"It is quite notorious that, for the greater part of the last two centuries, subjects of the British crown have been *permitted* to engage in foreign wars, both national and civil, and, in the latter, in every stage of their progress ; and yet it has not been imagined that England has at any time *allowed* her subjects to turn '*pirates*.' Indeed, in our times, not only have individual subjects of that crown gone abroad to engage in civil wars, but we have seen whole regiments openly recruited, embodied, armed, and disciplined in England, with the avowed purpose of aiding a rebellion against a nation with which England was at peace. An act of Parliament was passed to prevent transactions so nearly approaching to public war without license from the crown.

"It may be said that there is a difference between the

case of a civil war arising from a disputed succession, or a protracted revolt of a colony against a mother country, and the case of a fresh outbreak or commencement of a rebellion. The undersigned does not deny that such distinction may for certain purposes be deemed well-founded. He admits that *a government* called upon to consider *its own* rights, interests, and duties, when civil wars break out in other countries, may decide on all the circumstances of the particular case upon its own existing stipulations, on probable results, *on what its own security requires*, and on many other considerations. It may be already bound to assist one party, or it may become bound, if it so chooses, to assist the other, and to meet the consequences of such assistance.

"But whether the revolt be recent or long-continued, they who join those concerned in it, whatever may be their offense *against their own country*, or however they may be treated if taken with arms in their hands in the territory of the government against which the standard of revolt is raised, can not be denominated '*pirates*' without departing from all ordinary use of language in the definition of offenses. A cause which has so foul an origin as '*piracy*' can not, in its progress or by its success, obtain a claim to any degree of respectability or tolerance among nations; and civil wars, therefore, are not understood to have such a commencement.

"It is well known to Mr. Fox that authorities of the highest eminence in Great Britain, living and dead, have maintained that THE GENERAL LAW OF NATIONS *does not forbid the citizens or subjects of one government from taking part in the civil commotions of another.* There is some reason, indeed, to think that such may be the opinion of her majesty's government at the present moment.

"The undersigned has made these remarks from the conviction that it is important to regard established distinctions, and to view the acts and offenses of individuals in their exactly proper light."

The fact that few or no Cubans repaired to the standard of Lopez is no argument against the legitimacy of his mission, but was rather the consequence of his unfor-. tunate selection of the point of debarkation—so near the focus of the Spanish power, its arsenals, garrisons, rail-roads, and steam marine. He was thus overthrown before his friends had notice of his arrival. They had relied on him for arms and men, and he was too remote for a junction with them. In Havana, where Lopez counted on material aid, incessant espionage, the want of weapons, the presence of a powerful force, and the terrors of martial law, rendered any movement impossible. In other portions of Cuba the standard of independence had been unfurled, and a desultory war had been waged, with the constant expectation of auxiliaries from the United States. Many a gallant Cuban had been driven into exile or hurried to summary execution.

The right of revolution belongs to the people; they never resort to it but when oppression becomes intolerable, and then the law of nations, founded on humanity and justice, makes it lawful to assist the oppressed.

The Fillmore policy gratified the Spaniards, and squared with the policy of Great Britain, and elicited Lord Palmerston's congratulations and co-operation. But what owe we to her? She has never been disposed to mete out justice to us, and seldom has rendered it unless from selfish considerations. We have not to thank her for a single act of disinterested friendship or one concession of generous magnanimity. Occasional displays of reciprocal courtesy, and a few instances of considerate civility may be singled out of her ledger of exaction, surliness, and pride. But in any thing essential, involving international law, who can point to any example of British liberality? From the close of the Revolution to the war of 1812, her bearing toward us was not that of a parent nation to a young and rising people of kindred blood, but that of an insolent tyrant, conscious of superior strength and resources. The Earl of Chatham, in one of his loftiest flights of cloquence, reproached her for arming the savages against us in our war for independence.   And yet in 1812 she did not scruple to incite the Shawnee and Seminole, and teach them how to use the scalping-knives of Birmingham against our wives and children, our prisoners and our wounded.   She has since made a systematic effort to retard our progress and expansion, to denationalize and disturb our internal tranquillity, and so to act upon neighboring nations as to affect our institutions.   Her proceedings in Texas, Oregon, Mexico, Cuba, and Central America have long since demanded the interposition of the Monroe doctrine, but successive administrations have submitted to her diplomacy.   Her own policy, as it regards British interests, is the reverse of ours.   It is to-day what it has been for centuries—shrewd, far-seeing, and inexorable.   Wherever her flag floats there is protection for British property, and the credential of a British subject is a passport and a safeguard.   She contemplates five, ten, or twenty years in advance the territory she means to subject to her dominion, and then she does not entice it like a serpent, but seizes it at a bound.   She makes no apology for spoliations, and is so little ashamed of them that, at the World's Fair, she exhibited, as the special property of the crown, that peerless gem, " the mountain of light," which she had torn from the diadem of the last of the Moguls.   By her navigation laws and commercial code she lays half the world under contribution, and peacefully accomplishes what Napoleon, in the plenitude of his power, attempted in vain.   Whether under the rule of Whig or Tory, she is equally formidable to her friends and her foes.   It is fashionable to speak of the rapacity of England ; of her unbridled ambition ; of the tears, the groans, the rivers of blood that mark her footsteps in every quarter of the earth ; her licensed piracies on the ocean ; her outrages on inferior powers ; her military and judicial murders in Ireland; her hypocritical philanthropy for the African; her mission of Christianity and civilization into distant lands, while she afflicts them with fire and sword, transportation and servitude. But it is impossible not to admire a great and brave people, who, whatever be their faults, have never surrendered their constitutional liberty, never circumscribed their giant energies, and never proclaimed their own citizens, when arming and aiding the oppressed, as " outlaws and pirates."

The American chief magistrate sought to conciliate England. His conduct squared with the policy of the British government, but provoked the surprise and contempt of the British people.

France claims to be the rival of England in its love of free principles. The French people may, the English people certainly do love liberty, but their governments manifest no such feeling. France permitted the annihilation of Poland—Poland that led the van in the march to Moscow, and fought in the rear in the retreat—when one tap of the French drum would have preserved her nationality and secured her independence.

Did not France see Russia pour her Cossacks into Hungary without drawing a sabre to repel them? Has she not more than once trifled with and crushed the great heart of Italy? Did not her legions bivouac on the seven hills of Rome, and repress with their bayonets the aspirations of freedom?

France and England have had many opportunities to give to Europe constitutional governments. The great Napoleon, despotic as he was in all that concerned his personal ambition, was the only man of his century on the Continent who achieved any thing for public liberty. He taught the world that men are equal. He converted every throne into a magazine, and left it for circumstances to apply the match. He dragged down the hoary monster LEGITIMACY, surrounded by the household traditions of ages, and cast it among the despised things of earth. He fell, but the lesson of his life survived, and again France had it in her power to be free, and to emancipate Europe. She consented to a throne for a Bourbon, when a republic might have been established in defiance of the doted and quaking monarchies around her. France might then have become a vast intrench-ment bristling with bayonets. Poland would have vault-ed into the saddle. Spain would have posted herself on the Pyrenees and shouted for freedom. The heart-yearnings of Germany would have sprung into armor—those yearnings for freedom that stir the soul in her lit-erature—that shine out from the depths of her transcen-dentalism—that lurk in her theological controversies, and glow with supernatural lustre from the broken sword of Korner!

But, alas! the French preferred a citizen king, who cast aside the silver lilies to obtain power, and then tar-nished the tri-color by becoming the ally of England in a crusade against liberal principles.

The republic that followed his expulsion was a repub-lic only in name. France is now ruled by the imperial sword, England by an aristocracy. Neither are fit al-lies for us. We are a free people; and we should ex-press our sympathy for the oppressed, and assume, in this hemisphere, the attitude of control that becomes a republic.

Shall we "hide our light under a bushel" instead of diffusing its radiance over benighted nations? Shall we waste the "talent" committed to our care? Must we not "love our neighbor as ourself," and extend to him the blessings we enjoy? Are not nations the instru-ments of Providence? Have they a mission? What higher commission can we have than to resist the introduction of foreign influence and systems on this continent, and extend and establish our own? Had this been boldly executed when our standard was planted on the capitol of Mexico, or when Cuba implored our assistance, we should have acquitted ourselves of a great debt incurred by our fathers when they accepted assistance; and this great republic, instead of exhausting its energies over its own dissensions, would now stand before the world united and impregnable.

We proceed upon the theory that the condition of a republic is repose. What an error! That is the normal condition of absolutism. The law of a republic is progress. Its nature is aggressive. It is founded on the conflagration of ancient and polluted things, and it must have play and action on surrounding nations, or, like Saturn, devour its own offspring.

Kossuth's idea of the "solidarity" or unity of nations, is neither historical or practical. Nor, if practical, would such a condition be desirable. Even a united church would cease to be evangelical, and become corrupt. Our true policy is entire isolation as to our own sovereignty, and a fearless and controlling exercise of power over contiguous governments. We are deficient, as yet, in nationality. War is not to be dreaded when it develops this sentiment. Make the republic as national as some of the older countries of Europe, and it would have little to fear from its enemies. Nationality alone has arrested the march of the conqueror when all other efforts had failed. When associated with republican institutions the moral force of a nation is invincible. The ancient republics enacted prodigies. Their soldiers fought not for their own glory, but for the glory of Greece and Rome. "I am a Roman citizen," was the proudest boast of antiquity. Venice, in her era of independence, flaunted her flag over two continents. The Dutch republic wielded the trident of the seas. The commonwealth of England domineered over Europe. The French republic shook the dynasties of a thousand years.

What, then, is there to dread, so long as we are true to ourselves, if we see fit to extend the power and the principles of the republic? Other governments may feebly object, and their objections can be satisfactorily answered. Should they prefer war, what would be its effect but to develop our internal resources, and consolidate American nationality? In a struggle of ten years, with due allowance for the vicissitudes of war, we should become richer and more powerful, while they would stagger under the burden of their own debts.*

What have we to fear, that we should truckle to all the world, and quarrel for their amusement, instead of pursuing our natural instinct for expansion? Why shut our ears to the appeals of humanity and stifle a sympathy we inherited with our blood? Boldly administered, the republic is invincible. Our commerce, our mighty rivers and lakes, our mountains and prairies, are the nurses of enterprise. We occupy a country, not, like the tropics, producing food without labor, and therefore a redundant and effeminate population, nor, like the arctic regions, supporting a sparse and apathetic people, icebound as their climate, and incapable of emotion, but a latitude where labor is essential to production, and production is the sure reward of labor; where the faculties are neither emasculated or deadened by the extremes of temperature; where the physical conditions of nurture,

---

* The Walcheren expedition alone, which begun and failed in six weeks, just across the Channel, besides thousands of lives and a great loss of reputation, cost the British people £20,000,000, and added £1,000,000 a year in perpetuity to the national taxes.—*Edinburgh Review, April,* 1860, p. 212.

diet, education, and the institutions of government are all most favorable to development and power.

Why, then, should we regulate our policy by the views of European cabinets, or play the part of subordinates when we should be dictators in the affairs of this hemisphere? " One battle for liberty," says Bulwer, " quickens and exalts that proud and emulous spirit, from which are called forth the civilization and the arts that liberty should produce, more rapidly than centuries of repose."

We are in the restless period of youth; the law of the age is progress; let our flag be given to the winds, and our principles go with it wherever it is unfurled. Conquest is essential to our internal repose. War sometimes becomes the best security for peace.

CHAPTER XVI.

Effects of the Compromise in Mississippi.—Reorganization of Parties.—Union Party.—Southern Rights Party.—Foote nominated for Governor.—Influence and Patronage of the Federal Government.—Mr. Webster.—Letter from Judge Clayton.—Quitman's Position.—South Carolina Correspondence.—Renominated for Governor.—Contrast between Quitman and Foote.—Their Canvass. —Rupture.—Success of the Unionists.—Declension of Quitman.

1851. The prosecution against General Quitman, as we have seen, was abandoned, but the government had, in part, accomplished its purpose. It had hauled down the flag of Mississippi from her capitol, and forced her chief magistrate to resign, though it had not the power to arrest a fugitive slave in the city of Boston. It could not enforce the provisions of the Compromise, and negro thieves and assassins defied its authority. But it could exclude the citizens of Charleston from Fort Moultrie, consecrated by the blood of their ancestors, because their expressions on the fourth of July exhibited more devotion to Carolina than reverence for the national government.

When Quitman returned home he found the compromise measures, recently enacted by Congress, the great issue of the day. On the 30th of November, 1850, an act had been passed by the Legislature, apparently with the approbation of a great majority of the community, providing for a convention of the people of Mississippi, to consider the state of our federal relations and the remedies to be applied. It solemnly recited the evils complained of as destructive of our domestic institutions and of the sovereignty of the states, and provided for the election of delegates on the 1st Monday of September, 1851, and the meeting of the convention on the 2d Monday of November following. Great excitement now pervaded the state, over-riding the old political organizations. The friends of the Compromise took the name of the Union party, and styled its opponents disunionists. They, on the other hand, assumed the title of the Southern party, and referred to their adversaries as "submissionists." The Southern party embraced a large proportion of the old Democratic party, with a small class of what were termed state-rights Whigs. The Union party consisted of the great body of the old-line Whigs, and a strong detachment of Democrats, who regarded nullification, secession, or any other mode of state resistance as more to be dreaded than the evils complained of. The great names from both parties that had sanctioned the Compromise blinded many to the aggressions it covered, and thousands who disapproved it as an original measure felt it to be a duty to acquiesce in it as a law of the land, rather hoping than expecting from it the restoration of tranquillity and the arrest of encroachment. This party, thus composed of many who approved the Compromise as a matter of policy, and of others who merely acquiesced in it as preferable to a severance of the Union, nominated General H. Stuart Foote, then a senator in Congress, as their candidate for governor. From an attitude of opposition to it in its details, he had suddenly become prominent in his support of the measure, and avowed himself its champion on its merits. Up to this nomination the Southern party had not expected a serious contest. The people of the state, in their primary and mass meetings, and in political conventions, irrespective of party, had so often denounced the very measures recognized by the adjustment; successive Legislatures had spoken in the same tone with so much emphasis, it was presumed a similar sentiment would be expressed by the people. It soon became evident, however, that a serious contest was on hand. Mr. Fillmore—President by the death of General Taylor—expected to obtain a new lease of power by the popularity of a measure which had converted many of his lifetime opponents into his most confidential friends, and he exerted, of course, the whole power and patronage of the federal government to sustain it. Mr. Webster, who, with his rival and fellow-commoner, the illustrious Clay, had been twice disappointed by the nominations of Harrison and Taylor, regarded the Compromise as his last card for the presidency, and forgot his habitual propriety in the blindness of his zeal. In a speech delivered at Annapolis in the latter part of March he expressed "the most devoted attachment to the Union, and proclaimed the obligation to support it to be as binding as the obligation to support the Constitution. He regarded the recent compromise measures as the salvation of the country, and denounced the opponents of those measures as *disunionists.*"

The author of this biography, then editor of the Louisiana Courier, on the 30th of March, referred to this speech as follows:

"This, then, is the decree of Mr. Webster, the American secretary of state, and, after Mr. Clay, the most powerful man in the Whig party. In a speech deliberately made, every word and sentiment of which he knew would carry with it the authority of his illustrious name, he singles out a numerous class of his fellow-citizens, embracing men of the most eminent public and private worth, and proscribes them as 'disunionists.' Such language from ordinary men may be passed by with contempt; but when it eminates from Daniel Webster, the effect amounts to proscription. It has the force of a decree. It makes public opinion. In many quarters it will expose an opponent of the Compromise to insult and oppression.

"Now what is the Compromise? Is it part or parcel of the Constitution? Is it a pact or compact, intangible and inviolable, for any given number of years? Is it any thing more than an ordinary law, as to whose merits, or expediency, or constitutionality, men may honestly differ, and which may be modified or repealed, relaxed or made more stringent, by any subsequent Congress? It is not. How, then, can it be made a test of union or disunion? Can it imply a want of patriotism to oppose a statute of experimental policy, the effect of which no one was sure of at the moment of its passage, and whose merits are now, as much as ever, a matter of controversy? Human judgments are fallible. Is there equity or reason in assuming that a body of legislators may construct a remedy for an existing evil, and then consider as criminals all who deny the efficacy of that remedy? The idea is monstrous. As well might they tear down the altars of the Lord God Almighty, and compel Christians to worship some idol erected by their own hands.

"It can not be pretended that the statutes of compromise have the same sanctity and authority as the Constitution of the United States. And yet that Constitution, the sacred charter of our liberties, has been, from time to time, amended, and alterations are often proposed, without subjecting any one to suspicion or censure. Can, then, a majority of Congress throw such sanctity around a law as to subject those who dispute its efficacy to the charge of treason? Unquestionably not. Yet this is the assumption of Mr. Webster. It is the very essence of tyranny, it is the incarnation of the administration of the elder Adams, when a difference of opinion was construed as criminal, and citizens rotted in dungeons for daring to question the enactments of Congress.

"This very assumption hurled that dynasty from power. The election of Mr. Jefferson, though conducted according to the forms of the Constitution, had the force and effect of a revolution. From that moment dates the era of free discussion, and this is the first bold attempt that has been since made to stifle it by terrorism and proscription. The position of Mr. Webster brings us back to the despotism of John Adams, and denounces as seditious and treasonable all who oppose the series of acts of Congress termed the Compromise.

"If this is to be made an issue it is easy to foresee how it will end. Not only those who oppose the Compromise as unconstitutional and destructive, but thousands who reluctantly acquiesce in it will rise against a proscription so detestable. Never—no, not even for the Constitution itself, much less for an experimental patch-work of ephemeral legislation, of doubtful wisdom and wholly inefficacious—never will the American people surrender the right of free discussion, and of amending and repealing charters and laws. This dictum of Daniel Webster converts Congress into a king, and subjects to the penalty of rebellion every man who disputes its will. Every opponent of the Compromise a traitor! God of heaven! Could the Shah of Persia utter a sentiment more tyrannical, or more pregnant with that spirit which exacts absolute submission, or vengeance and blood?

"It is such sentiments as these—implying despotic assumption and slavish submission—that drive a brave, and proud, and sensitive people into ultraism and resistance. The Compromise, if we may believe its authors, and as the term implies, was adopted in a spirit of conciliation; and statesmen, who had their misgivings, voted for it more with the hope than the conviction that it would save the Union. But when the monstrous assumption of infallibility is set up for it—when the oracle and apotheosis of a powerful party proclaims for it absolute submission—the submission not only of acquiescence, but of silence, and demands this under the penalty of treason—every man who feels the instincts of freedom and cherishes its privileges will resist.

"The doctrine of Mr. Webster implies serfdom, and he who acquiesces in it is fit for slavery.

"When Mr. Webster, in a celebrated speech, first defined his position on the compromise bills, his views were received with favor throughout the United States. His antecedents and relations on the subject of slavery had been suspicious. He had, at various times and places, deliberately avowed opinions construed as hostile to the rights and institutions of the Southern States, and decidedly encouraging to the fanaticism that the free states have arrayed against us. He had even publicly claimed, in his speech at Abington, opposition to slavery and to the extension of slave territory as the peculiar merit of his party. When, therefore, he took occasion to express himself in favor of the Compromise on grounds the reverse of those he had previously occupied, and declared his resolution to maintain the guarantees of the Constitution, the whole country received his declarations with a shout of welcome. But now, seizing upon the Compromise, and his support of it, as a great political machine to lift him up to the presidency—now drunk with excitement and ambition—he sets up his new idol as a GOD, and with a dagger and brand would compel us to worship it. 'He denounced the opponents of the Compromise as disunionists.'

"That the spirit of this sentiment pervades many of Mr. Webster's admirers in this section there is little doubt. They would extort by threat, by proscription, an acquiescence and approval of a great measure which the judgment revolts from. They would overawe when they fail to convince. But they should open the pages of history and learn that men are prone to meet this spirit with a dogged resolution, and that for centuries the fagot and the scaffold failed to make a single convert. The hunted Waldenses perished one by one, and saw their wives polluted and their children thrown to the dogs, and would not surrender the right of conscience. The Jews braved confiscation, exile, degradation, the whole apparatus of torture and death, to preserve their faith. The Catholics of Ireland gave up their country to the baptism of blood and fire, and would not compromise with an enemy that demanded compromise with an iron foot upon their breasts and a dagger at their throats. And can Mr. Webster and his followers, in and out of the Whig party, expect to enforce this new TEST more successfully? Can they proselyte us with threats? Do they look to see the opponents of compromise dwindle into slaves? Do they expect us to tremble when they speak? If they proscribe us as *disunionists*, may we not proscribe them as *tyrants?* And when the oppressor lifts his arm to strike, the poniards of the down-trodden will clash against his ribs.

"Let them try the issue when they choose. Let the Websterians carry out, if they dare, the doctrine of their leader. Let them back the opponent of the war of 1812, and of the Mexican war, in his declaration of war against the opponents of the Compromise. We are not to be taught our duty by a man but yesterday an abolitionist, nor to be intimidated into silence by a pensioner's menace of proscription. The integrity of Mr. Webster has in times past been attacked. His patriotism has been impeached. When, for factious purposes, he, by parliamentary trickery, defeated a great measure which Andrew Jackson demanded of Congress for the honor of the nation, an illustrious representative from his own state declared that 'He need take but one step more to surrender to the enemy the capitol of his country!' And yet, this man is to discipline the South to its duty, to pass laws, and extort an approval of them.

"Stern and bitter opposition, resistance to the last extremity, will be the inevitable results of these monstrous and insulting assumptions. In their atrocity will be found a plea, even with moderate men, for the most extreme measures."

The intrigues of presidential aspirants and the enginery of the federal government were at work throughout the South to paralyze, distract, intimidate, or tempt the timid, the mercenary, and the ambitious; and this, with the dread of change and our hereditary love for the republic, rendered the so-called "Union party" formidable from the outset.

The Southern party wavered. With a preponderance of the talent of the state in their ranks, they did not exhibit the confidence and concert of their adversaries. They were not intimidated, but rather astounded by the inconsistency with which men but recently their coadjutors now openly clamored for "Union at any price," or found in the duty of acquiescence a plea for their desertion. The audacity of their leader and his energy inspired his party, while their opponents had several aspirants for the leadership, and were by no means unanimous as to the platform to stand upon. The following plausible letter to Governor Quitman from one of the ablest and purest men of his party, a state-rights man of the strictest sect, and of great influence, will show the flutter and uncertainty that prevailed:

"May 20th, 1851.

"My dear Sir,—The nomination of General Foote for the office of governor took us, in this region, somewhat by surprise. It proves one thing beyond question, that the self-styled Union party means to use every possible exertion to carry the state. Corresponding efforts must be used by the State-rights party.

"It is believed on all hands that you will be nominated to oppose him. I have no doubt that will be the case. One of the first considerations that will be presented to your mind, in entering upon the contest, will be the platform on which you are to rest. What ground can you take and maintain? How far will the people consent to go?

"This cry of union and disunion has frightened many of the timid but well-meaning Democrats. They have come to a pause, and scarce know what to do. Their prayer, in the first place, is for *light.*

"I have taken some pains to ascertain the state of public feeling and opinion here on the subject, and the purpose of this letter is to show you my conclusion, that it may have such influence with you as you may think it deserves. Secession on the part of this state, under the circumstances which now surround her, can not be carried. It will defeat the most popular man in existence. A convention to form a plan of ultimate disunion can not now be carried. If the issue be made approval or disapproval of the adjustment measures, then I am confident the non-contents have the majority. That majority will show there is still some spirit left in the South. When that majority is secured, what should be done I am not wise enough to undertake to say; that will be

Vol. II.—F

for after reflection. But the lowest point short of acquiescence, and short of an abandonment of state rights, will be most certain to secure the majority. Success with a very moderate platform is better than defeat with one based upon higher ground. The battle to be fought will be a hard one; every topic will be urged, and every argument insisted on that will at all subserve their ends, by the Foote men. Disunion *per se*—secession—a small spice of treason, just enough to escape the traitor's doom, will be charged upon the state-rights men.. All this must be repelled, and must be met by a moderation which, while it does not surrender our rights, adopts that show of remedy which is most in accordance with the spirit of the times. Should it be said that the State-rights party has abandoned its position, all that is necessary to reply is to show the changes and tergiversations of their leader.

"Surely they do not desire a monopoly on that score. The change in Virginia, in Georgia, in Alabama, indeed in all the slave states, fully justifies Mississippi in saying she will not take a step which those whose interests are identical will not aid her in maintaining. The question is to be looked at practically. What Mississippi ought to do, under the altered circumstances which surround her, is the true point, not what she ought to do if all her sister Southern States sustained her. The mere abstract point of right will seldom do to stand upon in public affairs. The sentiments expressed in your last message, even the more subdued tone of what is styled the Clayton address, are too strong for the popular feeling in this section. Perhaps the public mind might be brought up to that standard, but I do not believe it can.

"What, then, can be done? But little, I fear. First, it can be declared that our state thinks the Compromise Acts were unjust to the South; next, that while she is unwilling to secede, in the present posture of affairs, she will always be ready to go hand in hand with her sisters of the South in repelling aggression. Non-intercourse with abolition states, as far as practicable, may also be recommended.

"Now, my dear sir, this letter is written in no spirit of dictation. I feel a deep interest in this contest. I wished to lay before you, faithfully, my views of public opinion in this region. Doubtless, others will do so, and from among them I hope you will be able to select a position that will bear you successfully through. It will be more difficult and more dangerous to change after the canvass is commenced.

"I know you will take what I have said in good part, because you will know my motive is good. How far you may adopt or act on any suggestions of mine must, of course, be left to your own clear judgment."

This course did not square with the severe notions of Quitman. He was not a man of expedients. He was struggling for principles, in his opinion, vital to the South, and victory had no charms unless those principles prevailed. His own letters of that period will best define his position.

To Col. John S. Preston, of South Carolina.

"Monmouth, March 29th, 1851.

"First, then, in regard to public sentiment in this state. It is unquestionably hostile to the so-called compromise measures of the last Congress, and daily becoming more so. We have not, however, sufficient evidence that this feeling has settled down into any definite plan of action. Our population, composed largely of comparatively recent immigrants, is not entirely homogeneous. It partakes especially of that strong Southern characteristic individual independence of thought and action. There is, therefore, no man or set of men, however popular, who can do much to give particular direction to its elements unused to control or political discipline. I believe, however, that an increasing majority regard the present state of things as inconsistent with the safety of the Southern States, are not disposed to acquiesce in its continuance, and are ready to adopt some practicable mode of resistance. If, in the coming contest for the convention, our members of Congress, state officers, and other prominent friends of Southern rights, act in concert in support of some efficient measure of resistance, I have no fears of our success. The plan proposed by the address of the Central Committee, which I have forwarded to you, is, that the convention demand redress for past aggressions, and guarantees against future assaults upon our rights, and in the mean time provide for meeting our sympathizing sister states in a Southern congress.

"The proposed redress is:

"1. A repeal of the law suppressing the slave-trade in the federal district.

"2. Opening the territories to the admission of the states.

"3. Concessions of California south of 36° 30'. The guarantees to be amendments to the Constitution explicitly to protect slavery from hostile interference by Congress or states, and to restrain unequal taxation, direct or indirect.

"In case the redress and guarantees be refused, the state to make formal propositions to her Southern sisters for a separate confederation, and to unite with any number of them sufficient to secure national independence.

"I give it as my opinion that some such plan will be adopted by the convention. There are many of us who believe, indeed are well assured, that neither the majority in Congress nor the non-slaveholding states will assent to either of these just propositions, unless demanded by the Southern States with a unanimity not to be expected; but still we think the propositions are due to our confederates before we part from them, and again, there are some among us who still have some hopes that the people of the North, when deliberately and solemnly appealed to with the alternative of separation distinctly made, will yield to our demands.

"From this state of public sentiment there is but a step to that which prevails in South Carolina. But this step, the last in anticipation of unconditional separation, is likely to be long and cautiously deliberated on, because the next places them across the Rubicon. The people of Mississippi have advanced thus far steadily and firmly. The slightest exciting cause would carry them onward, yet without it, public sentiment, alarmed by the imaginary evils of an unknown future, may recoil and pause a long time in doubt and uncertainty. I believe, then, from present indications, that Mississippi, if her propositions are not promptly acceded to, will invite her neighboring sister states to form with her a new confederacy. · She may, from her weakness and the inconvenience of her position, withhold the final act until one of her immediate neighbors shall also be willing to join her. She will not, probably, even if redress and guarantees be. absolutely refused, venture to secede alone. Many of her boldest and stanchest Southern-rights men would not advise separate secession under any circumstances. A few with myself think that there are evils in the future even greater than separate secession.

"I concur with you in the opinion that the political equality of the slaveholding states is incompatible with the present confederation as construed and acted on by the majority, and that the present union and slavery can not coexist; but I fear that these momentous truths have not yet become fully impressed upon the public mind in the South. In the cotton states such sentiments prevail and are growing; but there are some indications of their existence in Maryland, Virginia, North Carolina, Tennessee, Kentucky, and Missouri, and although, to some extent, avowed in Texas and Louisiana, they are frowned down by most of their public men as treasonable and revolutionary. There is, then, no present hope that a majority of the slaveholding states will unite in any effective measures for curing the evils. It is vain to look for it or to expect it. On the contrary, the measures proposed to be adopted in some of the states, particularly Virginia, of a system of petty hostilities within the Union, would not only divert attention from sanative remedies, but would really increase the evil. There is no hope whatever of united action beyond the cotton states.

"For my part, I have long ceased to look beyond the cotton states for any united action, unless the North should pursue her aggressions so madly and indiscreetly as to shock good taste, and insult pride as well as violate justice. Indeed, I fear that the frontier states—I mean those bordering on the free states—will never abandon the present Union, however great its oppressions, unless rudely driven from it by the North, or forced to choose between a Southern and a Northern confederacy. There is even danger in case of the assembling of a Southern congress that Virginia, uniting with the other slaveholding states now disposed to submit, will attempt to force upon us some new '*compromise*' to preserve the shadow of the Union when the substance is gone. There is danger, too, except in those states in which proposed state action keeps up agitation, that the public sense of the insult, injury, and oppression inflicted upon the slaveholding states will become blunted by time and acquiescence, until it will be very difficult to arouse the people to a proper estimate of the extent of the danger which threatens them. While it is true that in some of the states, particularly Alabama, Florida, and Louisiana, much discontent with the late action of Congress prevails, and the spirit of resistance is extending itself among the people, yet nowhere, except in South Carolina and Mississippi, is it proposed to act authoritatively on these questions. To those two states alone, then, can we look to any efficient action. The latter is not yet fully prepared for final action; she has less capital, is younger and weaker than the former, and has no sea-port. The former should, then, take the lead, and fearlessly and confidently act for herself. This would prevent practical issues from her neighbors. Mississippi would, I feel assured, take position by her side, and soon all the adjoining states would follow her example. Thus you will perceive that I think united action on the part of the slaveholding states, or even a majority of them, out of the question; that there is not even a present prospect of the cotton states authoritatively taking joint action. I feel, therefore, convinced that no effective measures will be taken of the states separately. The time and energy of the states would be wasted in fruitless contests about the proper remedy, and differences of opinion on this point would defeat any action at all, even though all the consulting states should favor some remedy. If, therefore, the people of South Carolina have made up their minds to withdraw from the Union at all events, whether joined by other states or not, my advice would be to do so without waiting for the action of any other state, as I believe there would be more probability of favorable action on the part of other Southern States after her secession than before. So long as the several aggrieved states wait for one another, their action will be over-cautious and timid. Great political movements, to be successful, must be bold, and must present practical and simple issues. There is, therefore, in my opinion, greater probability of the dissatisfied states uniting with a seceding state than of their union for the purpose of secession. The secession of a Southern state would startle the whole South, and force the other states to meet the issue plainly; it would present practical issues, and exhibit every where a wider-spread discontent than politicians have imagined. In less than two years all the states south of you would unite their destiny to yours. Should the federal government attempt to employ force, an active and cordial union of the whole South would be instantly effected, and a complete Southern confederacy organized. All these results are problems which the future alone can solve."

On the 19th of March a committee of the citizens of Jackson addressed him the following letter:

"Jackson, 19th March, 1851.

"GEN. JOHN A. QUITMAN: DEAR SIR,—Your fellow-citizens of the State of Mississippi have witnessed, with sincere admiration, your chivalrous and patriotic defense not only of the rights of our common country upon the battle-field, but the rights of the South against the assaults of its enemies both at home and abroad, whose success in their efforts to prostrate the constitutional rights of the South was to be deplored almost as much as the success of a foreign foe; and for this you have been defamed and persecuted, driven to the necessity either of resigning the high trust committed to your keeping by the people of the state, or of having that state degraded by submitting its chief executive officer to be carried away as a captive to be tried by a foreign tribunal; and we have witnessed with delight and gratitude your triumphant acquittal, by the admission of your enemies that they had no proof to sustain their accusations (evidently gotten up for sectional and party purposes). These things, sir, have had a tendency to endear you still more to the people of your own state, with whom you are most familiar, and who best know how to appreciate you ; and, as a token of their respect for your services as a soldier, for your able efforts as a patriot in behalf of Southern rights, and their high appreciation of your character as a citizen, they have (as you will see by the inclosed resolutions) determined to give you a barbecue at the seat of government at such time as may suit your convenience to attend, and have appointed the undersigned as a committee to invite you to honor the festival by your presence. In the performance of this duty, we respectfully request that you will designate an early day when you can attend and receive the congratulations of your fellow-citizens.

"We have the honor to be, very respectfully, your fellow-citizens,   C. S. TARPLEY, Chairman."

Gen. Quitman to C. S. Tarpley, G. T. Swann, and E. Barksdale, Esqrs., Committee of the Central S. R. Association.

"Monmouth, March 31st, 1851.

"I have the honor to acknowledge the receipt of your letter of the 19th inst., inclosing sundry resolutions passed at a meeting of the Central Southern Rights Association, and inviting me, in behalf of that association, and other personal and political friends, to partake of a barbecue at the seat of government at such time as may be convenient to me.

"The circumstances under which this compliment is tendered render it peculiarly gratifying to me, because it assures me that you approve of my conduct under trying circumstances, and that I am still honored with your confidence and esteem.

"My position as governor of a state which had been the first to recommend measures of resistance to the anti-slavery movements, and my firm determination, in my official action, not to recede from the position which had been taken by the state, and which I heartily approved of, have subjected me to much bitter abuse and detraction. Such is ever the fate of those who seek to restrain the abuses of power. The priests, who derived honor and profit from the worship of the Ephesian Diana, and the goldsmiths, who enriched themselves by it, cried aloud and furiously assailed him who proclaimed truths that threatened to destroy the source of their power and wealth. These interested patriots, in answer to every argument, shouted, 'Great is Diana,' and 'Stone the traitor.' The selfish politicians of our day, who worship around the presidential altar with similar motives, drown all reason and argument in hosannas to the 'glorious Union,' and in abuse of those who will not submit to be quietly despoiled of their dearest rights in the name of the Union. I know of no reason for it, except that while governor I have fearlessly endeavored to maintain the rights of the state, and with you and thousands of the purest patriots of the South, have advanced opinions that the present state of the slavery question is incompatible with the equality of the slaveholding states in the confederacy, and have advocated some efficient state action to protect us from the oppressive measures of the federal government.

"Whether the prosecution against me for an alleged violation of the neutrality laws had its origin in these causes, I have not sufficient evidence to assert; but I do say that the prosecution was wholly unfounded; that not a single charge of the indictment was true; and that there never was, so far as I have been able to discover, any legal evidence to support it. Provoking and oppressive as was this prosecution toward me personally, it would not have deserved public consideration but for the manner, contemptuous and insulting, and disrespectful to the state, in which it was carried on. In urging the arrest and immediate removal of the governor, there was deliberation and design, and it is fair to infer that design was to humble the State of Mississippi, and to prostrate her before the federal power. The power that could dictate a eulogistic apology to the abolition city of Boston, after a most scandalous outrage upon law as well as the principles of common honesty, is fit for the service of perverting the power of executing the laws to insult a Southern State. In the acts of the administration, as well as in those of the government and the antislavery states, we may read the signs of the times. We would be blind not to see them, and infatuated not to prepare for them. They thicken around us, so that we can no longer avoid them. We must meet them face to face. We have been swindled by them out of the public domain. Even a portion of Texas, supposed to be secured as slaveholding, has been wrested from us. Every outlet to the extension of our institutions has been firmly closed. The golden shores of the Pacific, open to the adventurers of the wide earth, is denied to Southern labor, though in part acquired with our blood and purchased with our treasures. We are now hemmed in on the west as well as the north. The line once fixed, to save the Union, has been contemptuously disregarded. The area for the employment of our labor has been circumscribed by the fiat, 'Thus far shalt thou go, and no farther;' and while non-slaveholding states may be indefinitely increased, the number of slaveholding states and their political power must remain stationary or diminish. An effective step to the entire abolition of slavery in the federal district, surrounded on all sides by slave states, has been adopted. The provision of the Constitution for the reclamation of fugitive slaves has not only been disregarded, but a number of the leading free states have passed laws to prevent its execution within their limits, and, since the passage of the Fugitive Slave Bill, its operation has generally been defeated by cunning legal devices, vexatious intervention, and sometimes by open violence.

"A spirit hostile to slavery pervades the non-slaveholding states, and, in my judgment, it is becoming daily more active, more practical, and, consequently, more dangerous. The so-called compromise, instead of allaying it, by yielding to it all the public territory, appears to have stimulated it to more efficient action.

"In the great States of New York and Ohio the recent contests for senator have resulted in the election of men prominent for their principles; in Massachusetts the contest lies between a Free-soiler (extreme abolition) and an avowed Abolitionist. Not one of the states whose statute-books contain laws to prevent the delivery of fugitives has formally responded to the late Clay and Foote compromise by repealing their obnoxious laws, and complying with their constitutional duty, and most influential non-slaveholding states, in spite of the exertions of those whose political fate hangs on the success of their so-called compromise, show a fixed determination to repeal the Fugitive Slave Law or essentially to change it. In fine, hostility to slavery has never, in my opinion, assumed so systematic and dangerous a character as since the Wilmot Proviso was settled by excluding slavery from the public territories by the new and more effective means of the California and Mexican Proviso.

" If there have heretofore been any grounds for action on the part of the Southern States to avert the impending evil, or to prepare for self-protection if the evil could not be arrested, they exist now in a much greater degree than when the people of Mississippi, under the advice of distinguished citizens of both parties, assembled in convention, declared that the time was come when the aggrieved states should assemble and confer together upon proper measures of resistance, and resolved that we ought not to submit to an exclusion from the public domain, nor to any act which would impair the equality of the states.

" To the substance of these resolutions, which appeared at that time to meet with general approbation, I trust and hope the people of Mississippi will adhere, regardless of the senseless cry of disunion. The political equality of the states is the vital principle of the Constitution. Upon its strict maintenance depend our liberties. We are not permitted to surrender it even to purchase temporary peace for ourselves. It is a sacred inheritance, bequeathed by our sires, which it is our duty to transmit unimpaired to our children. If assailed, we must defend it, even though the Union perish in the contest. But firmly and inflexibly to insist upon all our constitutional rights, and to maintain them at all hazards, is the only mode of preserving the Union of the Constitution. All that we ask is justice and equal rights. If they have been extended to us, we have no right to complain. If not, we should demand them, insist upon them with confidence and without fear of consequences.

" Those who counsel acquiescence and submission to sovereign states must defend the measures complained of as right, proper, and constitutional. A free people, jealous of their liberties, will not listen to those who advise submission to wrong and oppression. Humility and forbearance are sometimes virtues in individuals, but they are faults, if not crimes, in states. Political communities must assert their rights, or none will concede them. The true issue, then, in our state is acquiescence and concurrence in the late compromise bills, or opposition and resistance to them.

"My message to the Legislature at their late called session, and the address of the central committee of the friends of Southern rights, contain formally my views of the proper measures of resistance which should be taken by the state. As a state-rights man, I shall yield obedience to the acts of the convention shortly to assemble, whatever they may be. I have thought proper to say thus much upon this occasion; I have only to add that I gratefully accept your civilities, and as I have been indirectly advised that the 14th of May next would be agreeable to you, with your approbation I designate that day for the proposed barbecue."

Though at this period a private citizen, Quitman's moral influence was felt in all the Southern States. In South Carolina there was a singular unanimity as to the necessity of resisting the unconstitutional legislation of Congress, but there was a division of opinion as to the mode of proceeding. One portion favored separate state action; the other preferred a Southern congress and the co-operation of the Southern States. Quitman was appealed to by the prominent men on both sides of the question, and as they are of a race of statesmen that never traffic principles for office, and boldly avow their opinions to the world, some of these letters are here published. They shed a flood of light on the history of the times.

From Colonel Maxy Gregg.

"Charleston, S. C., May 9th, 1851.

" Sir,—The movement in South Carolina toward final action has now commenced.

"The movement party from this time marches forward steadily to its object.

"There are few downright Submissionists, but many resistance men who waver and hesitate at decisive action. The bonds of friendship between the two sections of the Resistance party which are ready and not ready to move on, are not yet broken. Slight circumstance may decide whether the movement is to proceed with almost unexampled unanimity, or whether an opposition is to be organized of sufficient vigor to cause serious embarrassment.

"I beg of you to withhold any expression of opinion against the movement until you have had time for a deliberate survey of the new position of affairs. An expression of opinion by you (even if made in reply to some private and confidential communication from a wavering leader) against the policy which has been adopted by an overwhelming majority of the meeting just adjourned, might cause some fatal defection. For God's sake, let the resistance leaders of Mississippi express no hasty opinion against us."

From Governor Means.

"Executive Department, South Carolina, May 12th, 1851.

"My dear Sir,—Although I have not the pleasure of a personal acquaintance with you, I take the liberty of addressing a letter to you upon a subject which I feel satisfied, from the deep interest you have always taken in the defense of Southern rights, will not be entirely distasteful to you.

"A convention of delegates from the Southern Rights Associations of the state has just adjourned, and the resolutions passed by that convention may be looked upon as a fair exponent of the opinions of the state, and as indications of the course it will pursue.

"There is now not the slightest doubt but that the next Legislature will call the convention together at a period during the ensuing year, and when *that* convention meets the state will secede.

"I send you this information that you may have something more than mere newspaper reports to rely upon, and that our friends in your state and the other Southern States may shape their course to suit a contingency which will certainly happen.

"I will not presume to advise you as to the best policy to be pursued by the friends of the Southern cause in your state. Of this you are a better judge than I am. But I think it better to make this communication to you, as I have been informed that the Southern party in many of the states have been discouraged by the supposition that South Carolina did not intend to act.

"We have a *small* party opposed to separate state action, but that party will go with the state when it moves. There are a *very few* persons in favor of final submission, but so few as not to be worthy of notice. Depend upon it, our people are actuated by the true spirit, and are ready to encounter any danger they may be called upon to face in defense of their rights and honor.

"We are anxious for co-operation, and also anxious that some other state should take the lead, but from recent developments we are satisfied that South Carolina is the only state in which sufficient unanimity exists to commence the movement. We will therefore lead off, even if we are to stand alone, but trust that our sister states, who are threatened by the same dangers, whose interest and honor are at stake in common with ours, will unite with us in this our honest attempt to save our institutions from ruin and the South from degradation."

From Colonel Maxy Gregg.

"Columbia, May 15th, 1851.

"Sir,—I took the liberty, a few days ago, of addressing you on the subject of the policy which has been decided upon in South Carolina. A sense of the importance of your position in the present critical state of affairs induces me to venture on a second communication.

"I believe that if the Resistance party in Mississippi will now abandon all temporizing, and come out boldly for secession, they will greatly increase the chance of success in the struggle with the Submissionists. But if they flinch from the issue of disunion, they will suffer at once from all the odium of the measures of South Carolina and all the weakness of a false position. Let them contend manfully for secession, and, even if beaten in the elections, they will form a minority so powerful in moral influence that, when South Carolina secedes, the first drop of blood that is shed will cause an irresistible popular impulse in their favor, and the Submissionists will be crushed. Let the example be set in Mississippi, and it will be followed in Alabama and Georgia. Imparting and receiving courage from each other's efforts, the Southern-rights men will be ready to carry every thing before them in all the three states the moment the first blow is struck in South Carolina.

"In this great struggle the South wants a great leader, with the mind and the nerve to impel and guide revolution. Be that leader, and your place in history will remain conspicuous for the admiration of all ages to come.

"I earnestly hope you will suffer no inventions of the enemy to make you doubt the determination of South Carolina. There is no temporary excitement here, but a deep resolution and a fixed purpose, which will be steadily carried out. Very probably there will be no division at all in the ranks of the Resistance party, and that party is the state."

Gen. Quitman to Gov. Means.

"Monmouth, May 25th, 1851.

"MY DEAR SIR,—Your letter of the 12th of May, but post-marked at Orangeburg the 17th instant, has just come to my hands. I am greatly obliged to you for the kindness and confidence evinced by your communication, and I trust they will be continued.

"We are separated by state lines, but a common cause and common dangers unite us. From the letters of distinguished citizens of your state, I had anticipated the result of the secret convention of delegates in your state. Indeed I could see no other course left to your noble and gallant commonwealth consistent with her honor and character. Every other Southern state, except Mississippi, has bowed her neck to the yoke or silently submitted. Nowhere but in Mississippi has even any authoritative step been taken to meet you in a Southern congress. No alternative was therefore left to you but to retrace your steps and patiently submit, or to take separate state action.

"Experience has fully demonstrated that united action can not be had; the frontier slave states are even now indicating a disposition to cling to the Union at the hazard of their slave institutions. They will not, in my opinion, unite in any effective remedies unless forced to choose between a Northern and Southern confederacy. My opinions on these subjects having been more fully expressed in a letter which I addressed to a distinguished citizen of your state on the 29th of March last,* I have concluded to inclose an extract from that letter. I will only add that my opinions of the state of public sentiment here remain unchanged; at the same time, it becomes more manifest every day that we are to have a fearful, excited, and angry contest, in which the patronage and influence of the federal administration, and perhaps Northern capital, will be used against the friends of the South. We have high confidence in the result of the canvass before the people; but however that may be, you may rest assured that I and my associates regard the cause of Carolina as the cause of Mississippi, and will never cease our exertions, so far as they are consistent with our allegiance to our own sovereignty, to support and sustain your noble state in her determination to regain her equality in the Union, or, that failing, to maintain her independence out of it."

1851. On the 13th of May Quitman was received at Vicksburg with a salute of 100 guns, and escorted by the military—many of whom had served with him at Monterey—to the seat of government, where he was welcomed with the greatest enthusiasm. On the morning of the 14th a grand salute was fired, and by 12 A.M. 5000 citizens had assembled to welcome the patriot. He was welcomed in their name by Hon. T. J. Wharton, in an eloquent address. Gen. Quitman, deeply touched by his reception, and by the burning words of the orator, rose with evident emotion. He made an appropriate allusion to the presence of the Hon. Geo. Poindexter, so long identified with the history of the state. He refer-

* Letter to Col. Preston.

red to his recent arrest, and modestly construed the great assemblage of citizens not so much as a compliment to him, but as meant to express their indignation at the attempt of the federal authorities to humiliate the state. As governor he would resist any such attempt, but now gladly surrendered himself a prisoner to his friends. He spoke for an hour, and clearly defined his relations with Cuba, and his views on the absorbing issues of the day.

He was then presented with a beautiful and highly-wrought box by Dr. B. F. Johnstone, of Warren County, bearing the following inscription:

"On the evening before the battle of Yorktown Gen. Washington was reclining under a tulip-tree in the vicinity, surrounded by a group of officers. The remark was made, that ' the fate of our country will now be decided, and if we fail we may all soon dangle from this very tree.' The chief replied, ' Gentlemen, we may all be cut to pieces, but this country was never designed for submission, nor our necks for the halter of a tyrant.'

"This box is wrought of wood taken from that historic tree, and presented to Gen. John A. Quitman for his inflexible patriotism and exalted moral worth."

After a sumptuous repast the Hon. Wm. M'Willie addressed the assembled thousands in a masterly manner on the rights and duties of the South. This was followed by a torch-light procession, and by addresses in the Hall of Representatives from Hon. George Poindexter, D. C. Glenn, E. C. Hooker, G. W. Smith, and other distinguished speakers.

The ovation closed with a splendid ball.*

In June the Democratic State Rights Convention assembled at Jackson. Diverse shades of opinion prevailed. Many thought the position heretofore assumed by

* Condensed from a letter in the Natchez Free Trader, written by Col. J. D. Elliott.

the party, and which Quitman maintained with characteristic inflexibility, wholly untenable. They insisted that the issue should be made on the merits of the Compromise as an original question, thus waiving all measures of redress and resistance, and virtually acquiescing in it. Upon this ground, it was contended that Foote and the Union party might be successfully met. This half-way ground had already been taken by candidates for Congress, and in many of the counties by the Southern-rights candidates for the State Convention, which was then agitating the state. As the consequence of this modification of position, there were many who considered the nomination of Quitman inexpedient. He was not a strategist, nor a half-way man, nor a temporizer. He put no value on victory apart from principles; he preferred defeat to equivocation. The attitude of the convention was by no means firm and decided. It was influenced by the inexorable necessities of national politics. He, however, received the nomination; it being distinctly understood that he stood upon his own platform, and demanded nothing less than the substantial repeal of the Compromise, or decided state action to oppose its operation, as indicated in his letter to Hon. J. S. Preston, of South Carolina. Of all the public men in the state, of either party, he was most thoroughly controlled by convictions of right and wrong. Others were, doubtless, as honest and sincere, but were more or less under the bias of political feelings and associations. Men disciplined in the Democratic party, taught from boyhood that the security of our free institutions depended on its success, saw no dereliction on this occasion, but rather a duty, in a change of front or a waiver of principle to insure a triumph. But Quitman had never been, strictly speaking, a party man. During a portion of his life his opinions had thrown him into the opposition, and he had united with the Democracy only because it approached nearer his standard of principles. Upon the questions that now distracted Mississippi he was far in advance of his party and of the Democratic Convention. His moral courage —his personal popularity—his brilliant success in Mexico—resentment for the indignity recently offered to him by the federal authorities, and the enthusiasm and exertions of a few men as zealous and as ultra as himself—prevailed with the convention. And without qualifying an opinion he had ever given, he entered upon the canvass for governor.

About this period he was thus consulted by the ex-governor of South Carolina, a thorough advocate for separate secession, in contradistinction to the co-operation movement favored by Judge Butler, Senator Barnwell, and other leading Carolinians.

Whitemarsh B. Seabrook to Gen. Quitman.

"Edisto Island, June 9th, 1851.

"DEAR SIR,—Although both of us are now private citizens, yet good reasons exist why we should continue, confidentially, to interchange opinions and information concerning the critical situation and future prospects of the slaveholding states. It seems to be generally conceded that, unless your state or this makes an issue which will compel the states North and South to support her position or take sides with the federal government, for all past aggressions the assailed party will have to use the sponge of oblivion. In my own judgment, submission now will seal the fate of our institutions. The operations of the 'Compromise' measures, and the influence and patronage of the central authorities, will prove sufficient not only to maintain the division that unhappily exists in the South, but in time to effect the very end at which our enemies aim. Under this belief, the Convention of Southern Rights Associations, held lately in Charleston, arrived at the conclusion, with but few dissenting voices, that although co-operation was in every respect desirable, still, resistance alone by

South Carolina was to be preferred to obedience to the recent dangerous and unwarrantable enactments of Congress. Whether the Convention faithfully reflected the opinion and determination of the people I can not positively speak. That they are unanimous on the question of secession is beyond all doubt, but that there is a two-thirds majority at this time in favor of separate state action is questioned by many, though not by myself. Opposition in different parts of the state begins to disclose itself. At present it is confined to Charleston and the villages where Northern men are to be found in numbers.

"The views lately submitted to the public by Butler, Barnwell, Orr, and other public men of our state, have had, or will have the effect of bringing together every class of our population hostile to unaided action at the present time. Although Butler, Barnwell, and probably Orr, will in future attend no public meetings, or make speeches any where, yet their settled conviction of the extreme danger of secession by South Carolina alone will continue to exercise an influence on our people. Farther, the leaders in the late convention are men comparatively unknown to the public. It can not be said, therefore, that they have the confidence of the people. Without this support it is impossible for men, however distinguished for talent and patriotism, successfully to pull down one government and establish another. It is therefore probable that, the circumstances at the meeting of the State Convention being what they are, we shall not have in that body more than a two-thirds majority in favor of the separate secession of our state. With less than that majority it is admitted it would be dangerous to adopt so bold a measure.

"The course of the Convention will depend somewhat on our sister Southern States. If they affirm the right of secession, and the non-existence of a power to prevent a state from exercising it, the position of South Carolina will be greatly strengthened. On the contrary, if the Legislatures remain silent on the subject, or deny the right of a member to withdraw from the confederacy, it might prove injurious to the high purpose which we hope to accomplish. On this subject I request your views. What impression has been made on both parties, but especially the Southern-rights party of Mississippi, by the recent resolutions of the Charleston Convention? Is that party in the ascendant, and likely to continue so? Should South Carolina strike a decisive blow, may she confidently rely on the undivided support of her present friends in your state? What is the present issue before the people of Mississippi? What measures will probably be adopted by her convention? In your opinion, would it be wise and politic for South Carolina, unaided, to begin a conflict with the general government and the North, as some affirm, though we look to another and more glorious result?"

No copy of Quitman's reply has been found among his papers, but its tenor may be inferred from what follows.

Whitemarsh B. Seabrook to General Quitman.

"Edisto Island, July 15th, 1851.

"MY DEAR SIR,—I have the honor to acknowledge the receipt of your favor of the 26th ult. No letter that has reached me for several years has given me more real satisfaction. The facts that the party of which you are the head and ornament will succeed, and that you are prepared with a suitable programme to be presented to the State Convention, is indeed highly inspiriting intelligence. Were I at liberty to give even a limited circulation to your opinion concerning the course which it is expected South Carolina will pursue, it would have the happiest effect on every fence politician in the state. It would certainly remove the unfavorable impression which has been made on the minds of many by one of the resolutions of your June convention, that Mississippi ought not, under 'existing circumstances,' to secede. The co-operationists maintain that this declaration is an argument in favor of their position. In my opinion, it has destroyed the last foot of ground on which they rested.

"Information from the cotton states assures us that Butler, Barnwell, and others were wrong in the assertion that it would be fatal to our cause in that region for the Convention of Southern Rights Associations to declare that, on failure to secure aid within a reasonable time, South Carolina should decide alone. On the contrary, the organization of the Southern-rights party in all of those states, instead of being broken up, has been completed, and men hitherto lukewarm have become active in the secession. I speak advisedly when I say that volunteers by thousands are signifying their wish to be received into our ranks. Still, my dear sir, we have great difficulties to encounter. The state is prosperous; the imminency of the danger is not seen by the masses; many of our most prominent and faithful sentinels entreat us to pause; the consequences of separate state secession can not with certainty be foretold, and a lingering hope still exists that some Southern state, especially Mississippi, will yet show by action that it would be treason ever to expect from it any symbol of submission. My thorough conviction now is, that the only danger to our course is the want of moral courage by this state to strike a decisive blow. At present her resolution is apparently fixed and immutable; but federal gold and promises, added to the thousand circumstances that may occur, institute obstacles in her way, which together are not easily surmounted. Our final course will depend much on Mississippi. Let her, therefore, beware of the measures she adopts. If she demand of the central government indemnity for the past and security for the future, South Carolina will undoubtedly second the movement. If this scheme fail, what then? Let this state proclaim to the world that, at a time to be designated, say in six months, she will withdraw from the Union. If Mississippi be not prepared to follow her example, a simple annunciation on her part that any hostile attempt, direct or indirect, by Congress to prevent her (South Carolina) from exercising the rights of an independent nation, or to keep her in the confederacy, would be considered by your commonwealth as a subversion of the fundamental principle on which the states confederated, and, consequently, a full release for her obligations to the Union. If these events take place, the confusion and excitement that would follow would, after reflection, not only prepare the Northern mind for conciliation and compromise, but induce Virginia, Georgia, and indeed all the Southern States, to meet in convention, in order to unite in the demand which Mississippi had already made for new safeguards for the future. My fears are, that such a convention, in being too easily satisfied, might inflict an irreparable injury on the South. As an individual, I advocate an eternal separation from the North. A majority of the states, however, or of the people of your state or of this, would probably be content with the erection of other and more formidable barriers against Congressional usurpation and Northern fanaticism. Additional constitutional provisions would take several years to be made. In the mean while, the excitement of the public mind might be so entirely subdued as to pass by unnoticed all apparently unimportant infractions of the new compact. We now live under an anti-slavery government, whose will, openly hostile to the institutions of the South, is expressed at all times by a majority. What security can such a government give to the endangered party? None whatever.

The character and extent of the opposition in this state will, I apprehend, be fully known in a month or two. Of thirty papers, two in Charleston, one in Columbia, and one in Greenville (the last a submission paper), are against the secession cause. On the 28th of June, Col. Ervin, commanding United States troops at Fort Moultrie, Sullivan's Island, refused to allow the Moultrie Guards to celebrate their anniversary at their usual place —the battery of the fort—*because he could not permit language like that expressed by the orator at the last anniversary to be repeated in his hearing.* This seemingly little matter involves a great principle, which, the more it is examined, the greater will be its effects on the public mind. It has already induced many of the wavering to declare for early action by the state."

The relations between the rival candidates for governor had been always friendly. In the senatorial contest Foote had defended Quitman against the assaults of M'Nutt, and in the subsequent ballotings, on the failure of Quitman's chances, his friends in the Legislature had voted for Foote. During the war a correspondence of a confidential nature had passed between them. It was apparent, however, at the outset, that these relations of amity and courtesy could not be maintained. Quitman's friends, in letters that he carefully preserved, complained that he was too tame, too abstract, and not sufficiently severe on the tergiversations of his adversary. They demanded that he should be crushed with personalities, but Quitman never yielded to the demand. His habitual gravity, his personal dignity, the stern and deep convictions that occupied his mind, rendered him incapable of such a warfare. His speeches were arguments that might have been regarded as cold, but for the earnestness that gave them vitality and warmth. Gen. Foote, on the other hand, has a style and manner that may be called provoking. He has a diarrhœa of words; irony and satire are his favorite weapons, and, when driven from his position into a corner, he has a plausibility offensive to a plain-dealing, matter-of-fact man. Quitman would fight as long as he believed himself to be right, but no longer. Foote will fight for the pleasure of fighting. Quitman stood square upon his platform, and would debate no other issues. Foote wriggled around it, and employed his powers to tantalize and provoke. He had, beyond doubt, great personal respect for Quitman, but his tactics were indispensable to his success. He gave the cue to his followers, and taught them to evade the true issues, while boldly challenging discussion. He adopted Danton's maxim, " De l'audace, de l'audace, toujours de l'audace." And while Quitman stood as firm as Dentatus, Foote played the part sometimes of Suchet the tactician, and sometimes of Murat leading his squadrons to the charge. Gen. Foote gradually, as the canvass progressed, became more heated and personal, declaiming about traitors and treason, and other innuendoes, too much for the forbearance of his adversary.

Quitman, on the other hand, brought forward specifications against Foote:

" 1st. For advocating, planning, and urging the admission of California as a sovereign state with an anti-slavery proviso in her Constitution, and thus aiding to pass the Wilmot Proviso in another form.

" 2d. For advocating and supporting the dismemberment of Texas, by which 60,000 square miles of slave territory were virtually converted to free soil.

" 3d. For encouraging and supporting the bill to suppress the slave-trade in the District of Columbia, consenting thereby to affix a brand of opprobrium upon the purchase and sale of slaves, and admitting the right of Congress conditionally to abolish slavery in the district.

" 4th. For abandoning and opposing the assumed position of the state, and setting up a new platform for himself.

" 5th. For disregarding and disobeying the instructions of the Legislature which he himself had called for.

" 6th. For combining with Clay and others to establish a new party to perpetuate the wrongs inflicted by the Compromise.

" 7th. For undertaking, by so-called compromise, to barter away some of the constitutional rights of his constituents without even sufficient equivalents.

" 8th. For assailing Southern States and Southern men, and apologizing for the hostile action of some of the Northern States on the subject of slavery.

" 9th. For disrespectful allusions, while senator, to the Legislature of his state.

" 10th. For assailing those who are opposed to the Compromise in this state as disunionists and factionists.

" 11th. For deserting the party which placed him in position and counseling with and co-operating with Clay, Webster, and Fillmore.

" 12th. For receiving a nomination from the Whigs of this state.

" 13th. For holding on to his place as senator after accepting the nomination for governor.

" 14th. For violently assailing the governor of his state
Vol. II.—G

for acting upon opinions which he himself had formally communicated.

"15th. For misrepresenting the opinion and sentiments of the people of Mississippi on the subject of the slave question.

"16th. For voting with the Abolitiōnists against striking out the first section of the bill to suppress the slave-trade.

"17th. For failing to insist upon extending the Missouri Compromise line."

The exciting canvass between these gentlemen terminated in a personal rencontre, in the county of Panolo, on the 18th of July, which both parties lived to regret.

1851. On the first Monday in September the election took place throughout the state for delegates to the Convention, as authorized by the Legislature. A very large majority of "Union" delegates was returned. As soon as this extraordinary result was ascertained, Gov. Quitman, mortified by an expression of public sentiment so wholly unexpected, felt that he could no longer, with due regard to his own dignity and position, be a candidate for office. He issued the following address:

" To the Democratic State-rights Party of Mississippi.

"The result of the recent election for the Convention, however brought about, must be regarded, at least for the present, as decisive of the position of the state on the great issues involved.

"The majority have declared that they are content with the late aggressive measures of Congress, and opposed to any remedial action by the state.

"Although this determination of the people is at variance with my fixed opinion of the true policy of the state, heretofore expressed and still conscientiously entertained, yet, as a state-rights man and a Democrat, I bow in respectful submission to the apparent will of the people.

"It is true the state has not yet spoken authoritatively; even the acts of the Convention will not be binding until they shall have been ratified by a vote of the peo-

ple; but by the election of Non-resisters to the Convention, a majority of the people have declared against the
course of policy on the slavery questions which I deemed
it my duty to pursue while governor, and against the
principles upon which I was nominated, and upon which
alone I had consented to run as a candidate. I might,
perhaps, be elected notwithstanding this demonstration
of public sentiment in the election for the Convention,
but as I have been mainly instrumental in seeking the
expression of the will of the people through a Convention,
I ought, in my political action, to abide by it.

" Therefore, upon full consideration of all the circumstances, respect for the apparent decision of the people,
duty to the noble and patriotic party who are struggling
to maintain the rights of the South against Northern aggression, and to preserve our institutions from the fatal
effects of consolidating all power in the federal government, and a sense of self-respect which inclines me not
to seek a public station in which my opinions upon vital
questions are not sustained by a majority of my constituents, all concur in inducing me to the opinion that my
duty requires me to retire from the position which I occupy as the Democratic State-rights candidate for governor. With emotions of the deepest gratitude to the
patriotic party by which I was nominated for the evidences of their unfaltering confidence, both in the nomination and in the warm and hearty reception with which
I have been met every where in the canvass, I tender my
resignation of the high and honorable post of their chief
standard-bearer in the pending canvass, pledging myself
to them and to the country that I will, to the last, serve
the great cause of State Rights as faithfully in the ranks
as I have endeavored to do in high position.

" J. A. QUITMAN.

"Monmouth, Sept. 6th, 1851."

CHAPTER XVII.

Colonel Davis.—Union Convention.—Governor Foote.—Quitman's Views. — Democratic State Convention. — Quitman's Speech.—Letter to B. F. Dill.—Presidential Election.—General Pierce.—Letter to Chapman. — Letter to Central Committee. — General Scott.—Correspondence with Judge Wilkinson.—Elwood Fisher.—R. D. Cralle. —Nominated for Vice-president in Alabama.—Memphis Convention.—The Doctrine of Protection.—Quitman at Rhinebeck.—Defends the Institutions of the South.—Meditates the Liberation of Cuba.—Arraigned in New Orleans.—His Defense.—Reply to Judge Campbell.—Letter to. Thomas Reed and H. T. Ellett.—His Relations with Cuba not yet to be explained.

In this contingency, the Democratic ticket being without a leader, and the election near at hand, the Central Democratic Executive Committee, backed by an emphatic appeal from the state-rights press, prevailed on Colonel Jefferson Davis to lead the forlorn hope. He was enfeebled by illness and almost blind, but he entered immediately on the canvass with characteristic energy. Ill health and the want of time prevented his success, but he gave a powerful impetus to the reaction which soon occurred.

The State Convention, otherwise called the Union Convention, assembled in the capitol on the 10th of November, 1851. It reversed all that had been hitherto done in Mississippi to embody Southern sentiment for resistance and defense.

The Position of Mississippi, declared in Convention at Jackson, which met on the 10th day of November, 1851.

The people of Mississippi, in convention assembled, as expressive of their deliberate judgment on the great questions involved in the sectional controversy between the slaveholding and non-slaveholding states of the American Union, adopt the following resolutions :

1st. *Resolved*, That, in the opinion of this Convention, the people of Mississippi, in a spirit of conciliation and compromise, have maturely considered the action of Congress, embracing a series of measures for the admission of California as a state into the Union, the organization of territorial governments for Utah and New Mexico, the establishment of a boundary between the latter and the State of Texas, the suppression of the slave-trade in the District of Columbia, and the extradition of fugitive slaves; and, connected with them, the rejection of the proposition to exclude slavery from the territories of the United States and to abolish it in the District of Columbia; and while they do not entirely approve, will abide by it as a permanent adjustment of this sectional controversy, so long as the same, in all its features, shall be faithfully adhered to and enforced.

2d. *Resolved*, That we perceive nothing in the above recited legislation of the Congress of the United States which should be permitted to disturb the friendly and peaceful "existing relations between the government of the United States and the government and people of the State of Mississippi."

3d. *Therefore resolved*, That, in the opinion of this Convention, the people of the State of Mississippi will abide by the Union as it is, and by the Constitution of the United States without amendment. That they hold the Union secondary in importance only to the rights and principles it was designed to perpetuate; that past associations, present fruition, and future prospects will bind them to it so long as it continues to be the safeguard of those rights and principles.

4th. *Resolved farther*, That, in the opinion of this Convention, the asserted right of secession from the Union, on the part of a state or states, is utterly unsanctioned by the federal Constitution, which was framed to "establish" and not to destroy the Union of the states, and that no secession can, in fact, take place without a subversion of the Union established, and which will not virtually amount in its effects and consequences to a civil revolution.

5th. *Resolved farther*, That while, in the opinion of this Convention, such are the sentiments and opinions of the people of the State of Mississippi, still, violations of the rights of the people of the state may occur, which would amount to intolerable oppression, and would justify a resort to measures of resistance, among which, in the opinion of the Convention, the people of the state have designated the following:

1st. The interference by Congressional legislation with the institution of slavery in the states.

2d. The interference with the trade in slaves between the states.

3d. Any action of Congress on the subject of slavery in the District of Columbia, or in places subject to the jurisdiction of Congress, incompatible with the safety and domestic tranquillity—the rights and honor of the slaveholding states.

4th. The refusal by Congress to admit a new state into the Union on the ground of her tolerating slavery within her limits.

5th. The passage of any law by Congress prohibiting slavery in any one of the territories.

6th. The repeal of the fugitive slave law and the neglect or refusal by the general government to enforce the constitutional provisions for the reclamation of fugitive slaves.

6th. *Resolved farther*, That, in the opinion of this Convention, the people, in the recent elections, have been governed by an abiding confidence that the said adjustment measures of Congress would be enforced in good faith in every section of the land.

7th. *Resolved farther*, That, as the people of the State of Mississippi, in the opinion of this Convention, desire all farther agitation of the slavery question to cease, and have acted upon and decided all the foregoing questions, thereby making it the duty of this Convention to pass no acts within the purview and spirit of the law under which it is called, this Convention deems it unnecessary to refer to the people, for their approval or disapproval at the ballot-box, its action in the premises.

8th. *Resolved*, That, in the opinion of this Convention, without intending to call in question the motives of the members of the Legislature, the call of this Convention by the Legislature, at its late extraordinary session, was unauthorized by the people, and that said act, in peremptorily ordering a convention of the people of the state without first submitting to them the question whether there should be a convention or no convention, was an unwarranted assumption of power by the Legislature, at war with the spirit of republican institutions, an encroachment upon the rights of the people, and can never be rightfully invoked as a precedent.

It is not in place here to follow this matter farther. It belongs rather to the history of the state.* But it may be observed that the concessions made by that body, and especially the repudiation of the great fundamental attribute of sovereignty, the right of secession, gave a fatal blow to the so-called Union party, and terminated its existence in less than two years. The Nashville Convention turned out to be an abortion. Foote had been elected governor by a lean majority, with the general understanding that he should be returned to the Senate on the expiration of his term. But before that period arrived the Democratic State-rights party was again in power; one of its most gifted and consistent leaders, the warm personal and political friend of Quitman,† had been elected to the chief magistracy, and a large majority of the Legislature was of the same complexion. Governor Foote declined a poll for the Senate, and left the state for California, without even a demonstration of gratitude from a party whose heterogeneous ranks he had consolidated and disciplined, and whom, in the face of a tempest of opposition, he had conducted to victory.

The following letter from Gen. Quitman, dated Dec. 29th, 1851, will be read with interest, foreshadowing, as it does, the line of conduct recently adopted by the Mis-

* A complete history of Mississippi will soon appear, from the pen of B. W. Sanders, one of the most brilliant writers in the South.
† Hon. John J. M'Rae.

sissippi and other Southern delegates, in the Charleston Convention.

To W. D. Chapman, Editor of the Standard, Columbus, Mississippi.

* * * * * "The feverish anxiety to bury the past in oblivion, exhibited by many presses and state-rights men, carries with it a reproach upon ourselves for having raised opposition to the compromise measures. We, nine tenths of the Democratic party of the state, were the agitators. We proposed to meet what we deemed fatal encroachment upon our state as well as personal rights promptly and effectually at the threshold. We were beaten by our old foe, the Federal Whigs, aided by desertions from the democratic faith, and now we most anxiously implore the latter to forget the past, as if the error was ours and not theirs. The foreshadowing influence of the next presidential campaign may procure our pardon, but not, I predict, without our submitting to the decimation of our front rank in the late fight. I regret exceedingly that your very civil letter, asking my opinion in relation to uniting with Northern Democrats in nominating a candidate for President, did not reach my hands in time to render my answer of any value to you. The die is now cast. The press, with scarce an exception that I have seen, and apparently the great body of our party, not only seem to concur in the proposal, but are disposed to read out of the party those who think differently. It is still open for discussion in our proposed state convention. I hope it will then receive a most serious consideration. A concurrence of leading men in that body can only check the strong propensity to take part in a fight in which sixty millions of annual revenue and thirty thousand public offices are to be divided. From the highest statesman down to the smallest village politician there is in that great lottery a chance for a prize, if he shall have had the luck to shout on the successful side. Could there be a stronger evidence of the central tendency of our government than is exhibited in our own case? We of the State-rights party complain of the overshadowing influence of federal power. We profess to be organized in opposition to that influence, and

yet, as the trial of our principles approaches, we can not resist the temptation which that influence presents. We not only rush wildly into the contest for the possession of that power, but become so absorbed in its very influence that we propose to leave our political principles behind while engaged in the contest. Since the people of this state authoritatively declared in the September elections their opposition to all schemes of resistance to the aggressive acts of Congress, it would be both improper and impracticable to keep up an organization founded alone upon the question of state resistance. But the organization of the Democratic State-rights party embraced other great and permanent principles, as broad and lasting as the protection of the institution of slavery, and the preservation of the rights of the states. It furnished a platform broad enough and strong enough for every true Southern Democrat to stand upon. Had I, then, been originally consulted by our party, I would have advised preserving the Democratic State-rights organization, with effective associations in every county, and would have left those of the Union Democrats who concur in general principles with us, but merely were opposed to our remedial action, to unite with us, as such undoubtedly would. As such party, we might have declared our abandonment of the practical question of state resistance, yielding it up to the will of the people, but we might have left on record our protest against the aggression, and our condemnation of those false Southern men who had aided to impose on us the necessity of submitting to wrong. Standing thus organized upon the great slavery and state-rights principles, we should have assumed toward the great national parties, whatever names or shapes they might assume, an armed neutrality; but we should have tendered to the Northern Democracy our cordial co-operation, on condition that they would assume positions consistent with our equality and safety in the Union. In case such concession could not be obtained, we should have proclaimed our determination not to support their candidate for the presidency unless made acceptable to us by pledges or otherwise. This course would, in my opinion, have been more likely to secure the nomination of a candidate acceptable to us, than would be our presence in the Convention and taking part in the proceedings. Greater respect would have been paid to our position, because we would have been deemed to be in earnest. We might, at least, have forced the selection of a state-rights Southern man for the vice-presidency. As it is, we shall get some wishy-washy general resolutions, and Cobb, King, or Foote for the vice-presidency.

"Such are my opinions, but the great mass of our party seem bent upon a convention at home and a fusion with the Northern Democracy in a general convention; and are amiable enough to be content with platforms from which Cass and Foote and others insisted that they could rob us of the public domain, so it was not done à la Wilmot. It seems now pretty well understood that we are to meet on the 8th proximo, to select delegates to a Baltimore Convention, and to suggest Buchanan and Davis as our choice of candidates; and I am apprehensive that, in the present sociable temper of our friends, strong efforts will be made to keep out of our Convention all questions but a reaffirmance of old Baltimore platforms, upon which Foote, and Cobb, and Cass, and Sam. Houston profess to repose with so much self-complacency. I take occasion to say, from the heart, that the selection by a Baltimore Convention, even for the second place, of some sterling Southern patriot, such as Davis, Mason, or Hunter, would go far with me to make the ticket acceptable; but it is wild fancy to suppose that any prominent man who has opposed the admission of California, etc., etc., will be nominated, unless it is made the price of our own co-operation. Our delegates may fret a little, but they will be overruled, under the supposition that the same influences which brought them to the Convention will carry them to the support of any ticket called Democratic. We have lost our influence. Southern thunder is now regarded but a '*brutum fulmen*' as harmless as the rattling behind the scenes. Considering, then, all things, the mind of our party made up, and the justification we appear to have—in the attempt of the Union Democrats to get up a representation to Baltimore, and thereby to rob us of our good name—I have concluded we must meet on the 8th of January. What shall we do there?   I would reaffirm all the general principles asserted at our last June Convention ; declare that we will not support for President or Vice-president any Southern man who supported the admission of California, Slave-trade Bill, or the Texas Bill ; prescribe the terms on which we are willing to act with the Northern Democracy, and appoint delegates instructed to retire if our terms are not acceded to by the Baltimore Convention. We should make no nominations, unless we think fit to present the name of Col. Davis for Vice-president.

"I wish, if possible, to act with the mass of our party, but I will not vote for any nominee tainted with federalism, or hostile to us on the slavery question ; nor will I support or associate politically with any Southern man who advocated or aided to bring about the 'Compromise,' who assisted to rob us of our equality, and to cheat us out of the public domain.   I would as soon fraternize with the Abolitionist.

"Before three weeks pass there will be a new and powerful party in the country.   The electric fire of the great Magyar is now creating its elements.   Our quandam little friend, R. J. Walker, physically little, but a giant in vast political schemes, will form it into shape, and move it majestically down into the political plain like a Macedonian phalanx, united by one principle into a solid mass.   Perhaps we may make the best terms with these new progressives, for I fear that good old-fashioned Jeffersonian Democracy is about to be among the things that were.   'Fuit Ilium et ingens gloria Dardanidum.' "

The Democratic State Rights Convention assembled in great strength on the 8th of January, 1852.   A general spirit of harmony and conciliation prevailed, and it was considered expedient, with a view of uniting the entire Democracy of the state, merely to adopt the Virginia and Kentucky resolutions, and reaffirm the Baltimore Convention resolutions, as embodying the creed of the party.   Mr. Barry, of Lownds, one of the ablest and most eloquent members of the Convention, and Mr. Fontaine, an influential member from Pontotoc, submitted some additional ones. The chair ruled these amendments out of order, and, on an appeal from the decision, Quitman spoke in substance as follows:

"MR. PRESIDENT,—I do not expect, from any thing I shall say, to change the apparent determination of this body to reject any resolution of the character now presented. I would not speak did I not feel, from the position I have held, that my silence might be misconstrued. I know that the question before the Convention is upon the appeal taken from the decision of the chair, declaring the resolution offered by my friend, Mr. Barry, out of order, and that it is not strictly parliamentary on this question to discuss the merits of the resolution; but the distinguished gentleman who has just spoken (Col. Davis) has been permitted to discuss the subject generally, and, as it is not probable, from the apparent disposition of the Convention, that any other opportunity will occur, I respectfully ask leave, briefly, to present my opinions upon this subject. But, first, let me ask those gentlemen who would dispose of these resolutions so unceremoniously, in what are they out of order? If the general committee, to which all resolutions involving principle were to be referred, still exists, these resolutions ought to be entertained and referred. If the committee is defunct, they should be considered and debated on here. I see no good reason to exclude them, save that the mind of the majority is made up against them. I ask, however, that no technical forms shall deprive us who favor these resolutions from the privilege of recording our votes for them.

"I, for one, deem it of the utmost importance, both to principle and policy, upon this first occasion that the Democratic party have assembled round their council-fires since the great contest through which we have just passed, that we should fully define our position upon the leading political issues now occupying the public attention. I would go farther than these resolutions, or even those heretofore presented by my friend, Mr. Handy. I would exactly define how the proceedings of the late State Convention are obligatory upon us as citizens, and

so far I would declare our submission to them; but with
that exception I would reaffirm all the general principles
asserted by the June Convention of the Democratic
State-rights party; principles which we then deemed to
be elementary in our system of government, and essential to the preservation of the rights of the states, and
the protection of our especial property interests. Is
there any gentleman on this floor who will deny that
they are less so now than they were then? The least we
can do to preserve our consistency and to maintain that
frank and bold character which has heretofore marked
the Democratic party, is to adopt these resolutions or
some similar ones. If we give them the go-by, will it
not be said that we dared not to meet the question of
the right of secession? But gentlemen say that it is unnecessary to assert abstract rights. Why, then, did we
adopt the resolutions of 1798 and '9, and those of the Baltimore Convention? Let me remind you that, though it
may be an abstract right, it is not an abstract question.
Unfortunately, this great question involving the whole
of state-rights is now pressed upon us from every quarter. In the rapid strides we are making toward centralism, the defenders of state-rights find their doctrine neither fashionable nor profitable. Allured by the splendor
of a government which dispenses fifty millions per annum and thirty thousand offices, few politicians are disposed to come to the aid of the Spartan band who are
yet defending this last defile against the hosts of consolidation. It seems to me that the assertion of this great
elementary principle which distinguishes the Democrat
from the Federalist is more than ever demanded from us.
A regular convention of delegates elected by the people
of this state assembled in November last to take into
consideration the question of resistance to the late aggressive acts of Congress. That Convention overstep-
ped its powers, and passed a resolution denying to the
state the right of secession; that is, the right of the people of the state to resume the political powers delegated
to the federal government, asserting that such act would
be revolutionary, and, by implication, admitting the right
on the part of the federal government not only to coerce
a state by military force, but to prosecute and execute

her citizens for obeying the sovereign act of the state. If this act of the Convention was authorized, it is a formal surrender of the sovereignty of the state, an abandonment of her rights, a voluntary suicide.

"Now while I deny that this act of the Convention was authoritative or within the scope of its powers, it can not be denied that the declaration will be regarded by all the world as indicating the opinions of the people of Mississippi, as, in fact, the position of our state on that subject. If, then, we, the Democratic party, at the first great family meeting which has occurred after this position has been given to our state, shall fail to negative that degrading resolution, will not our silence imply our assent to it? Come what will, I am for meeting such position promptly and emphatically. Let us leave nothing to implication. Let our disclaimer of concessions, so degrading in a sovereign state, be as loud as their utterance; ay, let it reverberate in thunder tones throughout the land! Why should we hesitate for a moment to utter our firm conviction of a principle that lies at the foundation of our government? Gentlemen say it is superfluous, that it is contained in the Virginia and Kentucky resolutions which we have adopted, and yet they know that those who most loudly denounce this great sovereign state right profess to stand upon the platform of these celebrated resolutions. The same may be said of the Baltimore resolutions. Both have been frittered away by cunning sophistries. To a plain man, it is true, it would appear that the admission of the right of a state to judge of infractions of the Constitution, as well as the mode and measure of redress, is an acknowledgment of her right to seek that redress by withdrawing from the confederation, and, in like manner, the Baltimore resolutions on the subject of slavery and the equality of the states would appear to be sufficient for the protection of both; but did they shield the Southern States from being despoiled of their share of the domain, or save them from the insulting discrimination against their citizens made by the bill to suppress the slave-trade in the federal district? If, in passing these resolutions, we have a purpose, let us boldly avow it? Let us no longer deceive ourselves. These resolutions, like the Bible and the Constitution, are, as we know from experience, variously construed. Our purpose should be to let the world know what we mean.

"But it is urged against the resolutions now before the Convention that the introduction of any new issue might prejudice the claims of a favorite son of this state to a nomination for the vice-presidency—might cause the exclusion of our delegates from the Baltimore Convention, and might impair the prospects of harmony in the Democratic ranks. I propose briefly to notice each of them. I speak from the heart when I say that there is no man in this convention who would be more gratified than I would be at the selection by the Baltimore Convention of Col. Davis for the distinguished station to which he is recommended. It would be regarded by me as a great point gained; not because he is my neighbor and friend, not because he is eminent as a statesman and soldier, but because he is a firm defender of the rights of the states, and a true friend of the South; because, in short, I think his opinions upon state rights and slavery concur with my own. I would, therefore, be the last man to place any obstacles in the way of so great a good; but I am at a loss to conceive how any plain declaration of principles which that distinguished gentleman, as well as most of us, are known to entertain, can have such effect. On the contrary, my impression is, that any appearance of evasion on our part will have the effect not only to weaken our cause, but to injure those who have been prominent in the advocacy of our principles.

"As to our being excluded from the Baltimore Convention, let that alarm no one. I assure you, Mr. President, that the aspirants for the presidency and their friends are more afraid that the State-rights Democrats will not be there than disposed to shut the door against them if they come. They know full well that, in the present divisions of public sentiment, no Democrat can be elected without the support of the state-rights men. Take from the Democratic party those who assert the right of a state as a sovereign to resume her delegated powers, and scarce a corporal's guard would be left. This state of things furnishes an additional reason why we should avail ourselves of this important occasion to obtain the recognition of sound principles. Of what consequence is it who is elected President beyond the securing a principle? Without this the contest would be a mere struggle for office, interesting only to those who expected a share of the spoils. I came here in the hope that, through the Democratic party, something might be gained to preserve the remaining rights of the South, and protect us from the great evil now staring us in the face—the proclivity of our system to the consolidation of all power in the federal head. But for that I would not be here: as I want no office, I could have no motive to embark in the presidential contest but the success of principle. We favor a democratic organization as a means of effecting something to check federalism and centralism. I freely confess that, had I originally been consulted in regard to this movement, I would have advised the Democratic party of the state to remain organized, and to tender to the national Democratic party our co-operation only on condition that the nominations were made acceptable to us. Such a position would, I think, in the present crisis, have given us more weight and influence than we will have if present and acting in the national convention. It is, however, deemed proper to send delegates to the general convention. Let us, then, by the declaration of principles, furnish our representation in that body with a chart to guide them.

"I have thus briefly, Mr. President, presented my views. It is apparent that they are not acceptable to the majority: I shall, however, respect the action of the Convention, and, unless I am called on to sacrifice a principle, I shall conform to it, because I know not where else to look except to the Democracy for effective help in this day of tribulation to the South. I expect to support the nominees of the Democratic Convention for president and vice-president; but I will not vote for any Southern man who advocated that cunning series of measures called the adjustment, by which the slaveholding states were stripped of their equal rights in the public territory, and degraded from the position of equals in the confederacy. I may pardon the advocacy of these measures by a Northern man, because, in the struggle for supremacy, he but sided with his section; but the Southern man who deserted us in the hour of need I can never trust. I speak not of the great mass of those who acquiesced in the wrong, because to them the remedy appeared a greater evil than submission, but of those who were active agents in the support of disastrous measures, that time will show constitute but the first chapter in the history of the decline and fall of our domestic institutions and the final degradation of the Southern States."

On the 20th of February, in a letter to B. F. Dill, editor of the Oxford Organizer, he comments on the recent Democratic Convention:

* * * * "I am forced to acknowledge that I take but little interest in the struggle now going on in our state. I can scarcely make out what it is. Last summer the contest was noble and sublime: it involved questions the greatest which can arise under our system of government, and practically affecting our civil liberty and prosperity.

"Spoils, office, even men were forgotten in the contest; intellect and patriotism were every where aroused and warmed into action; our presses were honest, fearless, and manly; the State-rights party engaged in the conflict like men who felt that they were right—that truth, justice, and virtue were on their side. How is it now? You have well said that the struggle seems to be merely to break down Foote, and I fear that many are willing to sacrifice important principles to effect it. For that purpose the Democracy is to be rallied; we are asked not only to join our voices with Cass, and Chase, and Benton, and Rantoul, the Van Burens, and Donelson, the veriest puppy of the pack, in shouting hosanna to a name, but also to repudiate what we said six months ago, or, what is as bad, preserve a deceptive silence in regard to aggressions which, but a short time since, we thought almost justified extreme resorts.

"Foote is now assailed, not for his agency in robbing us of the public domain, and stigmatizing our institutions by odious discriminations. No, a discussion of these acts would revive a subject which we are required to forget. Many of our politicians seem to shrink from it as if they were touched in a sore place. The hard blow of a defeat and exclusion from office makes them sensitive at the very idea of state rights. For his course on the Compromise measures, which ought to consign him to political infamy, Foote is not now attacked. The war is now upon him for his finality resolutions in the Senate. Now seriously, being in the habit of thinking for myself and speaking boldly, I consider this act of Foote's commendable. In his canvass the burden of his song every where was, that the adjustment was a final settlement of the slavery question, and he pledged himself, under the witness's oath, that the Northern people would so recognize it. It was therefore honest in him to submit the test to them. In this he was consistent and bold. Why should we, who complained of the Compromise as. a gross wrong, and who declared that although the North received the lion's share, she would not stand by it, complain of Foote submitting the test to the Northern people? We were but lately for agitating against the outrage. Has our defeat caused any real affection for the measure, or does not our peaceable disposition arise from the desire to control a government which distributes fifty millions per annum and dispenses thirty thousand offices? Is not this the reason why we denounce the agitation of a question which may disorganize the Democratic party? This may be politic to obtain power, but it is not the way to secure principle. In my judgment, however, the question will come up. All appears now quiet; but why is it that so many presses devote column after column to efforts to keep down the question? It is because the politicians see and know that there are many thousands who, like you and I, feel ashamed of the present position of our party; who are not disposed to stultify ourselves by admitting that, plundered and oppressed as we have been, after all there is nothing like old party issues. Had I been originally consulted, I would have recommended that we should have retained our old Democratic State-rights organization. I am a Democrat, because democracy has heretofore sustained state rights. When it shall cease to do so, the name will have no charm for me. Democracy has generally boldly met practical issues as they came up. She has generally boldly thrown herself in the breach when assaults were made upon the Constitution or the rights of the states. I think I see, at the present time, a strong tendency to centralism, to the destruction of the federal character of our system, to the sapping and mining of the sovereignty of the states. Our doctrines are becoming unfashionable. Soon they will be held *criminal.* The oft-repeated phrases of '*loyalty to the Union*' is but the precursor of *laws* to suppress disloyal sentiments. There is every indication now, from the timidity of state-rights men, that we, I mean you and I, will live to see and feel such laws.

"I attended the late Democratic Convention in the hope that there we might do something to secure the remaining rights that are left to us, but I soon found that the majority had come there to combine against Foote, and to unite with Northern Democrats to make a President. Barry, Fontaine, Handy, and a few others of the Old Guard, with myself, stood alone in favor of a bold and frank exposition of our political principles and position.

"We were told that as Democrats we must not only acquiesce in the Compromise, but we must do nothing to bring back the recollection of the late contest, and say not a word about the rights of secession.

"The great object was to cover every thing under the broad shield of Democracy, and the greatest impatience was manifested at the bare mention of any resolution but those general ones which have before been adopted.

"Now, I acquiesce in the Compromise precisely as I did in the election of Foote. I submit to both, because the people have refused to resist the former, and have put the latter in the calendar as a political saint. It would be well for those who now so strenuously press us to forget the wrong which has been inflicted on us, also for the same reason to forget the offenses which the saint has committed.

"I am thus entirely out of the contest. I speak of the political contest now going on in the state, and can look on calmly. I believe it will be difficult to bring the great mass of the people to take any interest in old issues when new ones of greater magnitude press themselves on the public attention.

"The question now presents itself: What shall we of the strict state-rights school, what shall the 'Old Guard' do? It is not the part of a statesman to despair of the country.

"I can suggest no better means of preserving our principles than to form associations without reference to elections. The sacred fire was preserved in the deep recesses of the temple for centuries by the vestal virgins; thus we may preserve and extend sound principles, until the day shall come when it may be necessary to strike a blow for their defense. But upon this subject we should consult together.

"I now expect to support the Democratic candidate for President, but I will not pledge myself until I know who is nominated. If I felt disposed to act the seer, I would predict that Kossuth will elect the next President. If Walker becomes a candidate on his principles he will be formidable. I think there will be more than two candidates, and if two of them should be Democrats, the party, under that name, will be disbanded forever, and the true, unterrified Democrats, will unite to preserve state rights. I propose to call them the 'Old Guard.' The corps that never faltered, never turned their backs; whose motto was, ' We may die, but can not be conquered.' The monarchists, privilege men, and Tories, will rally under the banner of King Union."

1852. The National Democratic Convention, which assembled in Baltimore in May, nominated Franklin Pierce and William R. King, old-line Jackson Democrats, for President and Vice-president. In a letter to John T. M'Murran, Esq., Quitman thus refers to the subject: "I have just received the news that my old friend General Pierce is nominated by the Democracy for President. By the time this reaches you we shall probably have heard of the nomination of Scott on the other side. It will be well for these gentlemen to cast lots as to who shall occupy the White House. As we are to have a

Northern master, either of these generals will do as well as any other person."

General Quitman to W. D. Chapman.

"Monmouth, June 9th, 1852.

* * * "Nothing in my whole life has mortified me more than the backing out, I may call it defection, of leading men of the Democratic State-rights party of this state. Charity would persuade me to excuse those whose bread is dependent on their being of the successful party, as it would to excuse a starving man for stealing a loaf, but I can feel nothing but contempt for the blustering politician who, the moment he finds that he is not sustained by a majority, puts off his principles, as a deserter casts off his uniform. It can not be denied that the events of the last ten months have demoralized the Democratic party of the South to such an extent as to make regeneration hopeless. What a history would a faithful detail of the events of the last year in our state present! While as a Mississippian I feel disposed to bow my head in shame at the retrospect, I feel some pride in the thought that my name was blotted out when treachery commenced. I feel the force of your philosophy when you remark, 'Let the past take care of itself.' It is only a guide to the future. The question you proposed is, what is now the duty of state-rights men, for we are no longer a party? Even the 'Southern Press' has abandoned the idea of a party. I have just read with mingled feelings of surprise and sorrow, the article in the Press of the 28th of May, under the head of 'The present position of parties.' That hitherto independent press seems also to have been drawn into the absorbing vortex of the presidential maelstrom. I shall expect soon to find it glorifying *our candidates* for devotion to the great measure of pacification. What then shall we do? Could I speak for all true men of our own creed I would say, from the bottom of my heart, 'It is a duty to stand by our flag so long as a shred remains.' It is to be expected that, in the heat of the presidential contest, the battle-cries of the rival parties will drown the still small voice of reason and principle; but when the contest shall have ended, when differences of opinion shall have

led to dissensions, strifes, and collisions, then the eyes of the whole South will be directed to the patriotic banner of the 'Old Guard.' By sternly standing by our principles, a time may come for us to strike with effect. We may succeed in securing an equality in the Union, or our independence out of it, or at least fall gloriously. I say gloriously, for there is something soul-stirring in the sentiment, 'Dulce et decorum est pro patria mori.'

"Your inquiry, however, also covers the ground, what course we shall pursue while the absorbing contest goes on? Shall we mingle in it, or stand aloof? With General Pierce I have an agreeable personal acquaintance. We are friends, and, in selecting a Northern man, I know none less exceptionable. My personal feelings incline me to acquiesce in his nomination, and to give him my support, if I can consistently do so. This will depend upon the platform upon which the Convention has placed him. If they have indorsed the compromise measures, or if those are to be elementary principles of the reorganization of the party, I shall stand aloof, and be ready to unite with any forlorn hope to raise aloft the independent standard of state rights, and to stand by it or fall under it.

"We now have rumors that the Compromise has been adopted by the Convention. If so, I can not perceive how Southern-rights men can support such a platform. It was but a short time since we regarded some of the compromise measures as unjust, destructive of the equality of the Southern States, against the spirit, if not the letter, of the Constitution, and evidence of a fixed design to abolish slavery every where. If our opinions are changed—if we have found ourselves mistaken, if these measures are so benign as to deserve a place in our political creed—let us honestly make proclamation to that effect, and raise altars to its authors, Clay, Cass, and Foote. But if not, let us not write ourselves down as asses or rogues. How would Colonel Davis, Governor Brown, or I appear, vindicating, defending, and approving such a platform? Why, those political chameleons, Foote and Sharkey, could not beat it. But I must conclude by summing up: My present opinion, then, is, that if Pierce be nominated without any indorsement of the compromise measures, and if he assume no other objectional positions, state-rights men should give him their support. If, on the other hand, the Convention have placed him on that ebony and topaz platform, I think it will become our duty to stand aloof, or, what would be better, if we can muster spirit, use our exertions to rouse up and rally the old State-rights Guard, form societies, hold conventions, nominate a separate ticket, and declare war to the knife.

"But it may be said that such action on our part might, perhaps, result in the defeat of the Democratic ticket and success of the Whig. All the answer I have to this is, that if Democracy is to retain power by striding this centaur hobby, with abolition head and Southern tail, it had better be unhorsed. If reorganized Democracy admits the absolute doctrines of the existence and sovereignty of a supreme national government, possessing power to coerce the states, nothing will be lost by its defeat and destruction. On the other hand, by means of a bold and talented press, we may rouse the honest state-rights men throughout the land, and present an array that would command respect, and perhaps eventually be the means of saving our country. I know the corrupting influences which the distribution of sixty millions of revenue and thirty thousand offices exercise, yet I flatter myself that state rights, state sovereignty, and constitutional limitation to the federal power, will still find favor and support among the people.

"I regret that my pressing engagements have not permitted me a more elaborate reply to your inquiries; but I may at another time resume the subject. In the mean time I shall be happy to receive your views with equal freedom."

It is certain that he declined to take any part in the presidential contest, for reasons that will appear in his correspondence. His neutral position was perverted into a passive support of Scott, and, to counteract the impression, the Central Democratic Association, on the 6th of June, invited him to deliver an address at its next regular meeting. He responded in the subjoined elaborate paper:

"Monmouth, July 17th, 1852.

"GENTLEMEN,—Recently, on my return from Arkansas, I had the honor to receive your note of the 6th inst., inviting me, on behalf of the Democratic Central Association, to address them at their next regular meeting, or so soon thereafter as might suit my engagements. Appreciating highly the compliment tendered by an association that numbers among its members so many valued personal friends and so many intelligent citizens, in whose devotion to the true principles of old Jeffersonian Democracy, to states' rights, and to the protection of Southern interests, I have so much confidence, it is with some regret that I announce to you my determination, under present circumstances, not to take a prominent or active part in the pending presidential canvass.

"It is due to you as well as to myself that I should at once and frankly state the reasons that have influenced this course; the more so, that in this conclusion I have the misfortune to differ from so many political friends who have warmly embarked in this contest, and whose opinions I so highly respect, that nothing short of very strong convictions of propriety could have induced me to adopt a different rule of conduct for my own guidance; but with me it is a matter which involves not only political consistency but fidelity to principle.

"My personal inclinations also prompted a different course. I knew General Franklin Pierce personally while we were in the service together and since. His high intellectual qualities, his quick perception, and accurate judgment of men, secured my respect, while his nice sense of honor, his sincerity, and his pure-minded, disinterested integrity won my warm regard and friendship. His nomination was highly acceptable to me. When the intelligence of this event first reached us by telegraph, I promptly wrote to some friends, who had asked my advice, recommending him warmly to their support, unless the Convention should place him upon a false platform by adopting the so-called '*Compromise*' as an article of the party creed. I feared such might be the case from the nomination of Mr. King, whose course on some of the compromise measures was not approved by a large majority of the Democracy of Mississippi, but until it was known that the Convention had in substance indorsed the 'compromise' and declared it a finality, I had determined to give a sincere and active support to the ticket.

"That ill-judged act has, however, created objections which seem to me insuperable to those who have taken the positions and maintain the opinions that I do.

"Since my first connection with public life, my convictions have ever led me to adopt the doctrines of that political school in which Jefferson and Calhoun were illustrious teachers; to assume that, under our system, the sovereign power resides in the people of the several states, and the powers of both federal and state governments are merely delegated trusts which can be resumed by the sovereign at pleasure; that when the federal government transcends the powers delegated to it by the Constitution, each state for itself in its sovereign character has a right to interfere and protect its citizens from unwarranted aggressions; and, consequently, as each state is the sole judge of the mode and measure of redress, she can, whenever in her judgment the reasons are sufficient, resume the delegated powers, and secede from the Union.

"The result of many years of experience, observation, and reflection, has also established in my mind the conviction that the subjection of the negro to the white race is in conformity with the designs of Providence, that slavery is the natural, and, of course, the best condition of the negro, and that this social institution, so far from being an evil, moral, social, or political, is beneficial to both races, and has been, and now is, a chief element of the wealth, prosperity, and power of these United States.

"With these opinions of our political and social systems, I have jealously watched every encroachment of the government upon the rights of the states, and every attempt to make odious discriminations against the institution of slavery, and have sympathized and acted with the patriotic band who, for a time, dared to breast the overwhelming tide of consolidation and anti-slavery.

"When the compromise measures of the last session of Congress were first introduced, they were generally

Vol. II.—H

regarded by the Southern people, with the exception of those whose instincts lead them to favor a strong government, as unjust encroachments upon the rights of the slaveholding states. They were looked upon as indirect means to secure the effects of the Wilmot Proviso. It was supposed that the tendency of these measures would be not only to destroy the equilibrium of power between the two sections, till then preserved in the Senate, and thus transfer all the political power of the government to the opposite section, but eventually, by the addition of new states, to enable the states hostile to slavery, by a change of the Constitution, violently to destroy the domestic institutions of the minority section.

"It was my opinion and is now, that the spirit and the letter of the Constitution were violated in the admission of California; that the power to "admit new states" was, in that instance, abused for the purpose of excluding slavery from her broad limits. It was my opinion then and is now, that the unprecedented means used to bring about a dismemberment of Texas grew out of a disposition to curtail the territorial area of slavery. I believed and still believe, that the bill to suppress the slave-trade in the federal district, and which also asserts the right to emancipate slaves therein, makes an insulting discrimination between the institutions of states that, by the Constitution and bond of union, are equals in rights, interests, and dignity. I believed and still believe, that, by these oppressive measures, a fatal blow has been struck at states' rights, and that, under their influence, if not averted by Providence, the institution of slavery must perish, or the union of these states be dissolved. I believed and still believe, that the Fugitive Slave Law, passed mainly by Southern votes, and worthless, unless sustained by public sentiment in the free states, was merely permitted to become a law as a blind to hide the vast sacrifices demanded of the South.

" Of such material is the boasted ' compromise.' How fallen from her high estate is the South, when she can ask its maintenance as an extreme concession from the North! For myself, as an humble citizen, I reject the terms.

"As it is easier to defend a fortress against an open

daylight attack than to guard against the secret approach of the sap and the mine, so I have less fears of the open war of abolition and free-soilism than the more slow and insidious, but not less dangerous effects of compromises that take away, but never give. I regarded these aggressions so serious as to require extraordinary action on the part of the aggrieved states to ward off, if possible, the impending peril.

"These views and opinions were formally, and without reserve, communicated to the public in my message to the special Legislature of 1851. Subsequent events have impaired my confidence in the resolutions of meetings, conventions, and even legislative bodies, but they have not diminished my apprehensions of the tendency of these measures. Painful as these conclusions are, they are the convictions of my judgment, founded on the history of the past. I devoutly pray that my gloomy anticipations may never be realized. While they exist, however, I would be faithless to my section of the Union were I to sustain these acts; yet such pledge is required from the supporters of the platform adopted by the Democratic Convention at Baltimore. The record of the proceedings of the Convention does not furnish us with a sufficient reason why the support of measures so obnoxious to a large majority of the Southern democracy was engrafted into the Democratic creed. The object, probably, was to commit the Northern democracy to the execution of the Fugitive Slave Law. But the terms of the resolutions go farther: they require that State-rights Democrats, on their part, shall not disturb, or even complain of measures by which they believe that the South is virtually excluded from all share in the common territory of the states, and by which the slaveholder is disfranchised in the federal district. If there be any meaning in these resolutions, they constitute a contract between the democracy, North and South, that the former will abstain from repealing the law for the restoration of fugitive slaves; and the latter, admitting the right and justice of the precedents established by the admission of California, the dismemberment of Texas, and the bill to abolish the slave-trade in the federal district, will adhere to and abide by them: in other words, so far as the democracy is concerned, to make the 'compromise' a 'finality.'

"If these measures are so benign as to deserve a place in the Democratic creed, we should raise altars to those who planned them and put them in operation; if they are not, we who opposed them should not stultify ourselves by formal pledges to maintain them as elementary principles of party faith. As I believe the principal measures of the miscalled compromise will be fatal in their results to the Southern section of the Union, I can not, even for the sake of attaining a temporary good, pledge myself to sustain them. I submit to them as evils for which I see no present means of correction; but it is asking too much of sincere Southern State-rights Democrats, who last year advocated united resistance against them, now to pledge themselves to sustain them, and to forbear the use of such means as time shall disclose to correct them, and thus avert from ourselves and our posterity the fatal consequences which we believe will follow in their train.

"As I heartily concur in all the remaining articles of the platform announced by the Convention, and hold the qualifications and character of its nominee in high estimation, I shall, while the present issues are before the country, vote that ticket; but, for the reasons assigned, I decline to take an active part in the canvass, that may, directly or indirectly, be construed into a support of the obnoxious portion of the platform.

"Regretting the necessity of speaking so much of my own position and opinions, I remain, gentlemen, with the highest respect, your obedient servant,

"J. A. QUITMAN.

"Messrs. J. C. Carpenter, R. P. Winslow, W. S. Langley, H. Napier, A. G. Haley, E. P. Russell, committee, Jackson."

On the same day he sent the following note to his friend, Wm. P. Mellen, Esq., of Natchez, declining to appear at a Pierce and King meeting:

"I have concluded not to take an active part in this canvass, at least unless circumstances should require it. I will vote for Pierce cheerfully. I heartily approve all the proceedings of the National Democratic Convention except the indorsement of the Compromise. I will never consent, expressly or impliedly, to sustain measures which I believe, and have declared to be fatal to state rights and slavery. This pledge is required by the resolutions of the Convention. I can not, therefore, be an active participator in the canvass, and shall not be in at the meeting."

The letter to the Central Committee, so full of his characteristics, was widely circulated. General Aiken, of South Carolina, wrote him: "I feel gratified at the position you have taken, and rejoice at the noble and self-sacrificing indorsement you have given the doctrine of state sovereignty. Your views have met with the approbation of nearly every person, secessionist and co-operationist, with whom I have conversed. Your letter has been widely circulated throughout the upper districts to suppress any interest in the election of presidential electors."

"Monmouth, July 23d, 1852.

"EDITOR OF THE FREE TRADER: DEAR SIR,—Some friends who appear to attribute more consequence to newspaper reports of my opinions than I do, have specially called my attention to the following article from the Memphis Eagle and Enquirer of the 4th instant:

'*Testimony of a Democrat and Southerner.*

'We presume that, among our Democratic fellow-citizens at least, the opinion of Ex-governor John A. Quitman, of Mississippi, is entitled to some weight. The genuineness of his "democracy," and his honest but somewhat misdirected devotion to the South, have, we believe, never been questioned even by the bitterest of his political opponents. A gentleman of New Orleans, who was a fellow-passenger of Governor Quitman a few days since in a steamer bound up the river, asked his opinion of General Scott.

'"Sir," said the governor, in reply, "the American people have never done General Scott justice! The more that man's character and claims of distinction are canvassed, the higher will be the stand he will take in the admiration and gratitude of his countrymen.

' "I have been surprised and astonished," continued Governor Quitman, "that among the Whig party there should be found a single man unwilling to give him a cordial and hearty support. As to his being ' controlled by Seward'—*that is mere stuff!* I know the man, and he will be controlled by no one contrary to his own convictions of what is right. And as to his being true to the South, I consider him the most unexceptionable man, on that score, among all the Whigs who have been named in connection with the presidency. I am a Democrat; and consequently, differing widely as I do from General Scott on every political question, can never give him my support; but if there is a Whig in the Union for whom, under any circumstances, I could cast my vote for President, that Whig is Winfield Scott!"

' Such, in substance, we understand, was the reply of a brave and gallant old soldier, when his opinion of a noble and much-abused companion-in-arms was asked. We have before heard that these were the sentiments of Governor Quitman. If we mistake not, there is a gentleman in this city (a Democrat), and another at Holly Springs, Miss., who served with Governor Quitman in the Mexican war, to whom, some months since, he made declarations almost identical with the foregoing. This testimony, from one of the highest Democratic sources, taken in connection with Gen. Scott's hearty, unqualified, and enthusiastic approval of the Whig platform (which it is now PLAIN AND PALPABLE TO THE WORLD, IS SOUNDER, STRONGER, and MORE JUST TO THE SOUTH, on sectional questions, than the Democratic platform), these facts, we say, OUGHT to be, and, we doubt not, WILL be satisfactory, not only to all Whigs, but to every man in the country.'

"The zealous friend of General Scott who reported to the editors of the Eagle and Enquirer the conversation above alluded to has, no doubt unintentionally, placed in my mouth language stronger than I used, and thus attributed to me sentiments which I do not entertain, and could not utter.

"The conversation alluded to occurred on the deck of a steamer, in the presence of several gentlemen of both parties. In reply to various opinions expressed by others, I said in substance that the Southern Whigs, in their opposition to General Scott, had done him injustice; that his opinions on the slavery question were less obnoxious than those heretofore publicly expressed by Fillmore and Webster, and I would sooner trust him on that subject than either of those gentlemen; that if there was any merit in the 'Compromise,' which I did not admit, Scott should be preferred by them, because he openly declared for it before Fillmore's opinion was known. For these reasons, it appeared to me strange that men who were willing to support Fillmore or Webster should make objections to Scott; that my objections to Scott applied equally to the other gentlemen—they were founded on radical differences of opinion in regard to the structure and character of our political system; that General Scott was an advocate of a strong national government, while I was a state-rights man of the strictest school; that for this reason I should not vote for him, but would always do him justice, although I had reason to complain of some of his official acts in regard to myself as an officer of the army.

"A Whig gentleman present having remarked that the apprehension was that Scott would be controlled by Seward and politicians of his stripe, I smiled and said: 'You mistake the character of the man. The danger lies in the opposite extreme. Always accustomed to command, General Scott prides himself specially upon the infallibility of his own judgment. He rarely asks or takes advice. He will be controlled by no man, not the whole Whig party, against his own convictions.'

"Some allusion having been made to his military reputation, and my opinion asked, I said it would be unwise in us (the Democratic party) to deny to him the highest military distinction; that his Mexican campaign, from the first gun at Vera Cruz to the fall of the capitol, was one of the most brilliant on military record. Its lustre was dimmed by some blemishes, about which I would not now speak; but that when the history of his victorious march, from the sea-board to the national palace, shall be faithfully detailed and popularized, it will greatly add to the high military fame he at present enjoys, not only in America, but abroad.

"The conversation was casual and desultory. I have merely endeavored to present my share in it correctly. It is known that in private conversation I am in the habit of expressing my opinions frankly, without looking to political consequences.

"Very respectfully yours,   J. A. QUITMAN."

The three letters that follow are from state-rights men, among the most intellectual members of the party.

Hon. E. C. Wilkinson to Gen. Quitman.

"Yazoo, August 18th, 1852.

" MY DEAR SIR,—Constant engagements have so far prevented my answering your letter, and giving, as you requested, an opinion of your recent publications. It would doubtless have been better for the party with which I am now acting,* if you had not pursued this course, but I can not say that I see any thing in what you have published inconsistent with your own antecedents. Yours is a position somewhat different from that of any other state-rights man in Mississippi. You are expected to carry out your creed in all its severity, and not to flinch in the least from its conclusions. The time may come, and I do not doubt it will, when you will find your advantage in it; for when the State-rights party is formed again (and who can tell how soon it may be reorganized?) it will naturally turn at once to you, who have stood, and stand now, like old Torquil in the romance of Scott, all alone, battered, but not beaten, while every living soul has fallen around you. But, to be perfectly frank with you, for this must be what you would wish, your writings, although singularly well expressed, appear to me to go too far, or else they (the card especially) have been misunderstood, and are now, and with great force, urged against us by the Whig electors. I feel sure it is the platform and not Pierce that you object to, and that you can not admire the political character of Scott, for he has none. Moreover, I must be-

* He was a presidential elector on the Pierce ticket.

lieve that you regard the Whig platform as far more objectionable than the Democratic. But be assured of one thing. I, for one, shall never criticise or comment upon these writings in a manner the least injurious to you. It will be constantly thrown in my teeth in public discussion, and it has already been. But I am not quite so much of a party man as to attempt to disparage a friend to serve a party.

" * * * * Sir, the State-rights party owes you an everlasting, an eternal debt of gratitude. When asked at Nashville by Mr. Pickens to point to our future leader, I pointed to you. That party is not dead—it sleepeth only. In thinking, writing, and acting, you are qualified to act the part that future developments must ere long require of you. Do nothing, say nothing to mar the full reliance that the earnest-minded of the party— the Old Guard—still have on you."

Elwood Fisher, Editor of the Southern Press, to Gen. Quitman.

"Washington, August 17th, 1852.

"DEAR SIR,—Yours of the 26th ultimo was duly received. The request to publish your answer to the Democratic Committee had already been anticipated, and I was gratified to find, amid the general defection, that you had not given way. I must, however, express my regret at your determination to vote for Pierce. I would have supported him myself but for the platform, and on such a platform I would not have supported Calhoun himself, if living and a candidate.

"You, and I, and others took a very distinct position as to the Compromise. We were not sustained by any of the states but South Carolina. But I thought, nevertheless, that we ought to maintain our opinions individually with the more firmness and inflexibility. Hence I regretted your retirement from the gubernatorial canvass of Mississippi, and regretted the position General Davis assumed afterward, as I wrote him, in reply to a letter from him to me, in which he gave his reasons. I thought them unsatisfactory.

"It is true we had been defeated in every state but South Carolina. But in Georgia, Alabama, and Mississippi we had a powerful party—one that held the destiny of the Democratic party of the *nation* in its hands. It is true that, in a presidential election, we would have lost some strength, perhaps a good deal—but all that would have been much more than restored after the election was over, and the disappointed office-seekers had been demoralized. We would, I think, have succeeded in obtaining the ascendency along the whole line of cotton states, from South Carolina to the Mississippi. This would have secured Florida and Louisiana, and it would have compelled Tennessee, Virginia, and Kentucky to rectify themselves. For they would have lost the power they now possess of betraying the South for federal favor.

"I can not concur in the support of Pierce at all with such a platform, and I can not isolate him from it when he says it is in accordance with his judgment. If a Southern-rights party had resolved to support him with a distinct repudiation of the platform, and with a power, from its own separate organization, of resisting his administration in any attempt to pursue the compromise policy, I could have co-operated. But you must forgive me for saying that I consider it one of the most disastrous signs of the times that men of the two extremes, Free-soilers and Fire-eaters, hasten into parties, and yet repudiate the platforms. It looks like a love of party for the sake of party. The consequence is, the success of the Democratic party will be the complete ascendency of the Compromise faction, and the continual defection of Southern-rights men in order to obtain place.

" Although your letter is marked private, I have taken the liberty of sending it to a very decided friend of the cause in Alabama, who is opposed to union with national parties, and in favor of a separate organization, as, he says, the great mass of the party there is. If they persist in so thinking, the standard may be still upheld, and you be called on to sustain it. I wrote him recently after receiving your letter, and, in answer to his request to suggest some names, suggested Mr. Paulding's and yours. I advised Mr. Paulding's for the presidency, yours for the vice-presidency, on the ground that such a compliment was due to the only remaining Northern man who was faithful, and with the understanding that after the pending contest yours should be the *first*—there to remain until victory crowned the struggle. If such a ticket were made, I believe South Carolina would vote for it this time."

R. D. Crallé, Biographer of John C. Calhoun, to Gen. Quitman.

"Lynchburg, Va., Sept. 3d, 1852.

"MY DEAR SIR,—I had the pleasure to receive your favor of the 15th ult. (with the accompanying documents) a few days since.

"I do not know whether I ought to thank you more for the personal or political reminiscences which they are so well calculated to revive. The history of the past has become as a dream, though its records are not quite so easily effaced. The actors, too, are, for the most part, gone; but they have left behind them memorials whereby posterity will determine the meed of praise or censure. The part we have borne has also been, in some measure, jotted down; and I am sure neither of us would desire now that any page should be blotted out. For one, I stand still, as I stood in 1832, on the side of the Constitution as interpreted in 1788–89. I know well that to talk now in behalf of state rights and state remedies, is to speak in an unknown tongue. The cause is gone, and forever!. But woe to the memory of those through whose treachery and baseness it was lost. The time can not be far distant when the evils of consolidation shall develop themselves to a much abused and betrayed people; and then will come the day of reckoning, the day of retribution. If I do not much mistake the signs of the times, a very few years will be sufficient to make us fully realize the folly and madness of that policy which the Southern States have been compelled to adopt. The old adage of '*Quem deus vult perdere,*' applies, I fear, with fatal force to the entire southern section of this *nation*, for *Union* it ought no longer to be called. We have now no other business than to elect presidents and vice-presidents. The spirit of the country has sunk down to this. One step lower—and this is easily taken —and our masters will arm us, for this ignoble conflict, not with the ballot-box, but the bayonet. To this issue it is rapidly hastening; and many now, I doubt not, will still be living when this once vaunted experiment of self-government will end in one of the sternest and most corrupt despotisms that ever overshadowed the earth. 'Will,' did I say? It is already ended in one of the most *corrupt*, and only not the most despotic government, *in position*, on the globe, because not yet fully armed to carry out its *theory*. This, beyond doubt, involves every power that appertains to unlimited authority. I know of no power which, according to the prevalent theory of our institutions, can not be lawfully exercised by the *national* government, and as to its disposition to stretch to the utmost its arm of authority, we need look only to the late 'Compromise Acts,' as they are called—the blackest and basest, in motives and in aims, that ever stained the records of civilized man. It will be incredible to posterity that these most nefarious enactments were the work of *Southern* men; and yet it is most true. And equally true is it that the sole motive which moved them was the *hope* of place and plunder. Is it not amazing that every one of these 'compromises' (or, to call them more properly), these *surrenders* of Southern rights, interests, and honor, have been voluntarily tendered to the North by Southern representatives. These last—the most shameful, the most audacious, and by far the most dangerous of all, inasmuch as they have not only grossly outraged the Constitution, but forever sealed the destiny of the Southern States—were commenced, urged forward, and consummated with an eye single to the presidency. I thank God that the principal actors have been consigned by the Baltimore Convention to that seclusion which their conduct so justly merited, while I deeply regret that any supposed necessity should have induced that Convention to recognize these infamous measures as a part of its 'platform.' I for one can never give countenance to them in any manner or form whatever. I agree, entirely and cordially, in the views contained in your letter. I shall vote for Mr. Pierce—from my personal knowledge and admiration of the man; but never will I consent to acknowledge the validity of acts originating in treachery and corruption, and dooming the slaveholding states to certain and irretrievable ruin; for I hold it as absolute destiny, that acts destroying the equilibrium established by the Constitution, degrading one half of the states to the condition of colonies, converting a federative republic into a national consolidated despotism, recognizing public robbery as the true basis of popular sovereignty, and, above all (to us), damming back upon us our surplus slave property, can, by possibility, lead to no other result. The present temper of the North—the still rampant spirit of aggression and fanaticism—the supineness, if not cowardice of the South, with the increasing spirit of insubordination on the part of our slaves, fill me with fearful apprehensions in regard to the future. God alone can educe good out of so much evil.

"In regard to the presidency I see no other course left us than the one you recommend. To trust the now unlimited powers of government in the hands of such a man as General Scott, with his absolute want of civil qualifications, combined with his Whig sympathies and associations, would, in my judgment, be an act of madness. He would necessarily become the mere instrument of others, and these the most hostile to us. They would soon bring him into their toils, and we should hear, in brief time, thunders against the ' sedition' of whole states, as his late letter intimates. On the contrary, if we elect Mr. Pierce we shall secure a man of sense, of considerable experience in public affairs, of sound *head*, and (what is better still) sound *heart*, and one who, in the trials of the past, has proved himself far more reliable, in respect to our rights and safety, than the traitorous representatives who have staked our property and lives in exchange for an office. You know these men well enough, and I need not name them. I would this day rather trust my private property, my political rights, my peace and security, in the hands of Mr. Pierce than any Southern man who recommended or *connived* at the passage of the infamous ' adjustment.' I say '*connived at*,' for there are many names in the *negative* on the Journal that ought to be put in the *affirmative*. Had you sounded the undercurrents, as I did, and watched the course of individuals during the parturition of the monster, you would be able to put your finger on many a caitiff and traitor whose names appear in the negative, only because they desire to cover the treason of Judas by the kiss of Judas. But the end is not yet, as they will find to their cost. They have sold us out, it is true, but the thirty pieces of silver are not yet paid. Perhaps they may hereafter find the cord instead, and be made to 'play out the play' of their Galilean exemplar.

"It would afford me much pleasure in my retirement to hear frequently from you; for, besides yourself, there scarcely remains a single individual of distinction among old acquaintances who has withstood the blandishment of place and plunder, and stood firmly up in support of a most sacred cause."

1852. On the 13th of September the Southern-rights party of Alabama met in convention in Montgomery. Hon. Thomas Williams, the president thereof, submitted the following communication from General Quitman:

"Monmouth, near Natchez, September 5th, 1852.
"DEAR SIR,—The mail of yesterday brought your letter of the 24th ult., requesting my views upon several matters presented; and especially asking responses to some interrogations inclosed.

"Honored by the assurance which you give me that the Southern-rights party of Alabama have unshaken confidence in the existence of common feeling and sentiment on Southern rights between them and myself, I can only express my regret that the necessity of an immediate and prompt reply to reach you in time will compel me to dispense with that full expression of my views which the importance of the subject, and my high respect for those who solicit my opinions, would render so desirable to me. I shall therefore briefly respond, and refer you to the documents which I forward herewith, viz.: An address written by me in 1834, my message to the special Legislature of this state in 1851, and my late published letter to the Democratic Central Committee, for a fuller exposition of my views on some of the subjects presented by your letter.

"I rejoice to learn that the Southern-rights party of

Alabama still retains its organization. An organized opposition to the despotic doctrines which gave birth to the obnoxious compromise measures is indispensable to the safety of the South and the preservation of state rights. If the people of the whole South finally settle down into quiet acquiescence in the precedent set, and the encroachments made by these aggressive measures, they will soon have nothing worth contending for. Their equality lost, their constitutional rights scoffed at, their institutions branded with obloquy, their property not only placed without the pale of the protection of the common government, but its powerful agency used to render it more precarious and hazardous, and less valuable, and by these means their state credit impaired, their spirit broken by a sense of inferiority, and their confidence in themselves lost, they will gradually sink into hopeless dependence, and be content with holding their political rights, and their slave property, at the mercy of their more powerful confederates.

"Whether as an organized party you shall enter into the presidential contest, is a question of policy which you alone can decide. If it be likely to give strength to the party or the cause, it should be done regardless of other consequences. But as I am pushed for time, I beg to refer you to my views on this subject communicated a few days since to one of your committee, Mr. Moore, in reply to a letter from him. I proceed to the interrogatories; my answers are:

" 1st. The federal government has no right any where to interfere with the institution of slavery in such manner as to impair the relation of master and slave.

" 2d. A citizen of the United States, possessing slaves, has a right to carry them into the territory belonging to the United States, and hold them there as property, and it is the duty of Congress, within their constitutional jurisdiction, to pass such law as may be necessary to protect such property as well as any other. When the common government refuse such protection, it would disregard the objects which called it into existence.

" 3d. The abuse, by Congress, of the power delegated to regulate commerce between the states, by interfering in any wise with the free transportation of slaves from one slaveholding state to another, would be a violation of the spirit of the compact, so flagrant an insult to a portion of the sovereign states of the Union, and so dangerous to the harmony of the whole, as to demand the executive veto to any bill having such purpose.

"4th and 5th. By *sovereignty* I understand that political power which can ultimately control all other powers. This power in our system resides alone in the respective states, and not elsewhere. As sovereigns, the states have merely delegated to their state governments and to their common government certain specified powers to be exercised for their benefit. These may be resumed by each sovereign at pleasure. There exists, however, a moral obligation on the part of each not to resume the powers delegated in the federal compact, unless the compact be violated by the other parties, or used to oppress the people. As this right of secession exists in the states, it would be as absurd on the part of the federal government to claim the right of using force to bring back a seceding state, as to attempt by force to bring a neighboring state, Mexico, for instance, into the Union.

"6th. Whenever a duly-organized Territory shall take steps for admission into the Union as a state, and shall prefer to recognize African slavery in her Constitution, the President or other public officer, opposing it on that ground, would deserve impeachment, for a violation of the clear intent of the Constitution.

"7th. Congress having taken jurisdiction over the subject of the extradition of fugitive slaves, it would now be a fraud on the slaveholding states to repeal or impair the efficiency of the fugitive slave law.

"I have thus, out of respect for the committee, and a sincere desire to promote a cause with which I feel identified, briefly answered your inquiries.

"You will meet in convention on the anniversary of a day when Southern as well as Northern blood flowed freely, to acquire the rich and broad domain of which we have been plundered. On that day, amid a sheet of flame, and in the very face of thirty pieces of artillery, the Palmetto banner was *first* planted on the gates of Mexico.

"May Providence guide your councils and smile upon

your patriotic endeavors. I am with you heart and soul, but I desire no other position than a place in the ranks.

"With the highest respect, your fellow-citizen,

"J. A. QUITMAN.

"Thos. Williams, Esq."

The following report was then unanimously adopted:

"The committee of two from each county, to which was referred the report of the executive committee and sundry resolutions, submit the following:

"The nominees of the Whig and Democratic parties for the presidency having failed to answer the interrogatories propounded to them, the Southern-rights party of Alabama can not with consistency vote for either. We believe it to be the true policy of the Southern-rights party to nominate a ticket which shall at once embody its sentiments and preserve its organization. We therefore recommend the nomination of Ex-gov. GEORGE M. TROUP, of Georgia, for the presidency, and Gen. JOHN A. QUITMAN, of Mississippi, for the vice-presidency. These gentlemen are known to be true to the rights of the South, and are eminently worthy of the support of Southern men."

In the existing state of parties this nomination was considered only as a complimentary recognition of Quitman's eminent merits and services. Gen. Pierce was elected by a large majority.

1853. In June Quitman attended a convention at Memphis called to deliberate over the commercial and other interests of the South and West, upon which the protective tariff and other sectional legislation of Congress had long acted injuriously.

One of the most graphic orators our country has produced summed up his objections to the protective principle in a single line: "It claims for Congress the power of organizing the labor of the country." This is the power of controlling the mind and the muscles of every citizen—of employing his time, his strength, his ability, and his capital, according to the wisdom, the caprice, or the folly of the government—of confiscating the ships of the merchant for the benefit of the wool-grower—of driving the farmer from his field into the manufactory—of starving one portion of society that another may become opulent.

If Congress can regulate the labor of the country according to the character of the laborer, may it not distinguish between the labor of a slave and the labor of a freeman? In fact, has it not already done so? The protective principle is an extortion from slave labor. Although the tariff laws are general in their terms, their operation is uniformly partial and sectional. Most of the manufactories are in one section; the staples that feel the severity of the law are in another section; and it is practically much the same as if Congress, intending to support the government by a direct tax, should levy it upon all slaves within the United States. The tariff laws may not be so decisively exclusive, but they approximate it. They, in a measure, separate the Southern States from the rest of the Union. They select the slaveholder as their victim. They operate to the injury of every man, woman, and child in the South.

Look around at the decay and poverty which, in spite of our enormous exports, are visible in parts of the Southern States. Our immense annual income is not expended in luxurious living, nor in magnificent buildings, nor in public improvements and gigantic enterprises with a view to future improvements. Where does it go? With the cheapest labor, the finest climate, the most fertile lands, and the four great staples, cotton, sugar, tobacco, and rice, the South is the poorest section of the United States. Why is this? Can any one assign any other cause than the operation of unwise and partial

revenue laws? To these we attribute, in a great measure, the declension of the South and the prosperity of
the North.

New England is our opposite in every thing. A black
and wintry sky frowns upon a sterile and rock-bound
soil. Her forest, compared with ours, is a wood of
dwarfs. Industry, and science, and labor, and capital are
indispensable there to production. Nothing comes spontaneously or kindly; and with all the caressing and pam-
pering, she never produces enough for her own consump-
tion. Her factories would stop, and her operatives starve
but for the fleecy staple and the cereal crops of the
South. Winter binds up her water power, and her rivers and canals, four months in the year; and the cost of
fuel, much of which is brought from the South, diminish-
es the profits of her steam-machinery. She relieves herself every year of a redundant population by sending
South for a living thousands of her stoutest-bodied men,
and other thousands tempt seas the most remote, leaving
at home a large majority of females and consumers.

Yet, in despite of all this annual expenditure of capital
and productive labor, she is ahead of us in the career of
prosperity. Her population multiplies faster. She has
ten school-houses where we have one. She has whole
navies of merchantmen and lines of steam-ships. Where
are ours? She has millions invested in insurance companies, in national stocks, and in the English funds. She
buys from us our staples to sell them again, transformed
into starch, maccaroni, arrow-root, biscuit, whisky, brandy, rum, candies, snuff, prints, cambrics, Lowells, and a
thousand other fabrics, under the protection of a principle which gives her a decided advantage in our markets
over the foreign manufacturer of the same articles. And,
under this system, she grows rich and richer, and more
importunate and more exacting every year; and in the

same ratio we become poor, and more cringing and more timid.

Our Revolutionary fathers rose in arms, at the hazard of property and life, to resist a tax not half so unjust and oppressive. A single obnoxious law overthrew the administration of John Adams, a statesman burnished with the lustre of the Revolution, and surrounded and supported by its ablest and bravest instruments. The legislative action of Virginia alone more than once rolled back the tide of federal aggression that threatened to submerge and destroy the limited and strictly defined character of our government. But now, so much are we accustomed to encroachment—so drilled to act as "hewers of wood and drawers of water" for the North—so much absorbed and distracted by their war on our institutions, which, under the most insidious professions, they continue to wage, that we scarcely see, or, if seen, we dare not denounce the colossal evil which has so long pressed us to the ground. We see, and we are ready to resist, the flaming brand that fanaticism levels at our institutions, but we do not perceive that the PROTECTIVE SYSTEM is a fiend, in the shape of a trusted domestic, who drugs our food and our cup, and slowly, but surely, drains away our vitality.*

This monster haunts us like a phantom in all the occu-

* Gouverneur Morris, a great statesman of New York, writing to Randolph Harrison, of Virginia, concludes a strong condemnation of the protective system thus: "You can not have manufactories. We can. We already have some, and shall soon have many poor children, who can be put up to march backward and forward with a spinning-jenny, *till they are old enough to become drunkards or prostitutes.*" —Sparks's Life of Morris, vol. iii., p. 351. This is not a Southern sentiment; no Southerner would speak thus of the free laborers of the North. But it was deliberately uttered by a man of great capital, talents, and influence, deeply interested in all that concerned New York, and was deliberately published by a distinguished citizen of Massachusetts, a pet of Harvard University, who did not scruple to alter the expressions and suppress the opinions of *Washington* whenever they conflicted with his taste or his sentiments.

pations of life; is a tax on our labor and on our pleasures; drives us from our fields, and, like the obscene birds of Virgil, pollutes even our feasts.

Professing loyalty to the Union—which implies a defense of the South against the fanaticism of the North—the government supports a system which effectually strengthens the party it proposes to rebuke, and cripples the party it promises to defend. There is just this difference. The Abolitionist would rob us of our slaves; the government will let us retain them, but contrives to diminish the profits of their labor, well knowing that thus the institution itself is sapped. So they each accomplish, by different means, the same end—the ruin of the slaveholder.

1853. In July, Gen. Quitman revisited his native place, Rhinebeck, where he was received with military ceremonies and a generous enthusiasm.

From the N. Y. Herald.

"The arrival of Major General John A. Quitman having become known, citizens of the towns of Red Hook and Rhinebeck, formerly the town of Rhinebeck, assembled *en masse*, to the number of several hundred, at the hotel of Stephen Lasher, in the village of Red Hook, to welcome the gallant general at the place of his nativity. A committee was hastily organized, consisting of William Chamberlain, Jacob Benner, and James B. Fisk, of Red Hook, and Ambrose Wager and Gouverneur Tillottson, of Rhinebeck, to wait on the distinguished and gallant general, who in a short time returned and presented him in the large dining-hall of the hotel, where he was received, on the part of his old friends and neighbors, by John Elseffer, Esq., and welcomed in the following manner. A sketch only can be given. He said:

"'Sir,—I have the honor, in behalf of the citizens of the towns of Red Hook and Rhinebeck, spontaneously assembled, to tender you a cordial and heartfelt welcome to the place of your nativity. The associations connected with the name of Quitman in this vicinity, owing to the high respect felt for your honored father, and associations of a more recent occurrence connected with the name of Gen. John A. Quitman, make a visit from you to the place of your nativity highly interesting to us. There are many within the hearing of my voice who knew you personally from your youth, and many remember that you, when comparatively but a stripling, with a satchel under your arm, but with a stout heart and a fixed determination, went out from among us and traversed the Alleghanies alone and on foot. Stretching to the outskirts of civilization, you entered into the broad and fertile valley of the West, and, planting yourself in the State of Mississippi, you conducted an honorable professional business, acquiring, by your industry and talents, such a standing that the people of that state conferred on you the highest offices in their gift, both executive and judicial. Sir, we rejoiced at your success. We hail you this evening also as a soldier and a patriot, who, at a sacrifice of domestic and private enjoyments, has defended the honor and dignity of our beloved country. The country witnessed your military career with pride— the friends of your youth looked on with great anxiety and high hope, traversing with you the sandy plains of Mexico under a tropical sun, passing through their mountain gorges, surrounded by an insidious foe, demolishing the strongholds and fortresses of the enemy, scattering their armies, and taking possession of their cities. Yes, sir, and it was our joy that the volunteer brigade under command of General Quitman first entered the city of Monterey, and bore the heat of the battle at the storming of Chapultepec, first broke down the Belen gate, and that your foot, sir, was the first American foot that entered the city of Mexico, and that by your orders the stars and stripes of our glorious Union were unfurled from the Halls of the Montezumas. (Cheers.) Sir, we are proud of the fame you have won; we love the men who love their country; we love to honor the men who stand by and honor their country. He said there were many subjects to which he would like to advert. During an absence of thirty-four years many changes had been wrought in his native state—

the unparalleled growth of our cities and villages—the
works of internal improvement carried on mainly by individual enterprise—the progress in agriculture, churches, and schools, those great nurseries of freemen—all must
convince him that the gentler arts of peace had not been
neglected at home while he had been abroad rearing for
himself a world-wide fame. He again welcomed him as
a citizen by adoption of a Southern state, and though petty jealousies might arise for a time, yet the intelligent
men of the North, and the chivalrous men of the South,
with an eye to the peculiar interests of each sovereign
state, and the reserved rights of each, would preserve
the Constitution and the Union.' (Cheers.)

"When the enthusiasm subsided, General Quitman responded in substance as follows:

"He expressed the deep emotion with which he now,
after so long an absence from his native place, received
the welcome congratulations of the friends of his child-
hood, and of those whose fathers had been the friends
of his honored father. The tide of early recollection
which overwhelmed him rendered him unable to respond
to the complimentary address which had just been uttered by his honored friend, the playmate and companion of his early days. The allusions of his friend had
been so personal, that he would be excused in adverting
for a moment to himself. He had gone forth from his native place thirty-four years since a portionless adventurer,
armed only with the stern energies, the untiring industry
and perseverance, and the good principles which the fathers of this good old county of Dutchess had imparted
to their children. Success had crowned his efforts, as
well in his professional as in his civil and military career.
Through the vicissitudes of an eventful life, in his contest
for professional reputation, for civil distinction, and for
military fame, his energies had been aroused, his ambition stimulated, and his heart nerved by the fond hope
that his name would be honorably mentioned around the
firesides of those who now stood about him. In all his
wanderings his heart often reverted to the scenes which
now surrounded him—to this fair land, unsurpassed in
the beauty of its quiet rural landscapes, skirted by pic-
turesque mountain outline which bounds the western

horizon. Nowhere was there a fairer land or a better
people. He then adverted to the late war, in which he
had borne a part. Glorious as were its results, he preferred to contemplate it in its effects upon the public
opinion of other countries. It had been said by those
who profess to distrust the efficiency of our free and liberal system of government, that while it must be admitted that it was well adapted to a state of peace, it would
utterly fail in war. Well, we had been compelled to
wage an aggressive war with a neighboring people; the
small standing army which it had been the policy of the
government to retain was inadequate to the emergency.
The President issued his call for volunteers. At once
two hundred thousand men, from all parts of the country, offered their services. The contest was, who should
be permitted to go and who obliged to remain. Less
than one tenth of this number were required and accepted into the service. They proved themselves not only
men but soldiers. He said it had been his lot to command principally volunteers during the war, and it gave
him pleasure and pride to say that on many occasions
they had shown themselves not inferior to veteran regulars. It was a volunteer brigade that had burst through
the strong defenses of Monterey, and it was the volunteer division, associated with a brigade of regulars, that
had first entered the imperial city of Mexico and planted
upon its capitol the glorious stars and stripes of our
country. (Cheers.) Who will now say that our institutions are not adapted to a state of war as well as of
peace? We have secured the respect of Europe, even
our great commercial rival England—that great power
upon whose empire it is said the sun never sets—now
treats us with respectful civility. (Cheers.) Yes, he
said, John Bull is polite to Young America. (Three
cheers.) The valor of our citizen soldiers has secured
peace with all nations. We are safe from dangers abroad.
He next alluded to other dangers that menaced our system of government. To avoid them was our duty, to
preserve our institutions in their purity. The great feature of our system, which distinguishes it from former
republics, is its federative principle; it is not a consolidated government, and he trusted it never would be. It

consists of sovereign states, by whom as sovereign communities the powers delegated in the Constitution have been conferred upon the general government, and no other. An absorption of the rights of the states would as certainly destroy that Constitution, and with it the Union which it established, as would the separation of the states. We of the South have domestic institutions dissimilar from those of the North; we know that in the federal system we are in the minority; we can not intrust the control of our peculiar policy to those who do not understand it, and therefore may have prejudices against it, as you would not intrust yours to us. We ask not to interfere with yours; we demand only that we should be permitted to regulate our own. Our safety, as we are in a minority, requires us, therefore, in accordance with the true principles of the Constitution, to insist upon the strict preservation of the reserved rights of the states. A sacred regard to these principles will alone preserve the Union; a systematic disregard of them may destroy it. Let us preserve our glorious Union. Standing here among his countrymen, a native of the Empire State, yet owing his allegiance to, and bound by interest, inclination, and gratitude to a noble and gallant Southern state, in whose bosom he had cast his lot, it was his duty, as a candid and honorable man, to say here to the men who rule the destinies of this mighty state, that this Union can only be preserved by a sacred adherence to the mutual engagements entered into between the states in the formation of the Constitution. From what he had seen and heard he believed this to be the prevailing sentiment in this the honored county of his birth, and among those stern freemen who surrounded him, who knew how to defend their rights as well as to abstain from violating the rights of others. (Cheers.) He concluded with again returning his thanks for his hearty welcome. (Enthusiastic cheers.)

" When the gallant general had concluded his remarks, of which the above is but a meagre outline, Nelson Barnes, a volunteer in the New York regiment, was introduced by Mr. Elseffer to General Quitman. The general gave him a shake with both hands. Their congratulations were hearty and earnest. After a personal introduction to all who had come to testify their respect, Rev. Dr. Strobel submitted a few congratulatory remarks, alluding to his position as successor to and pastor of the congregation of the honoréd Frederick H. Quitman, D.D.; to the fact that he had succeeded the honored guest of the evening in his early instruction through several schools—it was true, about ten years his junior; and, as if to increase the interest between them, he had become a member of a literary society founded by the general, all which rendered the present meeting highly interesting; and in every relation in which he had heard his name mentioned, the same gallant, noble, and honorable bearing which so highly adorns his mature years was accorded to him in youth.

"Gouverneur Tillottson, Esq., on the part of a delegation who had arrived from the village of Rhinebeck, was introduced, who alluded to the distinguished civil and military career of Gen. Quitman, the claims that the citizens of his native place held on him, and the respect they bore for his name and fame, and that, though he had by adoption become a gallant son of the South, their confidence in him was unshaken, inasmuch as he asked only constitutional and civil rights—rights guaranteed by the mutual compact; if he asked less their confidence in him would be impaired. But because he was true to the place of his adoption, he believed him to be so to the place of his nativity; that his adopted and his native state alike had claims on him, and the country at large, and those duties were best discharged by preserving the rights of each sovereign state inviolate, and raising high over the head of sectional and petty feeling the federative, civil, and constitutional rights of our great charter and of the Union. To which Gen. Quitman heartily responded, and begged him to testify to the delegation whom he represented, and to his old friends in Rhinebeck, considerations of esteem and regard.

"The party partook of a collation, and about ten o'clock the gallant general was conducted to his rooms. Thus closed one of the most interesting and gratifying interviews that has ever been had by the people of this vicinity."

The chief motive that prompted this visit to New

York at this period was to concert arrangements for the liberation of Cuba. He had long been earnestly appealed to by natives of the island, deeply interested in its prosperity, and anxious to strike for its political freedom, to give to that sacred cause the aid of his name and his talents. The cause was near his heart; he felt for the oppressed; and, in his judgment, Cuba was closely connected with the fortunes of his own country. He entered warmly into the enterprise, meaning carefully to abstain from violating the laws of the United States or existing treaties with Spain.*

In pursuance of his mission he visited New York, Philadelphia, Baltimore, Washington, and other points. His designs were frankly communicated to distinguished persons at the seat of government, and he left there with the distinct impression upon his mind not only that he had their sympathies, but that there could be no pretext for the intervention of the federal authorities. He left the capital buoyant with hope, and during the year devoted his energies to the cause. He was spoken of again in connection with the Senate, but took no part in the matter.

* One of his most intimate friends, Wm. P. Mellen, Esq., of Natchez, thus writes me: "I presume you are familiar with Quitman's position as to Cuba. He made all his arrangements to avoid any infringement of the laws. He never intended, as he often assured me, to violate the laws. Although he might leave the United States before hostilities commenced on the island, he did not intend to disembark before there had been a formal declaration of independence. This was for two purposes—to forestall the emancipation of the negroes threatened by Concha, and to place himself in the position of Lafayette when he landed on our shores. The priority of hostilities before embarking would have been the only difference. The down-trodden and feeble Cuban required *immediate* aid.

"Of all the men whom I have ever known, Quitman was the most law-abiding. When I was a member of his company, the Fencibles, immediately after its organization, he impressed the duty of submitting to and enforcing the laws on all suitable occasions, and so earnestly that I never forgot his lessons; nor do I believe that any member of the company was ever engaged in or sanctioned any disrespect of the laws."

1854. At the April term of the United States Circuit Court for the Eastern District of Louisiana, Judge Campbell charged the grand jury at great length in reference to the neutrality laws. On the 19th of June they requested the court to have summoned before them, as witnesses, John Henderson, Sen., Samuel J. Peters, P. Sauvé, A. L. Saunders, J. S. Thrasher, and John A. Quitman. On the 1st of July the grand jury came into court with the names of the three last, who had refused to testify before them. The grand jury likewise presented an elaborate report upon the subject of their investigation. On the same day, Messrs. Saunders, Thrasher, and Quitman, being present in court, were called upon by the court to show cause why they should not be required to enter into recognizance to observe, for the term of nine months, the laws of the United States in general, and specially the act of Congress approved April 20th, 1818.

The matter was argued by General Quitman for himself in person, in behalf of the others by eminent counsel. The order of the court was made on the same day. It recited the statements of the grand jury, and concluded with the mandate that each of the above-named parties be required to enter into a recognizance in the penal sum of $3000 to observe the laws, etc., and especially the act of 1818, for the term of nine months, and remain in the custody of the marshal until they comply with the order.

On the 3d of July, the court, reciting the fact that the said persons had not entered into the required recognizance, ordered that a mittimus be issued, and that they be committed until they complied with the order of the court.

Under this order they were arrested by the marshal.*

---

* J. M. Kennedy, Esq., of New Orleans. He conducted Messrs. Quitman and Thrasher to their quarters at the City Hotel, and at the

Quitman was disposed to go to jail; but his friends, on the plea of other and higher duties in reserve for him, prevailed on him to give bond. The parties appeared and entered into recognizances, and were discharged.

Some weeks thereafter Gen. Quitman arraigned the conduct of the presiding judge through the columns of the New Orleans Delta:

"*Judge John A. Campbell.*—This gentleman, who lately presided in the United States Circuit Court at New Orleans, appears to have come to the South full of zeal to ferret out some infraction of the neutrality laws.

"Upon taking the bench, he announced that he would hold his court open for six months, if necessary, to prevent our people from aiding their neighbors of Cuba to shake off the grinding despotism of Spain. He seemed desirous of correcting the common error into which the best men of our country had fallen, that there was neither crime nor dishonor in individuals advocating and aiding the extension of American institutions on this continent, by the same means by which they were established in our country—by revolution. He held that those who contributed money to such a purpose were criminal, and those who, by speeches, incited 'incautious young men' to take part in such enterprises were 'most criminal.'

"Repeated charges were made to the grand jury, and when, after diligent inquiry, they reported to the court briefly, that they could find no infraction of the laws, Judge Campbell sent them back again, with instructions to make a fuller and more detailed report, with a view, as it afterward appeared, of giving color to his subsequent arbitrary proceedings.

"Upon the coming in of the desired report, the judge, who, throughout, seemed to be familiar with the secrets of the jury-room, stated that he should direct a copy to be transmitted to the secretary of state at Washington,

social dinner which soon followed, being called on for a sentiment, gave the following impromptu—"CUBA :

    · "We'll buy or fight, but to our shore we'll lash her;
    If Spain won't sell, we'll then turn in and *thrash-her.*"

and, without any affidavit, charge, or accusation of offense against us, ordered Mr. Thrasher, Dr. Saunders, and myself, severally, to enter into recognizances, with sureties, to observe the laws of the United States in general, and the neutrality laws in particular, for the space of nine months.

"Upon my refusal to comply with this illegal demand, I was committed to the custody of the marshal, and afterward directed to be imprisoned in the Parish Jail of New Orleans for nine months.

"After the final adjournment of the court, I entered into the required recognizance, under the following protest, made before the clerk of the court in the presence of witnesses:

"'I regard the order of Judge Campbell, one of the justices of the Supreme Court of the United States, requiring me to give bond and security that I will, for the space of nine months, observe the laws of the United States in general, and especially the so-called Neutrality Act of 1818, as an unconstitutional, illegal, and arbitrary exercise of power. I refused a voluntary obedience to it, because I deemed it my duty not to yield, upon a mere demand, my sacred rights as an American citizen. I am now, by the order of the same judge, a close prisoner in the hands of the marshal. I yield to this illegal demand only because I have no appeal from a power which, practically, is absolute and irresponsible.

"'Under duress of punishment, and with a solemn protest against the assumption of power claimed by the aforesaid judge in this case, I am compelled to sign this bond or recognizance.

"' (Signed),   J. A. QUITMAN.

"'New Orleans, July 3d, 1854.'

"Judge Campbell, finding that public opinion condemned his arbitrary and oppressive acts, has recently caused to be published in the Delta a written opinion, differing essentially from that orally delivered by him in court at the time of his demanding recognizances from Mr. Thrasher, Dr. Saunders, and myself.

"Until the appearance of this posthumous opinion, I had no intention of appearing before the public, content to leave the imputations attempted to be cast upon me

and many good and patriotic citizens to the test of time
and the good, honest sense of the great mass of our countrymen, who, however they may be divided in opinion on
questions of temporary policy, will not, on great and interesting questions, fail to distinguish between right and
wrong, though timid, time-serving politicians, and pharisaical professors of national morality, with selfish purposes, may conspire to mystify the question and delude
the public mind.

"Had Judge Campbell, in his posthumous opinion—
the after-birth of an uneasy mind—confined himself to
the facts as they were, however odious his opinions may
have been to every sound idea of the constitutional rights
and liberty of the citizen, I would have left them to the
criticism of an enlightened republican bar, and to the serious reflection of the statesmen of a free people; but I
regret to say that his statement of the facts is so entirely destitute of foundation in truth as to be libelous, and
to compel me reluctantly to deny them through the same
channel by which they were propagated.

"I have said that this posthumous 'opinion' differs in
toto from the oral opinion delivered by the judge in
court in my presence and that of a number of gentlemen
in attendance. It is due to myself to say that, had any
of the statements upon which I shall comment been made
in my presence, they would have been contradicted on
the spot in as strong terms as my respect for the court
would have permitted.

"But inasmuch as this opinion has first recently been
brought to light through the press, I have no choice but
to expose this judicial manufacture of facts by the same
means. I again repeat that I do not now intend to present to the public the side-bar efforts of Judge Campbell
to influence the grand jury to find bills against the friends
of Cuban independence, nor will I comment upon the
legal argument of his opinion, except to say that it is
obscure, evasive, and sometimes disingenuous. Its leading feature is a studied effort to show the existence of
arbitrary power in a federal judge to imprison citizens at
his pleasure—a power which he claims to derive, not
from the Constitution of the United States nor the laws
thereof, but from the common law of England and from

monarchical precedents. For this I refer to his published opinion. My purpose is to show briefly his perversion and misrepresentation of the facts, and to defend myself against charges and insinuations contained in the published opinion, which were wholly unsupported by the evidence, and are *not true*.

"1. To give dignity and consequence to his assumption of power, Judge Campbell heads his publication with the title, 'United States of America *vs.* John A. Quitman.'

"Why this heading, unless to insinuate that there was a prosecution pending against me? Now, there was no such case in court. No charge, no accusation, no affidavit of any offense; nothing of the kind of record. The *case* was made by Judge Campbell; it grew out of his opinion. My name is not even contained in the grand jury's report. Judge Campbell alone is my accuser; he made the case and gave it a name.

"There was neither charge, accusation, nor complaint against me by the government. There being no such entitled case, why, unless to convey a false impression, was such title assumed to the published opinion?

"2. The first line of the published opinion of Judge Campbell is not true. It recites, 'This case originated in a requisition by the court upon the defendant to show cause why he should not give bond,' etc. Now, I assert that no such requisition or rule was ever served on me. There is none on record; no such rule was ever made. The first order of record in regard to myself was a positive order, requiring me to give a recognizance, with sureties, that I would observe the laws of the United States, etc., and, upon my prompt refusal to do so, it was followed by an order of commitment to the custody of the marshal, and afterward by an order of close confinement in the Parish Jail for nine months.

"3. The third statement in Judge Campbell's published opinion which I shall notice may be true, but, if so, it exhibits a proceeding not creditable to the dignity and impartiality of a court of justice. He says that, 'at the time the report was made,' my name 'was returned with others who had declined to answer the interrogatories of the jury.' I doubt this fact, because it does not appear in the published report of the grand jury, and I know of no other report made by them. If my name, then, was returned, I pray to ask, by whom? · Was this return secretly made? In writing, or verbally? Was it at the instance of the court? None of these questions are met in Judge Campbell's published opinion, and no allusion to my name is made in the published report of the grand jury. I had not then declined to answer any question. I so stated in open court. There is some mystery attending these transactions, and, unless explained, inference will be drawn not favorable to the impartiality of the court.

"4. The opinion again states 'that a printed statement of the facts which had occurred while he (I) was before the grand jury has been filed.' Filed where? by whom? by whose authority? How did a 'printed statement' get on file? This important link in the chain of facts —deemed sufficient by Judge Campbell to authorize the imprisonment of a citizen for nine months — deserves some notice. Will the public credit it that this 'printed statement' referred to by him, in his labored opinion, was the following jeu d'esprit of the accomplished editor of the Delta, published in his morning paper of the 30th of June?

"'Our description of the interview between General Quitman, the suspected head and front of the filibuster offenders, did not do full justice to the scene. We therefore reproduce it in a fuller and more accurate form. The general appeared before the grand jury on Wednesday afternoon—one of the hottest afternoons ever experienced in New Orleans—as cool and calm as an autumnal eve. He was received with great courtesy and consideration. There could not have been a more studied respect and politeness in a coterie of European diplomatists which assembled for purposes the reverse of amicable. As soon as the parties were seated, and the ardor of their mutual admiration and respect had subsided into the requisite gravity and self-possession of high officials charged with very important duties, the district attorney handed to the general a printed circular, which purported to contain a report of a meeting held at some unnamed place relative to the island of Cuba, and of certain eloquent speeches delivered on that occasion by certain alphabetical gentlemen.' The general very coolly inspected this document, after which he was asked if he knew any thing about said meeting, or of any other meeting which contemplated any expedition or enterprise of a revolutionary character against the island of Cuba. Thereupon the general addressed the grand jury substantially as follows:

"' "Gentlemen,—I have no knowledge of any act or speeches of the character referred to, or of any other contemplating a revolutionary movement in the island of Cuba, in which I have not participated to as great an extent as any other person. I have done nothing, however, which, in my judgment, is lawless or dishonorable. My conscience is clear on these points. But, after the interpretations that have recently been given to the law, I submit it to your sense of honor, justice, and propriety, if I can be expected to answer any questions relating to such movements or purposes." "Certainly not," remarked several of the jurors. "If it is your pleasure, then, gentlemen, I will retire," said the general. "You can go," said the foreman, as if he regretted to part with the general; and thereupon the gallant gentleman bowed himself out. Whether the grand inquest will base an indictment on this response of General Quitman, will be known when they come into court to-morrow.'

"This humorous newspaper morceau, it appears, was filed by Judge Campbell. Referring to it as a 'printed statement,' he says that 'it therein appears that, after being asked to give an account of the meeting alluded to in the circular, the witness (I) declined to give information, because his answering would criminate him.'

"Now, the reader will perceive that the Delta's article does not bear out this assertion of Judge Campbell; nor is it true in point of fact. I have never said, I could not say, that my answer to any inquiry would criminate me. Unconscious of any violation of law, or plots to do so, I could not suppose that I would criminate myself before any enlightened and unprejudiced tribunal. My position, according to this newspaper statement, which the judge had caused to be filed to give it judicial sanctity, was this: that I was a participator in some acts and designs having reference to a revolutionary movement in Cuba; that these acts and designs were neither illegal nor dishonorable; that, if so, they were entirely irrelevant to the present inquiry into a breach of the laws. But if deemed illegal, which I denied, as a participator in them, I ought not to be questioned about them. The grand jury, concurring in this sentiment, asked me no questions. In this particular, therefore, Judge Campbell, in his opinion, or indictment against me, states what is neither true by the 'printed statements,' nor in fact.

"5. The judge farther adduces, as testimony against me, the loose and vague charge, that 'the report of the grand jury is, that his (my) name has figured prominently with the rumored expedition.' The report states no such thing. My name is not therein mentioned. Judge Campbell, not under oath, has supplied it.

"6. In the next sentence of his opinion he descends from the dignity of a judge to become the retailer of petty scandal, by supposing that a speech referred to in the printed circular, 'perhaps might be attributed to the defendant (myself) without *great injustice*, when the fact is ascertained that he would commit himself with an enterprise like that set forth.' This language might better become a Solomon Swap in a horse-trade, than a judge of the Supreme Court presenting the facts upon which he concluded to deprive an American citizen of his liberty for nine months. His honor's train of argument is this: Supposing it to be ascertained that I would connect myself with some unknown enterprise, then, '*perhaps*,' a certain speech found in a printed statement might, with *some*, but not *great injustice*, be attributed to me. On such inferences and suspicions, presented with an obliquity leaving a doubt whether they are not said in jest and irony, depends the liberty of a freeman!

"7. In connection with this subject Judge Campbell farther says: 'The defendant confessed the fact of a connection of a kind which rendered it a matter of impropriety for the grand jury to press any question upon him relative to the details of the movement.' There is a palpable untruth in this insinuation; but it is worthy of a place in this opinion, which, throughout, as I have already shown, garbles the facts, and mystifies them when it does not wholly misrepresent them. An honorable mind can find abundant reason why a grand jury should not inquire into irrelevant matters which involved private confidence. But the reader will remark that the judge here admits the fact that no inquiry was pressed upon me, when, in other portions of his opinion, he repeatedly asserts that I refused to answer on the ground ' *that he* (I) *would criminate himself.*'

" 8. After proceeding with cautious art to cull scraps from the report of the grand jury, this posthumous opinion proceeds to say: 'They (the grand jurors) *find* from other evidence that an expedition is on foot for the purpose of assisting a Cuban revolution, or of making a demonstration on the island."

" The judge has evidently critically inspected the report, and it would be uncharitable to suppose that, as a lawyer, he does not know well that the word '*find*' is a technical word. It means a solemn presentation of a fact. Now the grand jurors *have found* no such thing. They merely use the cautious phrase ' strongly incline to the opinion;" they lean that way. They have not found an opinion, much less do they profess to *find* the fact; and even this inclination of opinion is still farther qualified by their positive declaration that nothing like a military organization or preparation had been brought to their notice. How thoroughly the meaning of the report is perverted by Judge Campbell, in this particular, the public will judge by the following extract from the report of the grand jury: 'Although the grand jury strongly incline to the opinion that these meetings and collections of funds have for their end the organization of an expedition, either for the purpose of assisting in a Cuban revolution, or making a demonstration upon that island, yet the plan, *whatever it may be*, seems altogether in the perspective; and aware, as we are, that a great deal has been said and written about the extensive and formidable preparations on foot for the purpose of revolutionizing Cuba, we believe it has been very much over-rated and magnified, nothing like a military organization or preparation having been brought to our notice.'

" 9. The opinion goes on to imply that I made an argument. I neither had counsel, quoted authorities, nor made an argument on the legal question, except to refer for my rights as a citizen and witness to the Constitution of the United States. I desired to know whether any charge or accusation had been made against me, and if so, what was its nature, and by whom made; and I denied the authority of a federal court to exercise any powers but such as were fairly deducible from the third article of the Constitution. General Waul, of the New Orleans bar, it is true, at some stages of the proceedings, appeared for Mr. Thrasher and Dr. Saunders.

"10. When the judge, in a subsequent portion of his opinion, says, 'The assertion is direct and positive that his answer will implicate him in a prosecution or forfeiture,' if he refers to me, he states what is wholly gratuitous, and without the least foundation in fact. If intended as a quotation, he has strangely omitted the usual quotation marks, which he has studiously preserved even when disconnected sentences from the report of the grand jury are inserted.

"11. The fact stated in the opinion, that I had declared my inability, from some undisclosed connection with those engaged, 'of affording information of practices involving a breach of the neutrality laws,' is also a misrepresentation. I made no such declaration, but more than once declared that I knew of no practices involving a breach of the laws.

"12. In fine, Judge Campbell, in his manifesto, refers to his leading witness, public rumor, 'that brazen-mouthed monster, with her hundred tongues.'

"'Public rumor,' says he, 'has attached suspicion to the name of the defendant, according to the certificate.' This concluding sentence may be considered the summing up or recapitulation of the evidence on which my character is to be assailed by a judicial libel, and my liberty restrained for nine months.

"'Public rumor,' aided by her fit associate, John A. Campbell, is engaged in trumpeting to the world that suspicion attaches to my name. Suspicion of what? Of being the open advocate of state rights, strict construction, free trade, direct taxation, the remodeling of the federal judicial system, the limitation of the tenure of office of the federal judges, and their election by the people? Suspicion of having aided and abetted the independence and annexation of Texas, and the conquest of Mexico? Suspicion of never having faltered in the defense of Southern rights' and of the equality of the states? Of admiring American institutions, and desiring their extension over this continent? Suspicion of cordially hating the stupid and barbarous despotism of Spain over the people of Cuba? Of planning, in conjunction with other patriotic citizens, some lawful measures to aid an oppressed people to overthrow a tyrannical and usurping government, and thus averting from ourselves and our children the dire calamity which would befall us if the cherished European policy of establishing a hostile negro or mongrel empire on our borders, at the very mouth of. the great outlet of the Southwestern States, should be carried into execution? Of doubting the ability or disposition of our common government, distracted already by the slavery question, to remedy the impending evil?

"If such suspicions attach to my name, before the world I confess myself liable to the honor or reproach which belongs to them. If, however, Judge Campbell means to insinuate that suspicions dishonorable to me attach to my name, he but adds a falsehood to the many misrepresentations of facts contained in his published opinion. Suspicion to my name! The name is Saxon. It means freeman. It has never been disgraced by falsehood, cowardice, or base truckling to power. May those who inherit it be ever worthy to bear it, by opposition to all political despotism, and by stern, unyielding resistance to tyranny, whether boldly attempted to be enforced by the bayonet, or slyly and stealthily by the perversion of judicial powers.   J. A. QUITMAN.
"Monmouth, August 15th, 1854."

General Quitman to Thomas Reed.

"Monmouth, August 24th, 1854.

"DEAR SIR,—Your kind letter of the 15th was very gratifying to me. To find those who have known me so long and so well giving their hearty approbation to my course at a time when so many pharisaical professors of national morality individually reflect upon it is truly consoling. I do not wonder that you, as a lawyer, educated to revere the safeguards which are thrown around the liberty of the citizen, should condemn the course of Judge Campbell. It was even worse and more arbitrary than has been represented in the public press. Aware of the general condemnation of his positions in my case, he has recently published a long and labored written opinion, in which I am sorry to say that he grossly misstates the facts. This has compelled me to come out with an answer in which I handle the judge with severity. It will be published in the Delta next week, and I will send you a copy. I owe you and my friends a debt of gratitude personally for the kind notice taken of me in your meeting. In another particular of vastly more moment, however, the movers in that meeting deserve praise. They have drawn public attention to the great question of our age and generation, the question whether American or European policy shall prevail on this continent. Of this great question, Cuba is the battle-ground for its solution. The erection of a strong negro or mongrel empire opposite to the mouth of the great outlet of the commerce of the Southwestern States, an empire included within the European scheme of the 'balance of power,' would forever put a stop to American progress and expansion on this continent, and very probably eventually crown their scheme by bringing about a dissolution of this Union. We are a strong people when united, but weak whenever the slavery question is started. Spain and her allies, by the possession of Cuba, have it in their power at all times to distract the United States with this question. We must disarm them of this power to injure us. How shall we do it? I say by encouraging a revolution in Cuba. The moral influence of our example has always made the people of the island ripe for the movement. They only ask the assistance of American intellect and American arms. Shall we be told that it is immoral or dishonorable in an American in his individual character to respond to such a call? Suppose the people of Cuba, groaning under the worst tyranny now known in the civilized world, should concert a revolution, gather the means, and invite me to aid them to lay the deep foundations of liberal institutions and American principles in their country, would I perform my duty to God, to my country, to humanity,

and to civil freedom, were I to refuse to devote a portion
of my life to such a cause?   Would the American citizen, seizing his rifle to strike the shackles of despotism
from the minds and bodies of his neighbors of his own
race, deserve censure or praise?

"This question is not even an abstract one to us.   The
European policy is to establish near us negro or mongrel
states.   Such a result would be fatal to us.   Our destiny
is intertwined with that of Cuba.   If slave institutions
perish there they will perish here.   Thus interested, we
must act. . Our government, already distracted with the
slavery question, can not or will not act.   We must do
it as individuals."

Gen. Quitman to Hon. H. T. Ellet.

"Monmouth, Sept. 11th, 1854.

"DEAR SIR,—Well assured from your temper that you
would not take your pen to pass an empty compliment,
I appreciate highly the expressions of your note just received, approving the matter and manner of my comments on Judge Campbell's opinion, and I thank you for
the pleasure its perusal gave me.

"Next to the desire of shaking from my name the insidious imputations on my character contained in that
published opinion, my great object was to lend my assistance to check the increasing judicial encroachments
of the federal court by holding the judges amenable to
the only power which they fear—*the force of public opinion.*   I am glad to perceive that you think I have so far
succeeded in this purpose as to destroy at least the effect of the alarming precedent set by this federal judge,
as I believe, with the connivance of his brethren on the
supreme bench.   For I can not believe that he would
have dared thus boldly to disregard the liberty of the
citizen, against the plain injunctions of the Constitution,
if the matter had not been previously planned at Washington.   I appeared before the public very reluctantly,
and when forced by considerations of self-respect to do
so, you will perceive that I have confined myself to the
exposure of Judge Campbell's subterfuges to bolster up
his violent assumptions of power.   I there left the subject, but most sincerely hope that some more able pen
will take up that important branch of the controversy

which so deeply concerns the civil liberty of every American citizen.

"I will only add, that in my strictures I sought to be temperate and respectful. If the article is severe, its severity consists in the disclosure of the facts, not one of which, of importance, but might, with strict truth, have been more highly colored.

"The poor attempt made by some volunteer friends of Judge Campbell to answer me, does not touch any fact that I have distinctly charged."

With these letters must be dismissed, for the present, his connection with Cuba and the Cubans—a connection that exposed him to prosecution on the part of the government and to misapprehension and defamation from a thousand sources. Calumnies have been uttered since his death. But the same potent considerations—considerations connected with the cause itself and with humanity—that sealed his lips still exist. Until these determine, the silence and the mystery must remain unbroken; and his pure and unsullied character in private life—his proverbial fidelity to pecuniary engagements—his inflexible resolution, and his great name, must be his defense against falsehood and detraction. The materials for his vindication—his notes of what transpired at Washington—his correspondence with the friends of Cuba—the evidence of his business arrangements, receipts and expenditures—the programme of his intended operations, showing how closely he had studied the laws of nations, the statutes of his country, and the opinions of celebrated jurists of this country and of England, will, at a proper time, be given to the world; and they will place his memory even on a higher pedestal than it now occupies in the public mind.

Note.—Had the war in the Crimea continued, and had Spain sent a contingent to the Allies, as was anticipated, Russia, in all probability, would have furnished means for the invasion of Cuba. The want of money, at a critical juncture, on the part of the friends of Cuba, was the sole obstacle to her liberation.

CHAPTER XVIII.

Fifth Congressional District.—Letter to Judge Stone.—Is nominated for Congress.—Know Nothing Party.—The Canvass.—Letters.—His Position in Congress.—Great Speech on the Neutrality Laws.—Its Effect.—Letter from James K. Paulding.—Col. E. G. W. Butler.—Dr. Samuel A. Cartwright.

1855. On the 23d of July the democracy of the fifth congressional district (so long and so ably represented by a distinguished senator from Mississippi that it is still called Brown's district) assembled in convention at Monticello. Several prominent gentlemen were spoken of as candidates. It being announced that one of the delegates had a letter from Gen. Quitman, the reading was called for.

"Monmouth, July 19th, 1855.

"DEAR SIR,—I was prevented by some pressing cares from replying promptly to your letter of the 27th ult., and I now have the pleasure to acknowledge the receipt of that of the 15th inst. I feel grateful to you and my friends in the east for this kind consideration, and, without troubling you with the detail of my own reflections upon the subject of this unexpected proposal, I will frankly and briefly state the conclusions to which I have arrived.

"As to my own personal inclinations, I am not *solicitous* of a nomination to Congress; and, at any time when the danger to Southern rights and institutions was less imminent, I would decline it, but I feel that when the enemies of our domestic institutions are marshaling their forces for a deadly assault upon us, no Southern man has a right to decline any post of duty to which the public voice may assign him.

, "If, therefore, the convention assembled to nominate a candidate for Congress in this district shall see fit to select me, such as I am, with the opinions and positions which I hold, and upon which I have ever boldly acted, I would accept the nomination, and, if elected, endeavor to represent the people of this district faithfully, truly, and fearlessly.

"My political opinions and positions are so well known that I need not refer to them. To avoid misconception on some points, however, I will remark that they remain unchanged, as when you and I acted together in 1850. A State-rights Democrat of the strictest school, I have no political connection or affinity with any other party. More devoted to principles than party, I would support no measures emanating from any source that conflicted with these cherished principles.

"I believe that the institution of negro slavery is not only right and proper, but the natural and normal condi-. tion of the superior and inferior races when in contact; that, as the chief element of our country's prosperity, it constitutes a great interest, which is entitled, like other great interests, to the fostering care and protection of the federal government, within the sphere of its powers; that legislation or action directly or indirectly hostile to this interest, is at war with our compact of union, and should be resisted by the states and the people affected by it at all hazards; that the preservation of the institution of slavery in Cuba, which can only be effected by her independence and separation from the malign influence of European governments is essential to the safety and preservation of our own system; that our government ought not to thwart, but rather encourage, by all proper means, the diffusion of American republican institutions on this continent; that it is consistent with the designs of Providence, and our right and duty not to restrain, but to encourage the Caucasian white race to carry humanity, civilization, and progress to the rich and fertile countries south of us, which now, in the occupation of inferior and mixed races, lie undeveloped and useless, furnishing only a theatre of operations for British intrigue to annoy us; that the policy of our government, in regard to these momentous questions, has been too much influenced by the prevalent spirit of hostility to negro slavery, and the determination not to permit its extension; that, upon all matters connected with our peculiar domestic institution, the South must look to herself; that no national party organization will fully protect us; that, while honestly differing on other subjects, the patriot should seek to keep our people united on this, and that, therefore, it is highly impolitic and injurious, in our party contests about issues less vital, to indulge in violent denunciation of those who differ from us politically. I should, therefore, in a canvass principally discuss these momentous issues, and, while freely criticising erroneous or false doctrine, endeavor to calm, not to excite high party feeling on other subjects less vital and important.

"If left free to urge these views in connection with the great and permanent principles of democracy, I should not feel at liberty to decline the nomination if it should be tendered to me.

"While this letter is private, in answer to your suggestions, you are at liberty to make such use of it as you think proper.

"Appreciating sincerely the kindness which prompted your communications, I remain, very respectfully, your friend and obedient servant,   J. A. QUITMAN.

"To Hon. W. A. Stone, Monticello."

These sentiments were received with acclamations. The names of all the other gentlemen were voluntarily withdrawn, and John A. Quitman was declared the nominee of the Convention.

The Know Nothing organization—the strangest infatuation of our times—was then sweeping over the country like a tornado, obliterating the ancient and wholesome landmarks of parties, and setting up a new idol in the temples where our fathers had worshiped. Concealing its illegal tests, its oaths, and its ambitious designs under the disguise of Americanism, it appealed to a national sentiment which, for the time, was irresistible, and which never could have been resisted but for the fearful evils that lurked beneath, and had been concealed from the masses of its neophytes. It practically repudiated the fundamental principles of civil and religious liberty, rejected the right of free discussion and freedom of conscience, required the sacrifice of personal independence, threatened the subversion of the rights of the states as sovereign members of the confederacy, and, in the assertion of the inexorable sway of the majority, would, in time, have reversed the character and terms of our government, substituting the decrees of its clubs for the reserved rights of the states and the covenants of the Union.

The whole tendency of the organization was to centralization, like the clubs of Paris, that commenced with philosophical declamations against political evils, and ended in the most fearful and bloody tyranny that ever afflicted mankind. Regarding it in this light, as hostile to his long-cherished principles of conservative and constitutionnal guarantees, Quitman accepted a nomination when it was claimed that over two thirds of the voters of the district had been inducted into the order. He had, however, no apprehension. He considered its tenure of short duration, and that its greatest present practical evil was to divert the public mind in the South from great issues and principles that should not be lost sight of, and which were at that moment subjected to the crucible in Kansas. Indeed, he believed that this was the real motive of the Northern politicians who organized the order. He therefore paid but little attention to it in his canvass, considering it as but a nightmare which would be dispelled when the sleeper awoke, but usually confined himself, and thus compelled his adroit and talented opponent, to the discussion of the vital principles that control the relations of the states to the federal government.

The following notes of his opening speech will show the character of the whole:

" 1. My position : since 1851 have not mingled in party strifes : devoted to Southern rights, and to the cause of liberty : I am no mere party man : have little faith in national organization to secure our national rights.

" 2. Nominated by the Democratic Convention with a full knowledge of my peculiar views : nomination generously conferred without solicitation or intrigue : demanded no pledges : knew that the temptations of national popularity would not seduce me, nor menaces deter me, nor party zeal decoy me from defending Southern rights : that I would never sacrifice principle to support men : with a toleration that distinguishes the Democracy, they exacted no pledges, but found them in my past life.

" 3. Thus I enter the canvass; and I shall not, if it can be avoided, permit myself to be drawn from great and vital issues to mere party discussion : such discussions are for place-hunters, not for statesmen or the people.

" 4. The great overshadowing question of our time is the question of races, philosophically, as connected with society, and politically, as recognized and defined in the Constitution of the United States.

" 5. Influence of the institution of slavery on morals, national wealth, production, progress, war, and peace.

" 6. Effect of its abolition.

" 7. Political abolition : its growth and power : effects in California, Kansas, and in the North and East : now violently aggressive : threatens to control our foreign policy : to discriminate against our production : to change our judicial system : to repeal the Fugitive Slave Law : to abolish slavery in the district : to refuse admittance to any slave state : to exclude it from the territories : to encourage abolition in Cuba : to circumscribe it with free territory : to foment and aid domestic insurrection.

" 8. The resources of the anti-slavery organization.

" 9. Duty of the South : their means of resistance : the necessity of resistance."

These views he elaborated with great vigor and earnestness. He had been long represented as a disunionist among a people proverbial for their attachment to the Union, and who had stood by Jackson, and by every successive Democratic administration, with unbroken ranks. But when they heard his real sentiments from the lips of the veteran, and saw sincerity and firmness stamped on his manly brow, the cry was, "If *this* be treason, make the most of it."

Confining himself thus to the discussion of cardinal principles, he avoided the bitterness and humiliation of mere party wrangling. The Know Nothings themselves specially invited him to address them, and many, after hearing him, renounced the order. On one occasion, when rather pertly asked on the stand what he thought of Know-nothingdom, he replied, "We must not speak evil of the dead or assault the dying. The order will die and leave no sign. No friend will close its eyes or write its epitaph! Men boast of being Democrats, men glory in being Whigs; but, in two years from this day, who will glory in having been a Know Nothing? Ask one of them, and he will be as explicit as a certain lady I heard of. She and her husband were on the point of being shipwrecked. He requested her, in that solemn moment, to tell him whether she had ever been false to his bed. 'My dear,' said she, 'sink or swim, that secret shall never be told.'"

To J. F. H. Claiborne.

"Monmouth, November 18th, 1855.

"DEAR CLAIBORNE,—Although we have not yet received full returns from the district (none from the seashore counties except Harrison), the certificate of election has been forwarded to me. So far as heard from, my majority is 1756—Perry, Green, Hancock, and Jackson Counties yet to hear from. You know better than I do how much they will add to my vote. Your last letter put them down as 'all right.' I am content with this, and shall act in my official career as boldly as if I had been unanimously elected. On Southern and state-rights questions I shall claim to be the chosen representative of the 'tenth legion' of old Mississippi—the heart and soul of the state. In popular governments the representative of a principle is stronger, elected upon a contest, than if elected by acclamation. I do not look for unanimity in the South, even if slavery in the states should be assailed. There were Tories in '76, there will be Tories in '56. *We* shall have to serve the latter as the patriots of the Revolution treated the former. Taking all in all, both Mississippi and Louisiana have done well. Your calculation of the vote in the latter has turned out to be wonderfully exact, failing only in two parishes, and there from local divisions. Our people have had much to resist: a politically corrupt combination, planned by cute Yankee genius, addressing itself to the passions and prejudices, supplied with a patent machinery of vast power, had to be encountered by our party organization alone, and by calm appeals to the good sense of the people. The federal administration gave us no strength; on the contrary, its weakness is deplorable. We have triumphed. Let us, by honest adherence to the principles upon which we rallied, maintain our position. I advise you of the sea-shore and contiguous counties, by all means, to organize Democratic State-rights associations, and maintain your discipline. Carry out your own just views of conciliation. Two thirds of the members of the order in your section are undoubtedly (as you wrote me six weeks since) 'Democrats at heart; natives of our state, or fully identified with it, and true to the South.' They joined the order under a delusion, and will abandon it the moment their eyes are open to its anti-Southern tendencies.'"*

1855. On taking his seat in Congress he was appointed chairman of the committee on military affairs, a position that he retained during his entire term of service, notwithstanding the subsequent change in the political complexion of the House. His appointment gave general satisfaction to the army. Though he had led a di-

* These were correct views, and things turned out as Quitman had predicted.

vision of volunteers during the war, and retained an almost enthusiastic confidence in their efficiency, no man had a more exalted appreciation of the regular service, or recollected more minutely the constancy, the energy, and the heroism it had exhibited against the heaviest odds from Palo Alto to the gates of Mexico. He knew the value of a military education—of the training at West Point—of discipline and *esprit du corps*, and he believed that the enthusiasm of our volunteers (and their familiarity with the use of arms), controlled by the science of our officers and the steadiness of our regulars, constituted an army more effective than any in Europe.* With these just and liberal views, he soon became, in the House of Representatives, more than the nominal organ of the army. He was its champion and friend. Hundreds of letters, from veteran and junior officers, even from the most remote posts, attest the confidence they had in him. He introduced and carried through a bill to increase their pay, a measure that had been too long postponed.

1856. On the 29th of April, 1856, he delivered, in the House of Representatives, his great speech on the repeal of the neutrality laws. It will be found in the Appendix. No speech ever made a deeper impression on the American people. It was commended for the justice of its views and the vigor of the argument by the public journals in every quarter. He received upward of one thousand letters from every state and Territory in the Union, from officers afloat and at the frontier posts, from associations of students, from learned and unlearned men, and of every shade of political opinion, thanking him for that speech. Many of these letters, as manifestations of public opinion and from their intrinsic merits, would be read

---

* His views on this subject, and in relation to West Point, are stated explicitly in his letter to Capt. Lovell, Chapter XIV.

with interest, but there is room only for a few.   The first was written in a hand so tremulous, and in characters so indistinct, that it has been a work of labor to decipher it. Age and infirmity were pressing the writer, but the sentiments are those of a man in the full vigor of masculine intellect, and who properly appreciated the mission of the republic.   He has recently gone to receive the reward of a well-spent life, leaving many honorable memorials on the public records and in the literature of his country, but none that will survive longer than the following letter.

From Hon. J. K. Paulding.

"Hyde Park, Dutchess County, May 23d, 1856.

" SIR,—I yesterday received a copy of your speech on the neutrality laws, which, coming under your frank, affords me an occasion to express to you the high regard I have always entertained for your services, character, and talents, of the latter of which your speech affords ample testimony.   It is that of a statesman—a character, I may venture to say, seldom found among the one hundred and fifty pettifoggers in Congress, who discuss great national questions as they would an action of assault and battery, or a suit of ejectment between John Doe and Richard Roe.

" Ever since the Spanish possessions in America became independent of the mother country—as these unnatural step-dames are styled—it has been obvious to me that their habits, manners, and, above all, their ignorance, bigotry, and that mixture of races, which can never be amalgamated or reconciled, would for a long time, if not forever, present insuperable obstacles to the establishment of a permanent system of rational liberty.   The entire structure of society among these mongrels afforded no sufficient materials either for the foundation or superstructure of the temple of freedom ; and when they adopted the language, principles, and forms of the Constitution of the United States, it was with an utter incapacity either to comprehend or reduce them to practice.

" In such a state of things, I thought I saw, very distinctly, that they had only emancipated themselves from the colonial despotism of Spain to sink into incurable anarchy, and, as an inevitable consequence, become the mere foot-ball of some other European power, whose interference could give a preponderancy to one or other of the contending factions. In short, it was evident to me, that, unless shielded by some influence still more powerful, these infant states would so weaken and exhaust themselves by their internal struggles in the very cradle, that they would never be able to walk alone. Their inevitable destiny would be a series of internal struggles, a perpetual succession of revolutions, ending at length in that chronic anarchy which hardly ever fails to result in a return, like the dog to his vomit, to a voluntary submission to the chains of despotism.

"The only influence I looked to as the great obstacle to this impending fate was that of the United States, and it is to them I now look as the sole obstacle to the relapse of the so-called republican states of this continent into a condition far worse than their primeval barbarism, or to their recent state of colonial dependence, not on Spain, but on Great Britain and France, which are aiming, by conjoint efforts, to subjugate once more the New World to the Old.

"The United States present the only serious obstacle to this policy; and it rests with them to decide whether, in the course of a few years, they are to be every where surrounded by kindred republics, united by common principles and common interests, or by those who, if their present policy is persevered in, will become their inveterate enemies. I fear it is already too late to remedy the past. The course pursued by Mr. Webster (now become one of the adopted pets of the Democracy), while conducting the foreign policy of this government, was eminently calculated to alienate the states of Central America, whose friendship is, of all others, the most important to the United States, most especially since the acquisition of California. On the achievement of their independence, both Mexico and all the South American states looked up to us as their monitor, guide, and protector; and had the United States fulfilled this mission of high and holy duty, they could and would have established an influence on this wide continent which would not only have counteracted, but triumphantly overborne all the intrigues and intimidation of England and France, always dangerous even when in opposition, and now ten times more dangerous when combined.

"It is my practice to speak what I believe to be truth of the dead as well as the living, and I have therefore no hesitation in affirming that, in my opinion, during the whole of his administration of the foreign affairs of the United States, Mr. Webster was little better than a pliant tool of the policy of Great Britain, to which every leading Eastern Federalist has always been more or less subservient. He fell into the hands of Sir Henry Bulwer, the most artful and intriguing of all the pupils of Lord Palmerston, himself the most artful and intriguing of all ministers, and permitted himself to be led into a series of blunders, which will require all the wisdom, and firmness, and courage of his successors to remedy. He turned his back on the defenseless states of Central America; treated their ministers with rudeness and contempt; despised their friendly advances; derided their weakness; and finally deluded the United States into becoming a party to a convention for dismembering the State of Nicaragua of a large portion of its territory. In short, he not only left these defenseless states to the mercy of Great Britain, but became an auxiliary in oppressing them. This act in due time followed by an abortion of a treaty, entered into by the United States with a view of obtaining the co-operation of Great Britain in a project for cutting her own throat, and by Great Britain, it would seem, for the sole purpose of deceiving them into a belief that she had relinquished what she now affirms the United States absolutely conceded to her forever.

"Thus have the United States been gradually involved in a predicament which will, in all probability, end where it ought to have begun, by a total and final severance of all the interests of the two countries with respect to American affairs, and an abandonment of the farce of fruitless negotiations. They have no common interests; their interests are every where in collision, and totally irreconcilable without sacrifices on the part of the United States, to which they can not submit without enormous loss and irretrievable disgrace. The result of Mr. Webster's blundering subserviency to Great Britain is, that the United States have lost the confidence and affection of the states of Central America, and Great Britain acquired a paramount control in Costa Rica and Guatemala, if not in the two sturdy little republics of Honduras and St. Salvador.

"It seems to me it is high time for the United States to cut themselves loose from all entanglements with Great Britain in relation to Central American affairs, with which that power has no right to interfere. She has no possessions but those she has usurped in that portion of America. She belongs to another world, and her interference with the policy of the United States is founded in an insatiable appetite for new acquisitions, coupled with a sleepless jealousy of our growth. Her intervention, therefore, is in the highest degree offensive and impertinent; and, in my opinion, the United States committed a great error in recognizing her right to become a party with them in any system of policy relating to Central, or any other portion of independent America. While thus entangled in the web of British policy, we may be assured that neither at Tehuantepec nor any where else will there ever be established a water communication, much less a ship canal, connecting the two great oceans of the world.

"As matters now stand, and if we may judge from the past, there is little dependence to be placed in the good offices of the government of the United States in fostering the prosperity and establishing the real and substantial independence of Central America. As you justly state, this can now be accomplished by the people of the United States alone; and this they can and will do if left to themselves, without either violating the law of nations, or the neutrality law if construed strictly according both to its letter and spirit, and not by over-zealous pettifoggers hungering as well for fees of office as for the reputation of vigilant officers. The laws of nature as well as of nations (except in unmitigated despotisms) permit every man to expatriate himself at pleasure. A large portion of the present citizens of the United States availed themselves of this natural right to leave their country and come hither to live and die. The Germans especially have been in the habit of organizing into little communities at home, under the eye of their own government, for the purpose of emigration, and no one ever inquired whether they furnished themselves with arms or not, or whether they became soldiers, or artisans, or husbandmen, on their arrival in this country, or at any subsequent period. All know, however, that one of the highest obligations of an emigrant citizen is that of bearing arms in defense of his adopted country against the world.

"But, in what is called the freest country in the world, it seems, by the construction given to our neutrality law, our citizens are prohibited from the exercise of this universal right of expatriation; or, if they emigrate, they must go singly and without arms, though their journey may be full of perils, and their destined home in a country where there is great reason to apprehend they may be placed under the necessity of defending themselves, their property, their wives, and their children by force of arms. In this point of view, the neutrality law of 1819 is a gross infringement of the favored rights of the citizen. It confers on every foreign minister, foreign consul, or foreign agent, the power to arrest the lawful business of every free citizen, by simply testifying himself, or suborning some instrument to testify, that he has reason to believe or suspect that he *contemplates* a violation of the neutrality laws. Such cases have happened in New York, and might have occurred at any other port, had there been such a loyal consul as Mr. Barclay, and such a vigilant district attorney as Mr. M'Keon, who seems at least as zealous in indicting so-called filibusters as actual kidnappers. I could say much more on this subject, most especially on the danger of conferring on government or any of its officers the right of arresting citizens on mere suspicion—not of having violated, but of intending to violate a law. Such a power ought never to be conferred on any government, much less on any public officer. It may, as you well know, be converted into an engine of oppression as dangerous to the rights of our citizens as the unbridled will of a despot. Suspicion, like necessity, has no law, but may be excited by the most innocent actions; and the greatest coward is always the most suspicious. It is only in time of war, or when the existence of our country is in imminent peril, that mere suspicion is a justifiable ground for outraging the favored rights of the citizen.

"I have merely reiterated your own ideas and arguments, and you will be pleased to consider this long letter as a commentary on your speech, which meets my unqualified approbation. The Central American question has occupied much of my attention during my retirement from public life, and I have, from first to last, written much on this subject in more than one of the Washington journals. I have always believed that and the Cuba question as the two by far most important points of our foreign policy, and, between ourselves, the article from which you quoted in your speech was from my pen. They are daily assuming still greater importance, and approaching a crisis in which we must either give all or take all. There is no other alternative; for if we succeed in patching up a Joseph's coat of many colors, it will only be rent in twain the first breeze that blows.

"I was therefore highly gratified to see you taking up this subject, and handling it with such statesman-like ability. I say, let the energy and enterprise of the people of the United States have their way, for that they will have whether you let them or not. In their expansion, they are but obeying the law of God and nature. It suits the organs of Europe, the London Times, and their docile echoes here, who have no opinions but what they derive from these 'legitimate' sources, to brand every citizen of the United States who goes to Nicaragua as a filibuster; but we hear nothing amiss of the German, French, and English filibusters who are abetting the Costa Ricans in murdering our countrymen in cold blood. All this is legitimate and orthodox; it accords with the humanity of legitimacy. It is no violation of the neutrality laws, and in strict conformity with the decalogue!

"Our countrymen don't seem to see it, but it is clear to me as the light of day, that the perpetual clamor of the British journals, led by the Times, against what they are pleased to call filibustering, originates in the convic-

tion that the spirit which animated these gallant mission-
aries of civilization and liberty is the most formidable
of all the obstacles to the cherished purpose of Great
Britain for the subjugation of Central America.   It is
our great weapon of defense against British encroachments; it is the best and deepest bulwark of the liberties
of the New World, and the strongest barrier against the
encroachments of the Old.   Hence it is that the British
journals are perpetually harping on filibustering, and
the Anglo-American papers responding to their principles, until our people have become persuaded they can
not go to any part of Central America to better their
fortunes, aid the progress of free principles, teach the
people how to govern themselves, or exercise any attribute of personable liberty, without violating either municipal or international law.   The honest truth of the
matter is, we have no opinions of our own; we are led
by the nose by the British press; we are the footballs of
British opinions, and, what is worst of all, we are cowed
by the apprehension of British power.   We can not take
a single step, or contemplate a single movement of policy, without asking ourselves whether it will give offense
to Great Britain, which is always on the look-out, and always ready to place herself in our way.   The statesmen
of England know this, and consequently despise our
threats, and persevere in their policy.   In the whole
course of our history we have never gained any thing
from Great Britain by negotiation, complaint, or remonstrance, but a repetition of insults and injuries.   As in
the past, so will it be in the future, so long as we rely
on her friendship, her magnanimity, or her justice, and
most especially, so long as she sees we are afraid of her.

"You will, I hope, pardon me for inflicting this long
letter on you, in consideration of the deep interest I take
in the subject, and especially as I do not expect an answer.   If it should chance to afford you any hints that
may be useful, they are heartily at your service for any
purpose you may deem proper.   Permit me to express a
hope that you will use every effort to bring this question to an issue before Congress during the present session.   With such material to deal with, I confess my
hopes are not very sanguine.   But if you fail now, I trust

you will not be deterred from repeating the effort at some propitious period. You have the right, the truth, and the Constitution on your side, and these will prevail at last, for under them the people will rally and conquer."

The next is from a citizen of Louisiana, of a family gloriously identified with the Revolution, and with every subsequent war in which we have been engaged, himself a gallant officer, the ward and confidential friend of the illustrious Jackson. The insight it gives into the sentiments of that great man is of special interest.

From Colonel E. G. W. Butler.

"Bayou Goula, La., June 9th, 1856.

"DEAR GENERAL,—I return you many thanks for the copy of your most excellent speech upon the subject of the neutrality laws, which you were so kind as to send to me; and, although I have not gone along, *pari passu*, with you, in your views of these laws (deeming something of the sort necessary to curb the military and adventurous proclivities of our people, and thereby prevent collisions with foreign nations), I could not avoid a feeling of indignation at the false construction placed upon them by Webster, Fillmore, and others of less ability, by which our people were made pirates and robbers, and placed at the mercy of England and France.

"The high and apposite authority which you adduce, in regard to the importance to us of Cuba, in a military, political, and commercial point of view, recalled to my recollections the opinions and remarks of my lamented and venerated friend, Andrew Jackson, and, on turning to a file of his letters to me, I find, under date of March 3d, 1823, the following characteristic remarks: 'If it is true that Spain is about to cede Cuba to England, good policy points to the course the United States ought to adopt.

"'There can not be an American who does not see that, if Britain obtains the Gibraltar of the Gulf, as she holds the Gibraltar of the Mediterranean, she controls the commerce of the world, and embargoes the mouth of the Mississippi when she pleases.

"'The wisdom and energy of America must prevent this, or we are involved in a perpetual war until Great Britain shall be dispossessed of it.'

"Immediately preceding this is the following paragraph, which can not but interest you. 'I have declined the mission to Mexico. I could be of no benefit to my country there: and, in the present state of revolution, a minister from the United States, to present credentials to the tyrant Iturbide, might strengthen him on his tottering throne, and aid him in riveting the chains of despotism upon the Mexican people.

"'I can never do an act to aid tyranny and oppression. I have therefore declined.'

"What a wonderful and noble old man he was! The letter from which these extracts were taken is one of advice, principally, on the commencement of my military career; and, after commending to me the study and imitation of the life of Sir William Wallace, he remarks: 'It is in the scenes of military life that you can judge properly of men.'

"I am looking with much interest to the result of the deliberations of the Democratic Convention at Cincinnati, and hope, for the sake of the Union and the great principles of democracy, that they will end in harmony, and in a fraternal and unanimous determination to give to the nominee, whoever he may be, a disinterested, patriotic, and zealous support."

The next is from a distinguished citizen, equally eminent for his enlightened and philosophical views of government and statesmanship, and for his profound researches in medical science.

From Dr. Samuel A. Cartwright.

"New Orleans, May 21st, 1856.

"DEAR GENERAL,—I have just read your speech on the '*Neutrality Laws*,' published in the Louisiana Courier of this morning, and am delighted with it.   *   *   *

"In a letter to Gallatin, June 16th, 1817 (see Correspondence, vol. iv., page 306), Thomas Jefferson says:

"'A law respecting our conduct as a neutral between Spain and her contending colonies was passed by a majority of one only, I believe, and against the very general sentiment of our country. It is thought to strain our complaisance to Spain beyond her right or merit, and almost against the right of the other party, and certainly against any claim they have to our good wishes and neighborly relations. That we should wish to see the people of other countries free, is as natural, and at least as justifiable, as that one king should wish to see the kings of other countries maintained in their despotism. Right to both parties, innocent favor to the juster cause, is our proper sentiment.'

"You have shown that our neutrality laws not only *strain* our complaisance to Spain and other monarchies of Europe, and against the rights of oppressed nations struggling to establish republican institutions, but they *strain* to violation our own Constitution by infringing on the reserved rights of American citizens themselves; and consequently the neutrality laws, as far as they encroach on the reserved rights of the people, are, or should be, null and void. The Constitution, which gives power to Congress 'to define and punish offenses against the law of nations,' gave no power to the Congress of 1817, or any other Congress, to alter or amend the law of nations, or to convert praiseworthy acts and chivalrous deeds, so considered by the world at large, into high crimes and misdemeanors, punishable with fine and imprisonment. Among the rights not delegated to the government, but reserved to the people, were the rights our fathers reserved of teaching their children virtues, and setting before them the lives and actions of such men as Lafayette, as worthy of imitation. Yet the Congress of 1817, by a majority of *one*, usurped the power and encroached upon the reserved rights of the people by declaring those very acts which had crowned the noble foreigners who came to our assistance during our revolutionary struggle with honor and glory as high crimes and misdemeanors against the United States. The government of the United States was prohibited from enacting any *ex post facto* law; yet the Congress of 1817 usurped that power by declaring those acts vices which our fathers taught their children to regard as virtues. Nay more: having, by an *ex post facto* act, changed virtue into a pretended vice, the Congress of 1817 usurped to itself the power of punishing the newly-made vice by fining and imprisoning all those who should dare exercise or practice the virtues they had been taught by the framers of our government.

"You not only very justly brand the neutrality laws of 1817 (1818) as usurpations on the reserved rights of the people, but you show very clearly that their origin is in 'the false assumption that government should direct the morals and sentiments of the people.' You refute that doctrine (which is an excrescence of the divine right of kings) by very clearly showing that the divine right is reserved to the people themselves:

"'*That the American citizen sits enthroned in the charmed circle of his reserved rights, the monarch of his own actions, and that the reservation of these individual rights is the noblest feature of our system ; and that he is the worst enemy who, by legislative usurpation or judicial construction, would seek to impair them.*'

"The Congress of 1817 did something more than impair an interesting class of reserved rights: it abolished them entirely; and, still worse, made the exercise of certain rights, which every preceding Congress of the American people regarded as virtues, punishable as high crimes and misdemeanors. The subsequent decisions of the courts riveted the usurpation, and have until now shackled the hands and caged the most patriotic sons of our republican land. Happy is it that the powers not directly granted to the legislative or executive department of our government were not confided to the judiciary, or to any other department, but reserved to the people of each state in the confederacy. Your movement to repeal the so-called neutrality laws of 1817 (1818) is, when properly interpreted, not a movement that any other nation has a right to take offense at, but a movement to reinvest the people of the United States with those reserved rights which the Congress of 1817 (1818) in an evil hour stole from them. HENRY CLAY descended from the speaker's chair, and accused Spain of rewarding her minister in the United States for the part he took in inducing the Congress of 1817 to commit the roguery on the reserved rights of the American

people, and intimated very clearly, in the speech which
you quoted, that other powers besides Spain exerted all
their influence to prevail with Congress to deprive our
people of that portion of their reserved rights which the
acts of 1817 took from them. That those acts were
passed against the general sentiment of our country at
the time, we have the authority of Thomas Jefferson for
believing.

"That the Neutrality Laws of 1817 (1818) always have
been, and are now against the general sentiment of our
country, can be easily proved by the nomination of a candidate for the presidency who would advocate their repeal. There is no doubt that such a candidate would be
elected by an overwhelming majority.

"If the Congress of 1817 (1818) had not tied the hands
of our people by stealing from them their reserved rights,
and making the acts which had nearly deified Lafayette
high crimes and misdemeanors, the British West Indies
would not now have been given over to free-negro barbarism. The Jamaica planters would have cried aloud
to the people of the United States against the tyranny
of Great Britain in reducing them to a level with their
own negroes. In the evidence taken before the House
of Commons, it leaked out that they were casting their
eyes toward us, and even contemplating annexation to
the United States, but became discouraged when they
found that the Neutrality Laws of 1817 (1818) had deprived our people of the liberty to assist them in throw-
ing off the British yoke. Hence they had to submit to
the policy of England in sacrificing the West Indies to
enhance the value of her immense East India empire,
and at the same time to hem in her great rival in agriculture, manufactures, and commerce by a free-negro
barbarism planted in the centre of our republican hemisphere. I perceive by your speech on the neutrality
laws that you understand English policy perfectly, which
so few of our prominent statesmen seem to do. With
that policy understood, none but downright traitors to
their country could have made the Clayton-Bulwer
Treaty, and none but enemies to their country would
oppose its annulment and the repeal of the neutrality
laws. The Clayton-Bulwer Treaty, the preposterous

claims set up to a large portion of Central America, and the Africanization of tropical America, are parts and parcels of the same policy that led Great Britain into the late war with Russia—the policy being to preserve and extend her East India and Asiatic conquests against American competition in the West and Russian progress in the East."

CHAPTER XIX.

Quitman and the Vice-presidency. — Buchanan and Fremont. — Speech on Federal Relations.—Its Influence on Public Opinion.—His Views on the Slave-trade.—The subject considered.—Views of Luther Martin.—Argument of Major Marshall.—Re-elected to Congress. — Decline of his Health.—His last political Letters.—The English-Kansas Bill.—Quitman's Vote.—The North and the South.—Alarming Posture of Affairs.—Can the Union be preserved? •

1856. WHEN the National Democratic Convention assembled at Cincinnati, it was believed that Quitman would receive the nomination for the vice-presidency. He was regarded as the representative man of the party—of the action, progress, and expansion policy, which, if allowed full scope, would subdue internal controversies, secure Democratic ascendency, and place the republic in its proper position before the world. Quitman coveted distinction only with these views. On the first ballot he received the highest number of votes. The combinations that would seem to be indispensable to the nomination of a president, and the construction of what is called a platform of principles for the concentration of discordant opinions, rendered his nomination impracticable.*

* What his views were in the canvass that followed may be learned from the following note :

"Monmouth, October 17th, 1856.

"MR. WALKER: DEAR SIR,—I have just received your letter of the 6th instant, in which you inform me that a report is circulated in your neighborhood, that lately, when passing through Atalanta, I had given it as my opinion that New York and Pennsylvania would vote for Fillmore, and that I therefore recommended all Southern men to vote for him, and thus exclude Fremont. The only truth in this re-

Shortly after resuming his seat in Congress he delivered his celebrated speech on the powers of the federal government with regard to the territories. It will be found in the Appendix. He took occasion to discuss, incidentally, all the stirring issues of the day; the policy and designs of the Black Republican party; the Central American states; General Walker and Nicaragua; the repeal of the laws making the slave-trade piracy; legislation for public morality; the folly of attempting to legislate for posterity; and the relation of the states to the federal government and to the territories. This speech produced a profound impression at the time, and it will bear the test of the severest criticism. It was published in Europe, as significant of the views of a section of the Democratic party certain to control the destinies of the republic, and just as certain to claim for it a broader and grander sphere of operations, and a controlling influence in the affairs of this hemisphere. His sentiments were warmly welcomed by the American people. His popularity overleaped sectional boundaries. In every quarter, from Maine to Wisconsin, from Oregon to Florida, the press responded to his manly and thoroughly American doctrines.

In regard to the slave-trade he did not favor the reopening of it, but he doubted the alleged power of Congress to prohibit it, or to declare it piracy.

port is, that I did pass through Atalanta on my journey homeward. It was the day after the Know Nothing meeting had been held there. From whatever source it sprang, the report is utterly false. On all occasions, and every where, when my opinions have been asked, I stated what I believe will occur, and that is, that Fillmore will not carry a single electoral vote North or South. In this contest I can scarcely excuse the Southern man who throws his vote away on Fillmore. I would as soon recommend the Southern people to stand aloof from a contest involving their dearest rights, as to advise them to desert Buchanan. I can make due allowance for political prejudice and partisanship, but non-committalism in this contest is almost a crime."

First, in regard to slaves as property :*_

A slave is recognized by the Supreme Court as property, and entitled to all its attributes. Under the Constitution, the owner is allowed special aid when his property is a fugitive in a free state, and he is enabled to demand its restoration.

As property, the slave had been an article of American commerce with foreign nations for upward of a century and a half prior to the adoption of the present federal Constitution. In that instrument it was specially exempted from prohibition for a period of twenty years longer.

Second, the power of Congress:

It was the opinion of Luther Martin, a delegate in the Convention which formed the Constitution, that there was no provision in it for prohibiting the foreign slave-trade after the year 1808. He says:

" You will perceive, sir, not only that the general government is prohibited from interfering in the slave-trade before the year 1808, but that there is no provision in the Constitution that it shall afterward be prohibited, nor any security that any such prohibition will ever take place."—*Luther Martin's letter on the Federal Convention of* 1787.

The power to prohibit the foreign slave-trade is not among the enumerated powers in section eight.

Then follow sections nine and ten: the former enumerates a class of powers which the federal government shall be prohibited from exercising, the latter specifies a class of powers which the states shall be prohibited from exercising.

In the former the federal government is expressly forbid prohibiting the foreign slave-trade prior to 1808.

* See Texas State Gazette, April 2d, 1859, where this subject, in reference to the views of Quitman, is discussed by its distinguished editor, John Marshall, Esq.

Mr. Martin held that the Constitution failed to provide for its extinction after that period.

The authority of Mr. Martin is an important and reliable one. In the original draft of the Constitution the clause stood thus:

"Sec. 4. No tax or duty shall be laid by the Legislature on articles exported from any state; nor on the migration or importation of such persons as the several states shall think proper to admit; *nor shall such migration or importation be prohibited.*"

Mr. Martin proposed to vary this section so as to allow a *prohibition* or tax on the importation of slaves.

This was opposed by Mr. Rutledge, of South Carolina.

Mr. Ellsworth, of Connecticut, was for leaving the clause as it stood.

Mr. Pinckney, of South Carolina, said that his state could never receive the Constitution if the trade was prohibited.

Considerable discussion ensued, and finally this section was altered so as to read as follows:

"The migration or importation of such persons as any of the states now existing shall think proper to admit shall not be prohibited by the Congress prior to the year 1808, but a tax or duty may be imposed on such importation not exceeding ten dollars for each person."

Mr. Martin was present during the whole discussion of this question and its final settlement. He was a member of the committee which reported the above substitute. He must, therefore, be regarded as high authority for the assertion that the Constitution did not provide for the prohibition of the slave-trade after the year 1808.

Mr. Martin was opposed to the foreign slave-trade, and insisted that slaves weakened the Union; and he, with some other delegates from slave states, went even so far as to assert that the importation of slaves was inconsistent with the principles of the Revolution. He was, therefore, not at all biased in his opinion by prejudices in favor of that trade or the institution of slavery itself. But for his hostility to the institution, and some other Southern men, we should now be spared the task of demonstrating this right as one among the reserved powers of the states.

In examining the powers of Congress over the question of slave property, we must not be misled by the opponents of the foreign slave-trade, who assert more enlarged powers for Congress than is here admitted. We must apply the doctrine of strict construction to every grant of the Constitution, and limit the exercise of power at all times to what may be clearly shown to be absolutely "*necessary and proper*" in the execution of said grant. We must bear in mind that loose constructionists have existed from the formation of the Constitution itself. We must not forget that when the opinion of Hamilton prevailed that a national bank was constitutional, but three years had elapsed from the period of the adoption of the Constitution itself, nor the farther fact that Congress sanctioned the charter and President Washington approved of it. And we should remember, also, that after the lapse of nearly a quarter of a century, this same bank was denounced as *unconstitutional* by President Madison, who, in 1815, vetoed the bill to recharter it. We must not forget that in 1798, or only ten years after the adoption of the Constitution, the most odious violations of that instrument were committed by Congress and sanctioned by President Adams. These were the passage of the alien and sedition laws. And we will remember that so gross was the sacrilege, that Virginia and Kentucky, acting through their Legislatures, appealed to other states to join in opposition to them. We must not forget, also, that stupendous systems of internal improvement, embracing the Erie Canal and Maysville Road, have been asserted as constitutional subjects for the appropriation of the federal revenues; nor that, in many instances, the blow has only been intercepted by presidential vetoes. We must not forget that Henry Clay assumed to trace the corner-stone of his protective policy to the act of 1789, and to lay claim to the prestige of its indorsement by President Washington. He declared that it was then "solemnly proclaimed to the American people and the world, that it was necessary for the *encouragement and protection of manufactures* that duties should be laid;" nor that the reasoning adopted for all the violations of the Constitution by protective tariffs was, that the power to regulate commerce was in its terms *unlimited*.

Nor must we forget, above all other things, that the very law which was placed on the statute-book in 1820, prohibiting the holding of slave property north of latitude 36° 30', has, after the lapse of *thirty-six years*, been pronounced unconstitutional by the highest judicial tribunal in the land.

If this testimony convinced us of any thing, it is the danger of attaching too much weight to pleas of implied or incidental powers. It more especially shows us the misconceptions of men who lived in times contemporaneous with the formation of the Constitution, in their latitudinous views of its balances and adjustments. Because the power to regulate commerce had been transferred to the federal government by the states, and because the states had at times prohibited the slave-trade, it by no means followed that the right to prohibit was coupled with the right to regulate that trade when the latter power was conceded. Slave states, before and after 1808, have, in pursuance of police regulations, prohibited slaves being brought into their territory for sale or barter. As a police regulation only this power has been exercised by the slave states. That it should remain in a state is evident from the fact that no other state, let alone the federal government, can be a judge of the necessity for such regulations, either in regard to slaves coming from another state of the Union or from a foreign country. If such commerce at any time conflicts with the domestic policy of a state, no other tribunal but such as may be established by the people of that state can be the true and proper exponent of its wants or wishes.

If the states had prohibited themselves from exercising this power, we ought to find the prohibition specifically expressed among the other class of powers prohibited to the states in the tenth section.

On the other hand, the whole history of the states shows that the power to control the entry of foreign slaves into the states was exercised by them from the earliest time down to the final prohibition of the trade in this country. During the colonial period, Great Britain assumed the exclusive power to control the slave-trade, to the great offense of the colonies, who always contended for the exercise of the right themselves. When a colony desired, either temporarily or permanently, to suspend the trade, she was met by the mother country with a total disregard of her wishes. The trade was lucrative to British shipping, and her ship-owners were privileged to carry slaves to the colonies against the consent of their people. Remonstrances were vainly made at different times by Virginia, Maryland, and Carolina, and they passed laws designed to restrict the importation. The deaf ear which England turned to the colonies was the cause of the retaliatory resolution of the Continental Congress of 1776, that "no slaves be imported in any of the thirteen colonies." When independence was achieved, the states assumed entire control of the importation of negroes. During the confederation, each state exercised the prohibiting power whenever necessary as a police regulation, either to guard against a temporary plethora of slaves, or to abolish the trade entirely. It was a power freely exercised by them, and without molestation from the federal government. As we have already noticed, a special guarantee was given the trade by the Constitution down to 1808. But the action of the states shows that they still adhered to their right to exercise the power themselves, and, consequently, although the trade was prohibited in 1808 by a law of Congress, it was really extinguished by the states themselves prior to that time. Georgia prohibited it by an organic act in 1798, and South Carolina had previously prohibited it by act of her Legislature. These were the last states which exercised the right to admit foreign slaves into their territories.

In attempting to assume for Congress a power that is not specially granted, expounders of the Constitution of a later date than Mr. Martin have proposed to locate the power to prohibit the slave-trade as an incident of the power to regulate commerce. We shall see how incompatible is the exercise of such a power under this clause.

The history of the power to regulate commerce is, in truth, the history of the federal Constitution itself. The chief defect of the articles of confederation was the want of this power. States on the sea-board oppressively taxed the imports and exports of the interior states, while there was little uniformity in any of the state tariffs. The individual attempts of states to retaliate upon the obnoxious regulations of foreign powers proved abortive, and were taken advantage of by other states of the confederacy. It was found impracticable for thirteen different Legislatures, acting separately and distinctly, to agree in the same interpretation of a commercial treaty, or to take uniform measures in carrying it out, and the strict maintenance of national faith became impracticable. In the navigation laws the citizens of one state were treated as aliens by another, and the same privileges extended to the foreign ship-owner as to the domestic. Great Britain having adopted regulations destructive of American commerce with the West Indies, it became a subject of serious consideration by the Congress. It was resolved by that body, in 1785, that, unless the federal government was invested with powers competent to the protection of commerce, reciprocal advantages could not be commanded from other nations, and that our foreign commerce must be ultimately annihilated. It was at first proposed that the states should cede the powers to the federal government for the space of fifteen years. Four states only agreed to fully comply with the recommendation. Georgia specially declared that the exercise of the power over commerce should not extend to prohibit the importation of negroes. At the same session, Mr. Monroe, as chairman of the committee which recommended a letter to be addressed to the states showing the principles on which an alteration of the Articles of Confederation was proposed, reported:

" That the 1st article of the 9th of the Articles of Confederation be altered so as to read thus:

" The United States in Congress assembled shall have the sole and exclusive right and power of determining on peace or war, except in the cases mentioned in the 6th article—of sending and receiving embassadors—entering into treaties and alliances—of regulating the trade of the states, as well with foreign nations *as with each other*, and of laying such imposts and duties upon imports and exports as may be necessary for the purpose; provided that the citizens of the states shall in no instance be subject to pay higher imposts and duties than those imposed on the subjects of foreign powers; *provided, also, that the legislative power of the several states shall not be restrained from prohibiting the importation or exportation of any species of goods or commodities whatever,"* etc.

Such was the scope of power proposed by the committee to be exercised by the federal government. That simple uniformity, and not prohibition, was intended, is evident from the fact that the power to regulate trade was asked as well to be exercised upon the *foreign* as upon the *domestic* trade of the states; and to the latter was guaranteed the exercise of the power to prohibit importations of "*any species of goods or commodities whatever.*" Georgia had likewise specially insisted that the power ceded to Congress should not extend to the prohibition of the slave-trade.

It was not until the State of Virginia, in 1786, proposed a convention of commissioners from the several states at Annapolis, Maryland, "to consider how far a *uniform* system in their commercial relations may be necessary to their *common interests* and their permanent harmony," that a demonstration on the part of the states was made in its favor. Only five states assembled, but they unanimously concurred in calling the convention which framed the present Constitution. The movement was sanctioned by the Congress of 1787, for the sole and express purpose of effecting a revision of the Articles of Confederation. When the convention assembled, the clause "to regulate commerce with foreign nations, and among the several states," as reported in the original draft, "was agreed to *nem. con.,*" without dissent (Debates, p. 434), "and with the Indian tribes," was afterward added by the committee of eleven; and this, also, "was agreed to *nem. con.*" (p. 507). The clause then stood as we now find it:

"The Congress shall have power—

"To regulate commerce with foreign nations, and among the several states, and with the Indian tribes."

Such is a brief history of this power. To state this clause specifically:

"The Congress shall have power—
"1. To regulate commerce with foreign nations.
"2. To regulate commerce among the several states.
"3. To regulate commerce with the Indian tribes."

The power given is the power to *regulate*. The subject is the *commerce*, as well with the *foreign nations* as among the *states* and with the *Indian* tribes.

The same amount of power is given to the federal government to regulate the one as the other commerce. Nor is there any concurrent power to be exercised by the states, either among themselves or with foreign nations. It is to be exclusively exercised by Congress in each case; and, consequently, if Congress can prohibit articles in the foreign trade from being imported into the states, it can likewise prohibit articles of commerce in the domestic trade from being imported into one state or territory from another. The power and the subject matter are the same. The former is the power to *regulate*, and the latter is *commerce*. And if Congress can assume the power to prohibit the foreign slave-trade under this clause, it must do so because slaves are an article of commerce. This would be the exercise of a discretionary power not conceded by the Constitution, or claimed by any respectable authority.

"No word can be found in the Constitution which gives Congress a greater power over slave property, or which entitles property of that kind to less protection than property of any other description."—*Opinion of the Court in the Dred Scott case.*

That article in the Constitution which declares the
VOL. II.—L

right of the people to be secure in their persons, houses, papers, and effects, against unreasonable search and seizure, shall not be violated; and the article which also declares that no person shall be deprived of " life, liberty, or property, without due process of law," applies as well to the property of the American citizen on shipboard on the ocean as in a private dwelling in the state or territory. The right follows the flag of the country wherever it may be; and whether the owner's " effects" may be slaves or dry-goods, brought to the country from distant lands for the purpose of trade or commerce, they must be alike exempted from unreasonable seizure.

" The rights of property are united with the rights of person, and placed on the same ground by the fifth amendment to the Constitution, which provides that no person shall be deprived of life, liberty, and property, without due process of law." * * * " The powers over person and property of which we speak, are not only not granted to Congress, but are in express terms denied, and they are forbidden to exercise them. And the prohibition is not confined to the states, but the words are general, and extend to the whole territory over which the Constitution gives the power to legislate." * * * " It is a total absence of power every where within the dominion of the United States."—P. 56, *Dred Scott decision.*

When Congress acquired Louisiana, only an inconsiderable portion of it was erected into a Territory. An immense region, inhabited chiefly by Indians, was held by the federal government in trust for the states. If Congress could successfully prohibit the slave-trade under the clause to regulate commerce, it might have exercised the power in this territory under pretext of regulating commerce with the Indian tribes; and, by " unfriendly legislation," have utterly excluded the institution of slavery in Arkansas and the Indian nation. This will but imperfectly shadow forth the gigantic power a latitudinous construction of the Constitution may sanction.

Congress did assume to declare that slavery and involuntary servitude, except as a punishment for crimes, should be forever prohibited in all that part of the territory ceded by France under the name of Louisiana lying north of 36° 30′ north latitude not included within the limits of Missouri; but, as we have seen, this act, after remaining on the statute-book for thirty-six years, was at last decided by the Supreme Court of the United States to be wholly unconstitutional. Congress had usurped its powers in passing the law; and if, as in the case of the law prohibiting the foreign slave-trade, Southern men aided in its accomplishment, it should never be justly cited as stultifying the South for asking for its repeal.

Congress now exercises the power of laying a tax upon slaves shipped from one state to another. It is itself an oppressive obstacle to the inter-commerce of the states. Should we acquire Cuba, it might be assumed that Congress could lay a prohibitory tax upon slaves imported from that island. It is exclusively a commercial regulation, and if we acknowledge the power to be unlimited, the tenure of slave property must become precarious. Indeed, all property would become insecure. The power to prohibit, and the denunciation of piracy and penalty of death might be invoked against the holder of any kind of property obnoxious to the arbitrary will of a majority in Congress; and no man could tell when he might wake up to-morrow for the halter as a pirate, for holding property which he legally acquires to-day.

We conclude with a quotation from the opinion of the Supreme Court in the Dred Scott case.

Before doing so, we will say that the whole subsequent action of Congress on the foreign slave-trade has been marked by a hostility to it founded alone upon the false philanthropy of European and Black Republican sentiment, and not upon purely commercial considerations. Congress never assumed to stigmatize the foreign slave-trade as piracy for other reasons than that it was an inhuman traffic—reasons which the governments of Europe and the Black Republicans at the North might assign for suppressing the trade, but which do not exist in the federal Constitution either in letter or in spirit. In carrying on this moral war against the outer slave-trade of the Union, instructions were at one time given under act of Congress to all the ministers of the United States accredited to the powers of Europe and America to propose the proscription of the African slave-trade by classing it under the denomination and inflicting on its perpetrators the punishment of piracy. Doubtless the failure of the United States to become a party with European powers for the suppression of the trade has arisen from other causes than hostility to the trade itself. Mr. Cass, in his opposition to the quintuple treaty, developed the main cause—the extension of the *right to search and police over vessels* on the ocean to foreign powers. John Quincy Adams, in his first message to Congress, denounced the trade as "*an abominable traffic.*" Its suppression was one of the measures proposed to be laid before the Congress of Panama. In 1825, RUFUS KING, then a senator from New York, and a leader of his party, proposed in the United States Senate, that after the payment of the public debt, the proceeds of the sales of the public lands should be applied to the aid of the states emancipating their slaves. A bonus was thus offered to tempt the weaker slave states to abolish the institution; and but for the violence of the Abolition party we can not tell how far even some of the slave states might have favored a system of gradual emancipation.

Thus it has been that opinions in Congress entirely at war with the Constitution have led to attacks upon the institution of slavery, and to attempts to cripple and enfeeble it as a political power in the confederacy. This was the paramount spirit which pervaded the mass of the supporters of the present law against the foreign slave-trade. With the facts of history before us, it is the duty of Southern men, above all other considerations, to demand a strict construction of the powers granted by the Constitution, and to devote their moral energies and their political strength to the resistance of all attempts by Congress to pass laws neither constitutionally "*necessary or proper*" to the administration of the government.

"But, in considering the question before us, it must be borne in mind that there is no law of nations standing between the people of the United States and their government, and interfering with their relations to each other. The powers of the government, and the rights of the citizen under it, are positive and practical regulations plainly written down. The people of the United States have delegated to it certain enumerated powers, and forbidden it to exercise others. It has no power over the person or property of the citizen but what the citizens of the United States have granted. And no laws or usages of other nations, or reasoning of statesmen or jurists upon the relations of master and slave, can enlarge the powers of the government, or take from the citizens the rights they have reserved. And if the Constitution recognizes the right of property of the master in the slave, and makes no distinction between that description of property and other property owned by a citizen, no tribunal, acting under the authority of the United States, whether it be legislative, executive, or judicial, has a right to draw such a distinction, or deny to it the benefit of the provisions and guarantees which have been provided for the protection of private property against the encroachments of the government."

The interdiction of the slave-trade was made with the apparent consent of the Southern States. It was made when the British auspices under which it had been fostered were hateful to the people of the South, and when the grand but delusive optimism of the French Revolution still influenced the public mind. Virginia, particularly, was deeply infected with the universal emancipation doctrines of the day, and received with rapture the eloquent platitudes of Lord Mansfield on the subject of slavery. The institution of slavery has since been more thoroughly studied. The normal condition of the negro, his slavery in Africa, his improvement, morally and physically, when brought in contact with civilization, the effect of his labor on the commerce of the world, on society and public morals, and the sanction for his subjection found in the Holy Scriptures, have changed the opinions of mankind. In Virginia, where fifty years ago her statesmen, her Legislature, and her judiciary all favored the policy of gradual emancipation, there is now a constitutional ordinance prohibiting the Legislature itself from setting free a slave, expelling from the commonwealth all set free by their owners, giving authority to the Legislature to forbid the power of emancipation in any case, giving like authority to reduce the free negro population into perpetual slavery, either by compulsion or by their own election, providing a mode for such reduction into slavery, and a farther act inflicting fine and imprisonment in the penitentiary upon any one maintaining the doctrine that Virginia masters have not the right of property in their slaves.*

Experience has demonstrated the erroneous notions that prevailed in former years, and it is due to posterity

---

* Code of Virginia, p. 745–6. Howard's argument in the Court of Appeals of Virginia—Bayley *vs.* Poindexter. Maryland has recently enacted a similar law.

to apply the remedy. When Quitman objected to the term "*settled policy of the country*" in the resolution of Mr. Orr declaring it inexpedient to repeal the laws prohibiting the African slave-trade, he meant that one generation can not impose laws on another.* "Sufficient for the day is the evil thereof." The law-making power carries with it the law-repealing power.

The slave-trade, as it formerly existed, was carried on, mainly, by English and New England traders. They were brutal and mercenary men, who purchased their commodities low, and put a low estimate on their value. They found the negro, in his native haunts, scarcely a grade above the monkey, and subjected to the most cruel oppression and to summary execution during the life and at the death of his barbarian master. The most abject and inexorable slavery has always prevailed in Africa, and their bloody *fetishes* are more revolting than the grossest superstitions of India.

Civilization and humanity rose up against the horrors of the slave-trade. This was rational and just. But in their sympathy with the poor victims of what was called "the middle passage," the statesman of that age overlooked the actual home condition of the African, now known to be even more wretched than the treatment they experienced on shipboard. They likewise at that day almost universally regarded slavery as an evil, and the interdiction of the trade and gradual emancipation constituted the process by which it was to be removed. It is now, by those who understand it best, no longer regarded as an evil, but as a necessity, a blessing, an instrumentality in the hands of Providence for the benefit of the two races. Emancipation is now discarded. The interdiction stands on no better grounds. It is, in fact, an act of humanity to export them from Africa, and, instead of

* See his speech, December 18th, 1856, Appendix.

prohibiting, our fathers should have applied themselves to *regulating* the mode and manner of conducting the trade.

A few years since the immigration from Europe was accompanied with privations and inhumanities. Starvation, thirst, pestilence, and indignities were the concomitants of the voyage, and the passengers, poor and friendless, had no redress. Many actually reduced themselves to bondage to escape the oppression of their native land, and to secure comfort and protection on the passage to America. No statesman thought of prohibiting the immigration, but they set to work to reform the abuses; and now ships are only allowed to bring a number consistent with their tonnage, a specified quantity of water and stores, allowing an ample margin for detention *in transitu*, and a competent surgeon must be on board. By these and other stringent and salutary regulations, the evils that formerly existed have been abated.

Apply a similar system to the trade for slaves: the business will soon be wrested from the hands of British buccaneers and Yankee smugglers. Southern ship-masters will engage in it. Associations of benevolent and Christian planters will send out their agents—men who know the value of slaves, and have no prejudices against them—who have been trained to regard the negro, not only as a fellow-man, but as a progressive man, capable of civilization, to be treated with kindness and worthy of confidence. The "horrors" of the slave-trade, by which Wilberforce (who was one of the most narrow-minded and bigoted statesmen that England ever gave birth to) accomplished its prohibition and the ruin of the West India colonies, will disappear, and we may satisfactorily work out the great problem of the civilization of Africa, and carry out, in this hemisphere, our manifest destiny.

England, and France, and Spain are now prosecuting the slave-trade under very transparent disguises. They have virtually ignored an interdiction which they find destructive to their interests. But, independent of them, we should pursue in this, and in all other matters, our own policy. It is not what they think or what they recommend, but what humanity and the interests of the republic demand—always to be pursued when they do not conflict with the comity and equity due to other nations. If the "institution" itself be wrong, the interdiction is right, and all our local laws interposing obstacles to emancipation are irrational, if not criminal, and should be repealed. But if African slavery be a social, industrial, and political good, and in the plan of Providence, as we of the South have demonstrated, its interdiction is absurd.

Free trade in this respect would evangelize and civilize Africa. It would bring the African potentate and his subjects, for the first time, in contact with the American slaveholders, the only class of men that understand and appreciate the negro. The man-stealing, the raids, pillage, and murder, set on foot by the dealers of former times, would be discountenanced. A system, conducted upon covenants and apprenticeship, would soon be instituted, giving to the African, as our laws now do to the free negro, the election of perpetual and hereditary slavery, which many now elect. And the result of the commerce would be the improvement of the native African at home, and the progress and development of our own country by the required addition of labor, diffusing its benefits over the world.

When Mr. Buchanan's election to the presidency was announced, there was a very general desire expressed by the press that Quitman should be called to the cabinet. The officers of the army were particularly anxious to see him at the head of the War Department.   But no arrangement of the kind was proposed.

1857. He was re-elected to Congress by acclamation, with the consent of all parties.   An analysis of his speeches, deduced from the Congressional Globe, would be a text-book for the student.   His interpretations of the Constitution were singularly logical and consistent. No emergency, however pressing or tempting, ever betrayed him from the plain and literal meaning of that instrument into the labyrinth of constructive doctrine. His inflexibility won the entire confidence of the House. No member that ever sat therein commanded more personal influence.   It was known that he was not only willing to suffer martyrdom for his faith, but that he was always prepared to sacrifice all advantages for an abstract truth or principle.   His course was governed by his convictions of duty and of abstract right, as determined by the severe judgment he always applied to such questions.

1858. His health during this protracted and laborious session, in which he took an active part in the debates, as well as in the labors of the military committee, visibly declined.   He was deeply interested in a bill for the promotion of the volunteer service, which, against a powerful opposition, and the positive disapproval of the secretary of war, he succeeded in carrying.   The following interesting letter to a valued friend shows that, if his physical powers were rapidly decaying, his vigilance was as sleepless, and his intellect as vigorous as ever :

To John Marshall.

"Washington, February 1st, 1858.

"MY DEAR FRIEND,—I have pushed from before me several formidable piles of papers, to make a brief acknowledgment of your interesting letter of the 10th ult., inclosing the resolutions of the Texas Democratic Convention. They come very opportunely; for to-morrow (Tuesday) we shall probably have the Kansas Constitution sent in to Congress, and then comes the test of the fidelity of the Northern Democrats.

"Before I present my views of the present crisis, I must make some explanations, which will also account to you for the apparent quiet of Southern State-rights Democrats. At the commencement of the session, we came here to force a test upon Walker's administration of affairs in Kansas, and to compel the administration to approve or disavow his leading acts. Before that could be matured, however, we learned that there would be a formidable defection from the Northern Democracy, on the pretense that the Constitution should have been submitted to the people. Mr. Buchanan took ground for the Constitution, not, however, without hesitation and apology, but still his position *quoad hoc* was for us. This put an entirely different phase upon the matter, and we determined to adjourn our complaints against the President for his support of Walker, up to his last act, until the controversy between Northern Democrats should be determined. While the results of the proceedings in Kansas were doubtful, and while this Northern controversy was pending, our best policy was to make no final issues. You will see, from these representations, why we of the extreme state rights wing were quiet, and presented no ultimatum. When the neutrality and Paulding questions came up, we were obliged, for the sake of principle, to come out; but aware that the great question was still before us, we were as moderate as possible. We wished to give the President no reason for shifting his position on the Kansas Constitution.

" We are now on the eve of the solution of the great questions: 1st. Whether the Northern Democrats will stick to the principles laid down on the slave question in the Cincinnati platform; and, 2d. Whether any new slave state can ever be admitted. These are the issues involved in the vote on the Kansas Constitution. All other questions are mere pretenses, flimsy as the mazy sophistries by which they are attempted to be sustained. Let it be known in the South that these are the true is-

sues. Let the people reflect on them. If they are de-
- cided in the negative, let them at once take their stand
firmly and irrevocably.

"In view of these important consequences pending,
you will desire to know what is the present aspect of
affairs, and what are the chances. Neither as yet are
certain; both are involved in some doubt. We have information, which I believe to be true, that in the late
elections for the Legislature the Pro-slavery party in
Kansas has prevailed; that Gen. Calhoun, late president
of the Convention, whom I believe to be an honest, impartial man, has so declared in canvassing the votes.
Thus Kansas, if she comes in, will not only be a slave
state but also have a pro-slavery government. Now, I
doubt whether, under these circumstances, we can rely
upon a sufficient number of Northern votes to carry her
through. Compromises, substitutes, supplements, pro-
visos, and all other means, will be resorted to to defeat
this result, and when finally it comes to the naked question, I predict the Constitution will be rejected. If the
administration falters in the least, and I fear a little that
it will, our defeat is certain. Public sentiment comes
down to us from the North and West like a Mississippi
flood. Few, I think, will be able to stand it. Well, suppose we carry the Constitution. National Democracy
will almost cease to exist in the free states. Every man
who votes with us will be swept off at the next election.
The Black Republicans, or the Anti-slavery party under
some other name, will sweep every free state at the next
contest for President. Parties will become purely sectional, and no remedy left to us of the minority but separation. On the other hand, should the Constitution be
rejected, the South must regard the plighted faith of the
Northern Democracy violated. It will assure us that no
more reliance can be placed on them to aid in protecting
our rights; that National Democracy is worthless. We
must also see in the act a fixed and inexorable determination on the part of the majority never to admit another slave state—to stop forever the extension of our
system of slavery, and thus to bind the South to the triumphant car of an antagonistic majority.

"Who can doubt what, under such a state of things,

the South ought to do? If she waits for the border states, Virginia, Maryland, Kentucky, and Missouri, or either of them, to move, she will never act, but gradually become the willing slave of an insatiate master. The cotton states must move first. Alabama and your own great state have already taken the first step, and I doubt not Georgia, South Carolina, Mississippi, and Arkansas are ready to fall into line. Let but five states determine upon secession and separation to preserve their social systems, and all the other states having similar systems must, sooner or later, unite with them. The rationale of effecting this great measure is a very delicate matter. The plan by which it is to be effected must be well digested, and then firmly pursued to the result. I propose that each state shall hold a convention, assert, by solemn resolutions, the right of withdrawing from the Union, declare the violation of the spirit and letter of the Constitution, and that the time has come when her honor, her interests, and her safety require such separation, but that she defers the act merely to confer with, and co-operate, if possible, with her sister states similarly situated, as to the proper time and manner of her withdrawal. Then appoint delegates, with proper powers, to consult with such of the slaveholding states as may *coincide* with her (not all the states, or we will perhaps be out-voted by the Submissionists), and may consent to meet her delegates. Let the delegates, when assembled, present the mode, manner, and time of withdrawal, to be adopted by the conventions of the respective states. After the act of secession, let delegates immediately assemble to form a Confederation or Constitution, to be submitted to the assenting states, etc., etc.

"February 5th, 1858.

"I kept open my letter, partly because I had much more to say, and partly because I desired to give you information of the reception of the President's Message on the Constitution. It was sent in on the 3d, and has just been taken up to-day, and here we are in the House at 11 o'clock P.M., taking ayes and noes on preliminary questions, and no prospect of adjournment yet. On the reception of the message, recommending unequivocally the recognition of the Lecompton Constitution, Mr. Harris, of Illinois, the friend of Douglas, moved it be referred to a committee of 15, to take evidence, etc., (another Kansas committee). On the test motion made by us to adjourn the motion was lost. This looks squally. I still fear, notwithstanding the strong message, that we shall be defeated."

To J. F. H. Claiborne.

"Washington, February 4th, 1858.

"MY DEAR CLAIBORNE,—Since the last session of Congress I have been much of an invalid, having carried home with me some of the National Hotel poison, which it took much time and medicine to eradicate. My inability during a great part of the summer to attend to business has left me but little time for friendly correspondence. I am now, however, quite well, and I trust will soon regain my usual vigor. I am pleased to receive your approval in my efforts to modify materially our neutrality laws; it is the only means of our acquiring slave territory in the South. The federal government will never lend its aid to that object. The present policy of the administration is, by making treaties and assuming the protection of the route of transit over the Isthmus, to uphold and maintain the petty chieftainisms that exist in Central America.

"While these exist, emigration thither can not go from the Southern States. The New York speculators will send their commercial agents and laborers there; and, under the protection of England, they and Jamaica negroes will soon become the prominent powers in the country, and will fix forever the policy of these countries in opposition to slavery. We must strip the federal government of its power to prevent private enterprises from attempts to extend our institutions, or we shall soon be surrounded by impassable barriers to our progress.

"Thayer's speech in the House, and other indications, show that the eye of the North is already directed to these points. Blair, in his speech on the Central America question, went a step farther, and proposed to make that country the receptacle of the free negroes of the

United States. At present I can scarcely hope to have the neutrality laws seriously modified; but I have succeeded in my purpose of forcing the subject on the attention of Congress, and, at the risk of failure, will attempt to bring it to a vote.

"February 6th.

"Having been interrupted before bringing this letter to a conclusion, I can now inform you that we have at last entered upon, in the House, the great question of the session. The President's Message on the Lecompton Constitution was taken up on Friday. Upon its introduction Mr. Stephens moved its reference to the Committee on Territories; Mr. Harris, the friend of Douglas, moved its reference to a select committee of fifteen, to inquire into election frauds, etc., with power to send for persons and papers. Some of our friends being absent, we were compelled to resort to dilatory proceedings to prevent a vote being taken on this amendment, and, as the Black Republicans obstinately refused to adjourn, the contest was carried on from Friday noon throughout the whole night to half past six this morning, when I succeeded in having passed a resolution to adjourn the whole subject over to Monday morning, and then take the question on Harris's amendment without debate.

"Thus it stands. The manner in which the subject was treated on its first introduction, which you will see in the papers, shows the intense interest taken in this question. I can not but think the passage of the Lecompton Constitution extremely doubtful. There are two powerful opposing influences at work: Northern public sentiment on one side, and administration influence on the other. Were it not for the latter, my opinion is we would not get half a dozen Northern votes. Should it be rejected, what will the South do?"

To Gen. W. W. W. Wood.

"Washington, April 3d, 1858.

"DEAR GENERAL,—I am happy to acknowledge the receipt of a line from you. I receive the Free Trader very irregularly, and have not seen any notice taken of my Volunteer Bill. There was quite an opposition to it, backed up by the influence of the secretary of war.

Good sense, however, has prevailed over prejudice, and even the Senate have adopted the principle of my bill, by sending it back to the House with amendments which do not affect the principle. One of these amendments, however, is, to cut off two of the proposed regiments, and thus restrict the President to three. According to the bill not less than a regiment can be received from any state. This provision was required by the necessity of expedition and the simplicity of organization. . Companies from two or three states may unite and form a regiment, however, and then report themselves. This I recommend to our friends in Natchez. They must act promptly, because if I yield to the amendment of the Senate the bill will become a law next week. It will be useless if delayed longer. I need not say to you that I will always be happy to serve my young friend Captain Wood.

"The Kansas Bill is lost in the House. Crittenden's substitute was passed by a majority of eight.

"You will perceive that, to put the state-rights men of the South on proper ground, I proposed the Senate Bill without the humiliating compromise provision which the Southern senators had allowed to go in, to smooth the way for fishy Northern Democrats. I am sick of compromises, and will not bend an inch to dodge the naked question."

The various distracting issues growing out of the organization of Kansas consumed most of the last session that Quitman sat in the House. Toward the last of April a compromise, called the English-Kansas Bill, was reported, and the Southern Democracy resolved to support it. There were two non-contents, however—Bonham, of South Carolina, a man of noble attributes, and Quitman.

April 30th, 1858. Mr. Millson, of Virginia, strongly advocating the passage of the bill, thus referred to Gen. Quitman:

"While gentlemen on the other side of the House complain of this bill, there are objections to it also on this side. The distinguished gentleman from Mississippi has objected to it. He has not indicated the character of those objections, but I know him too well not to understand that they are perfectly consistent with his devotedness to state rights and to the principles of the Democratic party."

Quitman desired Mr. Millson to yield the floor for a moment. He did so with pleasure, and the members, says Mr. Hooker, in his eloquent address before the Mississippi Legislature, "crowded around the venerable man to catch the last words of wisdom that fell from his lips. His form was already bowed, and his manly features marked with the fatal malady which was so soon to remove him from our midst." It was a painful moment, for he felt that he was about to separate from the Southern members in whose patriotism he confided, and especially from colleagues who were in daily consultation with him, and to whom he was fondly attached. But his opinions against compromises had long been fixed. And now he was not only willing to be a martyr to his faith, but he was one of the few who were willing to hazard every thing for an abstract truth or principle. Too feeble to speak at large, as he desired, he only said:

"I construe the bill reported by the committee of conference as an express submission of the question of the admission of Kansas under the Lecompton Constitution back to the people of Kansas, and thus virtually referring to them the adoption or rejection of the Constitution, the more objectionable because that reference is not made to the *quasi* sovereignty which acted upon that instrument originally, nor to the people acting under an organized government, but to a disorganized mass of voters who can not speak for the sovereignty of a state.

"I oppose the measure, in the second place, because it is a concession upon this question which I, as a Southern man, am not prepared to make. I regard this contest as a mere incident to the slavery question. I am desirous

of seeing this great issue between the North and South
brought to a fair, honest, and final settlement, which shall
forever recognize the full constitutional equality of the
slaveholding states. If we can come to terms, no man
in the House will rejoice more than I. If we can not,
let us separate. These are the main reasons why I oppose this bill.

"I will answer the other question propounded by the
gentleman, that I look upon the act of the people of Kansas as complete—as an act of *quasi* sovereignty, with the
consent of the United States, in the formation of a Constitution. I regard that act as complete and binding upon
the people of Kansas, and as the only voice that we have
received here in regard to their will. I have opposed
the reference of the whole question back to the people
of Kansas, or even to any political power in Kansas; and
I oppose it now the more because it is simply a reference
back to the individual men who may be entitled to vote
at the time this vote is to be taken. These are, in short,
some of the reasons why, with all respect for the opinions
of my political friends, I can not support this bill. I will
not take any more of the gentleman's time by saying
more."

" *Mr. Millson.* The House will now, I trust, perceive
the application of the views I was endeavoring to present at the time the gentleman from Mississippi asked
me to yield to him. The gentleman says he regards the
act as complete, and Kansas entitled to admission.
Would he yield to her demand for admission upon the
terms proposed by her, claiming twenty-five or thirty
million acres of the public land?"

" *Mr. Quitman.* I ask the gentleman to allow me to
say that I have never regarded these propositions, in respect to land grants, as forming any of the conditions on
which a state is admitted into the Union. I wish to
make this single other remark: that Congress either has
or has not the right to restrict the entire rights of a
state. If she does restrict them, then they are not binding upon the state, because she can only admit the state
upon one condition or the other."

The bill was subsequently passed, Quitman and Bonham being the only Southern Democrats who voted against it. He deeply felt the responsibility he had incurred, but, believing that the South should act and no longer deliberate, he never hesitated a moment. He was influenced by the same sentiments he had thus forcibly expressed, in 1850, in a letter to a friend:

"The South, anticipating, from the movements of the last two years, that they would be assailed through the Wilmot Proviso and kindred measures, prepared to meet the attack. Our noble state first led off, and dauntlessly took the right of the line, and soon, following her example, nearly the whole South was in battle array, firmly resolved to meet the shock. The North recoiled at her attitude, and proposed terms of adjustment. A Southern-born President, however, was found to advise the enemy to amuse us with proposals, while he pointed out to them how our position could be turned, and all the advantages of victory be secured for them without the risk of battle.

"The Southern ranks were thus broken, and before we can re-form to meet this new and insidious attack, we shall have lost all we proposed to contend for. I am convinced that the North will continue to press us to the extreme point of endurance. The equilibrium between the sections is now destroyed and forever. The free states will have the control of the government, and what is to restrain them? Forbearance and pity, or a sense of justice and fraternity? It is weakness to expect it. Such considerations never yet restrained the exercise of power. There is one thing that may restrain them for a time: the fear of losing us. Soon, however, confidence in themselves will grow, respect for us will be lost, and it will be regarded as a right and a duty—ay, a moral and religious duty—to regulate our institutions, and coerce us into submission. Even now, perhaps, nine tenths of the Northern people firmly believe that slavery is a social, moral, and political evil. A majority believe it to be a wrong and a sin, for which, in their consciences, they are individually responsible. Their sense of duty to God requires them to spare no exertion to remove this evil. To the extent that they can constitutionally act, they deem themselves responsible for the continuance of slavery, and, when the Constitution fails them, they appeal to 'the higher law.' Suppose, then—and we can not suppose any thing else—that they only bring to bear the means which they, under the loose construction of the Constitution now so common, claim that they possess, to restrain, depress, lessen, and remove this 'evil' and 'sin,' will not the Union become for us a curse instead of a blessing?

"But will they stop with the effort to exert constitutional power? Will they not find somewhere else the power they desire to exercise? They will soon have the executive branch of the government; they will have the majority in Congress; they will get the judiciary. What, then, is to be our fate? You say *compromise*. But can we compromise a question of conscience? Can we halve a moral duty? The commandments of the moral law are not discretionary, but imperative: 'Thou *shall*,' or 'thou *shall not*.'"

These were prophetic words, and events that have followed in an unbroken march show how accurately he had fathomed the future. In 1835, Mr. Webster, in a speech in New York intended to recommend himself in advance of Mr. Clay for the presidency, declared opposition to slavery "a religious sentiment which could not be disregarded." This was, substantially, the first avowal of the "irrepressible conflict," now elaborated by a more sagacious and resolute man than Webster. A large majority of the people of the free states entertain a religious and conscientious scruple against slavery. Their theory of our government supplies a plea for their interference with the subject, and while this theory prevails they will continue to interfere. They hold, very generally, that the federal Constitution or league emanated from the *people*, as one consolidated community; while, at the South, we insist that the Constitution and Union originated with the several *states*, as separate, independent political sovereignties. If it be granted that each man in this country had a separate and direct agency in establishing the Union, then, they contend, it is a logical inference that the citizens of each state are, to a certain extent, responsible for the institutions of the others, and thus they justify the intervention of Congress. These views make them responsible in their consciences for the extension, if not for the toleration of slavery. The few at the North who adopt the Southern view of the federal Union find, in the reservations and guaranties of the Constitution, sufficient answer to their scruples, but under the pervading theory taught by Webster, Kent, and Story, opposition to slavery is a logical result. It is absurd, then, to consider anti-slavery sentiment as a temporary distemper, to be cured by temporary remedies and expedients. Its foundations are deeply laid in the vitals of our system, and a political organization has sprung up from it that now flings its menacing shadow over the republic.* It has steadily grown

* Mr. Doolittle, United States senator from Wisconsin, in a recent speech distinctly intimated that the Wide-Awakes might be required to install Mr. Lincoln into the presidency by force of arms.

The Tribune, of the 27th of September, speaking of a trifling broil that occurred at or near Cranston's New York Hotel between two young New Yorkers and a party of Wide-Awakes, used the following significant language, and that, too, after the proprietor of the hotel had, in a card, expressly denied that any guest or employé of his hotel was implicated in the matter:

"The Wide-Awakes are a very thoroughly organized body of young men filled with the vigor and the excitability of youth. Is it from the moment of its birth until now—with none of the infirmity of precocious growth about it, but solid as it is colossal: it defies all parties at the North, and chäl-lenges the South to a trial of strength. As late as 1855 it had no organization. In 1856, when the first Black Republican Convention assembled, it was more a matter of ridicule than apprehension. Now its dark banners float in triumph over half the states. Shall we shut our eyes longer to its progress, and to the dangers that threaten us?

New England, formerly so conservative, and with whom we have ever had the closest social and commer-cial relations, is now under the dominion of a majority avowedly hostile to slavery in the territories and in the states, resolved never to cease the conflict until the " na-tion" be purged of this " deadly sin." Only two years ago Governor Banks disclaimed, for the Black Republi-cans of that commonwealth, the incendiary doctrines of Garrison, and now we find that party nominating for

quite a prudent thing to risk a collision with such a body? Is it not possible that some much more serious result may happen both to Mr. Cranston's house and Mr. Cranston's guests than occurred on Tuesday evening, should such a demonstration be repeated? As a matter of caution, we suggest that any public expression of the anti-Republican-ism of the establishment had better not be permitted to get outside öf it, except by way of the chimneys. It goes off there as harmless as the smoke, hurts nobody, and nobody complains. But, unless Mr. Cranston is disposed to see an influx of company in a guise and with a purpose which would make any tavern-keeping soul to tremble, we advise him, for peace' sake, either to turn out of doors or keep quiet the infatuated fools, both men and women, who endeavored to stir up a riot there on Tuesday evening."

No man who witnessed the grand Wide-Awake demonstration in the city of New York on the evening of the 3d of October, composed of 20,000 young men, in uniform and under military drill, can doubt the great political influence this organization will hereafter exert. The first club was instituted at *Hartford* (there is an evil omen in the name) only a few months since, and now they number near half a million of members—intelligent, active, resolute men, full of enthusi-asm, who know how to advance, without calculating where they are to stop!

governor a candidate who broadly and distinctly indorses and approves those very doctrines—the extinction of slavery by the power of the federal government, the social and political equality of the negro, and
the moral propriety of insurrection, and, of course, murder! That ancient and venerable commonwealth, with
all her glorious antecedents, her learning, and her refinement, is ruled on "higher law" or "mob principles;"
and, but for the excitement of the slavery question, which
arms her fanatics against sister states, would, in all probability, be convulsed by some social problem between
capital and labor. With the proud memorials of the
Revolution looking down upon her shame, she refused
burial to a gallant son, of heroic lineage, who fell at
Buena Vista,* but rendered funeral honors to the murderer John Brown and his incendiary crew. She heaps
indignities upon the statue of Webster, her most illustrious orator; turns her back on Everett, her most illustrious scholar, to lay her trophies and her homage at the
feet of Sumner and Wilson. She makes pigmies of her
great men and giants of her pigmies, converts her pulpits into rostrums, and tramples on the laws of the country to deify a fugitive slave. A voice from Faneuil Hall
once animated our whole country; but now the merchant princes of Boston tremble at the ruffian howl in
its consecrated precincts, and purchase a temporary
truce by heavy contributions to outlawry and brigandage. To divert the socialists and infidels from their
own palaces, they are forced to encourage the anti-slavery movement, forgetting that, when the knife of fanati-

* The major general of the Boston militia refused to order a military reception, when the body of Captain Lincoln, adjutant general
of the army, was brought there, on the ground that he fell in a war
for the extension of slavery. Lincoln was the son of a governor of
Massachusetts, a sterling patriot, and grandson of Gen. Lincoln, of
the army of the Revolution.

cism leaves its sheath, it soon ceases to discriminate between its victims. What cares the political or religious monomaniac for constitutional restraints or the rights of property?

The Black Republicans of New York, and of other states, disclaim—and doubtless honestly disclaim—the intention or the power to interfere with slavery within the states. But can they stand up against Garrisonism any longer than the Republicans of Massachusetts? Is the pressure upon them less strong? Are they capable of greater resistance? On the contrary, greater influences are operating upon New York than were ever brought to bear on New England. The ablest man in the free states, who forms and controls public opinion more imperatively than any man now living in any country, has dedicated himself to this crusade, and his march, wherever he goes, is the march of a conqueror. His doctrines, stripped of their plumage, are to the last degree revolutionary and incendiary. Not Danton, or St. Just, or any of the Jacobins of Paris ever preached doctrines more pregnant with deplorable results than the doctrines recently announced by William II. Seward, senator from New York, and which have been applauded and endorsed by enthusiastic multitudes. The New York Tribune and Evening Post—making an aggregate of enormous circulation, conducted by men of high social position and distinguished talent, exerting prodigious influence over public opinion, or rather creating and directing it in all the free states—disclaim the intention or the disposition to employ the agency of the government, or any other agency, to abolish slavery in the states. They are only opposed to its extension, without which, in their opinion, it will dwindle and die. There is little difference between the opinion thus expressed by these powerful journals, and the opinion entertained by nine tenths of what are called the " conservative" voters in the free states. Northern conservatism, as contradistinguished from abolitionism, "hath this extent, no more." The latter would expel slavery, wherever it be found, by compulsory laws, or by fire and sword if necessary. The former would merely confine it where it is, exclude it from all territories, in whatever latitude, hereafter acquired by the common blood and treasure, and thus slowly but surely accomplish its destruction. Both aim at the same end. One wing is represented by Garrison, Andrews, and Gerritt Smith, the other by the Republican press. The latter would accomplish, by obtaining the control of the government, and by the forms of law, what the former would do by poison, the knife, and the firebrand. When Mr. Seward recommends that the army and navy be dispensed with, is it with the hope that John Brownism will then have a fair field? Mr. Greeley anticipates the election of a Black Republican President, and, in due time, a party majority in both branches of Congress; then the multiplication of the federal judicial districts, the appointment of Black Republican judges, and the rescinding of the Dred Scott decision.

This grand result may be accomplished by the forms of law, but it would strike a deadly blow at an institution recognized by the Constitution, and by the rightful interpreter of the Constitution. It would destroy the independence of the judiciary, and be, in all its consequences, revolutionary and demoralizing.

There is in New York, and elsewhere at the North, a truly conservative element, reposing on the traditions of the past, exulting over our national prosperity, condemning agitation, and anxious for fellowship and union. It comprises most of the commercial interest, necessarily in close communion with the South; the manufacturers, who find there their best customers; the capitalists, who dread the agrarian feeling visible now in communities overcharged with adventurers from the clubs of Europe;* and the educated classes, for the most part, who have studied the history of their country, and appreciate the value and grandeur of its future. But all these rather waive than discuss the issue. They are opposed to agitation; they condemn the anti-slavery organization; they love the South; they love their whole country; but, when thrown into the political arena, not one in a thousand will or can conscientiously defend slavery on its merits, or on the true constitutional ground. They almost to a man treat our claim to equal rights in the Territories as an absurdity or an abstraction. To defend our claim would be fatal to any political man in the free states. Patriotic and loyal as many unquestionably are upon a great constitutional claim held by the South as sacred and indispensable, they can not, in their consciences, act with us. How long, then, can they main-

* One of these, Carl Schurz, a celebrated Black Republican orator, recently addressed an audience at Springfield, Massachusetts, as follows:

"There is your Declaration of Independence, a diplomatic dodge, adopted merely for the purpose of excusing the rebellious colonies in the eyes of civilized mankind. There is your Declaration of Independence, no longer the sacred code of the rights of man, but a hypocritical piece of special pleading, drawn up by a batch of artful pettifoggers, who, when speaking of the rights of man, meant but the privileges of a set of aristocratic slaveholders, but styled it ' the rights of man' in order to throw dust into the eyes of the world, and to inveigle noble-hearted fools into lending them aid and assistance. There are your boasted Revolutionary sires, no longer heroes and sages, but accomplished humbuggers and hypocrites, who said one thing and meant another; who passed counterfeit sentiments as genuine, and obtained arms and money, and assistance and sympathy, on false pretenses. There is your great American Revolution, no longer the great champion of universal principles, but a mean Yankee trick—a wooden nutmeg—the most impudent imposition ever practiced upon the whole world."

How utterly faithless to the traditions of our country, and to the fellowship of the Union, must be the people who listen to and applaud such language as this!

tain their present relations with us or with our adversaries? One by one the stanchest of them must give way, or be trampled down by the overwhelming masses of Black Republicans, whose ranks are rapidly swelled by immigration and the popular clamor for gratuitous distribution of the public lands—a cry that appeals directly to the pauperism of the Old World, and arrays it against the property and established usages and institutions of our country!

With the strongest appreciation of the patriotism of great masses in the free states—paying my willing homage to the talent, scholarship, and conscientiousness of many that oppose us—finding it most difficult to reconcile their personal virtues with their disorganizing doctrines, I can take no more encouraging view of the condition of things. To be conservative, loyal, or even moderate, in New York, is to occupy a post that promises neither honor nor reward. Pressed by numbers constantly accumulating, by the temptations of ambition and the contagion of majorities, and of an irresistible enthusiasm, the friends of to-day will become our opponents to-morrow. Clouds and darkness rest upon the future. Religious feeling operating on a puritan community— the equality of races and universal emancipation reviving the revolutionary cries of Europe in the minds of tumultuous and uneducated masses—licentious notions of liberty and the hope of plunder in the wreck of established institutions, these are fearful elements fermenting and underlying the social fabric. The same wild influences will, sooner or later, clamor against the unequal distribution of property, and the proprieties and barriers that separate the many from the few. In a word, from a government of restraints, of checks and balances, of judicious discriminations and reservations, we are rapidly drifting toward a government purely radical, popular, and Jacobinical, the end of which must be anarchy or despotism.

The South never has "calculated," and never will "calculate," the value of the Union. Without a trace of mercenary feeling in her nature, without counting its advantages or disadvantages, she clings to it with filial affection as a thing to be reverenced, and too sacred for traffic or speculation. We are well aware that, by enormous concessions of territory, and by acquiescing in a system of unequal taxation, we have contributed a large excess over our quota to the common stock; but we find our compensation in the development and prosperity of our common country. Whatever concerns it, or any part of it, interests us, and we have ever been willing to make any sacrifice short of a constitutional right. With this sentiment for the country and for the Union deeply rooted in the South, we contemplate a dissolution as men contemplate the extinction of their long-cherished and fondest hopes. But we have no misgivings as to our future. Our tranquillity would scarcely be disturbed. The state governments would quietly perform their functions, and in sixty days a new federation would be formed. We may be called secessionists, but may we not, in the event of a separation, claim to be *the* government *de jure?* We stand inside of and upon the Constitution, and only separate to maintain the guaranties of that sacred instrument. What should we have to fear? What army or navy would act against us? Where would the money come from to reduce us to subjection? Our physical power and military spirit are known to the world. "War," said Gen. Greene, in his Southern campaign, "war in the South is a very different thing from war at the North." The feeble colony of South Carolina exhausted the well-organized and powerful army of England, and her swamps and forests proved more formidable than British garrisons and forts. It is folly to talk of coercing the South. We laugh at such a threat, as we laugh at the mean and dastardly idea that our slaves would join our assailants. Why did they not join the British in the war of the Revolution and of 1812? On the contrary, in every crisis they have manifested their fidelity, and would fight, if necessary, by the side of their masters, for homesteads dear to them as to the whites, and which they rarely desert but when deluded by some scoundrel of lighter complexion. They constitute for us a material element of strength in war, and the means of subsistence for our armies in the field.

With respect to foreign powers, our productions will always secure for us their good-will. The South had little cause to quarrel with England for any local grievance in either the war of independence or the war of 1812. *We* might have lived unmolested under British dominion. But we took up arms for our Northern brethren, whose commerce was tampered with, and whose seamen were impressed. British negromania, which our Northern friends count on, has run its career. The practical lesson of the West Indies, once the most prosperous, now the most unprofitable part of her broad domain, has brought England to her senses. Our cotton crop is indispensable to her, and cotton can not be produced without slave labor, and *compulsory* slave labor. Algeria, India, Africa, as rivals of the South in the production of cotton, are humbugs. Production is regulated by laws more immutable and controlling than fanaticism. The laws of trade are omnipotent in England. We watch her harvest-weather, and she notes our sunshine and our showers. She buys our crops; we purchase her manufactures. The South-has similar relations with France. Our free-trade doctrines welcome her beautiful fabrics and her delicious wines. Our plantation necessities demand the manufactures of these great nations. They will take in return, *in their own shipping*, our cotton, sugar, tobacco, bread-stuffs, lumber, and naval-stores. We have neither manufactories nor shipping, but are purely agricultural, with free trade for our allies, and non-intercourse and prohibitory duties for our enemies. With such relations as these, is it likely that England or France will quarrel with the South about the institution of slavery?

When we are forced, in self-defense, to separate from the fanatic states; when our harbors are crowded, not with bottoms from Boston and New York, but with foreign shipping, and our warehouses are packed, not with the manufactures of Lowell and Newark, but of Manchester and Lyons; then, and not till then, will our Northern brethren perceive, in its whole extent, the folly of their course. The fall of real estate in their cities, the silence of their spindles, the stagnation of their commerce, the obstructions to their enterprise, will teach them how insane it was to intermeddle with a great interest antecedent to the Union, guaranteed by the Constitution, auxiliary to their prosperity, indispensable to ours, and the greatest consolidated element of national wealth.

When they ask us to surrender slavery, and its natural extension in territories adapted to its growth, they ask in the spirit of a footpad who demands your purse with a pistol at your breast. When they interfere with it by the law-making power, they exercise a function that finds no warrant in the Constitution. When they attempt, as they have attempted, to arm our slaves against us, and instigate a peaceful and contented people to the commission of crimes, *they* sever the bonds of Union, and drive us to seek shelter and safety under a separate and distinct government. We separated from England

for the mere assertion of a right which she was willing
to qualify or surrender, and which had never occasioned
any actual evil. When we leave the present Union, we
shall leave it to preserve our property from spoliation,
our homesteads from rapine and murder. We shall
stand justified in our own conscience and before mankind; justified as every people stand justified in history,
who, having patiently endured injustice for the sake of
peace, finally draw the sword for the sake of independence. We shall quit the Union, be that day of sorrow
early or late, as loyal to its covenants as when first our
fathers formed it, loving and regretting it to the last;
glorying in its early traditions and mourning its sudden
fall; ever mindful of the patriot friends at the North
who have co-operated with us to maintain it, and reserving for them the places of honor around our altars and
firesides; but with the resolution, inflexible as destiny,
to defend our rights in their whole extent, or perish
with them!

The election of a Black Republican President, under
the formalities of law, does not necessarily involve a dissolution of the Union, but it will be conclusive as to
the existence of a public sentiment that will abolish slavery if the present Union be continued. The election of
such a candidate now, or ten years hence, is only a question of time. In its practical teaching it is the same thing.
Political parties of fifty years' growth are powerless, and
now enjoy only a temporary and precarious lease by the
compulsory fusion of antagonistical materials; a compact
based on no common creed, no mutual concession of principle, but a mere bargain of individuals for office, dictated by inexorable necessity. On the other hand, opposition to slavery is a consolidated power, moving in one
direction, by one impulse, its whole strength concentrated upon a single object. But yesterday a "still, small

voice" whispering in tabernacles, to-day shaking the Alleghanies with its thunder, and sweeping like a hurricane from the Atlantic to the Missouri. Small rivers, thus directed, cut their way through mountains of granite. Parchment restraints and judicial interpretation oppose but feeble barriers to the force of numbers, composed of new elements and nationalities, and utterly indifferent to the traditions of *our* ancestors. The Puritan and the Jacobin are in fearful propinquity. Excited multitudes are not to be restrained even by their leaders, who, having tasted power, are apt to become conservative. Danton and his comrades were butchers of mankind, but butchers more sanguinary still demanded *their* blood. The great party that now demands the non-extension of slavery and the repeal of the Fugitive Slave Law will, in the next decade, demand universal emancipation! *This* is the danger we have to look in the face—not merely the election of a chief magistrate pledged to exclude slavery from the Territories, and to annul the decisions of the constitutional tribunal, but the next great act in the drama—the abolition of slavery itself! This is already down in the programme. Mr. Seward has foreshadowed it in all his recent speeches, and the deed will be accomplished if this Union be maintained. The weight of numbers, if not against us now, soon will be, if anti-slavery progress for the last five years be reliable data for calculating its future. Even now, when its preponderance is not firmly established, it proposes no compromise—if we could make any more compromises with safety or honor—but proclaims its purpose, and pledges itself never to recede. Our decision must be made, and made speedily, and there is no halfway ground to stand upon. Surrender or resist are the only alternatives of the South—*surrender* to an exacting party who advocate the debasing equality of races, and are deeply infected with the demoralizing theories of socialism, or *resistance* as remorseless and inflexible as the fanaticism arfayed against us.

Disunionism never flourished in the South. It is not the atmosphere for revolutions. The nature and occupation of our people demand stability, not change. Sedentary and agricultural, we cherish the homesteads and laws of our ancestors, and live among the reminiscences of the past. We claim only what we believe to be, and what the Supreme Court has decided to be, our right under the Constitution. It is sneered at as an abstraction; but all fundamental principles are abstractions, and this abstraction, in our view, and in the opinion of our opponents, is the one upon which the superstructure of slavery stands. We assert no claim to interfere with the concerns of other states. Reverence for the republic, a filial love of its flag, its progress and expansion, is the prevailing feeling of the South. We would take up arms to defend a disputed boundary in Maine or in Oregon, or the right of fishery on the banks of Newfoundland.* But if we can enjoy no repose in the Union, if one half of the Northern people advocate the curtailment of our rights with the hope of seeing our most valued resource perish, and the other half menace us with violence, we must of necessity retire from it. A brave people, with great resources for empire and independ-

* John Adams, in his private journal of the negotiations for peace with the British commissioners at Paris, has this entry: "Nov. 29, 1782. When we were upon the fishery question, the commissioners urged us to leave out the word '*right*,' and substitute the word 'liberty.' I told them I could never sign a treaty with such a qualification. Mr. Laurens (of South Carolina) upon this said, with great firmness, that he would never give his voice for any articles without this, etc."

When the controversy about the northeastern boundary occurred, the whole South stood up for the rights of Maine. In 1840, "Cass, Cuba, and Canada," were the watchwords of the Democracy of the South.

ence, impregnable to invasion, and inspired by a universal sense of the moderation of their course and the justice of their cause, will know how to act when the surrender of their rights is the price of submission.

No matter how the withdrawal of the Southern States be accomplished, whether peacefully or by violence, it will be the saddest exodus on record, and for centuries will wail along the pages of history like a funeral dirge. Other great nations have grown old and corrupt, decayed and died. But ours, yet in its youth and freshness, will perish like a gallant ship, complete in all her appointments, driven recklessly upon the rocks, her crew wandering for years upon the desert strand, to return at last, perhaps, and gather up the fragments of the wreck as their only means of escape. May the God of our fathers, who visibly guided them in their glorious efforts for independence, teach us, of all sections and all parties, moderation, and interpose his merciful providence to save the republic!

Our love of country amounts to enthusiasm. "Blood is thicker than water." Bonds of iron—yes, stronger than iron—unite us with our brethren. But all these, and more than these, will break when a free and proud people see their state sovereignty insulted, their constitutional rights denied, and their sanctuaries threatened by deluded masses.

Gen. Quitman was no disunionist. There was never a moment, from his first manhood to the hour of his death, that he would not have accepted the part of Decius to save the republic. Every dream of personal ambition was associated with its duration, grandeur, and expansion. He fought in Mexico not so much to win laurels for himself as glory for his country. He desired to see Mexico and Cuba under our dominion. He was equally anxious for the annexation of Canada, uninfluenced by

jealousy of the North. He regarded whatever concerned the power and prosperity of the country not as a
slaveholder, but as an American, confident of our ability,
under a proper administration of the Constitution, to control this whole continent as independent and sovereign
united states. But, with this deep and confirmed loyalty to the Union, he had long satisfied himself that the
Southern States could not remain in the Union and
preserve their domestic institutions and constitutional
rights. He saw a gulf between the North and the South,
spanned by a narrow bridge, built upon the single arch
of *expediency*, and when this arch breaks down the separation will be inevitable. Every year, as the non-slaveholding states grow in power, it becomes less necessary
to temporize with the South; the arch is weakened, and
the fathomless abyss of the untried future lies beneath.
With these convictions he opposed compromises, and
voted against the English-Kansas Bill. When he gave
this vote, he voted, substantially, for a direct issue, and
no more compromises. He had no wish to postpone the
question for posterity. The bill passed the House by a
majority of nine. It was reluctantly accepted and voted
for by the Southern Democrats (all except Quitman and
Bonham, of South Carolina), as the only practicable and
peaceable solution of a perplexing and threatening question. The whole country felt relieved, and patriotic citizens from all quarters hastened to congratulate the President of the United States. That eminent person, distinguished alike for his personal virtues and truly conservative principles—the last of a line of illustrious statesmen—shared the general satisfaction. But what have
we gained? Where is the repose and security it promised? Like Pyrrhus, the South may exclaim, "One more
such victory as this, and I am vanquished." New demands—stronger popular demonstrations in the North

and West—hostile accessions of strength in both branches of Congress—the chair and the committees in the
hands of our opponents—a nomination for the presidency
formidable for its sectional power and national organization, and the enthusiasm concentrated in its support—
and, finally, the rupture of the Democratic party, the only
anchor capable of holding the drifting ship!   What have
we a right to expect?   What should we do?

These are questions we shall have to answer.   There
is no escape.   Quitman gave his answer when he recorded his vote against the English-Kansas compromise; and
his deepest regret when dying—the last political thought
that struggled for expression on his lips—was that he
could not live " to vindicate that vote."

CHAPTER XX.

Quitman visits South Carolina.—His Appreciation of that State.—
Reception in Columbia.—The Palmetto Association.—Contrast
between Quitman and Calhoun.—His last Letter from Washington.—Decline of his Health.—Journey home.—Last Letters.—
His last Words: "I wish to vindicate my Vote."—Dr. Cartwright's
Narrative of the closing Scene.—Review and Analysis of his Character.—Dr. Perry's funeral Discourse.

1858. In April Gen. Quitman accepted an invitation
to address the Palmetto Association (the survivors of
the famous Palmetto regiment) at their anniversary
meeting at the capital of South Carolina. The invitation touched his heart, and revived, for a time, his failing
energies. He was proud of the regiment. It was closely associated with his own career. He greatly admired
South Carolina, her educated and high-toned statesmen,
and their enlightened administration of state affairs. In
their great contest in 1832, when, single-handed, they
fought the battle of the South, and maintained the doctrines that Virginia, in her best days, had enunciated as
authoritative and binding on the federal government, he
stood almost alone in Mississippi, not only sympathizing
with, but sustaining them. He had adopted the opinions of Mr. Calhoun as to the theory of our government,
and on all the great questions of the time, except that,
fired with the thirst for military fame, and with more of
the old Roman appetite for conquest, he was for putting
on steam and giving full play to the energy of the republic. The more matured and experienced Carolinian
had entered life with similar views. He strongly advo-

cated the war of 1812. Intrusted by President Monroe with the department of war, he infused an energy into its operations till then unknown, and inaugurated systems and improvements so comprehensive and splendid as almost to transcend the constitutional restraints. Subsequently, for a brief space, secretary of state, he pressed the acquisition of Texas with an energy that paralyzed the diplomacy of England and France, and soon overcame what many considered insuperable difficulties. There was scarcely any obstacle his genius and enthusiasm would not have encountered to push forward the republic, until he became convinced that all these energies and acquisitions were to be employed against the rights and institutions of the South, and then he grew rigidly conservative. He collected his great faculties and concentrated them into a lens, the focus being the Constitution, and there, by that powerful light, the country saw the danger that threatened it. Ardent by nature—the blood running impetuously through his veins—full of grand ideas, fitted for a career of splendor, he became reserved, circumspect, an austere constructionist, a penurious legislator, a stickler against appropriations, opposed pre-emptions and encouragements to Western immigration, and voted against the war with Mexico! The explanation of this surprising change is that he foresaw increased danger to the institutions of the South. The influx of foreigners, and their immediate investment with the privileges of citizens, he regarded as an evil. Most of them come here the victims of oppression and bad government, and with exaggerated and impracticable notions of liberty; it is natural that they should respond to the claim for the largest liberty. Those that settle in the North and West, unacquainted with our domestic system, and deriving all their information from abolitionists, naturally fall into their ranks. In the South, where the institution speaks for itself, the immigrant population soon become slaveholders. But the proportion flowing North and West is as four to one, and the element may be set down as antagonistical to the South.

In 1850, Quitman, when organizing Mississippi for resistance, found sympathy and co-operation in South Carolina. She was ready to second any movement he might make. Under the ban for her single-handed but glorious struggle for nullification, "the rightful remedy," she had deemed it prudent, and for the benefit of the common cause, that some other sister state should take the initiative in the pending struggle for our institutions; but she was prepared for the contest, and, had it come to an issue, would have chosen Quitman as the common leader. In his whole career, civil and military, he had her confidence and respect. He had been toasted in South Carolina in 1851 as the first President of the Southern republic. At that period the Union party of nullification times had disappeared in South Carolina. The whole state was for resistance, but the leaders were divided as to the proper method. They were called "Co-operationists" and "Secessionists;" the latter being for the immediate secession of the state without waiting for the action of other states; the former deeming it prudent, if not indispensable, to have the co-operation of one or more states. With the Secessionists were all the then representatives in Congress (except Col. Orr), Governor Means, Ex-governor Seabrook, J. H. Adams, since governor, Colonel Maxy Gregg, R. Barnwell Rhett, and others. On the other side were Senators Barnwell and Butler, Colonel Orr, Langdon Cheves, C. G. Memminger, John L. Manning, James Chesnut, John S. Preston, A. G. Magrath, W. D. Porter, J. W. Hayne, James Simons, etc. Many of these gentlemen consulted Gen. Quitman. He, of course, took as little part as possible in the controversy, though, when he found that other states that had been relied on, as Mississippi and Georgia, for example, receded from their position, he believed that South Carolina should act alone, and thus precipitate an issue. The controversy was ultimately tested by a popular vote, and the Co-operationists happily carried the state by a large majority. The present union of the South places in a very striking light the wisdom of the course then adopted.

It was a proud day for the veteran when he reached Columbia in the afternoon of the 3d of May. The Capitol artillery announced the approach of the train. The whole population of the city, and thousands from the surrounding country, had collected at the depôt to see the war-worn statesman. He was received by a committee of the Palmetto Association, and their chairman, Capt. W. B. Stanley, himself a gallant soldier, thus addressed him:

" GENERAL QUITMAN,—After the lapse of many years we meet again, yourself the illustrious guest, and I the humble representative of the survivors of the Palmetto Regiment organized into the Palmetto Association.

" On behalf of that Association, I thank God for the privilege which now crowns them of extending to you the hand of a joyful welcome to the capital of their state, and of assuring you that you are received alike in the arms and hearts of her people.

" The language of truth can not be confounded with the language of adulation, nor can just panegyric be offensive either to modesty or taste.

" Let me, sir, then, with the frankness of the soldier, and as the organ of soldiers, declare to you that the presence of no living man could enkindle nobler sentiments or awaken prouder recollections in the minds of South Carolinians than your own.

" We hail you as our comrade in arms, and as our brave general, and although the terrible conflicts of the valley of Mexico belong to history, we still hail you as our brave and dauntless chieftain, whose voice rang loud amid the bloody clamors of musketry and artillery, stimulating the Palmettos in their struggle to plant the first standard of victory on the walls of the fallen capital of Mexico. South Carolina loves you in peace because you first loved her sons in war, ministering to them in sickness and privation, kind and cordial to them in their hours of repose, sharing their perils, and imparting to their bosoms the fiery courage of your own in the stormy hour of battle and blood.

"Our Butler, our Dickinson, and many other Palmettos, are curtained by the rayless night of death; with them the fierce battle of life is ended forever. Sir, their dust, mingling with the soil of their beloved state as it does, breaks forth with our living voices to-day in sweet but mournful acclamation of welcome to you.

"The brave, the beautiful, the aged, and the young, all hands, all voices, all hearts, join to make you welcome to the capital of South Carolina.

"Her emblematic eagle, twin sister of Mississippi's own proud bird, displays her wings to greet you, and her emblematic tree freshens in its foliage at your approach. Smiles and tears, prayers and flowery wreaths, all that the beauty, and chivalry, and hospitality of South Carolina's capital can present you with, I place upon your brow.

"Again I say, welcome, welcome, thrice welcome be the general of our pride, affection, and veneration."

The general replied to this generous welcome in brief and feeling terms. He was pale, emaciated, and feeble, and doubtless was then in the first stage of his last fatal illness. He was taken immediately to the residence of his friend, Col. A. J. Green.

On the 4th Gen. Quitman was escorted to College Hall by the volunteer battalion, including the fire companies of the city, the Arsenal Cadets, the Sons of Temperance, Palmetto and Congaree Lodges I. O. O. F., the members of the Eutaw Encampment, the Independent Fire Engine

Company,* the students, graduates, and faculty of the university, the state and municipal authorities, and the Palmetto Association in the rear, 68 in number, survivors of many a hard-fought field. Three banners, battle-riven, were borne in the procession—the flags of the Fairfield, Chester, and Newberry companies. These banners floated over the orator on the platform, and his companions in arms were clustered around him. When the general entered the spacious hall, filled with the beauty and talent of South Carolina, he was received with a feeling not to be expressed by mere acclamations; then, indeed, were "tears, smiles, and flowery wreaths" lavished upon him. The order of exercises was as follows:

"PRAYER by Rev. Dr. Thornwell.
"ODE: '*Welcome to the Chief*' (sung in full choir). [By W. Gilmore Simms]:

"Open your gates, gay city, with a clang
    Of martial gong and trumpet, and a fire,
Such as on plains of Churubusco rang
    When your own forward sons went forth in ire;
Give voices to your hearts, that, when he hears,
    His heart shall whisper, 'These are brethren all
Of those who follow'd me with bended spears,
    When Mexico was stooping to her fall;
When, at Chapultepec, we crush'd her powers,
And storm'd, through all her gates, our way to Aztec towers.'

"Oh! these are glorious memories, which are best
    Treasur'd when thus ye welcome home the brave;
Thus keep ye shrin'd, within each martial breast,
    The glory of the gallant sons ye gave;
So honor ye the children of your care,
    Who thus go forth in confidence and pride,

---

* This company bore on their standard a wreath of *immortelles* encircling a key of their engine-house which had been found on the person of one of its members slain in the battle of Churubusco.

This touching incident reminds me of poor Stanford, adjutant of Crittenden's battalion, shot at Havana. When leaving New Orleans, he carried with him his masonic apron; it had belonged to his father. The moment before his execution he requested that it might be sent to his only sister, the wife of Wm. L. Patterson, Esq., United States Consul, Genoa.

Secure that love shall ever deck the bier
  Of those who welcome battle as a bride;
Nor, in the mournful tribute o'er their graves,
 ·Forget the homage due that welcomes living braves."

" ADDRESS by General John A. Quitman.

" ODE [written for the occasion by H. H. Caldwell,
Esq.].   (Sung in full choir.)

" Sing in loud, triumphal numbers,
    Sing a grateful nation's lay !
Dead must be the heart that slumbers
    Throbless, on this solemn day.
Sing the men, whose stout hearts beating,
    Recked not of the deathful strife;
Hearing Honor's voice repeating,
    ' Is not duty more than life ?'

" Twine the cypress, twine the laurel
    'Round brave BUTLER's honor'd name;
While to coming times, the moral
    He has taught us, gilds his fame: ·
Nobly for his country dying,
    Shouts of victory filled his ears;
While that soul to Heaven was flying,
    Who may count its rapturous prayers?

" Think we of the brave who perish'd
    Far beneath that tropic sky;
In our heart of hearts be cherish'd
    Memories all too deep to die.
'Tis not all a dark affliction,
    This stern thought of those who died;
But the nation's benediction,
    And that weeping nation's pride !

" By this pride, the surest token,
    Know your amaranthine fame,
More than may by words be spoken,
    Still through ceaseless years the same:
Wreathed in many a bardic story,
    Sung to many a mountain lyre,
Live, forever live your glory,
    In one blaze of hallowed fire !"

The oration will be found in the Appendix.   The
"South Carolinian" closed its account of the proceedings of the day with the following words:

"Thus concluded one of the most enthusiastic demonstrations that we have ever witnessed.   Long will it be

remembered.   It conveys to General Quitman some idea of the appreciation South Carolina attaches to his conduct both in war and iu the council.   In war he proved himself true to the honor of his whole country, and in the council he has proven his devotion to the home of his adoption and choice.   If the array of beauty, the assembly of the talent and wisdom of the state, the popular enthusiasm, be taken as evidence, then surely he must see the position he occupies in South Carolina, and the remnant of the Palmetto regiment will perceive the pride their fellow-citizens feel in their deeds, when they join with such spirit in doing honor to him whom, in the language of Captain Stanley, they have welcomed as 'the general of their pride, affection, and veneration.'"

The "Guardian," after a vivid description of the ball and supper in honor of the general, says:

"The distinguished orator, soldier, and statesman, must have deeply felt that South Carolina loves, esteems, and honors him for his many virtues, his gallant deeds, and his devoted attachment and patriotism as a statesman to the honor, rights, interest, and independence of that section of the confederacy which he has selected as his home, and whose citizenship he so nobly wears.   He returns to-day to the duties of his post at Washington; and in bidding him adieu, we tender to him our best wishes for his safety, and a long life of usefulness to the South, and happiness and prosperity to himself."

General Quitman took leave of his friends in the following note:

"Columbia, May 6th, 1858.

"DEAR SIR,—I can not leave this beautiful city without presenting my grateful acknowledgments to yourself and your associates, for the hearty welcome with which I was greeted on my arrival, and for the unremitted and kind attentions which I have received, both from the committee and from all classes of your citizens, during my brief visit to the capital of South Carolina.

"I remain, with the highest respect, your friend and obedient servant,   (Signed),   J. A. QUITMAN.

"Capt. W. B. Stanley, Chairman of Committee."

On his return to Washington he found an invitation from Natchez to command a grand encampment of volunteers.

To William Cannon and others.

"Washington, May 30th, 1858.

"GENTLEMEN,—I had the honor to receive, several days since, your letter of the 19th inst., tendering to me, on behalf of the general committee of arrangements, the command of the proposed grand military encampment to be held at the Pharsalia race-course on the 1st, 2d, and 3d days of July next. When your communication reached my hands, there appeared to be some probability that the resolution of Congress to adjourn on the 7th proximo would be rescinded, leaving it very uncertain whether I could consistently, with my duties here, accept the invitation. Now that there is a probability that Congress will adjourn on the day proposed, I am enabled to reply to your letter.

"I fully appreciate the high honor conferred upon me by your committee, and by the citizen soldiers, in designating me as the commander of the proposed encampment, and gratefully accept the honorable position assigned to me, dependent, however, upon the adjournment of Congress in time to enable me to reach home before the day proposed for the encampment. Should this uncertainty in any way conflict with your arrangements, I can but recommend that you select some other commander."

1858. This was his last letter from Washington. Immediately after the final adjournment, though ill able to travel, and too feeble to move without assistance, he set out to fulfill his engagement with the Mississippi Volunteers. During a great part of the journey in the cars he slept, supported by his friend, Mr. Wright, a representative from Tennessee, and by other members of the House. At Memphis he embarked in the J. C. Swan, and reached Natchez early on the morning of the 21st, and proceeded at once to his residence in the vicinity. From the moment of his arrival his family lost heart. He was a mere shadow, and evinced a constant inclination to sleep. Yet even in this condition his habits of exactitude and of duty prevailed over exhausted nature. With his own hand he wrote the following letters—the last lines he ever traced, and probably the last connected thoughts he ever expressed:

General Quitman to General W. W. W. Wood.

"Monmouth, June 30th, 1858.

"My dear Sir,—Please to read the inclosed letter, preserve a copy of it, and hand it to its destination. Entire silence on the subject of my not taking active command will injure me. I am quite unwell, constant fevers, and, since I saw you, I have not been out of bed for more than an hour at a time.

"When you have leisure I will be happy to see you."

From General Quitman to the members of the Executive Committee appointed to make arrangements for the Pharsalia Encampment.

"Monmouth, June 26th, 1858.

"Gentlemen,—At the time I accepted from Washington your very kind invitation to command the military encampment, I hoped my health would so improve as to enable me to perform its duties. I hoped especially that rest on my arrival home would soon entirely restore it. Anxious to comply with your wishes, and desirous myself of taking part in this laudable and public-spirited movement, I have continued to hope from day to day that my health would improve, but I find myself, on the contrary, prostrated by constant fever, and so weak as to be unable to sit up more than an hour at a time, leaving me no hope whatever of having health and strength sufficient, at the short day of the approaching military parade, to undergo the duties which the important position you have honored me with requires. I am, therefore, compelled, very reluctantly, at this late day to decline the high honor you have been disposed to confer on me.

"I am, gratefully and respectfully, your friend and fellow-citizen."

His friends now despaired.   He was attended day and night by his brother-in-law, Henry Turner, Esq., his former partner John T. M'Murran, Esq., his friend Josephus Hewitt, Esq., and other friends.   His able physician, Dr. Blackburn, desired a consultation, and Dr. Cartwright, of New Orleans, who had been long his friend and medical adviser, was telegraphed for.   The doctor's affecting letter relates the closing scene.

Dr. S. A. Cartwright to J. F. H. Claiborne.

"New Orleans, April 20th, 1860.

"MY DEAR SIR,—You inform me that you are writing a memoir of the illustrious Quitman, and, inasmuch as I 'knew him so well, had seen so much of him, and enjoyed his confidence,' you request me to send you my reminiscences of him; and also, as I was with him in his last moments, you ask me to depict, over my own signature, the sad scenes of his last hours, to close your volume. In regard to his last days on earth, as far as the great and good Quitman himself was concerned, I have no sad scenes to depict.   The universally-beloved citizen, patriot, and hero was spared the pains of death.   Neither bodily suffering nor mental anguish disturbed the happy quietude of the closing scenes of his eventful and useful life.

"You have no doubt observed how quickly soldiers or other persons on fatigue duty, involving protracted bodily and mental labor with loss of rest, fall into a wakeful, yet quiet and happy slumber at those intervals when duty does not demand their watchfulness and attention; a groan or a suppressed breath will awaken the watchful attendant on the sick, and the report of the sentry's gun, so distant as scarcely to be audible, will arouse the fatigued patriots of an army in danger from their slumbers to full consciousness in an instant, while loud talking, and noises ever so boisterous immediately around them, tend only to make them sleep the sounder. It was a similar disposition to sleep, and to sleep sweetly, yet easily aroused to perfect consciousness and mental activity by any thing in the shape of duty, which constituted the leading feature in the last illness of General Quitman.

"The attending physicians, alarmed at the somnolency arising from no apparent cause, and recognizing it as a dangerous, if not a fatal symptom, communicated their fears to his family. I was telegraphed to hasten to Monmouth. On my arrival, I ascertained that this somnolency had begun to creep upon him in Washington City about the time of the adjournment of Congress, and had been increasing ever since; that he had been more or less unwell all the session, but had, nevertheless, attended strictly to his duties, and, in fact, had not enjoyed his usual good health since he had suffered from the mysterious poisoning at the National Hotel. He thought he had slept all the way from Washington to Memphis in the cars. It was evidently not natural sleep, 'tired Nature's sweet restorer,' but a typhoid narcosis, the harbinger of exhausted vital power. His iron constitution, impaired by the poisoning at the National Hotel, had been overtaxed by the multiform labors his great soul, forgetful of self, imposed upon it in the service of his constituents, his family, his friends, and his country. After his return the somnolency continued, but his strong will shook it off for the time being whenever he had any thing he regarded as a duty to perform. At the marriage of his daughter, which took place soon after his return home, he received his friends in his usual happy, cordial, placid manner. When that event was over he took to his bed, complaining of some fullness about his forehead, and some pain and febrile symptoms for a few days, which subsided, leaving him, however, without any desire for food or drink of any kind; yet he did not seem to suffer from inanition, except that the prominent and alarming symptom, the drowsiness, continued to increase, and the power of his will to shake it off continued to diminish.

"When I arrived and spoke to him, he awoke, as if out of a tranquil sleep, and conversed for a few minutes, as if nothing was the matter. He had no fever, no pain, no thirst, no excitement of the pulse, and I was almost ready to announce to his family and friends that he was in no danger, when I fancied I saw an expression too sublime and blissful to be earthly play for an instant about his brow, and immediately his eyes closed, the muscles of his face relaxed, his jaw fell—he was asleep! My heart sunk within me when the inward voice of a long medical experience said, 'There is no hope; no mortal recovers after that unearthly expression; it is the *avant courier* of the immortal part to that "bourn from which no traveler returns."' Yet his natural expression was often so sublime and blissful, and so much akin to that seraphic radiance which occasionally lights up the countenance of the good man dying, as to leave some uncertainty in regard to its cause, and some grounds of hope that the world was not so soon to lose him.

"On feeling the surface, the temperature of his body was found to differ in no great degree from health; rather colder than natural, particularly the extremities; but this was readily accounted for from the empty, shrunken state of the cutaneous capillary vessels, so apt to occur in long abstinence from food and drink. But I was grieved to find that the skin itself had lost much of its vital tenacity. He had, as before said, no thirst, no appetite, no *wants*, and seemed perfectly happy when let alone. I induced him to take a little light nourishment by urging it upon him as a duty; no other consideration

VOL. II.—N

could induce him to touch it. It oppressed him, however, and made him feel uncomfortable until he threw it
up, as his stomach, like his skin, had lost much of its vital power, and could not digest it. He continued in
nearly the same state from Monday, the day of my arrival, until Friday, without much change, except that
the wakeful intervals grew shorter, and the sleep longer
and more profound. In his wakeful moments reason
was not clouded; I took means to ascertain this point,
and found him the veritable John A. Quitman I had
known so long, in possession, when roused from sleep,
of his vigorous mental faculties as in days of yore. On
Friday febrile reaction took place, as if Nature was making an effort to awaken the system from its long torpor.
But the absence of thirst, the relaxed state of the skin,
and the paralytic condition of the secretory organs
proved too clearly that it would be abortive. Until Saturday the respiratory muscles, called involuntary, had
continued to carry on respiration in the same quiet manner, both when asleep and awake, as in a healthy individual. The fever which set in the day before did not
seem to disturb them. But on Saturday, as the febrile
heat began to decline, they began to fail to perform their
functions, and the voluntary muscles came to their aid,
causing hard and laborious breathing, suggesting for the
first time the idea of physical suffering. The suffering,
however, was only apparent and not real suffering. He
was happy even then, and was unconscious how hard his
own powerful muscles were instinctively laboring to prolong life by keeping up the respiratory movements—unconscious also of the grief of his family and friends
around him, which could be restrained no longer, and
broke forth into open demonstrations. It would have
marred the happiness of his last hours to have heard
their groans, or to have seen their tears. In passing

through the death-struggle the typhoid narcosis, which
had caused him to fall into a state resembling sleep in
the cars from Washington to Memphis, began at length
to weigh so heavily on his senses as to obliterate all
sense of pain or fatigue in closing the journey of life.
When that journey was over, and the contracted muscles, which had been laboring to keep up respiration,
ceased to act and had time to relax, his features, temporarily distorted by their violent contraction, became placid again, and his naturally benignant expression resumed
its sway over his noble countenance, proving that he died
happily.

"It is said that some who witnessed the funeral ceremonies of Lord Nelson expressed a wish to die, if they
could be buried with all the pomp and pageantry of that
renowned personage, and have a monument to their
memories in St. Paul's. But who would not be willing
to die if he could die as happily as did the great and
good Quitman, leaving a monument to his memory in
the hearts of his countrymen of his own building, to
grow in beauty and freshness with revolving years, and
to last as long as liberty and republican institutions shall
endure on earth?

"As a citizen, a politician, and a soldier, General Quitman's life has only to be studied, his character imitated,
and his example followed in all those walks of life, by
the present and succeeding generations, to insure a career of usefulness, prosperity, and happiness to our young
men while living, and a better recompense hereafter than
a "niche in St. Paul's or Westminster Abbey."

General Quitman expired at half past 5 P.M., July 17th,
1858, aged fifty-nine. His death spread a pall over the
smiling city he had loved so much. Its citizens mourn-
ed as members of his household. He was buried with

masonic and military honors, and the silent grief of the young and old, the white and the colored people who crowded round his remains. He sleeps in a secluded spot on his own homestead, by his stricken children, the brothers of his youth, and his devoted wife, who soon followed him to the tomb.

The Legislature and the bar of Mississippi, and the Congress of the United States paid every honor to his memory. The masonic fraternity, with which he became connected at Delaware, Ohio, and whose highest distinctions he attained, remembered him with their most impressive ceremonies, in which, as though to show how much more permanent and beautiful are the ties of affection and brotherhood than the bitterness of party, his late opponent for Congress, a gifted and generous man, was the officiating functionary and chief mourner.

His life, as here recorded chiefly by himself, will enable every reader to make an analysis of his character. He was never a brilliant man. He was no rhetorician. His strength lay in his earnestness, his constancy, and integrity, and the boldness of his views. The portrait drawn by an old writer of Sir Nicholas Bacon, Lord Chancellor of England, is a life-like portrait of Quitman. "He was a plain man, direct and constant, without finesse or doubleness, and one that was of a mind that a man in his private proceedings, and in the proceedings of state, should rest on the soundness and strength of his own courses, and not upon practice to circumvent others."

He was well educated, and fond of classical reading, but he was one of those men who ask counsel less of times past than of time to come. He studied the future more than the lessons of antiquity, and the actual present more than either. He had little faith in preparations for posterity, which, like the wills of Thelusson and John M'Donough, usually end in shadows and disappointment,

if not in positive evil. He had no worship for the ideal;
liberty was in his eyes no goddess as she is painted by
the poets, but something practical; an inheritance, or
a boon won from tyrants by the sword, and secured by
charters and muniments. Of mere democracy, in its
true meaning, as it existed in Athens, and as seen sometimes in the United States—the rule of the mob, or of
some ambitious demagogue who ruled the mob—he had
an instinctive horror. His notion of freedom was freedom defined and regulated by law, and the rigid enforcement of law as applied to persons, property, and
government. That government is best where good laws
are best administered. Hence, in politics, he classed
himself not as a Whig, not as a Democrat, but a State-
rights man. His politics were based on the covenants
of the constitutional compact, and he acted with the
party that, in his view, adhered most closely to them.*
As Caius Marius thought it mockery to learn the Greek
tongue, the masters whereof lived in bondage under others, so he considered it a mockery to fraternize with
those who habitually surrendered principles for expediency. He shunned all such alliances, as the old Romans
walked aloof from that soil which was blasted with
lightning. Thus, for the greater part of his life, he was

---

* His early political life was regarded as vacillating, and was a
failure. It was not until he became the type and representative of a
great principle that he began to triumph. I find the following apt
illustration in "The Caxtons," by Bulwer.

"I will tell you," said Trevanion, "one secret of my public life—
that which explains its failure (for in spite of my position I have failed)—*I want conviction.*"

"Exactly," said Mr. Caxton, "because to every question there
are two sides, and you look at them both."

"You have said it," interposed Trevanion. "For public life a
man should be one-sided; he must act with a party; and a party in-
sists that the shield is silver, when, if it will take the trouble to look,
it will see that the reverse is gold. Woe to the statesman who makes
that discovery alone, while his party is still swearing the shield is
silver."

in the minority in politics. But he lived to see the very doctrines which had formerly drawn upon him defamation and defeat accepted with singular unanimity by his district and state, and by the whole South, as the sheet-anchor of the Constitution and the republic. A very unsuccessful man, but a close student of mankind, Sir Egerton Brydges, remarks that "if we overlook little frauds great robberies will follow, as a hound that draws the first drop of blood will never cease until he has drained the whole." This was exactly Quitman's theory as to the relations between majorities and minorities, the federal and state governments, and he was for executing the bond to the letter, considering all compromises as concessions of right, and therefore to be dreaded. · These concessions, he long ago foresaw, would engulf the states and bring us to our present condition, so aptly illustrated by Lord Commissioner Whitelock, in speaking of the civil war in England: "We scarcely know how, but from paper combats by declarations, remonstrances, protestations, votes, messages, answers, and replies, we must soon come to the question of raising forces and naming the general of an army."

With all his inflexibility and stickling for right, Quitman had no inclination for political controversy. He was extremely sensitive to attack, as scrupulous and ambitious men usually are, but he rarely retaliated on his assailant. When I urged him, in the last years of his life, to reply to a malignant misrepresentation of his conduct in relation to Cuba, he quoted the remark of Bently, in reply to Atterbury, whose passion for controversy was insatiable: "No man was ever written down but by himself."

His temper, though ardent, was much under his control. The working of his mind was laborious, but it seldom failed of accurate results. He expressed himself sometimes with difficulty; he often stammered and hesitated, and was given to repetition, but he never said a foolish thing. Good sense, broad philosophical views, theories strictly consistent, and deductions strictly logical, characterized his forensic efforts.

He has often been accused of making Mr. Calhoun his model, and of the ambition of wearing the mantle of that great man. This accusation, in all its parts, is wholly unjust. There was little resemblance between the two intellectually or politically. They resembled each other in simplicity and straightforwardness of character, in conscientiousness, energy of purpose, and capacity of resistance; but for bold, comprehensive, and correct views of statesmanship, for grand conceptions of American policy, for political consistency proof against the temptations of ambition, Quitman must take precedence of Calhoun. Notwithstanding the great and almost matchless abilities of the latter, and the personal enthusiasm he rarely failed to inspire, there never was a period during his whole career when the South was willing to confide itself to his guardianship. His antecedents had been remarkable for the wildest latitudinarianism of the Monroe administration, a period when, though there were really no parties, the Constitution and its restraints existed. And he only ceased to be a latitudinarian to become a conservative, opposed to those incidents of national progress as natural and indispensable to the growth of nations as the development of muscle to the growth of a child. When he constituted a part of Mr. Monroe's cabinet he was the fast man of his times, and fell into excesses tolerated by no honest rule of constitutional construction. He gradually shifted to the opposite extreme, and often permitted his apprehensions to control his judgment, converting every passing shadow into the Brocken of the Alps. He was too much of a croaker and

Cassandra in politics, and lacked the heroic elements for a national popularity. These Quitman possessed in an eminent degree. He had just lived long enough to have his principles fairly understood, and even those who differed with him confided in his unquailing courage and firmness. He was, personally, the most popular man in America at the period of his death; and for six years previous to his death, could the machinery of parties have been dispensed with, the popularity he brought from Mexico, and his grand ideas of American progress, would have carried him to the head of affairs.

As a lawyer he was proud of a profession which, in every age, has stood as a rampart between the people and oppression. He regarded a thorough knowledge of the common law as the foundation of eminence at the bar, and agreed with Lord Eldon, and the most celebrated of his successors, that it constituted the best qualification for a chancellor, and should be constantly studied while on the bench.

A more ambitious man never lived. He desired office for its power and distinction. He was greedy of military fame. His nature was essentially military; and he was fond of the pomp and clash of arms.* Had he gone to Cuba or to Mexico, both of which enterprises were un-

---

* *Gen. Quitman to Col. Samuel Cooper, Adjutant General U. S. A.*

"Monmouth, February 14th, 1853.

"MY DEAR SIR,—I had the honor to receive to-day, under your frank, the official Army Register for 1853. My association during the war with many officers of our gallant army gives me an interest in their official history. I therefore highly appreciate all public documents connected with the service, and am gratefully sensible of the favor you have conferred in sending me the Register. I have some pride in having been connected with the service, and will not, I am sure, lessen myself in the estimation of an officer of the army when I say that I prefer the address of 'general' to that of 'honorable.' I still have, I think, proper claim to the title. Although my lineal rank and command expired with my regular commission, I still hold a brevet commission, which, if it carries with it no honorary rank, confers at least the title."

der consideration, he would have administered just laws by the compulsion of the sword, the only government fit for an imbecile, ignorant, and factious people.

His courage amounted to indifference to danger; he was cool and self-possessed, without a particle of bravado—the sublime courage which soldiers evince when standing firmly at a post where death is certain to be the compensation of fidelity—the impetuous daring that leads a general in great emergencies to place himself at the head of his men and rush into the deadly breach. In the fiercest battles of the war, and in the thickest of the fight, it is the universal testimony that he was as calm and cheerful as though merely on parade. With his faculties tasked to the utmost, and danger and death enveloping him, his habitual smile never left his countenance, and he only seemed to think of the safety of his men and the triumph of their arms. He was no actor. Naked heroism in battle, stripped of every thing like sham, sat upon him as gracefully as gentleness and goodness in private life. He was intuitively quick in his conceptions, and rapid and daring in his combinations. His conduct and generalship at Chapultepec, and in the advance and capture of the Belen, challenged the admiration of our veteran officers, and will long figure in military history.

His moral courage was equal to his personal. He had no dread of minorities; no fear of the mob; no shrinking from responsibility; no reverence for power, except the power of the law; and none of that every-day cowardice which makes a conscience and a God of public opinion. While he commanded the Natchez Fencibles, and the epidemic was sweeping over the city with fearful mortality, he made it a rule to attend their sick-beds, and to bury the dead with military honors.

His whole life was a beautiful harmony. He was

faithful to his promises. He was never false to a friend. He never evaded a duty. He stooped to no artifice, and even in war preferred the assault to strategy. In the family circle he was affectionate and cordial, playful and talkative; a hearty laugher; a favorite in society; partial to women, and fond of the good things of this world. In early life he had been strikingly handsome; a noble form, developed by athletic exercises; a benevolent and sunny countenance; a low and musical voice; a graceful and captivating manner. During the war his fair complexion was bronzed. His features became more rigid and austere; his mustache grizzled and grim; and he looked, when motionless and in thought, like the effigy of a warrior mossed and weather-beaten by the storms of sixty winters.

I close the record of his career with an extract from the funeral discourse delivered at the grave by the Rev. Dr. Perry, D.D., LL.D., Rector of Trinity Church, Natchez:

"It was once the remark of a distinguished officer that no man of true courage ever approached the hour of battle without experiencing a keen sensation of solicitude and responsibility not devoid of due desire to preserve his life. How forcibly is this sentiment expressed in the solemn service we have just read, 'O spare me a little, before I go home and be no more seen!'

"This was not said by one who shrunk from death when duty called him, but by one who shared that feeling the Creator inspires as innate regard for life. It is the boon we are all privileged to crave, and not less he whose office calls him to expose life to the vicissitudes of chance.

"Summoned as we are, on the present occasion, to follow an illustrious personage to his last resting-place, and that, too, amid a combination of imposing and affecting circumstances, how natural to reflect upon the history he leaves to the world.

"To me the honorable dead was not a stranger. I met him a few days after his return home to die.

"His closing sickness was of a nature that denied the ability of holding much conversation, scarcely none at all, even with intimate and most cherished friends: an admonition for us all timely to prepare to meet our GOD.

"I stand not here to pronounce his eulogy, but simply as the minister of Christ to utter a few brief thoughts which the solemnity of the hour naturally suggests.

"We are often prone to feel discouraged at the loss of eminently useful men, and to think that thereby the interests of the high posts they have occupied must suffer. This is usually the case with that order of mind which places little or no trust in Providence—no belief in the Omnipotence that guides and guards, scrutinizing the footsteps of mortals here—that HE who gives knows best when and how to take away, being the eternal measureless font whence are drawn sweet waters of hope and strength.

"When, therefore, comes the voice, 'Go thy way and let another take thy place and acquit himself nobly as thou hast done,' it is the height of moral courage to be able to say, 'Even so, O Lord God.'

"There before us this day lies coffined a man of preeminent ability. I intend thus to express the more in saying that we do not select this or that attribute of character to distinguish its eminence merely, so much as to indicate the far rarer ability of doing many great things well at the same time. There are men, not a few, intellectually but moderately endowed, who, by selecting some one thing in and of itself important, and by adhering devotedly to the same, are able to attain a noted degree of usefulness and success in that particular.

"Honorable and praiseworthy as all this may be, it falls short of and is not comparable with that career wherein are embraced many objects, all of the highest cast, and every one of them carried to the summit of their respective requisitions. But few men possess such ability; that our departed friend did, facts fully demonstrate. At the bar, on the bench, in the battle-field, as chief magistrate of his state, as an honored, active member of the United States Congress, outstripped by none, he was equaled by few. He was by nature gifted with elements of greatness—a clear brain, an honest heart, of righteous determination, with unflinching vigilance. Ever truthful, he knew what to do; prudent, he knew where to stop; fearless, he knew when to advance; sagacious, he possessed the skill of a profound leader. * * * *

"As a Christian, Gen. Quitman was the son of a worthy clergyman. He was early and carefully trained 'to fear God and keep his commandments.' This lesson, it would seem, was not lost to him.

"By Trinity Parish records it appears that he has acted as vestryman in the church of my present charge. All who knew him in this connection can testify with what reverence he always treated matters of religion, and how generously he contributed to their support. Kindness to the poor and sympathy with the afflicted ever distinguished him. 'The widow and the fatherless' were especially objects of his tender care, and in whose aid he gave abundantly of his means. He practiced CHARITY.

"Personal piety is something the reality of which can only be truly known between God and the individual heart. We all feel that, as a controlling sentiment, it can exist in the soul, while it may not prove a frequent subject of verbal conversation. In the case before us we notice a life of nearly 'threescore years and ten' passed in the turmoil and performance of forensic and other public duties, in the shock and discipline of arms, in contact with all grades of temper, in the exercise of various professions in places near and remote, under alternatives many, and yet our friend in no single instance was ever known to have uttered a syllable or hinted a sentiment derogatory to Christianity; but, on the other hand, he was the advocate and supporter of it, adorning his whole life with the purity and beauty of its attributes. Does not a life like this come fairly under the Savior's great rule, 'Not every one that saith unto me, Lord, Lord, shall enter into the kingdom of heaven; but he that doeth the will of my Father in heaven?'

"One notable certain instance, however, affords a still closer view of General Quitman's pious character. When dissolution was approaching him, a daughter (the widow of a distinguished minister of the Church) at his bedside, fully impressed with the importance of that final moment, taking his hand in her own, exclaimed, 'My father, look to Jesus; He is your only hope.' 'Yes, yes,' answered the dying parent, 'I know it; He is my trust!' Brief words, but O how full! General Quitman was not the man thus to say, even in death, unless he *meant* it.

"But he has gone. Oh, sacred scenes of home, where wife and children dwell, where friends and relatives assemble, and affection's current courses and warms the social heart—alas! how changed! There, on the warrior's coffin, are his equipage and trophies. He has laid aside his harness, and his battle-sword lies clasped in its scabbard.

"From the *mystic tie*, too, he has passed away. Over the curve of the ever-living arch hang the insignia of his office. The gavel and the plumb never more shall he use. Grant, that when the ROYAL MASTER, with the stamp of fate, shall bid us present our work for inspection, we also, like him who has gone before, may be able to render good work, such as HE shall approve who once proclaimed, 'Let there be light! and there was light!'

> "Peace, soldier and statesman, peace be to thy shade!
> Cold now thy heart indeed, sheathed ever thy blade.
> The forum no more shall re-echo thy speech;
> Nor meet thee the foeman in onset or breach.
> The stanch ship of state must stem now the wave
> Without thee, the loyal, the true man and brave:
> Deeds val'rous shall blazon thy name and thy worth,
> Long after thy form hath commingled with earth.
> But of LIFE thou hast ROOT to put forth again,
> Undying, 'mid glories supernal that reign!"

APPENDIX.

A.

BATTLE OF MONTEREY.

General Quitman to General Felix Huston.

"Camp Allen, near Monterey, November 23d, 1846.

"DEAR GENERAL,—I have just had the gratification to read your two letters of the 27th and 29th ult. They are especially gratifying to me, because they show the lively interest you take in my honor and reputation. They prove to me, too, how much those who have clear heads and only honest and patriotic intentions think alike on points of great public interest. I have been here since the battle, without the most remote idea that I had, since I left Camargo, done the slightest thing to deserve censure, and, in the honesty of my heart, believing that, in all my actions here, I had acted a conspicuous part in giving credit and honor to our arms, and especially to the volunteer service. Not a breath was whispered but that I had been especially fortunate in giving *the only success* to our arms in the hard-fought affair of the 21st, and had done something very handsome in promptly occupying the strong line of works on the morning of the 23d, and, with the permission of General Taylor, led the gallant Mississippi regiment and a portion of the Tennesseans up to the very plaza. I was here complimented on all hands. Judge of my surprise when I was informed, several days since, that, simultaneously in Baltimore, New Orleans, and Natchez, rumors prejudicial to my military character had been heard. I mean to trace them, and beg your assistance in doing so. These slanders, I am sorry to say, receive some countenance from the fact that, in the first reports of these transactions, in which my brigade did so much for the credit of our arms, my *name* was not mentioned. I doubt not this fact struck the whole army with some surprise. Had any regular officer had a horse shot down under him before the batteries, think you reports would have been silent upon the subject? But I fear to appear to you anxious to have my vanity fed with praises. I would have been satisfied to say nothing had I merely been treated with neglect, but I can not consent to be censured for conduct which, if known, should extract praise instead of blame.

"By this time you will have received my letter giving you more in detail the particulars of the battle, and will probably also have seen General Taylor's detailed account. I have seen a rough draft of the latter, but was only enabled to read it imperfectly and in a hurried manner. I am inclined to think he gives my command and myself more credit than in the first advices. There is a mistake that there were any participators with my brigade in the capture of the Fort Teneria. The regular troops had been repulsed and *scattered* before we came up, and some of our men were wounded after we had entered the salient redoubt. Mr. Bailie Peyton's statement has astonished me. He has done great injustice to, and grossly misrepresented the Mississippi regiment. Both regiments were charging on the fort at the same time, the Mississippians, with M'Clung at their head, most rapidly. The larger portion of the Tennessee regiment was impeded by a deep ditch, which was more shallow on the side on which Mississippi charged. There is a controversy which entered first. In this I, as the commander of both, should not take part. I can say, however, that I believe M'Clung was first on the rampart. The charge was made on both sides rapidly, and not one minute elapsed from the commencement of the actual charge before the greater part of both regiments were in the works, or part of them. I had just formed a new movement of the Mississippi regiment, and rode rapidly to the Tennessee troops and ordered a charge, when I looked over my shoulder and beheld our brave and gallant boys advancing, not in double-quick time, but as fast as every man could run, directly up to the crater of the bellowing volcano, and tumbling in upon the Mexicans. It is, however, impossible to make a particular description of the events of the three days without plots and drawings. Enough has occurred to prove all that ever you or I have maintained about American volunteers.

"Having been unable to finish my letter in time for last mail, I now resume it. In looking over the accounts of the battles of Monterey two things have struck me. Almost all the letter-writers were with Gen. Worth. They show an evident disposition to blazon the transactions at the other end of the town to the disparagement of the gallant deeds of the army on this side. No man feels more sorely this injustice than Gen. Taylor. The other remark I have to make is, that I have been treated with marked neglect by most of the writers, although victory followed where I led. But enough of this. My friends must see justice done me; I can not. Every examination shows more conclusively that we on this side had the bull by the horns. It was our vigorous attack that brought against *us* nearly the whole Mexican force, and drew them off from the rear, where Gen. Worth was operating. When the official reports of Gen. Taylor and Gen. Butler are published, I hope my friends will see them published in our papers. I have just this evening seen a paragraph in the Concordia Intelligencer calculated to injure me. It finds fault with me for speaking the truth, that I was not consulted and did not approve of the armistice. I had been charged with giving my sanction to it. In declaring my disapproval of it, do I censure or disparage those who approved of it? Gen. Taylor, in his first dispatches, says that he was very generous to the Mexicans. There is no officer in the army who doubts that the city was ours; that we could have taken it in a few hours. Who dares say that we could not? But suppose not, I have my own opinion. The Courier had stated that I concurred in the terms. Shall I be assailed for indiscretion for holding an opinion which Gen. Taylor held, and withal be told that others acted a more conspicuous part in the battles?

"Captain W. P. Rogers, of Houston, Texas, formerly captain of the 1st Mississippi Rifles, furnished me the following interesting account of the battle:

" 'Our first work was to carry a strong redoubt, but in approaching it we passed over a level plain for a mile or more, exposed to the cannon of the enemy from several batteries. When within 200 yards, or perhaps more, Quitman's brigade was, by an echelon movement, made to form line of battle in front of the redoubt. The Tennessee regiment was upon our left, and opened fire first upon the enemy. Forming thus in front of the redoubt, Quitman's brigade poured a murderous fire upon the enemy, and kept it up until five or six rounds were fired, when the order to charge was given. I heard the word first from Lieut. Col. M'Clung. It is, however, due to others to say that he was the officer nearest to me. During the time, however, I saw Quitman, Davis, and Bradford in the thickest of the fight, each encouraging, by acts and words, the spirits of their men. Bradford was still mounted, and remained so during the day. Quitman's horse was killed under him. Upon the order to charge a shout of triumph was raised, and every Mississippian sprang to the conflict, with M'Clung in front. The Mississippians were first in the fort, perhaps because they were nearer than the Tennesseans. The fort was soon swept of the enemy but the dead and wounded. Our halt was brief; on to the distillery we rushed; there M'Clung was wounded and fell. But on, on was the word, for the distillery had surrendered. Over the creek we went, Davis on foot and in our midst. Here the Mississippians were met by a most galling fire from Fort Diablo. Our men fell thick and fast. We were ordered to retire, and did so, passing to the right and rear about fifty yards over a creek. Here the main body of our regiment, with some of the Tennessee regiment, formed line of battle, and kept up, for two hours or more, a galling fire upon the enemy. Gen. Quitman and Major Bradford were the only field-officers that I saw for some time. Col. Davis had taken a small party with him, and passed up the Rio Monterey for the purpose of reconnoitring the position of the enemy and obtaining a better position for his regiment. About 4 P.M. we were ordered, probably by Gen. Taylor, to return to camp. We passed on under the command of Maj. Bradford for half a mile, when we were met by Col. Davis, who ordered us back to the redoubt. There we were halted to resist cavalry, which threatened us, but did not attack us. At night we were marched to camp.

" ' At dawn on the morning of the 22d we returned to our first position, and found that Gen. Quitman had, during the night, thrown up breast-works, with the aid of the Tennesseans (Campbell's regiment). He had been upon his post during the entire night, and remained so for the succeeding 24 hours, thus exhibiting that indomitable energy and will so necessary to the soldier. He remained in or near the breast-works alluded to during the 22d, exposed to occasional shots from the enemy's cannon. On the night of the 22d I returned to camp, and was not in the fight of the 23d, and can not, therefore, speak of it except from report.

"'The glorious achievements of the 21st had intimidated the enemy, and his subsequent resistance was feeble. A nobler specimen of a man than Gen. Quitman never lived, and to him perhaps as much as to any other man is our country indebted for the glorious achievements at Monterey. With his brigade he effected a lodgment in the lower end of the city, a position at once commanding and calculated to intimidate the enemy.'"

Extracts from Major A. B. Bradford's Letter.

"Monterey, 25th Sept., 1846.

"The great city of Monterey is taken. It capitulated after one of the most sanguinary battles that have been fought in modern times, and the Mississippians have covered themselves with glory, as also the Tennesseans. The 1st regiment of Tennesseans and the Mississippians, out of 700, have lost near 170 men in killed and wounded. Many of the wounded will die, having been struck with cannon balls, grape, and canister shot. I have no distinction to make, all did their duty.

"I was in all the fight, saw every thing, and was exposed fifteen hours to cannon balls, grape, canister, and musketry; grazed seven times, but escaped unhurt. My poor horse Henry was wounded three times slightly, but yet is able to carry me. The Mississippians and Tennesseans under the galling fire took two forts by storm, and bore off three pieces of cannon as trophies. I can not forget the bravery and coolness of the noble Texans, who showed themselves equal to any in the field. A part of two or three of Col. Wood's regiment of Texans were with me the last day, and fought under my directions, and won immortal honor, as did Captain Bennett's company of Tennesseans under the command of Col. Campbell.

"I am now satisfied, and am willing that heaven may make any disposition of me it pleases. I have had my health, done my duty as a soldier, and lived to see our brave regiment gain imperishable renown. No corps in the army stands above us. Each officer and soldier did his duty, and it would take a volume to record their deeds of daring.

"The battle raged three days almost incessantly, the 21st, 22d, and 23d inst., and the capitulation took place at twelve o'clock last night, the 24th."

Extracts from Capt. J. H. R. Taylor's Letter.

"Monterey, Sept. 25th.

"Monterey is ours. We reached here after a march of fourteen days through the scorching sun upon the plains, each day lessening our number by disease until the effective men were about three hundred and fifty, leaving the poor fellows along the road at every ranchero. On Sunday we marched up and planted our mortars. Sunday night Gen. Worth was sent around the city to attack the opposite side. Monday morning our division and the 2d division moved toward the city. Gen. Twiggs opened the engagement with the Baltimoreans and was repulsed. Then came the Tennesseans and Mississippians, who were brought up a mile under the most destructive fire from the cannon poured upon us from the fort. We were led up within a hundred yards of the fort, suffering from canister and grape, and balls from a thousand muskets. There we stood half an hour, our men falling around in heaps. Col. M'Clung ordered a charge; and unprecedented in history, the Mississippi rifle regiment charged the fort bristling with bayonets, followed by the Tennesseans. Through the fort we went, driving the Mexicans into another fort. We rushed on, and at the entrance of this second fort the brave M'Clung was shot, and I fear mortally. We then waded the river, with Col. Davis and our brave Bradford at our head, gallantly leading under a still more galling fire from the third fort, losing men at every step, and even charging at this third fort. We were now ordered to fall back over the river; here the troops within a hundred and fifty yards stood and fired their small arms for an hour, exposed to the cannon of several forts. During this whole time we were not assisted by a single piece of artillery. At length the flying artillery came up and covered the divided troops from a charge of the lancers. The action commenced at five minutes before ten, and lasted till half-past five in the evening. For the want of ammunition we were ordered to retire to camp, and for a mile and a half we received the fire of the enemy's cannon upon an open plain. Bombs and shots were passing all night from our forts and those still held by the enemy. Tuesday we were led back into the fort, exposed again to the cannon, and many a poor fellow lost his life before we reached it. We then opened our batteries upon the Cathedral from our fort. At night the Mexicans deserted the fort that we charged over the river. Wednesday, Col. Davis, with the rangers and regulars, and some Tennesseans, made another attack upon the fort, but did not succeed, and it turned into a street fight—not many killed. The bombs were flying all night, and on Thursday morning they sent us a flag of truce."

Extract of a Letter from Capt. S. A. D. Greaves to the Editors of the Mississippian, dated Monterey, Nov. 29th, 1846.

"General Quitman's brigade carried forts *Teneria*, the *Devil*, and *Rencon* without the assistance of the regulars, as stated by Gen. Butler in his letter, and Gen. Worth three batteries and the Bishop's Palace. Gens. Worth's and Quitman's brigade did all the hard fighting, and carried the city. If Gen. Quitman's command had been distinct, as was Gen. Worth's, he would have, beyond controversy, completely distinguished himself. As it is, he has gained a reputation that any commander might be proud of. Col. Davis in both battles showed himself to be an accomplished commander and gallant officer. He is the admiration of his regiment. They have the most unbounded confidence in him, and every man feels proud of him. No man displayed more true bravery than Col. M'Clung. His daring conduct elicited the admiration of all.

"I have seen a letter from Gen. Butler, published in the Louisville Courier of the 27th of October, in which he says: 'We took one battery and a house fitted up as a fortification, and assisted the regulars in taking a second.' Now, on Monday morning the 21st, Gen. Quitman's brigade, of Gen. Butler's division, composed of the Tennessee Volunteers and the Mississippi riflemen, carried by storm the 'battery and house fitted up as a fortification.' Thus far Gen. Butler's account of the fighting is correct. And here let me add, that the Mississippi riflemen were the first in said battery and ' house fitted up as a fortification.' Col. M'Clung was the first in the battery, for I saw that myself; and I am informed that Col. Davis was the first at the ' house fitted up as a fortification' directly behind the battery. There Col. M'Clung was shot by a Mexican as he was entering the door. After Col. M'Clung was shot, Col. Davis pressed on with some fifty men through a terrible fire, and was in the act of charging upon the second battery or field-work, when he was ordered back. We returned to the camp Monday night, and Tuesday morning the 22d went back to the battery and ' house fitted up as a fortification,' and remained there until Wednesday morning about half-past six o'clock. At this time Col. Davis called out the Raymond Fencibles and Vicksburg Volunteers (in the order mentioned), marched at their head, and took a ' second battery.' We then took possession of the third battery, and every other fortification and defense on that end and side of the city."

B.

QUITMAN'S RECONNOISSANCE AT CHAPULTEPEC — GALLANTRY OF LIEUTENANT (AFTERWARD CAPTAIN) LOVELL, U. S. A., AND LIEUTENANT HARE, PENNSYLVANIA VOLUNTEERS.

This was decidedly the boldest reconnoissance of the war. The following note of it I find among the papers of Gen. Quitman.

"During the morning of the 12th of September, 1847, while Drum's battery (No. 1) was playing upon Chapultepec and the enemy was briskly returning the fire, Gen. Quitman proposed a close and accurate reconnoissance of the preparations of the Mexicans to receive an attack, of their means of defense, the obstacles of ground, number and position of guns, etc. Accordingly it was determined we should proceed that afternoon up the road as close to their lines as practicable, and endeavor to get a sketch of their arrangements; and about 3 o'clock the general, with his A. A. A. general, Lieut. Lovell, and about 40 or 50 men under Maj. Twiggs of the marines, started on this expedition. The escort was composed of men of all regiments, and formed a portion of the command which had volunteered for the storming party of our division. We pushed along by file up the road, keeping ourselves screened as much as possible from the view of the castle by the magueys on our left, until we came to a small house on the left-hand side of the road; but, before we reached this point, the enemy in our front had discovered us, and opened a scattering fire from their sharp-shooters, who were considerably in front of their lines, and somewhat on our right. The escort was placed at the building aforesaid, being . pretty well protected by it and a few large trees from musketry in front, but within short range of their field-pieces, and exposed to a flank fire from the castle which overlooked us on the left. Lieutenant Hare of the 2d Pennsylvania regiment was sent with five men across the road to get into the fields on the right, and by a dropping fire keep back the enemy on that side from turning our flank. The general and Lieut. Lovell then proceeded about twenty or thirty yards in advance, being slightly protected by a tree from the fire in front, but exposed on both sides. These arrangements and dispositions had occupied half an hour, during the whole of which time the advanced skirmishers of the enemy had kept up a constant fire of small-arms upon us, though without much effect. The general and Lieut. Lovell were at the tree before mentioned, and the latter was preparing to take a sketch of the enemy's works and the approaches, which were closely and distinctly before us, when all at once there was a sound of trumpets and beating of drums, and an evident general movement and commotion along the whole of their lines extending from their position on the road in both directions for a long distance. Their troops stood to arms, and the regiments were paraded with flying colors, evidently expecting to receive an attack. The advanced parties of their sharp-shooters were increased, and the fire upon us now became pretty warm. They, seeing likewise the smallness of our party, began cautiously to envelop us on both sides. Their demonstrations were rapidly becoming of an alarming character, but the general and his aid remained quietly in advance, making accurate observation and perfecting their sketch with a view to the operations of the next day. The enemy, meanwhile, continued to advance, and their fire grew warmer, and it was also evident that we had attracted the notice of Chapultepec itself, which opened a plunging fire upon our left flank at short range. Our protection screened us in a great measure from the fire in front (except that of artillery), but our flanks were entirely exposed. About twenty minutes had been passed in this manner, when Lieut. Lovell told the general he had better retire, as 'this was rapidly becoming an unfit place for a general of division;' but no attention was paid by the latter to this remark, he being evidently intent upon knowing personally his own field of operations. Lieutenant Lovell then said, 'I have finished my sketch;' but the general replied, 'Let us wait a few moments and find out where these guns are; no one ever saw that number of Mexican soldiers together without artillery.' The words were scarcely uttered before *bang ! bang !* went two pieces directly in our front, and a round shot crashed through the house while a load of grape swept by within a few feet of our persons. These were followed in a moment by two more discharges of artillery, when, Lieutenant Lovell having dotted down the position of the battery, the general said, 'I am ready to move,' and they turned to go back to the escort, but to their surprise and astonishment saw them running to and fro evidently panic-stricken. The cry was raised, 'We are surrounded; the lancers are in the corn-fields on our left;' and they commenced huddling together in one spot, all seeming to be in a measure unaccountably bewildered. At this moment a couple of rounds of grape from our front increased the confusion. Lieut. Lovell said, 'What the devil do you mean by huddling together? One round of grape might destroy the whole of you; separate yourselves.' And the words were no sooner uttered before Chapultepec awoke, and a 68-pound howitzer vomited down upon us about two quarts of grape. The iron shower passed luckily a little too high, cutting through the trees directly over our heads and covering us with leaves. The men then lost all command, and commenced moving to the rear of the road and ditch, notwithstanding the orders and entreaties of the general and his aid. At this moment it occurred to the former that Lieut. Hare was still in his position, and he ordered several of the men to go and recall him, but no heed was paid to the order; the men could not be induced to stay where they were, much less to go again toward the enemy. And yet these same men behaved the next day with the greatest gallantry in advance of this very spot. But such is a panic. The order was repeated, but no one would go, whereupon Lieut. Lovell, seeing the emergency of the case and unwilling to have the little picket sacrificed to its gallantry, said, 'General, I will go and recall them.' The latter hesitated at first about permitting it, but finally said, 'Well, they must not be sacrificed.' Lieut. Lovell then started across the road, when a soldier, whose sense of duty had returned to him, sprung out and said, 'Hold on, captain, I'll go;' but Lieut. Lovell, merely exclaiming 'You are too late, my good fellow,' pushed on across the road, the soldier, however, accompanying him. But just as they reached the middle of the road a volley of musketry swept it, and the poor fellow fell shot through the body, a victim to his reawakened gallantry. The officer pushed on, crossed the ditch on the other side, and, advancing toward the enemy's works, recalled Lieut. Hare and his little party, and they moved off through the open fields under quite a severe fire and rejoined their own troops. The lieutenant had, in the mean time, restored some order among the escort, and moved down the road with them toward our own batteries. Two companies of the 2d Pennsylvania regiment, seeing our party falling back under a sharp fire, and the enemy coming out very boldly and insolently in our direction, had advanced some distance up the road, and by a well-timed fire induced the Mexicans to stop their advance. The general also, as soon as he had reached the batteries, directed a 12-pounder to be drawn out into the road and discharged at the sharp-shooters who were pushing quite toward our lines. These demonstrations had the desired effect, and they went back to their own works. Thus ended, after a sharp and protracted skirmish, in which we lost eleven men killed and wounded, one of the boldest and most determined reconnoissances made during the campaign, and one too, which, if it did not insure our success the next day, yet contributed to it in a great measure, and was the means of saving many valuable lives. It enabled the volunteer division to perform the duty assigned them in an expeditious and direct manner, and without losing time in feeling their way. The panic which seized upon the escort was one of those unaccountable things which often occur in war, and which sometimes affect veteran troops. The previous and subsequent gallantry of many of these same men amply redeemed them in the opinion of their officers."

C.

THE PALMETTO REGIMENT.

A high-toned, martial spirit has always characterized South Carolina. The great battles of the war of independence were within her territory. The death of Jasper, the martyrdom of Hayne, the victims of the prison ships, the imprisonment of Laurens, the forays of Tarlton, the enormities of the Tories, the brilliant partisanship of Sumpter, the *coups de main* of Marion, and the patriotic spirit of her daughters, are incidents never to be forgotten. Her habitual chivalry of character may be traced mainly to those glorious recollections. She entered warmly into the war of 1812 ; her great orators stood by the side of Henry Clay in defense of the national honor, and on the ocean and the battle-field her sons were conspicuous. In 1832, when there was a probability of collision with the federal government, and when her Southern sisters, though suffering a common grievance, gave her little aid or comfort, nothing daunted, she exerted her energies, and converted the state into a vast encampment. There was a general embodiment of her available strength ; volunteer companies, thoroughly drilled and ably officered, were organized in every district, and no people on earth were ever better prepared to resist invasion. This military spirit had not been extinguished when the war with Mexico commenced. But President Polk, with whom her statesmen were no favorites, made no call on South Carolina until after the fall of Monterey, when public opinion and the exigencies of the service compelled the call. It was promptly responded to from the seaboard to the mountains. The regiment was soon organized, each company, in their respective districts, voting for regimental officers. The result was—for colonel, Pierce M. Butler; for lieutenant-colonel, James P. Dickinson; for major, A. H. Gladden. It had been raised for twelve months; but before it was called into service, the term was changed by the War Department to "during the war with Mexico." Under this proceeding, in some quarters, a general disbandment would have occurred. The regiment was composed, for the most part, of husbandmen, and officered by affluent planters or eminent professional men, who had made special arrangements for twelve months only; but not a man faltering, the regiment was promptly reported ready. They landed at Vera Cruz, and there they met, for the first time, their future commander, General Quitman, "in the full harness of a soldier, with a blanket stretched over three muskets stuck in the sand, to screen him from the burning sun."*

Their protracted exposure on the route, and the long march to Alvarado and back, over a burning sand-beach, sowed thickly the seeds of disease, and many a gallant gentleman succumbed under its effects. When the regiment first mustered on the beach at Vera Cruz, 10th March, 1847, it numbered 974, rank and file. On the 19th of June, 1848, when formed on the same strand to embark for home, 433 had perished. And many subsequently died from the effects of wounds and exposure during that brief campaign. "From

* General M'Gowan's eloquent address before the Palmetto Association.

the commencement of the campaign," says Gen. M'Gowan, "Colonel Butler was in bad health, but he shrunk from no service, and courted every danger. When unable to march or ride, he was carried on an ambulance at the head of the Palmettos. On the 19th of August, though suffering severely, he led his regiment, on its midnight march, through the Pedrigal, and took part in the battle of Contreras. Without pausing for rest or refreshment, he plunged into the battle of Churubusco. His horse was shot down. Waving his sword, he received a ball in his leg. But still the heroic leader pressed forward. Human courage could scarcely withstand the overwhelming odds concentrated against Shields's shattered brigade. Its ranks began to waver, and the impetuous general, almost in despair, appealed to his men to advance. Butler cried out, ' *The South Carolinians will follow you to death;*' and his men ratified his words with a ringing cheer and a rushing charge. At this moment Butler received a ball through his head, and fell to rise no more. The gallant Worth, as he dashed by in hot pursuit of the enemy, on seeing the body of his friend, reined up his horse, and exclaimed, ' *Butler dead!* A spirit pure as the blade he wore has gone to God. His country will preserve his memory.' "

There was one sentiment that inspired this heroic man, and which he constantly impressed on his command. He would remind them that South Carolina had always claimed a character for spirit, which her enemies had denied her; that the regiment carried the flag of the state, the symbol of her sovereignty, and must perish man by man sooner than justify the taunts that had been cast upon her. An intense feeling of state pride and of personal responsibility for the honor of Carolina pervaded the Palmettos. The following—the last lines that Butler ever penned—is the letter of a thorough soldier, and contains one electrical line never equaled in military correspondence: "*He desires a place near the flashing of the guns.*"

Colonel P. M. Butler to General Worth.

"San Augustin, 19th August, 1847.

"DEAR GENERAL,—We are here in tribulation. I can but hope, however, it is but temporary. It is ordered that this division remain as protection to the train. There is gloom on us all, while I am one who believes that *there will be fighting enough for all.* The moral effect is withering. The regiment, though weak in numbers, is up to the full point, and I trust South Carolina may have a place in the picture. We have been watching you and your division for the last two days with fraternal affection; but the entire voice of the army where I have been or heard is unbounded confidence in 'Worth.' 'So mote it be.' But I have strayed from the principal point or purpose of my note, which is to say that our friend, Colonel DICKINSON, more impatient, and not so long a soldier as myself, *desires a place near the flashing of the guns,* and, with good taste, wishes to get near *you.* If you can make him useful, he will feel much gratified. I am aware you are surrounded with a talented staff, but a little more of a good thing will render it not the less complete or effectual.

"I am, my dear general, yours sincerely,

"P. M. BUTLER, S. C. V.

"General W. J. Worth, commanding, etc."

Gen. Worth to Hon. A. P. Butler, U. S. Senator.

"Tacubaya, Mexico, August 26th, 1847.

" Sir,—I trust a cordial intimacy and friendship of twenty-five years with your late brother, the gallant Col. Butler, will excuse the trespass of a stranger. Your brother fell most gloriously in the great battle of the 20th before the gates of Mexico. In that bloody conflict no man gave higher evidence of valor and patriotism, or exhibited a brighter example. He fell, when it was God's will, precisely as he would have desired to die. His body rests here; his memory in the hearts of his countrymen; his spirit, bright and pure as his blade, with his God.

" The inclosed letter, written the day before the battle, I did not receive until the day after, through the hands of Dickinson; and it is not because of the kind things said by a friend's partiality, but because it is perhaps the *last* letter he penned, that I send it to you, begging that at some future day it may be returned to me, to be preserved and cherished.

" The gallant Palmettos, who showed themselves worthy of their state and country, lost *nearly one half*. This victory will carry joy and sorrow into half the families in South Carolina. Col. Dickinson is getting on well, and will, it is hoped, save his leg. An armistice is concluded, and commissioners meet to-morrow to treat of peace.

" Very truly, your obedient servant,   W. J. Worth.
"Hon. A. P. Butler."

The following passages from a speech delivered by the Hon. L. M. Keitt at Lynchburg, Va., September 11th, 1856, are full of interest:

"In 1846 you carried your flag into a neighboring republic. We upheld it. The South sent forty thousand men to the scene of battle; the North sent twenty thousand. Go ask the graves upon those battle-fields, and they will tell you who occupies them. Massachusetts and South Carolina have been sometimes arrayed against each other. I will run the parallel between them. Col. Butler, the brother of the Hon. Mr. Butler, the senator from South Carolina, who was so basely slandered by a foul-mouthed abolitionist, was the leader of the Palmetto regiment in the Mexican war. General Quitman told me, when an order came to him for a regiment to engage in the battle of Chapultepec, Colonel Butler, who was sick, went to him and said, ' I demand a right to be in that battle.' Quitman replied, ' You can not go, sir—you are sick.' ' I am sufficiently well to go,' said Butler. Quitman remarked, ' I shall see,' and thereupon a physician was sent for. He declared him unfit for active service, and General Quitman insisted that he should not go. ' I ask it, then, as a favor,' said Butler, ' and I demand it as a right.' ' Go, then,' said Quitman. He led this Palmetto regiment on to the fight. In that battle-field two free-state regiments ran, while, exposed to the fire of the Mexican lines, stood this regiment from my own state, swept by grape and canister. That regiment stood, while each man was writhing in the blood of his companions. Exposed in this fire that regiment stood, firing not a gun, leveling not a bayonet. While men were falling by scores they stood there. (Loud cheers.) Free-state regiments had broken up and retreated. Most of the regular army was cut up, and there was nothing but disaster in the perspective. ' What regiment will fol-

Vol. II.—O

low me ?' said Shields.   Colonel Butler replied, 'The Palmetto regiment will follow you.'   (Cheers.)   That regiment did follow.   Ere the leader advanced twenty steps he fell dead.   Scarce had the regiment moved ere its banner was struck down ; before it was fallen its lieutenant colonel took it up, and ere he advanced two steps he too was struck down.   Another took it, and scarce had he raised it when he fell; and while he was falling a gallant Irishman took it, folded it round his body, and bore it on to victory.   (Enthusiastic cheers.)   There, too, was a young man—a college companion of mine, and brother of my colleague, Col. Brooks—a lieutenant in his company.   When Shields said, 'What regiment will follow me ?' and Col. Butler said, 'The Palmetto regiment will follow you,' Brooks said, 'Ay, they will follow you to death.'   With his sword flashing, leading on his men, this young man fell mortally wounded.   When he and his brother—my colleague —left home, their father took an old family servant and said to them, 'Take him along ; he may be of use to you hereafter.'   My colleague, struck down with sickness, was sent home.   He left this old servant to attend his brother.   For three days and nights this old negro laid by the bedside of his dying young master.   Without cessation, in camp and amid the rage of battle, he watched by his side.   The ball had pierced him through.   From the perforation of the ball came large splinters of bones.   These he gathered together.   His young master died, and the regiment, in consideration of his attention and fidelity, bought him a house and lot.   The old negro purchased a wagon for his master, put him into it, and from the city of Mexico he carried him to Vera Cruz, where he put him on board a vessel bound for the United States.   From the port of arrival he took him to his master, the father of the young man.   He said to the old man, gray-headed and weeping, 'Here, sir, are the bones which passed from the wound of your dead son.   Here,' said he to the mother, 'is the corpse of your son.'   (Loud cheers.)   And this is the institution which is slandered by Northern fanatics.''

James P. Dickinson, lieutenant colonel of the Palmetto regiment, was an only child, born in Camden, S. C., in 1814.   His father, a native of the British West Indies, married the only child of Dr. Ephraim Brevard, of Mecklenburg, N. C.   The wife of Dr. Brevard was a Miss Polk, sister of Col. William Polk of Revolutionary fame, aunt of the present Bishop Polk of the diocese of Louisiana.   The ancestors of Dickinson—his grandfather Brevard, and Col. Polk, the father of Mrs. Brevard—were both signers of the Mecklenburg Declaration of Independence, May 20th, 1775, from which Mr. Jefferson derived some of his finest thoughts and expressions.

The Mecklenburg Declaration was written by Dr. Ephraim Brevard, a man of great ability, and of a bold and lofty spirit.   He was a graduate of Princeton, and having qualified himself as a physician, he commenced the practice in Charlotte, N. C.   His talents, patriotism, and education, united with prudence and practical sense, made him a leader in the committees that preceded the Mecklenburg Convention, and designated him as secretary and draughtsman of that remarkable Declaration.   It was of his mother, the widow Brevard, of Centre Congregation, that a British officer remarked, as a plea for plundering and burning her dwelling, "She has seven sons in the rebel service."   When hostilities commenced, Dr. Brevard entered the army as a surgeon, his brothers being officers in the line. He was taken prisoner at the fall of Charleston in 1780. Returning to North Carolina, he soon died from the effects of disease contracted in the service. He lies buried in the church-yard of Hopewell Congregation, twelve miles from Charlotte, but there is no stone to designate the spot. He thought clearly, felt deeply, wrote well, resisted bravely, and died a martyr to that liberty none loved better and few understood so well.*

From the same patriotic lineage on the maternal side came the Hon. Isaac W. Hayne, the present learned and eloquent attorney general of South Carolina, son of Col. Isaac Hayne, who was hung by the British at Charleston in 1781. His brother, Abram Hayne (grandfather of the late Robert Y. Hayne and of the Hon. Arthur P. Hayne, inspector general on the staff of General Jackson in the war of 1812, and distinguished for his gallantry), perished in the British prison-ships about the same time.

After the sharp engagement at Vera Cruz, referred to in Chapter X., in which Dickinson was wounded, the impression prevailed that the general-in-chief intended to carry the city by assault. Though still suffering, the ardent Carolinian made the following application, never before in print:

"Camp opposite Vera Cruz, March 23d, 1847.

"*General John A. Quitman:*

"My dear Sir,—I am informed a breaching battery near the railroad will be opened to-morrow, and that it is possible an assault may be ordered if the resistance of the city proves obstinate. Gen. Patterson is of opinion that the forlorn hope which usually leads the assault will be composed of details from the different brigades; and the object of this note is to solicit the honor of leading the detail from your brigade. I am sufficiently strong for such a duty, and the only risk to me from my wound would be the after consequences, and those not serious. But as I am *deliberately* determined, even if it risks my commission, to accompany any such command, this is not to be considered, and ought to be left to myself. I will go as a volunteer if I can not as an officer. I sincerely hope, sir, that you may favor my request, and that it would prove agreeable to those I seek to command. I can assure you that the honor of your brigade shall not suffer in my hands."

Disappointed in this hope of distinction by the surrender of the city, the wounded soldier addressed another note to Gen. Quitman. The allusion to his young and beautiful wife, to whom he had been married not quite two years, will touch every manly heart:

"Dear General,—Colonel Butler has informed me that you made favorable mention of my name in your report of the affair of the 11th ult. I would be much gratified, indeed, if you would favor me with a copy of it as a record of my first battle. I would desire it more especially for my wife, who is in ill health, and suffering far more on account of my absence than I could have anticipated. I have an opportunity to send by a friend a package to my wife, and would be glad if you would let me have the copy to-day."

* Review of Foote's Early History of North Carolina.

At the battle of Churubusco, immediately after the fall of Butler, while leading his regiment to the charge, Dickinson was shot through the leg. The wound was not considered dangerous, but, debilitated by his previous suffering and chafing at confinement, he finally succumbed, and his impatient spirit took its flight amid the roar and crash of the assault upon Chapultepec. As Butler died, his eye fixed on the Palmetto banner borne *onward* where the "blows fell thickest and heaviest," so Dickinson expired at the moment that the same flag waved in triumph on the brow of Chapultepec. An appropriate close for the eventful drama of a soldier's life.

Dickinson, like Butler, was six feet four inches in height, straight as an Indian, and of commanding presence. Butler had a clear blue eye, features chiseled as though by the hand of Phidias, and altogether a singularly handsome face. Dickinson's figure was cast between that of Hercules and Apollo. He was by profession a lawyer, and had won considerable reputation at the bar and in the Legislature. He inherited the warm, impulsive temperament of his father, and the deeper enthusiasm of his maternal ancestry. In his general character he was more impetuous than painstaking and persevering.

Major Gladden, who succeeded to the command of the Palmettos on the fall of his colonel and lieutenant colonel, is now a citizen of New Orleans. He participated in all the battles with his regiment, and conducted it to the heights of Chapultepec. When ordered on its summit to form his regiment, he laconically replied, "*It is already formed.*" It had plunged through a morass, exposed to a terrific fire, and ascended to the fortress, without firing a shot or breaking its ranks. He led the regiment in the terrible assault on the Belen, carrying its consecrated banner, which seemed fatal to all who touched it, until he fell severely wounded.

On the 6th of October, 1847, a public meeting was called in Charleston to pay a fitting homage to the memory of the Palmettos that had fallen in battle. Many of the names that figured at the meeting are historical, closely associated with the trials of the war of independence: Johnson, Hayne, Hutchinson, Pringle, De Saussure, Peronneau, Huger, Rutledge, Gadsden, Furman, Pinckney, Heyward, Gaillard, Ravenel, Grayson, Aiken, Holmes, Carew, Petigru, Schnierle, Ashe, Bryan, Strobel, King, Magrath, Rhett, Brisbane, Elmore, Moise, Rose, Connor, Porter, Edmunston, Cogdell, and others.

In reporting a series of strong resolutions (particularly one pledging Carolina to provide for the families of her glorious dead, if destitute, which, it is hoped, has been carried out), Hon. Isaac W. Hayne, attorney general, after a graphic recital of the achievements of the regiment and a touching encomium on Butler and Dickinson, thus referred to some of the younger officers:

"I leave the filling up of the picture to those more fitted for the task. I will merely add that the blood of the 'Game Cock'* has proved game in the third generation; that the name of De Saussure again becomes historic; that Blanding, Dunovant, and Moffatt, familiar already in our ears, are henceforth household words; that the Cantey courage again becomes proverbial. I must be permitted," continued Mr. Hayne, "to pay a passing tribute of private friendship to

* The Revolutionary title of General Sumpter.

one not unworthy of public regard. Lieutenant Shubrick, U. S. N., two hundred miles from the sea, is found fighting the battles of his country, a private in the regiment of his native state. Late of the squadron of the Gulf, tired of inactivity, he returned to Charleston and applied to government for permission to try his fortune in the army. He was allowed to report himself to Commodore Perry, and, if his services were not required, he had permission to serve where he pleased. On his way to Mexico he heard of the surrender of Vera Cruz and the death of Midshipman Shubrick, who fell by his gun in the siege. Commodore Perry retained him on duty until after his capture of Tuspan. We then find him under the walls of Mexico in the staff of Gen. Shields, where his horse was killed under him; afterward fighting as a private in the ranks of the Palmettos. His conduct was worthy of his lineage. It was in the spirit of his grandfather in the war of the Revolution; of his father in the war of 1812; the same spirit which gave five gallant uncles of the same name to the service of their country.

"Mr. Chairman," said the eloquent speaker, "I feel peculiarly gratified that South Carolina has sustained herself. I was for ten years an exile from her soil; and I learned that, beyond her borders, there were those who affected to consider her courage as rather in words than deeds. A few years ago, in the phrensy of party excitement, there was a huge device originated somewhere in Ohio — a mighty ball in the shape of a balloon; it took its course down the great rivers; was received in processions at all the principal towns; thence from New Orleans by Mobile to Montgomery, and on to Georgia. It passed through some ten states of this Union, and was paraded as a party pageant in the great contest of 1840. On it were inscribed the names of the different states of this confederacy, with eulogistic mottoes deemed appropriate to each. And among these was, 'SOUTH CAROLINA — *Hemp for traitors.*' Through ten states this passed—'*rolled*' was the expression—hailed with loud huzzas. Sir, the 'treason' of South Carolina is to be read in the report of the battle of Churubusco.

"Mr. Chairman, on that same party symbol there was inscribed, in juxtaposition to South Carolina, another name and another motto, "MASSACHUSETTS—*Ever Faithful.*" Was *her* faith evinced, only a few weeks since, when her Major General Howe proclaimed the war sinful, and refused to pay military honors to the remains of the gallant Lincoln, who fell at Buena Vista?"

At a very large political meeting in Mississippi in 1840, shortly after the passage down the river of this "mighty ball," the American flag was displayed, with all the stars brightly burning on it but the star of South Carolina, which was so dim as to appear that it was about to be blotted out. Underneath that dim star was the coat of arms of South Carolina—a coil of rope substituted for her proud palmetto, and the words, "*Hemp for traitors.*"

"I was standing near QUITMAN," writes a friend, who was then acting with the Whig party, "when this banner passed. His countenance grew terrible. He made a movement as though he was about to spring upon the flag and tear it to pieces. I made a hasty step toward him to recall him to himself. Dr. Otts approached him

at that instant for the same purpose. He looked me in the face, and
seeing how deeply the sight of such a flag disgusted and pained me,
he became more calm, and cast his eyes over the immense audience
assembled to hear the renowned Prentiss, their orator on the occasion. But with all his art, and sarcasm, and denunciation, and pan-
egyrics on the Union, he could not remove the wide-spread disgust
that repulsive flag had produced in the popular mind." Excited by
partisanship and pageantry, the people, nevertheless, remembered
South Carolina; her Rutledge, the elected dictator of a free people;
her Pinckney, author of the memorable words, "Millions for defense—not a cent for tribute;" her Laurens's, father and son; her
Haynes, who perished on the scaffold and in the prison-ships for the
common liberty!

I can not close this sketch of the Palmetto regiment without the
following reference to the late lamented Preston S. Brooks, the friend
and comrade of Quitman. I am indebted for it to C. H. Suber, Esq.,
of South Carolina.

"Washington, August 7th, 1856.

"MR. EDITOR,—Yesterday our immediate representative in Congress, Hon. P. S. Brooks, completed his 37th year, and it was my
good fortune to be one of a pleasant party of his friends assembled to
dine with him on the occasion. The party consisted of Judge Butler, General Lane, General Quitman, Colonel Davis, secretary of
war, Judge Douglas, Mr. Edmondson, Mr. Bocock, Clingman, and
myself. Colonels Brooks, Orr, and Keitt mess together, and live
very handsomely. I do not remember when I passed a few hours of
more pleasure ; and while at the table an incident unexpectedly occurred, which to relate is the object of this communication. Toward
the close of the feast General Quitman rose, and in behalf of the citizens of Holmes County, Mississippi, presented Colonel Brooks a
beautiful cane, and uttered at the time a few remarks, with which all
present were so pleasingly impressed, that I appealed to him to furnish me with an abstract of what he had said for publication, where
the constituents of Colonel Brooks may read the judgment of a veteran warrior of the man who bears in honor the flag of the old '96'
district.

"'General Quitman rose, and spoke in substance as follows: ' I
ask permission of the gentlemen present to avail myself of this opportunity to perform a duty with which I have been charged by the citizens of Holmes County, Mississippi. It is to present my friend, who
sits at the head of the table, this beautiful cane, with the approving
resolutions which accompany their gift. Captain Brooks (for I prefer the title which brings back to memory my association with you in
the service of our country), this cane has been forwarded to me by a
committee of citizens of Holmes County, Mississippi, as a token of
respect and approval, accompanied by the following resolutions :

" ' 'Lexington, Miss., July 4.—At a meeting of the citizens of
Holmes County, held in Social Hall, on motion, Colonel Otho W.
Bealle was called to the chair, and F. C. Adams requested to act as
secretary. The chairman requested James M. Haynes, Esq., to explain the object of the meeting. Mr. Haynes arose, and said that the
meeting, according to previous notice, had been called to take into

consideration the propriety of presenting to the Hon. Preston S. Brooks, of South Carolina, a walking-cane, with appropriate inscription, for caning that vile abolitionist and foul-mouthed slanderer, Sumner, of Massachusetts, in the Senate Chamber, on the 22d of May last.

" 'On motion of James M. Haynes, Esq., a committee of three were appointed, consisting of James H. Haynes, John M. West, and Fleet C. Mercer, to report suitable resolutions expressive of the sense of this meeting. The committee, after a few minutes, reported the following, which were unanimously adopted:

" ' *Resolved*, 1. That we approve of and fully indorse the conduct of Hon. P. S. Brooks, of South Carolina, in inflicting the well-merited chastisement upon Charles Sumner, a senator in Congress from the State of Massachusetts.

" ' *Resolved*, 2. That as a testimonial of our regard for the Hon. P. S. Brooks, we present to him a cane with suitable inscriptions.

" ' *Resolved*, 3. That a committee of three be appointed to forward the cane to our distinguished representative, the Hon. John A. Quitman, to be presented in our name to the Hon. P. S. Brooks.

" ' *Resolved*, 4. That a copy of these resolutions be forwarded to General Quitman, to be presented with the cane.

" 'On motion, a committee of three, consisting of the Hon. W. Thomas, J. D. M'Farland, and Jesse Broadway, were appointed to receive contributions to pay for said walking-cane.

" 'On motion, John M. West, the Hon. Madison M'Afee, James W. Grace, and James M. Haynes, were appointed a committee to carry out the objects of the 3d and 4th resolutions.

" ' *Resolved*, That we tender to the Hon. Madison M'Afee our sincere thanks for his promptitude in having a suitable cane prepared to be presented to the Hon. P. S. Brooks, and that great credit is due him for the taste he has displayed in the inscription upon the cane.

" ' On motion, the meeting adjourned *sine die*.

" 'OTHO W. BEALLE, President.

" 'F. C. ADAMS, Secretary.

" ' Sir, the approval of such men should be a full *compensation* for the abuse which has from certain quarters been heaped on your head. In point of character, intelligence, and high and refined sense of honor, the gentlemen whose names are associated with these resolutions have no superiors. You may justly be proud of their approval of your conduct. They have honored me by selecting me as the organ of this presentation to yourself. I know that their gift is bestowed upon one who is worthy of it—one who is incapable of a dishonorable act. I recall to mind the young and almost beardless officer who, when captain in the gallant Palmetto Regiment in Mexico while under my command, was remarkable for his gallantry and for the performance of every duty in the camp and in the field, sharing with his men the privations of both spheres; nor can I forget, sir, that in the last bloody fields of that campaign the blood of four of your kinsmen flowed to secure the brilliant victories of our arms; or that in the last terrible charge on the Garita de Belen your nearest surviving kinsman gallantly fell within the fortifications of the enemy. I will not now dwell upon the sad recollections of those events. I will only add that I unite with my friends of Holmes County in their high estimate.of you personally, and also in their approval of the honorable and proper sentiments which actuated you in vindicating the honor of your state and the character of your venerable relative upon the occasion to which they refer.'

"Col. Brooks, accepting the gift, said that his feelings would not permit him then to respond to what had been addressèd to him, but he would reply by letter when he could better command his thoughts. His reply to General Quitman (a copy of which was kindly furnished me) is as follows:

"'House of Representatives, August 7th, 1856.

"'MY DEAR GENERAL,—I could not trust myself yesterday to reply to your kind and complimentary remarks upon presenting to me the beautiful cane which my friends of Holmes County, Mississippi, had commissioned you to present in their name.

"'Under ordinary circumstances I would have replied on the instant to your address, but I was not ordinarily situated.

"'Yesterday was my birth-day. The morning had been devoted to a successful effort to restore amicable relations between two gentlemen, each of whom have qualities which endear them to their friends and make them valuable citizens of any community.

"'My heart was full with the feeling that, in connection with others, I had contributed to *do good* on a day so interesting to myself. This was the mood in which you found me, and when "my old commander," under whose eye I had served in a foreign land, presented a testimonial of approval from strangers, and expressed words of compliment to me as a man, as a soldier, and a representative, I could find no words to speak in the tumult of feeling which possessed me.

"'I now request you to tender my grateful acknowledgments to those you represent, and accept yourself assurances of my profoundest esteem and affectionate regard.   P. S. BROOKS.
   "'General Quitman.'

"His calm, dignified, and chivalric bearing throughout the whole excitement growing out of the chastisement of Senator Sumner has won for Col. Brooks 'golden opinions from all classes of people,' but to retain the good opinion of his gallant chief in other days, who has closely watched his every step under these most trying circumstances, is the highest possible testimonial of the correctness of his course.

"His constituents have reason to feel proud of their representative.   C. H. S."

D.

ADVENTURES IN MEXICO.

General M'Laurin to J. F. H. Claiborne.

"Jackson, Mississippi, July 16th, 1860.

"Your note of the 5th instant, containing memoranda found among General Quitman's papers in relation to the little party which went from Covington County to Mexico in the winter of 1847 and attached themselves to his command, and of which you make inquiries, etc., has been received.

"In the month of January, 1847, a party of 'nine young men, all of us then residing in Covington County, in this state, determined to go to Mexico at their own expense, to engage in the exciting events then transpiring. At New Orleans we provided ourselves with complete suits of uniform for private soldiers; also a rifle apiece of the ordinary Kentucky make, but of the best quality, with all the accoutrements we conceived necessary for efficient service, such as bowie-knives, revolvers, etc., together with a box of superior medicines, and written directions for their use, for most of the diseases consequent upon the climate and life we were about to enter upon, prepared by our friend Dr. E. D. Fenner, of New Orleans. We then embarked for Tampico, the rendezvous of the American army previous to the attack on Vera Cruz. We landed at Tampico on the 28th of January, where General Quitman had arrived a few days before with his command of the Georgia and Alabama regiments, under the command respectively of Col. Jackson and Col. Coffee. On the day after our arrival I reported our presence to Gen. Quitman, who had known most of us at home, and who evinced every mark of pleasure and delight at our course, and immediately accepted our offer to attach ourselves to his command, and at the same time assured us that he would use every effort to make our position as pleasant as possible—all of which he redeemed *beyond* the pledge. On the 22d of February, at the suggestion of General Quitman, and by consent of Colonel Jackson, our little rifle squad connected ourselves to Company 'D,' of the 1st Georgia regiment (musketry), which company was, for the most part, composed of well educated and intelligent young men of the city of Columbus, Georgia, and commanded by Capt. Davis, who, though a tailor, as Gen. Quitman frequently remarked, was every inch a *man* and a *soldier*.

"General Quitman's command remained in their quarters at Tampico until the 7th or 8th of March, when his and General Shields's command were taken aboard the steamer New Orleans, and reached the point of rendezvous of Gen. Scott's division at Point Lizardo, some 18 or 20 miles south of Vera Cruz, on the 9th of March about noon. Ours was the last of that division that was expected to arrive, except the South Carolina regiment, which had been detained by adverse winds. About 4 o'clock P.M., at a given signal, the whole fleet containing that well-appointed army raised steam and hoisted sail, and in two hours were greeted by the castle San Juan d'Ulloa and the heavy artillery on the main land guarding Vera Cruz. It was a calm, clear, beautiful evening, and just as the sun was disappearing behind Mt. Orizaba, beyond Vera Cruz, the landing of General Scott's command commenced some four miles below the city. Gen. Quitman's command landed and 'formed' on the shore just at dark, in which ground we slept with our arms at hand. About 1 o'clock in the morning, while I was lying in the calm moonlight on my blanket on the sand-beach with a high fever on me, and awake, and when all around was as still as if all mankind were at peace with each other, a picket-guard gave an alarm, and in an instant line on line of arm-

ed men, as far as the eye could reach through the dim light, were in
position and ready for any foe.

"Next day General Quitman's command remained on the beach
where they landed. During that day the South Carolina regiment
landed, under the command of Col. Butler, and were placed under
Gen. Quitman.

"That evening, I think it was, Gen. Quitman was ordered to leave
his position. And that night the new recruits (the South Carolinians and our little squad of Mississippians) began to taste the first re-
alities of a soldier's life, by having to cut their way through dense
chapparal. By next morning they reached near the point occupied
by General Pillow the day before, who was ordered to fall back, and
Gen. Quitman ordered to occupy the same ground.

"I will here remark that Mr. Jasper M'Donald, son of Governor
M'Donald, of Georgia, who was in possession of a 'Mississippi rifle,'
attached himself to our little rifle squad at Tampico, and continued
with us. And I would farther remark, that Capt. Davis refused to
let me march with his company that night in consequence of my attack of fever, and ordered Mr. Wm. Laird, one of our mess, to remain
with me on the beach, where one of each mess in each regiment was
left to take care of the sick and baggage.

"Shortly after Col. Jackson, with the Georgia regiment, had
taken possession of some temporary trenches made by General Pillow
on the day previous, a party of Mexicans in considerable strength
came within three or four hundred yards and opened a harmless fire
upon that regiment. At the request of Mr. M'Donald and the squad
of Mississippians, Col. Jackson gave them permission to go without
any officer to a point on the sand-hills within efficient range and
commence war on 'their own hook;' this they quickly put into execution. But the sharp crack of the rifles soon attracted the attention
of Gen. Quitman, who, it seems, had given orders that no shot should
be fired without his express orders, but this order had not been delivered to Col. Jackson. Gen. Quitman was soon upon the ground, and
stopped the sport; but the matter was soon explained by Col. Jackson, and Gen. Quitman himself ordered the 'rifles' and some fifteen
of Capt. Davis's company to go to another point and attack the Mexicans. This party was commanded by Capt. Davis, and numbered
twenty-three, besides Capt. Davis; but before they reached the point
designated, while passing the sharp crest of a sand-hill, they were attacked by another party of Mexicans on their flank, at some hundred
and twenty yards distant. This was answered by Capt. Davis; and
Gen. Quitman, though on foot, was soon upon the ground, and ordered them to fight it out where they stood. The Mexicans being in
considerable strength, divided into companies of some fifty, by firing
and falling back kept up an incessant roll, showing generally but a
part of their persons above the sharp apex of the opposite ridge.
After this little fight had lasted some twenty-five or thirty minutes,
and Mr. Thos. J. Lott, of the Mississippi squad, Mr. M'Donald, and
some six or eight others were *hors de combat,* Gen. Quitman, whose
entire person had been exposed to the Mexican fire most of this time,
ordered up Lieut. Col. Dickerson and two companies of the South
Carolina regiment. Col. Dickerson was badly wounded almost as

soon as he reached the ground; the fight continued some ten or fifteen minutes after their arrival, when the Mexicans retired, and several ponies and other trophies were secured by the victors. These particulars I got from the actors and eye-witnesses, and among them Gen. Quitman, who frequently assured me that the little squad of Mississippians fully sustained the reputation of their state on that occasion, which was as warm while it lasted as need be, as not a single one of Capt. Davis's little command escaped without a brush or a wound from a Mexican ball.

"Some ten or twelve of those who were wounded were placed in hospital near the scene of the fight (which occurred on Thursday), and all seemed to be doing well, when, on Saturday night, by an unfeeling, or rather brutal command of Maj. Gen. Patterson, the wounded were ordered to be removed from the house they were in to a house some mile or two off, for no other purpose than to let this Gen. Patterson occupy the house for his head-quarters (Gen. Scott's and Gen. Quitman's head-quarters were in their marquees upon the sand); the weather at night was very warm. Mr. M'Donald and others, whose wounds were among the worst, refused to be removed; but after the officer who had been ordered to make the removal informed Gen. Patterson of this refusal, it was agreed that some of those who were most dangerously wounded should remain until near daylight the next morning (Sunday), when the atmosphere would be cooler, and the removal took place at that time, by four men carrying each one of the wounded in a blanket; this removal, however, irritated Mr. Lott's wound, which was in the thigh. A high fever supervened in an hour or two—the wounded thigh began to swell—that night mortification commenced, and at four o'clock on Monday morning he died. This removal retarded the recovery of many of the others who were wounded—but they *did* recover. I may be wrong in thus denouncing General Patterson, but I can not think so—I wish I could. Mr. Thos. J. Lott was about the only man I ever knew who was utterly incapable of fear, and, like nearly all truly brave men, he was generous and obliging, often to a fault. He was the grandson of your old friend, Joseph M'Afee, Sen., of Covington County, now dead for many years, and the nephew of Joseph M'Afee, Jun., late senator from that county, and of Madison M'Afee, our late popular auditor of popular accounts, and the cousin of your friend, Col. John Watts, a former senator from that county also.

"The siege of Vera Cruz progressed. Gen. Scott closed his lines around the city. Communication with it was cut off by land and by sea, under the command of Commodore Perry. About the 23d or 24th of March Gen. Scott made his last demand on the city to surrender, which, being refused, he gave them warning that at a certain hour he would open his batteries upon the city; and at the appointed hour he commenced a brisk and effective cannonade, which was answered by fifty guns to his one. This grand display continued for near three days.

"The day after it began my health had improved, so that Dr. Cuyler, of the regular army (a man as remarkable for his kindness of heart as he is distinguished in his profession), who had been my physician, permitted me to rejoin my company. On the 27th General

Quitman informed me that he had received instructions from headquarters, that, if the city did not capitulate before that time, at one o'clock next morning the whole American army would be ordered.to the attack. But the carnage and bloodshed consequent upon such an assault was averted by the cessation of hostilities, and the agreement to surrender by the enemy. On the 29th the city was formally surrendered.

"This siege of Vera Cruz cost the American army but seventeen lives lost by Mexican missiles, but hundreds by the climate and exposed life of the soldier. Not one of our little squad but what was more or less sick, and continued so until after we arrived at home.

"About the 1st of April Gen. Quitman was ordered to advance upon Alvarado to take that place, and secure as many horses as possible to enable Gen. Scott to move into the interior: the result of that expedition is a matter of history. It is needless to say how much disappointment was expressed by the whole command, when, about eighteen miles above Alvarado, word was received that the place had been evacuated by the Mexican soldiery (some three thousand in number), and the place had surrendered to the navy. The disappointment expressed by General Quitman's command (the Georgia, South Carolina, and Alabama regiments) was not at losing the *horses*, but at losing a chance for a *respectable fight*, his command being about fifteen hundred.

"After our return from Alvarado Gen. Quitman took up quarters on the plain south of the city of Vera Cruz. The only water we could get to drink was procured by digging some three feet into the loose sand, when the brackish sea-water percolated through, and afforded us an abundant supply, though very warm and disagreeable. This water excited that terrible scourge of armies, the diarrhœa. The Georgians and Alabamians were acclimated, and had learned to be prudent in their diet. The Mississippians, as we were called, were all sick, but no more of us died; but the South Carolinians suffered exceedingly, from three to nine dying every day from the time we returned from Alvarado until we left for home.

"General Quitman, at this time, was confident that no more active service would be had by the American army that summer, and he was confident that after the battle of Buena Vista and the fall of Vera Cruz the war was virtually closed. This opinion was at that time generally entertained both by the American army in Mexico and by the people at home. So with this prospect of an uneventful life in Mexico, and the wretched health of nearly all of us, we determined to return home; and, through the kindness of Gen. Quitman, we procured passage in the American store-ship 'America,' commanded by one Joseph P. Levy. We went on board about the 13th, together with some 150 invalid soldiers on deck, and some thirty, mostly invalid officers, in the cabin. We paid for cabin passage one dollar per day, and after a passage of *nineteen* days we landed at New Orleans. The captain having by that time sold out, at more than California prices, a large lot of his private stores, such as brandy, whisky, cigars, etc., which speculation and *quick trip* was duly reported by a committee appointed by the cabin passengers to Col. ——, of the commissary department, on our arrival in New Orleans, who did not wait to hear the whole story told, but gave Captain Levy permission to *retire* from the American service.

"I have extended this communication much beyond what I intended, but I do not wish to close without a slight tribute to real worth where it is due. While I lay sick, before the surrender of Vera Cruz, Dr. Cuyler directed Mr. M'Kenzie to procure certain articles of food, etc., suited to my condition. Mr. M'Kenzie sought for them at all the sutlers' booths, but could not find them. He then went to the quarter-master's department. He was told by the clerks that the things he wished were there, but were difficult to come at. He told them that Dr. Cuyler thought it absolutely necessary to his friend's recovery that these things should be obtained. This made no impression upon them. He came back and told Dr. Cuyler of his failure, who started him on a second search, but with no better success than before, until he reached the quarter-master's department again, where he became very importunate, and the clerks were about to put him out, when Captain Irwin, the chief of that department in Gen. Scott's division, entered, and by accident overheard a part of this conversation. He called Mr. M'Kenzie to him, heard his requests, and demanded of the clerks if these things were there. They said they were, but very difficult to get at. Captain Irwin ordered them to get the articles, and never to let him hear of a soldier applying for any thing and being refused under such circumstances; that difficulty of access must never be given as an excuse for not furnishing any article in that department. This produced the articles in a few minutes. While the clerks were thus engaged, he told Mr. M'Kenzie that hereafter, when any thing was wanting in that department, he must not hesitate to come directly to him, be it ever so small, and if it was to be had he should have it. This is but one of the least of the thousand good offices of Captain Irwin to the sick soldiers on that line, and he should have a monument to his memory.

"The names of this little party of Covington County boys are, Daniel C. M'Kenzie, George W. Steele, Arthur Lott, Wm. Laird, Wm. Blair Lord, Laurin Rankin Magee, Hugh A. M'Leod, Thomas J. Lott (killed), Cornelius M'Laurin.

"Pardon this very long and hasty document, prepared in the course of a few hours in one day, and from memory alone. Your note revived so many old associations that I found it very difficult to condense and say what I wished to. This has not been written with the anticipation that it will be published, but you can use it as you may choose in whole or in part."

E.

The following beautiful ballad appeared in Harper's Magazine for September, 1857. It is from the pen of L. A. Bargie, Esq., of Washington:

THE TAKING OF THE BELEN GATE.

BY MUDIL BRAIG.

"IT is an aged soldier,
  All seamed with ghastly scars—
A wreck cast up on the beach of peace
  From the foaming surge of wars.
He is resting, in the noontide,
  Beneath a beechen-tree,
And the village school-boys gather 'round
  Or clamber on his knee;
For they love the good old soldier
  With his tales of the long ago,
Of the battles won and the high deeds done
  On the plains of Mexico.

"'They tell me, boys, the moments
  With doubt and fear are rife,
And patriot-virtues can not thrive
  In the air of civil strife.
But it matters not; when danger
  Assails our native land,
Mark then how quickly faction flies,
  And brave souls take their stand.
A freeman's hardy courage
  Needs but a foreign foe;
And so we proved before the world
  In the war with Mexico.
They were martyrs, those who perished
  For their country's trust and fame;
And glorious in the after years
  Shall be each sainted name.
They were strong to toil and suffer,
  They were strong to dare and bleed,
They were hearts sent forth from the hand of God,
  To meet the time of need!'

"The eldest of the children
  Is a noble, fair-haired boy,
And he drinks the words with a willing ear
  And a kindling smile of joy;
And his little eyes are widened,
  As at a trumpet's call:
'Now tell us of the hottest fight,
  And the bravest deed of all.'

"'Ah!' cries the old man, grimly,
  'We had enough to do;
For ne'er unstained with native gore
  The starry banner flew;
But we owed the most to valor,
  And the least to favoring fate,

At the taking of the Belen Pass,
  And the storming of the Gate.

"'We had gone through fire and labor
  For many a night and day,
From Palo Alto's mournful field
  To the heights of Monterey.
We paused at Buena Vista,
  Contreras felt our blow,
And at last we saw the distant spires
  In the Vale of Mexico.

"'Chapultepec is taken!
  Upon her ruined walls
A huge and smoky canopy,
  Like a shroud of horror, falls.
The bee-like swarms that clustered,
  For life and home to strive,
Are routed from their broken halls
  Or burned within their hive.
The guns that woke the morning
  Are dumb beneath our tread,
As on we march, in serried files,
  Through a desert of the dead!

"'All faintly in the distance
  Are heard the foe's alarms;
And hot, and grimed with blood and dust,
  We are resting on our arms.
On every war-worn visage,
  Stern grief with triumph blends;
For each has sought among the ranks
  And missed his kin or friends.
The voices that were dearest,
  We ne'er shall hear them more;
Our butchered comrades lie behind,
  And Vengeance stalks before.

"'Well may we halt our column,
  On the steep so dearly won;
Much has been dared, and much is gained,
  But more must yet be done.
Well may we halt our column,
  To catch a moment's breath;
For the road in front is leading o'er
  To the very jaws of Death.

"'It is a narrow causeway
  Across that dark morass,
With heavy arches frowning down
  Upon the fearful pass;
And at the giant portal
  The City takes her stand,
Hurling defiance back upon
  The invaders of the land.

Like a grim and surly watch-dog
  Stares forth each deep-mouthed gun;
And plumes, and helms, and burnished steel
  Are gleaming in the sun.
We have chased the wounded tigress
  To the entrance of her lair;
And, mad to battle for her young,
  She turns upon us there.
And loudly rings the war-cry,
  And wide the flags are cast,
And Mexico will make this hour
  Her proudest, or her last;
For all of savage valor,
  And all of burning hate,
That have outlived the shocks of war,
  Are at the Belen Gate.

" 'He comes, our mighty leader,
  Along the wasted van;
There is no heart in all the ranks
  That does not love that man!
He passes 'mid the columns;
  And it is a glorious sight
To see him form them for the fray,
  But his brow is dark as night.
He is thinking of his brave ones,
  Who sleep the eternal sleep,
Among the slaughtered enemy,
  On yonder bloody steep.
He is thinking of the succors,
  That should have come ere now;
Such thoughts may dim the brightest eye,
  And cloud the fairest brow.
But he gazes o'er the causeway,
  And he hears the foeman's cry;
And the old stern look is on his face,
  And the fire is in his eye.

" ' "Forward!' and at the signal,
  Beneath the general's glance,
With dauntless mien and measured tread
  The lengthened lines advance.

" ' There comes a blaze of lightning
  From gate, and wall, and spire,
As though the city had put on
  A girdle all of fire!
There comes a burst of thunder,
  As though the teeming earth
Were laboring with volcanic throes,
  O'er some sulphureous birth!
There comes a pattering shower
  Of iron down the pass,

'Neath which the solid masonry
  Is chipped like broken glass!
It was as though the Demons
  Had risen 'gainst our plan,
And brought the guns of hell to bear
  Upon the march of man!

"'But where the invading army,
  That stood so proudly there?
Has it *all* so soon been swept away?
  Has it melted into air?
No: far beneath the arches,
  At the signal of command,
Protected by the friendly stone,
  Behold each little band.
But onward, ever onward!
  No time to pause or doubt!
The glancing shot that skip within
  Bespeak the storm without.
We are near upon our foemen,
  We can count their fierce array,
The bayonet now must do its part,
  And end the fearful fray.

"'"Charge!" and we break from cover,
  With the panther's spring and yell!
Cannon and musket from the gate
  Peal back the challenge well.
And now a bullet strikes me,
  And I stagger to my knee;
While past me rush, in headlong race,
  The champions of the free.
I rise and totter forward,
  Although with failing breath;
For who would follow such a chase
  So far, and miss the death?
The smoke has covered all things
  In its darkest battle-shroud,
Save where yon living line of fire
  Lights up the murky cloud;
And there our gallant fellows
  Are raging in the strife,
Before that stern and dangerous Gate,
  Whose toll is human life!
They are chafing like the billows
  Upon a midnight shore,
With a tempest driving on behind,
  And a wall of rock before!

"'I see our gallant chieftain
  In the hottest of the fire;
I see our soldiers gather near,
  Like children 'round their sire;

I see him at the portal,
  Still calling on his men :
And now the hot blood from my wound
  Has blinded me again.

" 'I hear our fellows cheering,
  As though to rend the skies ;
And hastily I wipe away
  The blood-gouts from my eyes.
And I, too, stand uncovered,
  And shout with joy elate ;
For the Stars and Stripes are waving high
  Above the Belen Gate !' "

F.

From the Mississippian.

QUITMAN AT MONTEREY.

BY JOHN S. MURPHY.

"On the morning of the battle of Monterey it was observed that
Gen. Quitman was the only field-officer of the army dressed in full
uniform. A friend remonstrated with the general, and said he would
be a conspicuous mark for the Mexicans. The writer of this heard
the reply, and challenges the pages of ancient and modern history for
a more heroic expression :

" 'The more balls aimed at me, the less will be directed at my
men.' "—*Brandon Platform.*

"Where Sierra Madre's summits sublimely raise their head,
And cast their mighty shadow athwart San Juan's bed,
A beauteous valley lieth, and from its breast of green,
And 'mid its forests olden a city fair is seen,
Before whose ramparts frowning, and battlemented walls,
The bugle of the Northman a band heroic calls.

"San Juan's murmuring river a dirge precursive sings ;
The trumpet of the Northman prelusive pæan rings ;
For banner'd hosts advancing to where yon walnut-trees[*]
Umbrageous hang their verdure, and whisper on the breeze
A requiem low chiming with Juan's sorrowing flood,
Speak to the Aztec chieftain of vanquishment and blood.

" 'Tis the army of Columbia ; their lurid battle eve
Gives to the anxious Mexican a bivouac and reprieve ;
But short from war the respite, for morning's dawning sun
Is heralded most grandly by Taylor's signal gun ;
And forth from groves cascaded the serried troops defile
'Neath bannered stars reflecting the sunlight's vestal smile.

[*] Gen. Taylor's troops encamped at Walnut Springs the night before the battle of
Monterey.

"Within thy moated bosom, O splendid Monterey,
Concealed by wall and turret, and firm in their array,
Ten thousand Mex'an soldiers await, with eager brand,
The onset of those squadrons, invasive of their land;
Seven thousand are the foemen; from victor strife they come;
And still, in soul invincible, exultant rolls their drum.

"And foremost, bravely foremost, is seen a small brigade;
Five hundred Tennesseans deploy from yonder glade;
While Mississippi's Rifles, by fearless Davis led,
Give presage to the Mexicans of conflict sternly dread.
Three suns will rise o'er carnage; a chill September night
Shall 'lume with Luna's silver the ghastly of that fight.

"Ho! on a prancing charger, with epaulet and plume,
And sword that swiftly sendeth each foeman to the tomb,
Amid the battle's clangor, confronting gun and spear,
And serried lines of lances in war's resplendent gear,
See yonder placid chieftain, all gaudily arrayed—
E'en as the courtly warrior on holiday parade.

"The sheen of fame already has 'lumed his lofty brow,
Though civic honor's laurel has circled it ere now;
And in the eagle brilliance of that dark, undaunted eye
Is flashed the high expression of the soul that dares to die—
Or conquer for the country that borrows from the stars
The splendors of the banner that guides her in her wars.

"Each gallant of the Mex'ans, who trophy proud would ask
When conflict's din is ended, and doff'd the soldier's casque,
Has marked with glance expectant that majesty of form,
Which, angel-like, is seeking the battle's fiercest storm:
Ay, trophy proud it would be—that falchion gleaming grand,
And cleaving glory's pathway, in Quitman's strong-nerv'd hand.

"An aid-de-camp upriding, in haste precipitant,
Just as a death-wing'd bullet the hero's cheek has glanc'd,
In accents earnest urgeth his chieftain to retire
Before the foe's persistent and well-concentred fire;
'Oh! see you not,' he pleadeth, 'Ampudia's design?
The city lost were conquest, if still'd that heart of thine!

"'My general, our soldiers would sorrow long this day—
Now promising from glory her most effulgent ray—
If muffled drums were pealing the death-roll for thy fall,
And triumph shouts repressed were by Quitman's martial pall!
Nor grant the Mex'an braggart this hour the vauntful boast,
That though we've slain his hundreds, in *you* we've lost a host.'

"As when with inspiration a prophet's face doth shine,
And dazzles the beholder with brilliancy divine,
So gleamed that hero visage, so mounted high that soul,
Estranged from fear's impellings, disdaining death's control;
While all on earth magnanimous, or god-like in yon sky
Was haloed round that presence, and flashing from that eye—

"As thus, with lips expanded, and battle-blade upraised
(Though oft death's leaden missive his glitt'ring person grazed).
The chieftain brief responded, ' 'Tis well at me they aim
The thickly-flying bullets that many braves might maim:
Depart! ambition 's sated, when on this gory field
Your Quitman is at once to you a leader and a shield !'

" 'Twas said ; and, onward dashing, the city's rear is won ;
The strong redoubt is captured, and silenced is each gun ;
And still, in trappings gorgeous, conspicuous appears,
Where hearts with joy o'erflowing, the astral standard rears,
That stately chief whose bosom had breasted many balls
That grief might be diverted from Mississippi's halls.

"Oh! mother of the soldier, perennial bay enweave !
Thou daughter of the rifleman, with laurel crown the brave !
And wives by war unwidow'd, and sons unreft of sires,
When, gay of heart, ye gather round your bright autumnal fires,
Remember, in your gladness, that hero's towering plume ;
A Quitman's valor peerless averted woe and gloom !"

G.

SPEECH OF JOHN A. QUITMAN, OF MISSISSIPPI, ON THE POWERS OF
THE FEDERAL GOVERNMENT WITH REGARD TO THE TERRITORIES:
DELIVERED DURING THE DEBATE ON THE PRESIDENT'S ANNUAL
MESSAGE, IN THE HOUSE OF REPRESENTATIVES, DECEMBER 18TH,
1856.

Mr. Speaker,—When I rose on yesterday it was my intention merely to explain my position on two points of the pending discussion ; but
since I have the floor this morning, by the courtesy of the house, and
have had a night to reflect upon the subject, I shall avail myself more
fully of the opportunity, and devote the allotted hour to such notice
of the various questions involved in this debate on the President's annual message as my limited time will permit.

The most striking feature of this debate consists in the differences
of opinion which exist, not only between the several political parties
represented on this floor, but, to some extent, even between members
of the same party, on the subject of the relations which the Territories
and their inhabitants bear toward the federal government and toward
the states. This arises sometimes from erroneous conceptions of the
theory of our government, and more frequently from the attempt to
apply rules of action to particular cases without reference to any theory whatever. It is my purpose, therefore, to go back to the fountain-
head and source of these differences of construction and opinion.
While I shall endeavor to present my views of the true theory of our
political system, I know that I must do it briefly, and confine myself
to a mere glance at the subject.

And here let me premise that, although desirous of hastening to the
consideration of that subject, I feel it proper to notice in passing one
or two other points of this debate. The first is the declaration of the

President's Message with regard to the present aspect of the slavery question. In my opinion, that able document on this subject proves itself. Mailed in truth, it stands impenetrable against all the assaults that can be made upon it. I regard it as well-timed, and its conclusions as strictly correct.

Had I before entertained any doubts of the ultimate aims and objects of the Anti-slavery, or self-styled "Republican" party, the developments which have been made in this discussion would have removed such doubts. The President speaks boldly, but with due caution. I, for one, indorse his language. Yet, I do not mean to say that you, Mr. Speaker, or others here of your party, directly propose, in the words of the President, "to effect a change in the relative condition of the white and black races in the slaveholding states." I mean to say that the avowed objects of your political association would, should you become successful, lead to such a result; and I mean to say farther, what no man will dare to contradict, that there are many distinguished members of the Anti-slavery party, constituting the very soul of that party, who have openly declared that their great purpose is the ultimate destruction of the institution of African slavery, intertwined as it is with the social systems of fifteen sovereign states of this Union. Your platforms, it is true, have not threatened *direct* interference in the affairs of the Southern States. No party dares do that. The North, the whole North, dares not directly assail the institution in the states. Were the North to make such an attempt, under our present system of government, we would not stoop to argue the point, but, confident of our own strength, would treat the assault with contempt and ridicule; and such, Mr. Speaker, would be your course, and that of your political friends, were the combined South to assail any essential domestic policy which you gentlemen of the North think fit to entertain in your social systems.

Believing that it can be very clearly shown that negro slavery, as it exists in the South, has not only been hitherto one of the chief sources of our national prosperity, but is, and must continue to be, an element of moral and military strength, I have never been disposed, with some timid politicians, to shrink from the discussion of these questions when obtruded upon us by the ignorant or designing. But, during the present debate, such discussion is unimportant; it is, at least, not the real issue. The practical question is, whether the slaveholding states, and the inhabitants of those states, are or are not entitled to an equal participation, not merely in a portion of the advantages of our system of government, but in *all* those advantages, in all acts of legislation, in all places, always and every where, as well within the limits of the respective states as in the Territories, the common property of all the states—whether, I repeat, we shall not have an equal participation in every right, both direct and collateral, which may be incident to the equality of the states. We claim the privilege of equal competition for political power in the government, unrestrained by the action of that government. We claim the right of expansion as essential to our future security and prosperity. We may hereafter require more elbow-room, to guard against the possibility that a system of labor now so beneficent and productive might, from a redundant slave population confined to narrow limits, become an ultimate evil. We claim peace and tranquillity from this war of hatred, malice, and uncharitableness.

For these reasons, I cordially thank the President of the United States for the bold, clear, and manly tone in which he has rebuked this anti-slavery organization. Instead of meeting this insidious and ill-disguised war upon the South with weak efforts at conciliation and compromise, he has repelled the enemy with an open defiance. I like the temper in which this is done, and my judgment approves the policy of such a course. The principles of this sectional anti-slavery organization leave no middle ground for concession or compromise. There is no half-way house for timid or time-serving politicians. The principle must be squarely met with its direct converse. It is a battle for victory or death. In this struggle either *you* must conquer and crush *us*, or *we* must succeed in defending the rights and privileges of our section. As the contest now stands, it is a war to the knife. You are the aggressors; you have brought about this issue. I am aware that the leaders of the Black Republican party—I qualify the term to distinguish this new organization from the Republican party of Jefferson's day—I am aware, I say, that the leaders of Black Republicanism have studiously denied the charge of aggression. To meet their denial, it is enough to point to the broad basis of their party, which, I am ready to admit, deserves the designation of "great" applied to it by their orators and presses. It is, unfortunately, great in its numbers, great in its power for evil, and, more than all, great in being founded upon a wide-spread sentiment of hostility to slavery. Upon that sentiment, Mr. Speaker, and not upon the Kansas Act, nor upon the repeal of the Missouri restriction, rests your political power and that of your party. That sentiment, inculcated in your schools and in your churches for a quarter of a century, is the cement which unites discordant political elements, and constitutes the grand basis of the organization of Black Republicanism. Even had this party never tendered political issues, or adopted a political platform, it would still deserve the rebuke of the President for the war of opinion which, from its constitutional elements, it wages against the social systems of the South. That alone, under a common government, in which public sentiment possesses so much influence, would sow the fruitful seeds of alienation of feeling between the sections, and would, therefore, lead to an eventual separation.

There is another point in this discussion, Mr. Speaker, upon which I must not forget to touch. While expressing my hearty concurrence with the views of the President on the slavery question, I will not conceal my regret that I can not also commend the course of the administration in regard to Central American affairs.

I listened yesterday with much pleasure to the eloquent remarks of the gentleman from Alabama (Mr. Walker) on that part of the message which refers to these matters. In most of the views presented by him I concur. The policy which has generally been pursued by our government in relation to Central America has been too narrow, too timid, and too much warped by European diplomacy. My judgment and my heart have always responded to the noble sentiments uttered by Mr. Clay in 1818, when the question was before Congress, as to the recognition of the young republics then springing into existence on our southern borders, and the propriety of adopting penal laws to restrain our citizens from aiding those republics to secure their independence. But having fully presented my opinions on this subject in a speech delivered during the last regular session of Congress on a bill introduced by me to modify our existing neutrality laws, I will not now repeat them. I am happy to hear the gentleman from Alabama expressing his agreement with me so far, at least, as to admit that those laws have been construed too broadly, and enforced with too much rigor; and I hope that, when the time shall come to act, that gentleman will be found standing by my side in the effort to repeal the odious features of an act which has too long been a stumbling-block in the path of our national destiny, and obstructed the progress of civilization and liberal government on this continent.

Mr. Walker. I beg leave to assure the gentleman from Mississippi that I read his argument with infinite pleasure; and I believe that I then told him that I stood side by side with him on that question.

Mr. Quitman. I remember the remark, and am happy to hear this reiteration of the gentleman's opinion. As his objections to the neutrality laws, in his speech of yesterday, were limited to the *mode* in which those laws have sometimes been enforced, and did not seem to extend to the laws themselves, I feared that I might have misunderstood him. I shall rejoice to have his efficient aid in adapting our legislation to more liberal and expanded views of policy. We are the great power of this continent, and have the right to adopt a policy purely American. I am utterly opposed to moulding our national policy in regard to American affairs to suit the views of England, France, or any of the great powers of Europe. We want no treaties with them to fix our relations with American states, or to define and regulate our connection with, or our duties toward those states. Great Britain does not deign to consult *us* in reference to her relations with the empires of Asia; and why should we administer to her pride by making her a party to our intercourse with the adjacent states of this continent?

The point of most interest to us at present is Nicaragua. I do not propose to pass an eulogium on General Walker, but I *do* regard him as one of those instruments which, in the hands of Providence, are used to facilitate the march of civilization and improvement, and the spread of liberal political principles throughout the fairest portions of the world. Shall our government, then, throw obstacles in the way of his progress? Should we not rather, by all proper means, encourage such desirable results? Had a liberal policy always been pursued, and had not our government, by the enactment of stringent and severe penal laws, adopted the narrow and suicidal policy of preventing our citizens from embarking in enterprises neither unconstitutional nor violative of our neutral duties, the liberal party in Nicaragua, of which Walker is now the chief, would be peacefully and firmly established in power and authority, instead of being threatened with annihilation by a combination of semi-savage foes. That party would now be left to lay the foundations of civil and religious liberty, and to develop the vast and varied resources of that rich and beautiful country—resources constituting mines of agricultural, mineral, and commercial wealth which will forever lie buried, unless brought to light by American enterprise.

Although, Mr. Speaker, I find the minutes of my hour rapidly gliding away, and although I have not yet touched the principal subject I rose to discuss, I can not permit the opportunity to pass without an allusion to another matter, which, though of little practical consequence in itself, derives some importance from its connection with the great issues of the day. On Monday last a member from Tennessee [Mr. Etheridge] introduced the following resolution:

"*Resolved*, That the House of Representatives regard all suggestions and propositions of every kind, by whomsoever made, for the revival of the African slave-trade, as shocking to the moral sentiment of the enlightened portion of mankind; and that any action on the part of Congress conniving at or legalizing that horrid and inhuman traffic, would justly subject the government and citizens of the United States to the reproach and execration of all civilized and Christian people throughout the world."

Upon objection made, the rules were suspended, and the resolution passed under the pressure of the previous question. Debate and even explanation were thus cut off, and our constituents, as well as the public, were left to guess at the reasons of our respective votes. After the passage of this resolution, the gentleman from South Carolina [Mr. Orr], who had in vain attempted to amend the former resolution, introduced another proposition, in the following words:

"*Resolved*, That it is inexpedient, unwise, and contrary to the settled policy of the United States to repeal the laws prohibiting the African slave-trade."

This also passed by a decisive majority; only eight members voted in the negative, debate and explanation having been again cut off by the application of the parliamentary thumb-screw.

I voted against both resolutions; and now take this first opportunity of stating the reasons of those votes. Both resolutions were, in my opinion, as objectionable in substance as the mode of forcing a vote on them under the pressure of the *previous question* was improper. The prominent features in the proposition of the member from Tennessee are its sinister expressions, and the intensely virtuous indignation manifested, not against the revival of the African slave-trade, but against the wickedness of those who would have the hardihood to make suggestions or propositions in relation thereto; and, as if to deter all good patriots from even harboring such suggestions, it invokes the reproach and execration of "the civilized and Christian people throughout the world" upon the government and people of the United States should Congress, by any action, connive at or listen to such suggestions. It denounces thoughts, propositions, and opinions, on the assumption that they are shocking to the moral sentiment of mankind. Now, sir, I find in the written chart of the duties and powers of this house no authority to take charge of the public or private morals of the good people of the country. It is a vain and pharisaical arrogance of superior virtue in us to assume such censorship. I intend no personal disrespect when I say that this house, constituted as it is, is one of the last tribunals to which questions of public morals or of private honor should be referred; and yet, sir, the resolution of the

gentleman from Tennessee, if it sprang from any higher motive than
that of entrapping political opponents, was a mere attempt to denounce as immoral and unchristian certain opinions known to be entertained by some of our fellow-citizens, and to invoke, in advance of
any proposed action, horrid imprecations on the country should Congress in any way connive at such sentiments by any political action.
I surely do the gentleman no injustice when I say that his object was
not merely to obtain an expression of the opinion of this house against
the African slave-trade. He will hardly venture to say that that
alone was his object. It went obviously farther. The studied phraseology in which the resolution is clothed, going to the very verge of
parliamentary license, indicates the purpose of obtaining the influence
of this house to put down and stifle opinions and propositions on subjects of legitimate inquiry, on the grounds that they are infamous and
detestable. It is a precedent full of mischief and danger, which I regret especially to see introduced by a *Southern* man. Under it, what
is to prevent the introduction of a resolution declaring the holding of
slaves to be immoral, inhuman, and contrary to the spirit of Christianity? There are probably some on this floor ready to present such
a proposition, and, from the complexion of this house, I am not certain it would not pass if propelled by the brute force of the previous
question. I repeat, the precedent is dangerous, and, in my opinion,
more pregnant of evil than the "suggestions" so much condemned by
the mover. I regret that it should have received the sanction of a
single Democrat on this floor. Were we sitting as a board of censors
upon the morality of practices affecting human happiness in general,
I would desire to include in our censures the cooley-trade now practiced by our refined and virtuous ally, England; for by that trade
white men, if I may so designate the Chinese, are carried into the
worst kind of slavery. I would wish also to embrace in our depreca-
tions the "shocking and unchristian" practice of immuring in the unhealthy and fetid prison-rooms of a factory for eleven hours of the day
white children of both sexes and of tender age, thereby destroying the
health and elasticity of their bodies, and blunting and stupefying their
intellects, by the constant employment of watching the interminable
whirling of the spinning-jenny. I protest, Mr. Speaker, against this
house establishing any code of morals for the country; but, if we are
to have one, let it be general.

Mr. Etheridge. Will the gentleman yield to me for a moment?

Mr. Quitman. My time is so short that I would rather not be diverted from my argument.

Mr. Etheridge. My object in rising was to ask the House to extend
the time of the gentleman, and give him an opportunity of discussing
these questions fully.

Mr. Quitman. I will now go on; and should my hour expire before I shall have concluded what I have to say, I would be happy to
accept the proffered courtesy. I do not often occupy the time of the
house, and would not do so now had I not been incidentally drawn
into this debate.

Before I leave these questions of ethics, I can not pass without notice a singular bill which quietly and silently glided through this
house the other day, apparently unobserved by the vigilant guardians

of the Constitution who sit near me. I allude to the bill presented by the chairman of the Committee of Ways and Means [Mr. Campbell], forbidding, under penal sanctions, the introduction of obscene, indecent, or immoral prints, statuary, etc. While the private motive may be proper, such a bill belongs to the description of legislation upon which I have been commenting, and, in my opinion, introduces a mischievous political precedent. In the first place, who are to constitute the censors? I doubt not that the Committee of Ways and Means would admit many specimens of art at which a portion of our sturdy countrymen and women, with a taste less artistically refined, but perhaps with more of virgin purity, would be shocked. We have statuary about this Capitol upon which some of my fair constituents could not look without a blush. But, sir, I would ask the chairman and Committee of Ways and Means, whence do they derive the power of supervising the public taste or morals? If they possess it, I also commend to their attention a bill to suppress the exhibition of model artists now so fashionable in our great cities.

I return, however, for a moment to the slave-trade resolutions of the gentleman from Tennessee. I was not at all surprised to see him refusing to suspend the previous question, at the request of my friend from South Carolina [Mr. Orr], to enable the latter gentleman to offer an amendment which would have brought the house to a direct vote on the expediency of reviving the African slave-trade; but I *was* surprised, in the sequel, to find the gentleman from South Carolina refusing a similar privilege to me. After the passage of the obnoxious resolution of the gentleman from Tennessee, my friend from South Carolina, with a view, no doubt, to put himself and friends right upon the journals, introduced a resolution differing from that he had originally proposed as a substitute. The first proposition would have been acceptable to all of us; the difference consisted in the addition of the words, " and contrary to the settled policy of the United States." The previous question having been called on this resolution, I appealed to the mover to permit an amendment, striking out the words *"contrary to the settled policy of the United States,"* in order that I, and those acting with me, might unite upon his resolution; but the gentleman refused to do for a political friend that which he complained had not been accorded to him by a political opponent. This want of courtesy compels me to make some explanation.

Mr. Orr. I did not complain of the refusal of the gentleman from Tennessee to let me offer an amendment to his resolution; I merely requested that he would afford me an opportunity so to do.

Mr. Quitman [addressing Mr. Orr]. Well, I recall the word "complain;" but, in making a request of a political opponent, you implied that it should have been granted. Now, Mr. Speaker, my position on this subject is simply this: I am *not* in favor of the revival of the African slave-trade. Not because I look upon it as " shocking, horrid, or deserving the execration of the civilized world;" for I believe it has resulted in practical benefit to the negro; not that I believe the transfer of a slave from benighted Africa to America—from the dominion of a cruel and despotic negro master to a kind and humane white master, does any harm to him or to the world; but I am opposed to the revival of the African slave-trade because, in my judgment, it is inexpedient, impolitic, and adverse to the interests of the section of country which I represent. Such, too, I believe to be the prevailing sentiment at the South. I should have voted, and am ready to vote, for any proposition which shall confine itself to a declaration against the policy or expediency of the African slave-trade; but I will not, by any fear of consequences or misconstruction, be driven to adopt the affectedly denunciatory language of the gentleman from Tennessee. It is the language either of cowardice or hypocrisy; not that of plain-dealing. I speak of the resolution, not of the gentleman. I should not be much surprised to find it followed by a resolution condemning the internal slave-trade. I say again, distinctly, that had these resolutions simply declared that the revival of the African slave-trade was inexpedient, and even against public policy, my voice would have been heard strongly in the affirmative; but I am opposed to lectures upon the morality of that trade. There I stand, and I can not be coaxed or dragooned into the support of resolutions which I do not believe to be true.

The resolution of the gentleman from South Carolina [Mr. Orr] was also objectionable, though not in the same degree. It proclaimed "*the settled policy of the country*" to be against a repeal of the present laws. Now, in the first place, in a progressive country like ours, where public sentiment sways the public policy, there is an impropriety in any Congress resolving what shall be the future or settled policy of the country. Every Congress will have enough to do to adapt its action and legislation to its own proper term of authority and power. I regard such language, to say the least of it, as empty declamation.

In the next place, it being admitted that treaties are laws, this language of the resolution goes to the extent of approving and perpetuating all our treaty stipulations in relation to the African slave-trade; and of some of these I do not approve, but, on the contrary, believe them to be unwise and impolitic. Such, for instance, is the stipulation to aid Great Britain in watching, with a naval force, the coast of Africa. Neither am I prepared to say, though opposed to the slave-trade, that it ought to be treated as piracy. I doubt much whether the horrors of the middle passage do not arise mainly from the false philanthropy of exaggerated punishments. Resting in this uncertainty, I could not, by my vote, declare the laws and treaties on this subject to be our "settled policy." For these reasons, now given because explanation was refused when the resolutions were offered, and because I regarded both resolutions as useless and unnecessary, I opposed them.

And now, Mr. Speaker, I come to the principal subject I rose to discuss, to which my mind has been led by observing the differences of opinion that exist, not only between the three political parties in this house, but between members of the same party, on the constitutional powers of Congress over the Territories. It is the fashion of the day to discuss pending questions rather as technical lawyers than as statesmen, and to treat them rather with reference to their political bearing than as parts of the true theory of government. The discordant opinions to which I have referred arise from different views of our political system. They could not exist to any considerable extent if elementary principles were well understood. Instead, then, of discussing in detail the various opinions that have been advanced on this floor, I propose to go back to the fountain-head and examine some of the cardinal principles of our system. If these be correctly understood, the conclusions which flow from them must either produce more uniformity of opinion on these subjects, or, at least, bring us to the point of divergence. There is a proneness in the human mind at all times toward strong government. One proof of this proneness is the prevalence, in all ages, of monarchies over free representative governments. In our system this feeling manifests itself in the tendency to centralism. It arises from the necessity of continuous intellectual efforts to maintain free government. There never was a more truthful remark than that uttered by Jefferson, "Eternal vigilance is the price of liberty." A people can not sleep and remain free. The *vis inertiæ* must be counteracted by frequent agitations of elementary principles.

In treating of the theory of our government, the great source of error lies in not defining and locating the SOVEREIGN POWER. I shall therefore endeavor to show what it is, and where it reposes. SOVEREIGNTY IS THAT HIGH POLITICAL POWER WHICH CAN CONTROL ALL OTHER POLITICAL POWERS. It can have no superior and no equal. If there be any other political power in the system higher, or greater, or more potent, then the former power is not sovereign. It admits of no rival. It can not be limited; for limitation proves the existence of a controlling power. It may act through different agencies, but can not itself be divided or parceled out. There can not be in the same system two sovereign powers. This is in politics as great an absurdity as the existence in mathematics of two longest lines or two highest numbers. In the moral world there is but one sovereign—God.

In every distinct political community the sovereign power must exist somewhere. It is impossible to conceive the one existing without the other. The moment the social compact is formed, that instant the sovereign power reposes somewhere. If it were possible to imagine a people springing, suddenly and at once, from a state of nature into political existence, the sovereignty would reside in the males of full age. It might be interesting to trace the existence of this high sovereign power among the civilized nations of the earth. I will allude to several, merely for the purpose of illustration. In Russia the sovereign power is in the autocrat. There is no power in that political organism to control his will. From his ukase there is no appeal. He can reverse judicial decisions, confiscate property, take life, and change the organic law. Respect for the revolutionary action of his subjects may restrain him, but there are no means of enforcing a political right against his sovereign will. In Great Britain, again, this high power rests in Parliament, comprised of the three great estates of the realm—King, Lords, and Commons. An act of Parliament is supreme. It can reverse the decisions of the courts, take away titles, confiscate estates, depose kings, destroy life, and change the organic law. There rests the sovereign power under that organism of government. Englishmen may talk about their rights, but they have none that may not be annihilated by an act of Parliament.

In the nations to which I have alluded, this high controlling power is so prominent as to be readily seen and fixed. In our system, the elaborate work of a more enlightened age of the world, and a more advanced stage of the human intellect, it is not so easy to trace clearly the location of the sovereign power. It exists, but where? Does it rest in the federal government? Let us apply the test of the definition I have given. Has the federal government power over all other powers? Not at all, sir. It is strictly limited; circumscribed by the most rigid limitations; forbidden, by its organic law, over which it has no control, from exercising many of the most important attributes of sovereignty. It can exercise no sovereign powers by its own intrinsic force. It is merely a part of the machinery of government, through which, as through an agency, some of the powers belonging to sovereignty are put into operation.

Do the state governments possess this high sovereign power? A mere glance at their structure shows that they do not. The state governments are the creatures of the state Constitutions. They may be enlarged, restricted, modified, and even annihilated by the organic law. They are, therefore, subject to a higher power, and are not supreme or sovereign. As in the case of the federal government, they are merely the agents through which the sovereign power is exercised, and have not that high attribute of themselves. We must look farther to find the deep sources of political authority. The origin, formation, and history of our system of government, as well as the frame-work of it, show clearly where this high power exists. It reposes in the sovereign states of this great confederacy—not in the state *governments*, but in the *states*. I emphasize the distinction, because the two are sometimes confounded. In a recent debate in the other wing of the Capitol, a senator, in alluding to the opinion of the Supreme Court that Congress possesses over the Territories the powers of the federal and state governments, drew the inference that Congress had power to establish or change the organic law. Now, neither the federal nor the state governments, nor both of them together, have any such power. The decision referred to does not, therefore, go to that extent. Neither the Legislature of the State of Mississippi, nor that of any other Southern state, can change or alter the status of a slave. The state alone, in its sovereign capacity, has the power of changing the organic law. Negro slavery constitutes a part of the social systems of these states, and, although their governments may regulate those systems, the sovereign power, which alone has the entire control of the organic law, can alone establish or destroy them. The states of this Union are *states* in every sense. I refer not only to the usual American sense of that word, but to the acceptation of the term as used by writers on the law of nations. They are separate political existences, each retaining within itself the entirety of its political sovereignty, and exercising the powers of government, in part, separately, through its state government, and in part, jointly with the other states, through the federal government, but all exercising their highest sovereign power only in convention, or such other mode as their Constitution or organic law shall prescribe. I know not, Mr. Speaker, whether I make myself distinctly understood. The opinions that I advance are the results of much reflection; but they are uttered without any previous preparation.

I have thus pointed out where, in my opinion, sovereignty rests in our complex system of government.

I know that opinions on this subject are widely different; but all must admit that, when the tie was severed which had bound the colonies to Great Britain, there sprang into existence thirteen sovereign and independent states, having with one another no connection save that produced by the presence of a common danger. They stood toward one another as separate, independent, friendly nations, each claiming for itself, and conceding to the rest, a distinct national existence. This character is stamped upon them, not only by all their political action, but by their formal acknowledgments to one another. In the articles of confederation entered into shortly after the conclusion of the Revolutionary War, at the time when men, North and South, understood the structure of our government certainly as well as they do now, this language is used:

"Each state retains its sovereignty, freedom, and independence, and every power, jurisdiction, and right which is not by these Articles of Confederation delegated to the United States in Congress assembled."

"*Each state retains its sovereignty, freedom, and independence.*" There was a separate sovereignty, a separate freedom, and a separate independence. Neither of these was delegated. Some powers, jurisdiction, and rights were alone for the time delegated—subject to be resumed by the sovereign.

Again, sir, upon the treaty of peace with Great Britain, how were the states then regarded? Although connected with one another by the articles of confederation, the King of England treated with them as distinct states, and not as a common nation. We are not a *nation*, but a union of states under a federal Constitution. It is a misnomer to style ourselves a "nation," though, since we act with other nations through a common government, they may with more propriety apply the term to us. The frequent use of the words "United States" as a substantive in the singular number, and of the term "nation" as applied to our union of states, is one of the evidences of the tendency of the public mind to political centralism. The first article of the treaty of peace with Great Britain, signed at Paris on the 30th of November, 1782, uses these significant terms:

"*Art.* 1. His Britannic majesty acknowledges the said United States, viz., New Hampshire, Massachusetts Bay, Rhode Island and Providence Plantations, Connecticut, New York, New Jersey, Pennsylvania, Delaware, Maryland, Virginia, North Carolina, South Carolina, and Georgia, to be free, sovereign, and independent STATES; that he treats with them as such; and for himself, his heirs, and successors, relinquishes all claims to the government, propriety, and territorial rights of the same, and every part thereof."

And so, Mr. Speaker, you may pursue the historic record of the formation of our political organism, and look in vain for any act by which that high power, which must exist in every political community, has been ceded from its original possessors—the states. The Constitution of the United States was acceded to by the states as states. Each for itself, in its sovereign capacity, entered into the compact. We find in it the delegation of some of the powers of government, but no cessions of sovereign power. That rested originally with the states; and there, I contend, it remains to-day. If it does not rest with the states where is it? I have shown that this government, being possessed only of limited powers, for specified purposes, can not be sovereign. That high power, I repeat, remains where it originally rested—in the states of this Union; and whenever it is called into action it must flow from its pristine source.

I may, Mr. Speaker, in the attempt to make myself understood, be charged with unnecessary repetition of the same idea; but our political system is very complex and much misapprehended. In its complicity, however, I recognize the great frame-work of the liberal age in which it was constructed; for that complicity was necessary to secure liberty by the protection of every interest involved.

I come now to apply this principle of sovereignty to the *Territories*. At the time of the formation of the federal Constitution there were not in existence any such municipal communities as those we now term Territories. Consequently the language of that instrument, which confers upon Congress the authority "to dispose of and make all needful rules and regulations for the territory and other property of the United States," was not intended to convey to Congress the right of legislation over the Territories as subsequently constituted. This is clear. The context itself shows that the word "territory" was palpably used in the sense of property, for the disposal of which Congress, the common agent of the states, was to make the "needful rules and regulations," such as to survey the lands and to provide for their sale. This is further shown by the stronger and more explicit language used in conferring the power of legislation over such cession as might be made by the states for the seat of government. Whence, then, is derived the power of Congress to legislate for a Territory as we now understand the term? Before I proceed to answer this question of the power of municipal legislation, I should state, what necessarily follows from the views which I have already presented, that the people of a Territory possess no sovereign power. They occupy the common territory of all the states, over which the states jointly not only possess the eminent domain, but also the ultimate sovereignty. The inhabitants of a Territory possess no more sovereignty over it than if they had established their residences in the Russian empire. All the political powers that the people of a Territory possess or acquire must come from the states, either by the common grant of all the states, or by cession from their agent, the federal government, under the Constitution. Now, sir, having fixed their true relations to the states, I shall proceed to answer the inquiry, whence does Congress derive the right of legislation over the Territories? It is, in my opinion, implied in the power delegated by the states to Congress in the Constitution to admit new states into the Union upon equal footing with the original states. This right necessarily implies the right of Congress to prepare the *people* (or rather the *inhabitants*, for the term "people" technically signifies a community politically organized, and can not, in that sense, be applied to the inhabitants of a Territory) for admission into the Union as a state. The major includes the minor—that is to say, under the power to "admit," Congress possesses the right of paving the way for that act—of making the preliminary arrangements for the important change of the political condition of a Territory. It is under that power, then, and not under the right to make "rules and regulations" for the disposal of the common territory that Congress can legislate for the Territories, or establish municipal governments therein. But, sir, this authority is limited to legislation, and does not extend to the exercise of any power properly appertaining to sovereignty, much less to the delegation of such attributes to the territorial government. The power of legislation, and that of making organic laws, are distinct things—the one may be exercised by the legislative branch of the government, the other is the exclusive attribute of the sovereign power. In the whole process, this high authority is brought into action in only one instance—on the admission of a new state. In the act of admission into the Union as a state, the people of a Territory are at once collectively invested with sovereignty. From that instant they stand as the peer of every other state. The sovereign power passes to them, not from the federal government (for that government can not hold it), but by the cession of the other states, in conformity with their constitutional compact, by which, by empowering Congress as their common agent to admit new states upon an equality with themselves, they have bound themselves to cede their joint sovereignty, until that moment retained, to their new sister.

From the principles I have laid down, Mr. Speaker, the inference clearly follows that Congress, possessing merely the power of municipal legislation to prepare the Territories for admission into the Union, has no power to exclude or abolish slavery in the Territories. Much less have the inhabitants of a Territory, possessing no inherent sovereignty, and having no political powers except those derived from Congress, this right.

A glance at the condition of the inhabitants of any portion of our common territory, before the establishment of any territorial government, may still farther tend to illustrate my views. What is the condition of the residents now upon the Gadsden purchase—the inhabitants of the rich and fruitful hills and dales of Arizonia? Are they in a state of nature, like the wild savage, without a political status, without laws to restrain them, or without rights to be protected? I think not; for I differ from my friend from South Carolina [Mr. Orr] in the opinion which he the other day advanced as to the state of a Territory. There is, sir, in my opinion, a common law, which exists in every portion of our common country, as well in the states as in the common territory, from the instant of its acquisition; and that law is the Constitution of the United States.

Mr. Orr. In speaking of the common law, I had reference to the common law of England. I stated expressly that, in my belief, the Constitution extended over the Territories.

Mr. Quitman. I then understood the gentleman to take the ground that no law for the protection of property existed in any of the Territories until made by the territorial Legislature. I think that I now comprehend his idea better. I maintain, in the first place, that the inhabitants of such portions of our territory have all the rights, privileges, and immunities provided or reserved in the Constitution. Furthermore, every citizen of any of the states, from whatever section of the country he goes, taking up his residence on the common territory of the states, carries with him all the essential rights which he possessed in his own state. The states being joint proprietors and co-sovereigns, the citizen of each state stands, as it were, upon the soil of his own state, as much so as if he stood upon the deck of an American vessel on the high seas. The general principles of law that are common to all the states, founded on usage and general conformity, prevail in and constitute the common law of the Territory. There may be no judicial organization to enforce that law, but it has its vitality, and exists; and, upon the establishment of judicial tribunals, would be recognized and acted upon without positive legislation on the subject of these rights. Prominent among these rights is that of property recognized by any of the states. When that right, as in the case of slaves, is recognized by the organic law of nearly one half of the states in the Union, and at least in one instance acknowledged by the Constitution of the United States, it not only exists and is available in the common territory of the states before the establishment of civil government there, but is far beyond the reach of both the federal and territorial governments when found on the common possessions of the states. There is but one power that can destroy my right to my slave, and that is the *state* in which I hold him, or to which I voluntarily carry him. If the federal government does not possess the right, it is absurd to say that one of its departments has it. While I concede to that high tribunal, the Supreme Court of the United States, the right to determine finally all cases of law and equity which come within its jurisdiction, I deny its authority to settle questions which involve the political rights of the states. The Constitution is the work of the states, and they must construe it for themselves upon all questions affecting their rights. These would cease to be rights, if subject to the antagonistic power against which they were limited. It is absurd to suppose that the states, in the formation of the Constitution, jealous of their great essential political rights, would have left them at the mercy of that very power against the encroachment of which they were erecting a barrier. It is yet more absurd to suppose that they would have left them, by construction, to one department of the government, and that department, both from its mode of appointment and its tenure of office, the least responsible to the people.

I approve, Mr. Speaker, the principles of the Kansas-Nebraska Act. I claim, under it, and under the Constitution, the right to carry my slave into either of those Territories. I know that this right, if a case can be made on it, may be the subject of the examination and decision of the Supreme Court of the United States, and that that decision, in any given case, would be final. I would abide by it, as a settlement of the case decided; but I am not willing to let it go to the world that I would respect the precedent, or that I would surrender the principle that the assertion of such essential rights belongs exclusively to the states aggrieved by their violation. The Supreme Court, in my opinion, possesses no jurisdiction to decide finally upon the political rights of the states. I am still old-fashioned enough to stand squarely upon the doctrines of the Virginia and Kentucky resolutions of 1798-'99.

At last, Mr. Speaker, this whole subject resolves itself into several great questions connected with the theory of our political system.

Is this essentially a *national* government, or is it a union of sovereign states?

Does the sovereignty or supreme power reside in the central government, or the mass of the people of our country as a nation, one and indivisible? or does it yet repose in the sovereign states?

The solution of these great questions has, at various periods of our political history, occupied the attention of the best statesmen of the country. The radical principles involved in them divided the gigantic intellects of Calhoun and Webster. Almost all the differences of opinion that exist as to the action of the federal government on the practical issues which spring up from day to day, grow out of the various solutions of these questions. Therefore they are, indeed, worthy of repeated discussion.

I had, Mr. Speaker, intended to notice some of the remarks made by the gentleman from Kentucky [Mr. Marshall] on the subject of "squatter sovereignty," but I find that my hour has expired. Whatever more I may have wished to say in this connection, I must, perforce, postpone the accomplishment of my wishes until some farther occasion.

H.

SPEECH OF JOHN A. QUITMAN, OF MISSISSIPPI, ON THE SUBJECT OF THE NEUTRALITY LAWS: DELIVERED IN COMMITTEE OF THE WHOLE HOUSE ON THE STATE OF THE UNION, APRIL 29TH, 1856.

MR. CHAIRMAN,—Since the opening of this session of Congress, the public mind has been almost exclusively absorbed by the slavery question—that great issue which distracts the entire country, and seems to menace with danger the integrity of the Union. Had it not been for the excitement produced by that paramount question, a high sense of duty would have impelled me, during even the first week of this session, to present to the consideration of the House, and of the country, a matter of deep and permanent interest to both. As I shall be necessarily absent for several weeks, I will avail myself of this opportunity, so kindly furnished by my friend from Florida [Mr. Maxwell], to present my views on the subject of certain laws which now encumber our statute-book; those laws which seek to enforce our supposed neutral obligations to other nations; those laws which, though acquiesced in for some years, are, in *my* opinion, injurious to the best interests of our country, and fatal to its hopes of future development. The peculiar condition of many neighboring states and colonies, and the influence which their condition must exercise upon our own prosperity, render it highly important at the present time that we should review this branch of our national policy. A radical change is required. For the purpose of effecting this, I yesterday gave notice that I would introduce a bill to repeal the objectionable provisions of the existing neutrality law. This bill proposes to repeal the first, second, third, fifth, sixth, eighth, tenth, and eleventh sections of "An act in addition to the act for the punishment of certain crimes against the United States, and to repeal the acts therein mentioned," approved April 20th, 1818. I frankly admit on the threshold that my bill contemplates an entire alteration of policy; it advocates a complete abandonment of that extraordinary system of legislative restriction by which the free action and enterprising spirit of our people are crippled, and to which it is a matter of surprise that they have so long submitted. But, Mr. Chairman, we live in an age of progress. Changes are constantly going on around us; and to them we must adapt our course. It is not to the past alone that we must look to learn our present duties or our future obligations. The conduct of other nations, the aspect of adjacent states, the circumstances of each teeming hour—all these must be taken into consideration. That which might, twenty years since, have been morally and politically right, may now be not only morally wrong, but politically suicidal. When one set of legislators may, by one act, bind down immutably the energies of unborn millions, liberty ceases to exist.

Our government, in its theory, is purely representative. It should, in reality, be the reflex of public sentiment; but it too often lags behind the march of opinion, and endeavors to control and direct that power, from which it should properly take its color, as it does always take its being. But when the full tide of popular principle is aroused, the government *must* ultimately be carried with it.

While I believe that public opinion demands the change of policy which I propose by this bill, I still approach the argument with diffidence, doubting whether the short space of time allowed me will suffice to render the conclusions as clearly forcible to the minds of others as they are to my own. But, Mr. Chairman, I act with a firm reliance upon the strong American intellect, and with a conviction that my proposition is founded on reason, justice, and sound policy.

"The law of nations," so called, does not profess to establish fixed and invariable rules, applicable to all cases. Its object is to define the moral relations that mutually exist between independent states, and the character of those relations is necessarily modified by the course of circumstances. To understand the obligations that we owe both to ourselves and to other nations, we must first survey the position of the political communities around us. A distant and cursory glance is all that I can now bestow upon this instructive picture.

Of Canada, and the vast British possessions that skirt our northern frontier, I will not speak. Under the mild rule to which they are now subjected by the mother government, the people of those colonies wear the appearance of content; and it *may* be that they are preparing, quietly and without violence, to take their place at the proper time in the family of separate nations.

Turning to Mexico, our neighbor on the south and west, we shall find her in a state of disintegration. Since 1820, when her mixed population banished the Spanish tyrants, she has been rapidly sinking in every moral and physical element; and, during the last eight years, she has preserved a state of sickly existence by selling portions of her territory to the United States. This method alone has sufficed to prop the tottering foundations of her nationality; and this is, indeed, a sign that she is rapidly hastening to her final dissolution. The whole history of man shows that the career of nations is upward or downward: there is no level on which to rest, no halting-point for repose. Mexico, with her delightful climate, her fertile soil, her jeweled mountains, and her rich valleys, holding in her possession the commercial "philosopher's stone"—the power to tax the commerce of the world by the junction of the two oceans—Mexico, I repeat, is convulsed with annual revolutions, is approaching a state of anarchy, and soon, wasted, plundered, and depopulated, will become derelict, and liable to be seized upon as a waif by some stronger power. She can be saved only by the advancing flood of our enterprising citizens.

Central America, though more distant, is brought into closer contact with us by the command which she exercises over an important route of travel between portions of our own country. She has now not even the pretense of nationality. Her petty states, assuming each a separate independence, torn by internal dissensions and pillaged by the avarice of rival chiefs, afford a fitting theatre for the display of those European intrigues which *do* annoy our trade, and *would* check our extension. The only hope of redeeming this beautiful country, by the establishment of good government, rests in that patriotic band which has lately transplanted the principles of democracy from the United States to Nicaraguan soil. Although the extreme caution of our government has left this new republic to sustain herself alone against the opposition of her prejudiced neighbors, still she has American energy to guide her advancement, and the sympathies of countless American breasts to cheer her in the hour of her perilous ordeal; and, with these, she must finally triumph; she can not fail to fulfill her glorious mission, and cultivate the growth of civil and religious liberty in Central America.

I now pass to Cuba—well termed, from her position, her fertility, her genial temperature, her lovely scenery, her noble harbors, and her natural wealth, the "GEM OF THE ANTILLES." She is the solitary remnant of that gigantic despotism which, stretching its arm across the broad ocean, shattered the empires of Montezuma and the Incas, and attempted to grasp and hold the fairest portions of this continent. Of all her vast colonial possessions Spain retains only this island. And how does she retain it? To keep in subjection an unarmed white population of little more than half a million of souls she places on guard a standing army of twenty thousand mercenaries—an army larger in proportion than that with which Great Britain, in the Revolutionary War, endeavored to subjugate these American states, with their three millions of inhabitants. The records of tyranny can not show in any other land a military force so proportionately great. It is kept in readiness to maintain a despotic colonial government; and this species of government is, at best, but a fraud, because it perverts, by its very nature, the true purposes for which government is constituted. Its object, instead of being to promote the prosperity of the governed, is to enchain and rob them for the benefit of foreign rulers, disconnected with them as well in feeling as in location. The *people* of Cuba, belonging to the pure white Caucasian race, and descended from the best blood of the old Hidalgos, have displayed, in their hostility to Spanish misrule, a unanimity unequaled in the annals of revolution. They have attempted, again and again, to assert their independence. Were it possible for them to do so, they would vindicate their rights by open rebellion; but, stripped of arms, and deprived, by a tyranny that penetrates to their very hearths, of the means of combining their efforts, they are subdued by the mere force of the bayonet. It seems, indeed, as though Spanish oppression, driven out from its hundred provinces, has centralized and intensified all its powers in this unhappy isle. And yet this iron system is protected, not only by the moral influence, but even by the active interference of England and France; and, sir, I regret to add that the schemes of our enemies are, to some extent, aided by the ill-advised course of our own authorities—that course of action which prevents the generous and noble emotions of the American heart from bursting forth and encouraging the people of Cuba to strike for justice and freedom.

In glancing at San Domingo we see a strange and grotesque power, under whose stupid sway that fair island, holding, with her commodious ports, the same relation to the Caribbean Sea that Cuba holds to the Gulf of Mexico, is fast relapsing into barbarism. This caricature of government is sustained by mighty European influences in its attempts to exterminate the small white Dominican republic which still retains a portion of the island. All the rest of insular America is European or African.

Now, Mr. Chairman, standing here among the statesmen of America, I point to the surrounding scene. Behold it as it is, and then look forward a few years and contemplate what it will be. What reflections does it not present? A world-startling drama is to be enacted, and are we, the guardians of our country's weal, to have no part in the performance? Do we not know that the development, the greatness, and the safety, even, of our beloved land are deeply concerned? Is it not our evident duty to aid in the accomplishment of that high DESTINY which Providence has assigned to our republic of states? Does not the splendor of that DESTINY already tinge the present with a glorious promise of the future? And is it not time now, if ever, to act boldly and vigorously?

There is no statesman, no writer on the law of nations, no political casuist even, who will deny that it is the right and duty of every independent nation, not only to adopt all measures necessary for her self-preservation, but also to remove all obstructions from the path of her just prosperity. Kent, whose opinions are extremely conservative, says, in his Commentaries,

"Every nation has an undoubted right to provide for its own safety, and to take due precaution against *distant* as well as impending danger. The right of self-preservation is paramount to all other considerations. A rational fear of an imminent danger is said to be a justifiable cause of war."—Vol. i., p. 23.

Vattel lays down the principle on this subject as follows:

"In vain does nature prescribe to nations as well as to individuals the care of their self-preservation, and of advancing their own perfection and happiness, if it does not give them a right to preserve themselves from every thing that can render this care ineffectual. * * * Every nation, as well as every man, has a right not to suffer any other to obstruct its preservation, its perfection, and happiness—that is, to preserve itself from all injuries, and this right is perfect, since it is given to satisfy a natural and indispensable obligation; for when we can not use constraint in order to cause our right to be respected, the effect is very uncertain. It is this right of preservation from all injury that is called the *right of security.* * * * It is safest to prevent the evil when it can be done. A nation has a right to resist an injurious attempt, and to make use of force and every honest means against the power that is actually engaged in opposition to it, and even to anticipate its machinations," etc., etc.—Vattel, b. ii., ch. iv., sec. 49, 50.

I shall now, Mr. Chairman, endeavor to apply these rules to our present position. The isthmus of America is the first point to be considered. A free, safe, and unobstructed passage across that isthmus, either through the Mexican State of Tehuantepec, above the peninsula of Yucatan, or south of the peninsula and through Central America, is indispensable to intercourse and internal commerce between the Atlantic and Pacific portions of our country. It is now the *only* road; for many years to come it will be the only *commodious* road of transit. I know that there has been projected a magnificent idea of effecting, at some distant day, a speedy and safe passage across the great plains of the West and over the rugged mountains that separate the Atlantic and Pacific slopes of our continent. I heartily wish success to this plan; it is a fitting subject for the individual enterprise of our citizens, and for such governmental encouragement as can be properly given; but, even if assisted by all the resources of our government, long years must elapse before this undertaking can furnish a sure and expeditious route across the continent within our own territory. Until then, and during the period of the greatest emigration, while our infant settlements on the Pacific coast especially require our fostering care and protection, the true and natural route of communication must be across the isthmus of America. The unobstructed passage of the isthmus is, therefore, a *necessity.* It can be secured only by becoming a part of our country—bone of our bone and flesh of our flesh—or by being held under our immediate protection. Treaties with all the powers of Europe would be insufficient to answer our purpose. At the moment when their use is most needed, treaties may be violated or abrogated. The isthmus must be in friendly hands or in our own. To delay in seizing or securing it is to commit an act of moral treason against ourselves. When I speak of a *friendly* power I mean one that is identified with us in common interests and with similar political institutions—a power that, when the mighty struggle between despotism and constitutional liberty shall take place, will be found at our side as a firm and reliable ally.

It is equally necessary that Cuba should be united with us in the ties of a common destiny. Her geographical position proclaims her ours. That magnificent island lies along our southern borders so near that the sound of the morning gun, booming on the dawn of our great anniversary of independence, awakes an echo among her cliffs.

A single glance at the map is sufficient to show that Cuba, with her numerous deep and commodious harbors, stretching across the mouth of the vast inland sea of America, commands the entire trade of the Gulf of Mexico. It is the commercial and naval strategic key of the richest products of the world. Not a bale, a barrel, or a box that passes from the valley of the Mississippi, or from the states bordering on the Gulf, can reach the high seas through their natural outlet without being exposed to the cannon that bristle from the fortresses of Cuba. Should this mistress of the Gulf ever be in the possession of a declared enemy, we would be effectually cut off from the proper path of our southern and western trade; the best productions of our country, amounting in value to one half of all its exports, would be at the mercy of the foe. From the Cuban ports, so strongly protected by both nature and art, would sally out daily fast war-steamers, swooping down like kites upon the white-winged carriers of our commerce, and even threatening our extensive and defenseless coasts.

The communication and transit-commerce between the Atlantic and Pacific coasts being thus dependent upon the disposition of the Cuban authorities, we can easily perceive the necessity for uniting that island with us by strong and lasting interests. But this is not all. If these considerations were not pressed upon us by the dictates of necessity, there are other vast and paramount reasons little short of absolute necessity—reasons which Vattel, in the quotation already presented, designates as the pursuit of perfection and happiness; reasons in which are involved our peace, our prosperity, and the progress of civilization on this continent; and it is to these reasons that our immediate and earnest attention must be directed.

As early as 1823, Mr. Jefferson, foreseeing the immense advantages, since so fully developed, of uniting our interests with Cuba, wrote to President Monroe as follows:

"I candidly confess I have ever looked on Cuba as the most interesting addition which could ever be made to our system of states. The control which, with the Florida point, this island would give us over the Gulf of Mexico and the countries and isthmus bordering on it, as well as those waters which flow into it, would fill up the measure of our political well-being."

Mr. Stevenson, while minister to England, in a letter to Mr. Forsyth, secretary of state, in 1837, says:

"The possession of Cuba by a great maritime power would be little less than the establishment of a fortification at the mouth of the Mississippi, commanding the Gulf of Mexico and Florida, and consequently the whole trade of the Western States, besides deeply affecting the interests and tranquillity of the southern portions of this Union."

J. Q. Adams, when secretary of state, in his instructions to Mr. Nelson in 1823, says:

"Cuba's commanding position, with reference to the Gulf of Mexico, and the West Indies, etc., gives it an importance in the sum of our national interests with which that of no other foreign territory can be compared."

In his letter to our minister at Madrid, written during the same year, Mr. A. further says:

"In looking forward to the probable course of events for the short period of half a century, it is scarcely possible to resist the conviction that the annexation of Cuba to our federal republic will be indispensable to the continuance and integrity of the Union itself."

In 1852, Mr. Everett, secretary of state, in reply to the French minister, writes:

"The United States, on the other hand, would, by the proposed convention, disable themselves from making an acquisition which might take place without any disturbance of existing foreign relations, and in the natural order of things. The island of Cuba lies at our doors. It commands the approach to the Gulf of Mexico, which washes the shores of five of our states. It bars the entrance of that great river which drains half the North American continent and with its tributaries forms the largest system of internal water communication in the world. It keeps watch at the doorway of our intercourse with California by the Isthmus route. If an island like Cuba, belonging to the Spanish crown, guarded the entrance of the Thames and the Seine, and the United States should propose a convention like this to France and England, those powers would assuredly feel that the disability assumed by ourselves was far less serious than that which we asked them to assume. * * * *

"But whatever may be thought of these last suggestions, it would seem impossible for any one who reflects upon the events glanced at in this note to mistake the law of American growth and progress, or think it can be ultimately arrested by a convention like that proposed. In the judgment of the President it would be as easy to throw a dam from Cape Florida to Cuba, in the hope of stopping the flow of the Gulf Stream, as to attempt, by a compact like this, to fix the fortunes of Cuba 'now and hereafter;' or, as expressed in the French text of the convention, 'for the present as for the future (*pour le present comme pour l'avenir*), that is, for all coming time." * * * *

Mr. Buchanan, Mr. Mason, and Mr. Soulé, our ministers to London, Paris, and Madrid, having, in compliance with the wish of the President, assembled at Ostend, in 1854, for the purpose of conferring on the subject of our relations with Spain, addressed a joint letter to the secretary of state, from which I read the following appropriate extract:

"But if Spain, dead to the voice of her own interest, and actuated by stubborn pride and a false sense of honor, should refuse to sell Cuba to the United States, then the question will arise, what ought to be the course of the American government under such circumstances?

"Self-preservation is the first law of nature with states as well as with individuals. All nations have, at different periods, acted upon this maxim. Although it has been made the pretext for committing flagrant injustice, as in the partition of Poland and other similar cases which history records, yet the principle itself, though often abused, has always been recognized. * * * *

"While pursuing this course, we can afford to disregard the censures of the world, to which we have been so often and so unjustly exposed.

"After we shall have offered Spain a price for Cuba far beyond its present value, and this shall have been refused, it will then be time to consider the question, Does Cuba, in the possession of Spain, seriously endanger our internal peace and the existence of our cherished Union? Should this question be answered in the affirmative, then, by every law, human and divine, we shall be justified in wresting it from Spain if we possess the power; and this upon the very same principle that would justify an individual in tearing down the burning house of his neighbor, if there were no other means of preventing the flames from destroying his own house.

"Under such circumstances, we ought neither to count the cost nor regard the odds which Spain might enlist against us. We forbear to enter into the question, whether the present condition of the island would justify such a measure? We should, however, be recreant to our duty, be unworthy of our gallant forefathers, and commit base treason against our posterity, should we permit Cuba to be Africanized and become a second St. Domingo, with all its attendant horrors to the white race, and suffer the flames to extend to our neighboring shores, seriously to endanger, or actually to consume the fair fabric of our Union. We fear that the course and current of events are rapidly tending toward such a catastrophe. We, however, hope for the best, though we ought certainly to be prepared for the worst."

From the earliest ages, the East India trade has been the most valuable object of commercial nations. The rise and fall of a hundred dynasties have been dependent upon it. This commerce, when borne on the backs of camels over the deserts of Asia, enriched Palmyra, and built up those splendid palaces whose ruins, even after the lapse of many centuries, are the wonder of travelers and the shame of modern art. It was afterward seized upon by the genius of Alexander, to found and stamp with a conqueror's name the glorious city of the Nile; and, during the Middle Ages, it was a source of unfailing wealth to the merchant-princes of Italy. After the southern capes of Africa had been rounded by the bold navigator, this commerce attracted the attention of England. She grasped it, and her hold upon it at this day is unloosened. From it she has derived the principal elements of her naval importance. To perfect it she has expended millions in attempts to find a shorter passage through the icebergs of the arctic seas. To retain it she has been engaged in numerous desperate struggles. Her wars with Napoleon, and, more lately, her conflict with Russia—no matter what may have been their alleged pretext—have, in reality, grown out of her jealousy against all nations that might dispute with her the exclusive control of this vast mine of commercial wealth.

This lucrative trade, during the next twenty years, is destined to take a new channel. When the isthmus of America shall be cut, the Gulf of Mexico will become the highway of communication, not only between the most distant portions of our own territory, but also between Europe and the East Indies and China. The island of Cuba is, as I have before shown, the key to this path of communication. The possessors of that island will have the control of all this mighty trade, and, consequently, will soon become the first naval power of the globe.

Such are the natural advantages of the American continent; and to us, not to Europe, do they belong. WE are the great power of this hemisphere; it is not only our right, it is our positive *duty*, so to direct our affairs that European interests and intrigues may gain no permanent foothold upon our shores. Shall we, who look upon our institutions as promotive of the highest civilization, intellectual improvement, and popular happiness—shall we permit the natural advantages of our land to be taken away? Shall we yield them up with calm indifference to the unfriendly powers of Europe?

We are not impelled only by the laudable and patriotic desire of advancing the interests of our own country; other considerations of a higher character are presented by the aspect of the neighboring states. Cuba has the most important claims upon our sympathy. There we find a people of our own race, the white Caucasian man—a race born for all noble endeavors, and capable of indefinite progression—we find that people crushed to earth by the brutal despotism of an old, effete, decayed, and corrupt nation, which is itself kept alive only by the principle adopted by the more vigorous European nations of preserving the "balance of power." The tyranny of Spain over the people of Cuba is a reproach to the age, a disgrace to Europe, and an insult to the United States. There is *no* legitimate government in Cuba; there is *no* law there. The will of a Spanish satrap changes the government from day to day, and makes the law a thing of caprice. The sword, the musket, and the garoté are the ministers of sway. The immense military force overawes the spirit of the inhabitants. The most sacred principles of the social compact are violated; yet Europe sustains this heinous fraud, and America tolerates it. Why is this? Because British statesmen, with wily policy, are determined to keep this commanding point in the Gulf of Mexico, this outlet to the richest commerce of the world, out of the hands of Americans and under their own control. They have seen its transcendent value, present and prospective. They know that, if revolutionized and independent, with a domestic system similar to that of this Union, Cuba would always be our steadfast ally, even though she should not, as she undoubtedly would, become a member of our confederacy. They know that, with a ship-canal across the isthmus of America, Cuba united with us, and the control of the great staples of sugar and tobacco under our hands, as that of cotton now is, the commercial world would become tributary to us. Hence it is that she has striven, with so much art and perseverance, to maintain an ascendency in Central America and Cuba. In the former instance, she has succeeded in procuring from us, during a period of political delirium, a most absurd treaty, and in placing upon it a construction still more absurd; in the latter, she has been pertinaciously engaged in protecting Spanish tyranny, and in the unnatural and anti-Christian attempt to establish, throughout the whole of insular America, a barbaric black empire. The germ of her plot was exhibited in laying waste Jamaica, by destroying the proper relations between the white and black races there, and endeavoring by law to make those equal whom God has made unequal. Her plot is farther exposed by her intrigues in San Domingo, where, unfortunately, she had the address to defeat the ratification by that government of highly favorable arrangements entered into by the United States commissioner, General Cazneau, with the Dominican authorities.* Pursuing her schemes with intense cunning and indefatigable zeal, she has used her strong influence with Spain to bring about the gradual abolition of negro slavery in Cuba. Her intent is plain.

* See letter of General Cazneau at the end of this speech.

She is well aware that, at some not distant day, public opinion in the United States, favoring the cause of Cuban independence, must control the action of our government. She has rallied all her skill to prevent this consummation so devoutly to be wished. She desires to devote the American archipelago, the great islands of the Caribbean Sea, to the negro race. The history of that race from the beginning of time shows that it is incapable of self-government — that constitutional government can not exist where that race predominates — that arbitrary despotism necessarily accompanies its social systems. Could this scheme be effected, the object of England would be attained; our progress in that quarter would be forever checked. The protectorate of the black empire, or states, thus brought into existence would, of course, be vested in Great Britain. She hesitates not, for purposes of interest or profit, to stoop to alliances with a negro boy. On the other hand, we need not argue long to prove that the United States could have no relations, political or diplomatic, with a black empire. Such intercourse would taint with incurable leprosy our political system, already affected to an alarming extent by negrophilism. The end would be internal convulsion, disunion, and death. Let Great Britain accomplish her ends (and accomplish them she will, if we, with folded arms, supinely await the result of her machinations), and she will not only reap the incalculable advantages connected with the possession of this Gibraltar of the American Mediterranean, and forever retard our commercial advancement, but she will also have the power to disturb at her pleasure the repose of the contiguous states, and to stimulate throughout our entire country the agitation of that slavery question which, even now, is so pregnant with mischief to the harmony of our institutions.

I am aware that the British minister has denied, somewhat informally, that it is the design of his government to urge upon Spain the emancipation of the negroes in Cuba. I have not time to present the many and conclusive proofs that the policy of England is such as I have attributed to her. Can we not point to the "mixed commission," English and Spanish, which her influence over Spain has enabled her to secure in Cuba, for the purpose of examining into the status of a portion of the negro population, with power to declare certain classes of that population free? Let us refer also to the instructions given by Lord Palmerston to the British minister at Madrid in 1851, in which he says:

"I have to instruct your lordship to say to the Spanish minister that the slaves form a large portion, and by no means an unimportant one, of the *people* of Cuba; and that any steps taken to provide for their emancipation would therefore, as far as the black population is concerned, be quite in unison with the recommendation made by her majesty's government, that measures should be adopted for contenting the people of Cuba, with a view to secure the connection between the Spanish crown and the island; and it must be evident that if the negro population of Cuba were rendered free, *that fact would create a most powerful element of resistance to any scheme for annexing Cuba to the United States, where slavery exists.*"

Here is the plan of England plainly laid open to the gaze of all civilized nations. She says to Spain that it would be quite in unison with the policy of her Britannic majesty's government that the negroes of Cuba should be set free, because their emancipation would create "a powerful element of resistance" to the annexation of that island to the United States. Unfortunately such would, indeed, be the case. This proud country, which, when united in sentiment, might stand against a world in arms, is unable to resent the insults of feeble Spain when the slavery question may be, even incidentally, involved. Full well does England appreciate this fact, and through its means she seeks to obtain over us a safe and bloodless triumph. She could thus place in our side a thorn which would cause our energies to fester and gangrene, and might, perhaps, bring about national dissolution. None but the perversely blind can fail to perceive her serpent-like policy—a policy in which France, since the advent of Louis Napoleon, has heartily coincided. This important circumstance was announced by Lord Clarendon, secretary of foreign affairs, to the British Parliament. He remarks:

"I will further add, that the union between the two governments has not been confined to the Eastern Question. The happy accord and good understanding between France and England have been extended beyond the Eastern policy to the policy affecting all parts of the world; and I am heartily rejoiced to say that there is no portion of the *two hemispheres*, with regard to which the policy of the two countries, however heretofore antagonistic, is not now in entire harmony."

I have thus taken a very cursory view of the condition of Cuba and the neighboring states of Central America and Mexico. I have shown that, to preserve a free communication between the Atlantic and Pacific portions of our Union, the right to the undisturbed transit of the American isthmus is absolutely necessary; and that, for the same purposes, and to secure an outlet for the productions of the great valley of the Mississippi and of the states bordering on the Gulf of Mexico, and to protect a commerce now valued at more than four hundred millions of dollars annually, the possession of Cuba by ourselves, or by some reliable friendly power identified with us in principles, is equally a necessity. I have shown farther that paramount interests, involving the safety, the prosperity, and the advancement of our beloved country, "the last and noblest realm of time," destined by Providence, as we fondly hope, to promote the civilization, the moral and physical improvement, the elevation and happiness of man on earth—that paramount interests not only justify us, but loudly urge us onward, in sweeping away every obstacle from the path of our glorious mission. I have still farther shown that, while we, from over-fastidious notions of our neutral obligations to other powers, supinely rest in fancied security, or, what is worse, restrain by laws and prosecutions the giant energies of our free and adventurous population, the never-slumbering vigilance of our great commercial rival is at work, weaving intricate meshes and planning dangerous combinations to entangle and destroy us. It is time for us to awaken from our lethargy. The matured, deliberate, and sound opinion of the people, I believe, demands our concurrence. The government, which should always be the follower, as it is the offspring of that opinion, is called upon to act. How shall we act?

By the Clayton-Bulwer Treaty, which I hold to be unconstitutional, because it professes to impair the right of Congress to admit new states, at least in Central America—by that treaty we have thus far most foolishly bound ourselves to exercise no dominion in Central America. Spain refuses to sell Cuba at any price. The hope of acquiring that island by purchase was always a delusion. The white people of Cuba, though crushed to earth by the iron heel of tyranny, are still too proud to give their assent to be transferred as chattels. They deny that Spain has the right to sell them. Were we to declare war against Spain, the evil would not be corrected. Were we to attempt an invasion of the island, the landing of our troops would be preceded by an edict emancipating the slave population. It is known that, in such event, the captain general has power to issue such edict. Yet there before us, pregnant with ruin, hangs the dark and terrible cloud. Cunning devices to cripple our commerce and check our prosperity are being rapidly matured. Public opinion cries out for action; and again I ask, how shall we act? My answer is, meet that opinion! Let it speak and be heard; ay, more, let it have way! Repeal your neutrality laws. If *you* can not or will not avert impending dangers, at least do not manacle the hands of your free citizens and prevent them from protecting themselves. If *you* can not or will not remove the barriers that obstruct the career of our brilliant future, leave them to the foresight, enterprise, and perseverance of the American people, and, my word for it, they will prove themselves equal to the emergency.

I wish not to be understood as the advocate or apologist of any act in violation of the moral obligations due from one nation to another. I would faithfully observe and stringently enforce all the duties imposed upon us by honor or good morals. As a legislator, I am ready to assent to any regulation that will punish offenses against the law of nations, provided that that regulation does not infringe upon the reserved rights of the citizen. Farther than this Congress must not go. This government has no powers beyond those delegated by the Constitution. If the power be not therein written, or clearly deducible therefrom, the acts of Congress are usurpations, and void. By these rules I am disposed, as my time will permit, to briefly examine our present neutrality laws. It has been my misfortune to become somewhat acquainted with them, and to witness the total disregard of the rights of the citizen with which they have sometimes been administered by courts and judges.

The leading features of the eight sections of the act of April 20, 1818, which my bill proposes to repeal, are, in my opinion, not only unnecessary and impolitic, but are repugnant to the intention of the Constitution, and must be regarded as infringements of the personal rights of the citizen. This act, as may be shown by the debates at the time of its passage, is supposed to have been suggested by the representatives of European courts for the purpose of crippling the practical sympathy manifested by the people of the United States in favor of some of the Spanish colonies in America then struggling for their freedom. Mr. Clay, then Speaker of the House, and a warm advocate of the cause of the young republics, descended from the Speaker's chair, and strenuously opposed some of the provisions of the act, denouncing them as placing our government in the attitude of an ally of European despotism, and an enemy to the extension of liberal political institutions on this continent. That bold and sagacious statesman saw the deep schemes of European sovereigns whose colonial possessions in America were jeopardized, and dared to assail the suicidal policy attempted to be foisted upon us under the specious pretense of non-interference and national morality. In the History of Congress, published by Gales & Seaton, p. 1403, in reference to the discussion of this bill, I find the following :

"Mr. Clay offered some general remarks on the offensive nature of the bill, which, he said, instead of an act to enforce neutrality, ought to be entitled an act for the benefit of his majesty the King of Spain."

Again, on the 18th of March, it is reported of Mr. Clay :

"In the threshold of this discussion, he confessed he did not like much the origin of that act. There had been some disclosures—not in an official form, but in such shape as to entitle them to credence —that showed that act to have been the result of a *teasing* on the part of foreign agents in this country which he regretted to have seen. But from whatever source it sprung, if it was an act necessary to preserve the neutral relations of the country it ought to be retained ; but this he denied. * * *

"In its provisions it went beyond the obligations of the United States to other powers, and that part of it was unprecedented in any nation which compelled citizens of the United States to give bonds not to commit acts without the jurisdiction of the United States which it is the business of foreign nations, and not of this government, to guard against."

Again, on the same day, this bill being still under consideration, Mr. Clay, alluding to the Spanish minister, said :

"He (Mr. C.) would not treat with disrespect even the minister of Ferdinand, whose cause this bill was intended to benefit : he is a faithful minister, if, not satisfied with making representations to the foreign department, he also attends the proceedings of the Supreme Court to watch its decisions ; he affords but so many proofs of the fidelity for which the representatives of Spain have always been distinguished. And how mortifying is it, sir, to hear of the honorary rewards and titles, and so forth, granted for these services ; for, if I am not mistaken, our act of 1817 produced the bestowal of some honor on this faithful representative of his majesty ; and, if this bill passes which is now before us, I have no doubt he will receive some new honor for his *farther success.*"

Mr. Clay concluded his speech thus :

"Let us put all these statutes out of our way except that of 1794. When was that passed ? At a moment when the enthusiasm of liberty ran through the country with electric rapidity ; when the whole country *en masse* was ready to lend a hand and aid the French nation in their struggle, General WASHINGTON, revered name ! the Father of his country, could hardly arrest this inclination. Yet, under such circumstances, the act of 1794 was found abundantly sufficient. There was, then, no gratuitous assumption of neutral debts. For twenty years that act has been found sufficient. But some keen-sighted, sagacious foreign minister finds out that it is not sufficient, and the act of 1817 is passed. That act we find condemned by the universal sentiment of the country; and I hope it will receive farther condemnation by the vote of the House this day."

In the course of the same debate, Mr. Robertson also intimated the charge that foreign influence, more than domestic policy, produced the passage of that law. He argues:

"This might be a sufficient ground for the ministers of Portugal, of England, and of France to proceed upon; but shall we sympathize in their feelings on the subject, and be induced by them to pass acts to shackle our citizens, when it is so easy to trace their remonstrances to a general hostility to the cause of any people who are engaged in a struggle to ameliorate their condition by changing their form of government? It does not appear now that that act was passed so much with a view to do what is just to ourselves as to accommodate the views of foreign nations."

But alas! European ideas were too much venerated; European influence prevailed, and this unfortunate system was ingrafted upon us.

The objections to this act, as interpreted in our day, are:

Its creation of constructive crimes;

Its denial of the right of expatriation, and, under certain circumstances, of emigration even;

Its prohibition of the right of the citizen, in some cases, to avail himself of the rewards of his skill, his ingenuity, or his labor;

Its loading with onerous burdens, and punishing with severe penalties, fair commercial enterprises and speculations;

Its conferring upon the President and the collectors of ports powers inconsistent with the principles and dangerous to the institutions of our country;

Its branding as criminal acts noble, generous, and patriotic in themselves;

Its assuming to treat the citizens of a free country as the subjects or property of the government.

If all these obnoxious features do not appear distinctly in the act, the construction which has been placed upon them by, at least, one of the judges of the Supreme Court, has marked them in bold and unmistakable outlines.

There is, however, at the start, a still more serious objection to the whole of this legislation. It is not only not warranted by the Constitution—it is an attempt to take away from a free people rights which they have never surrendered. It is, to say the least, founded on an entire misconception of the relations which exist between the government and the people under our peculiar system.

This federal government is a limited one. Constituted by the states in their sovereign capacity, it possesses no powers but those clearly delegated to it in the compact of union. This character of our government is not left to inference: it is stamped in express words upon the instrument that created it. There it rests, and casuistry can not blot it out. The "POWERS NOT DELEGATED ARE RESERVED." "The enumeration of certain rights shall not be construed to deny or disparage others retained by the people." When, therefore, it is proposed to legislate upon any subject, the first inquiry must be, whether that subject is within the jurisdiction of Congress. The broadest con-

structionist does not pretend that crimes and misdemeanors generally are within the jurisdiction of the federal government. Whence,
then, are derived the powers claimed under the act in question? To
what clause of the Constitution do you trace them? There is no sem-
blance of a warrant for them to be found in the Constitution, unless
they be included in the power to define and punish "*offenses* against
the law of nations." If the grant of power be not contained in that
clause, it is not to be found in any place. The act, to be defined and
punished, must be an offense *against the law of nations*. To offenses
of that class is this power limited ; to them alone can it be applied.
Will it be pretended that, under this power to define and punish, Congress has power to go out of the law of nations, and *make* offenses or
crimes of those acts which, by the law of nations, are not condemned?
If so, the whole field of criminal jurisprudence is thrown open to federal legislation, and the specification of a limitation becomes absurd.
For instance, the sale of breadstuffs or of clothing by one of our citizens to a nation at war with a friendly power is not forbidden by the
law of nations. Will it be assumed, then, that Congress, under the
power above quoted, can make such sale a penal offense? Why can
this not be done? Because the act is not an offense against the law
of nations. That law is referred to in the Constitution as a positive
existence. No authority is given to Congress to alter or change it,
or to create new offenses. Judging the act of 1818 by these rules,
its leading provisions are clearly without the pale of the authority of
Congress. The very title of the act, as if in contempt of the limitations of the Constitution, proclaims it a usurpation. Instead of an act
to define and punish offenses against the law of nations, it purports to be
"An act for the punishment of certain *crimes against the United
States*." Like the alien and sedition laws, it attempts to make a
crime of that which was before not even an offense. Now, the law
of nations, even as known and acted upon in Europe, where the government generally has entire control over the citizen, or rather the
subject—there, I repeat, the law of nations does not regard it as an offense for the citizen to take service under a foreign government at
war with a friendly power. The usage is the reverse.—Vattel, b. iii.,
ch. vii., sec. 110, gives the rule and example :

"The quarrels of another can not deprive me of the free disposition
of my rights in the pursuit of measures which I judge advantageous
to my country. Therefore, when it is a custom in a nation, in order
for employing and exercising its subjects, to permit levies of troops in
favor of a power in whom it is pleased to confide, the enemy of this
power can not call these permissions hostilities. * * He can not
even claim, with any right, that the like should be granted him, etc.
* * * The Switzers grant levies of troops to whom they please,
and nobody has thought proper to quarrel with them on this head."

If, then, it be not an offense against the law of nations, even according to the European code, for the citizen of any neutral state to take
service under a belligerent nation, what constitutional power has Congress to prohibit the right of a free American citizen to lend his intellect, his wealth, or his sword, to any cause which he believes to be
just? And yet the first and second sections of the act of 1818 declare
the exercise of this right to be a high crime, and worthy of fine and
imprisonment.

The third, fifth, eighth, ninth, and eleventh sections of the act are obnoxious to objections of a similar character. They, in substance, forbid, under severe penalties, the selling, fitting out, arming, furnishing, or adding to the force of any ship or vessel intended to be employed in the service of any foreign state, or to cruise or commit hostilities against the citizens, subjects, or property of any foreign state; and, furthermore, they invest the President and the collectors of ports with extraordinary powers to seize and detain suspected vessels. Now many of these acts, if not all of them, thus made criminal and severely penal, are in strict conformity with the rights of neutrals, acknowledged by the law of nations. The property thus risked may, if seized by a belligerent, be confiscated; but the neutrality of the country whose citizens are engaged in such trade has never been considered as violated thereby. Vattel, in the same connection, proceeds thus:

"Further, it may be affirmed, on the same principles, that if a nation trades in arms, timber, ships, military stores, etc., I can not take it amiss that it sells such things to my enemy, provided it does not refuse to sell them to me also. It carries on its trade without any design of injuring me; and in continuing it the same as if I was not engaged in war, that nation gives me no just cause of complaint. * * * It is certain that, as they have no part in my quarrel, they are under no obligations to abandon their trade that they may avoid furnishing my enemy with the means of making war. * * * They only exercise a *right* which they are under no obligations of sacrificing to me."

The question, then, recurs, has Congress a right to brand as criminal acts clearly permitted by the law of nations?

The sixth section of the act proposed to be repealed, although in its phraseology, and still more in the interpretation which judicial advocates of constructive powers have placed upon it, it is more odious to the unaffected impulses of the American heart than any of the others, is still not so palpably at variance with the rights of neutrals conceded by the laws of nations. This section forbids, under severe penalties, any person within our territory to begin, set on foot, provide, or prepare the means for any military expedition or enterprise to be carried from this country against the territories of any foreign prince or people with whom we are at peace. This clause, if strictly construed, according to the rules which should govern the interpretation of penal statutes, means only to forbid military associations in the United States intended to proceed from thence in full military organization; but it has been construed by government officials, executive and judicial, to embrace in its penal denunciations those who separately, as private individuals, and without military organization, may choose to leave our country, with or without arms, to combine together elsewhere for the purpose of aiding an oppressed people to achieve their political independence. Such acts on the part of citizens do not involve the neutrality of our country; therefore, penal laws to punish them are not only beyond the scope of congressional powers, but are also infringements on the unquestionable right of the citizen as well to expatriate himself and unite his fortunes with those of another political community, as to emigrate to foreign lands, and there follow pursuits which may not be inconsistent with his allegiance to his country.

I have thus, Mr. Chairman, in this brief argument, considered the constitutionality of this law with reference to the European views of the law of nations. I have shown that the act of 1818 restrains individual rights, private enterprise, and personal liberty beyond the requirements of the international code; and, consequently, is without the pale of congressional powers. The power "to define and punish offenses against the law of nations" was confided by the Constitution to Congress, not to the executive or judiciary, for the sole purpose of preventing individuals from compromising the neutrality of the United States. It was never intended to control the private enterprises or speculations of the people. So far, then, as these enterprises do not, according to the established international code, involve the neutrality of the government, it is powerless to restrain them, because the right to do so has never been delegated. The government is responsible *to* the citizen, but not *for* him. He may commit, without responsibility to any earthly power, many deeds which the government can not so commit. The latter is always responsible. The American citizen sits enthroned within the charmed circle of his reserved rights, the monarch of his own actions. The reservation of these individual rights is the noblest feature of our system; and he is its worst enemy who, by legislative usurpation or judicial construction, would seek to impair them. The true patriot should watch and guard them from secret as well as open foes.

Even if the penal laws which I have arraigned were strictly constitutional, I would still oppose them as unwise, impolitic, and against the genius of our free institutions. They are founded upon the false assumption that the government should direct the morals and control the sentiment of the people. It is sheer political hypocrisy, or, at least, self-stultification, to crown with honor the memory of the good man Lafayette, whose portrait is deemed worthy to decorate this republican hall in company with that of our own Washington, in our gratitude for the aid which, in despite of his country's laws, he rendered us in the dark hour of our Revolutionary struggle, if we are by legislation to stigmatize as criminal the efforts of our own citizens to bear assistance to a neigboring people groaning under the yoke of an iron despotism—a despotism to which the condition of our ancestors was almost a state of freedom.

If our moral and national obligations to other nations require us to curb, by severe penal statutes, the adventurous and progressive spirit of our people, and we have the constitutional right to do so, let the bond be executed. If no such obligations rest upon us, and we are left free to consult the best interests of our country, it is my opinion that, even if we had the power to retard the progression of the age, it would not be exactly the perfection of wisdom for us to do so. Keeping in view the remarkable and interesting condition of adjacent countries, we can not fail to perceive that we have reached an epoch pregnant with mighty events. A year, a month, even, may determine whether Mexico, Central America, and Cuba shall be European or American. If, as I fear, the eyes of the two great powers of Western Europe are directed to their acquisition, how easy would it be for them, with their fleets and their armies now unemployed, to effect their purposes? How long, bloody, and destructive would be the struggle, should we attempt to assert the rights which, since the days of Monroe, we have claimed upon this continent, and which, but for the ignorant policy of the act of 1818, we would now peaceably and without violence possess! But for that act, Tehuantepec, Nicaragua, and perhaps all Central America would be now Americanized, advancing and prosperous under a liberal and stable form of government. In Cuba the tyrant-flag of blood and gold would have given place to the tri-color of independence, or to the starry and more glorious banner that floats "o'er the land of the free and the home of the brave." The bayonets of Spain, with the war-ships of France and England, could not have supported in that lovely island an unrelenting despotism, had not the private American aid invoked by the patriots of Cuba been cut off by the stringent application of this law.

An able editorial of the "Union," under date of March 11th, 1855, truly says:

"The well-known fact that Spain is indebted to the United States for the continuance of her dominion in Cuba, so far from inclining her to be grateful or even just, has only made her more arrogant and insensible to reason or liberality. But for the neutrality laws of the United States, which are far more strict than those of any other government, Cuba would at this moment have been at least independent, if not annexed to this confederation, had such been its desire. The government of the United States was the great instrument that arrested what in a few months would have been an invasion that no power in or out of Cuba could have resisted. The government of the United States preserved Cuba to Spain," etc.

Who will say that liberal civil institutions, borne over our borders by the energy of freemen, and planted in the misruled countries around us, would not have promoted civilization, and added to the sum of human happiness? What American patriot, who appreciates the beneficent results to our country which might have flowed from such sources, by not only securing our safety, but also many incalculable commercial advantages, does not deeply regret the false policy that manacles our hands, while those of our rivals are unconfined? The monarchies of Europe are annexing to their dominions vast territories in Asia, Africa, Australasia, and the islands of the South Sea. They take away the liberties of the conquered people, and establish arbitrary colonial governments, without regard to the opinions of the governed. We carry to the annexed free representative systems, and unite them with us as equals. The oligarchs oppress and impoverish their possessions; yet the false sentiment of the world styles *them* philanthropists, and fastens on *us* the name of "filibusters." Let us accept the word. As the term "rebel" in Ireland designates the patriot, so let the term "filibuster" designate the bold, fearless man of thought and action in America.

I have, Mr. Chairman, reflected much upon the subject of these neutrality laws, and I believe that of 1818 such a departure from the theory of our institutions as to be incapable of amendment. I therefore propose to repeal all its prominent features at once. When it shall come up for consideration, I shall either propose to return to the act of 1794, or present some proper bill to perform our absolute duties to other nations and no more.

I know that the public voice calls for some action on this subject. The true secret of national prosperity is progress. Understanding the value of free institutions, we can not but wish to extend them wherever the force of our example may penetrate. A social system like ours is most secure when its range is widest, and its influence is most extensively felt. We can afford to profit by the follies of the past; we can still more afford to profit by the *prestige* of our name. We are too dangerous an element in politics to be loved by the monarchical governments of the Old World. They tolerate us only because they can not crush us; it is upon our own continent, within and around us, that they seek to fan the flames of discord. By firmly establishing our influence upon this continent, we wrench away the last offensive weapon from their hands. Shall we now pause in our career? I, for one, will not be satisfied that our experiment of free institutions has been fully tested until it has gained the fairest portions of this continent for its field, and the noblest types of the white race for its supporters. When I look back to the past, I can form but one conjecture for the future; I rest in the faith that our favored country will steadily ascend through all the grades of her glorious destiny.

Letter from General Cazneau, referred to on Page 354.

Washington, April 25th, 1856.

DEAR GENERAL,—Feeling, as every true citizen must, a deep interest in the vindication of the honor of my country, outraged by incessant acts of foreign aggression, I have heard with great satisfaction that you propose to arraign before Congress and the people that absurd contradiction to every independent principle of American policy, the neutrality act of 1818. That law, and the obsolete ideas on which it is founded, constitute the most efficient aid and support to European interference and dictation in American affairs.

Our country can never occupy its proper and honorable position among other nations while the freedom of our citizens is shackled by laws which seem made for the sole and exclusive benefit of foreign and unfriendly powers.

Among the many instances of European interference in American affairs, I wish to call your attention to one in which I have it in my power to place before you the most undeniable evidence of a direct and insulting attack on the freedom and dignity of our inter-American relations.

The Dominican republic had repeatedly and earnestly solicited the attention of the United States to its peculiar situation. It is the only territory in all that grand circle of islands which inclose the Caribbean Sea, and command our isthmus routes to the Pacific, under an independent American flag.

Of all that one hundred thousand square miles of tropical wealth, with their three and a half millions of inhabitants, the Dominican republic is the only free white and republican government; all the rest of the West India empire is European and African. The Dominicans alone have achieved by their unassisted courage an independent, constitutional, and American existence. Their central and commanding position, their splendid harbors and inexhaustible natural resources, offer great and peculiar advantages to our commerce, and it was manifestly our interest to encourage the prosperity and independence of this American state.

In pursuance of this just and enlightened policy, I was commissioned by President Pierce, in June, 1854, to negotiate a treaty with the Dominican republic; and, after encountering many difficulties, through the intrigues and false representations of the French and English agents—who notoriously make common cause with the negroes of Hayti against the whites—the terms were fully agreed upon, and the 8th of September, 1854, named for the final signature of the treaty.

Meantime, an allied squadron had been sent for by these agents, and, sustained by its presence before the Dominican capital, Sir Robert H. Schomburgh, acting, as he declared, under the directions of Lord Clarendon, warned the Dominican government that it could not be permitted to enter into treaty relations with "such a suspicious and dangerous power as the United States without the previous knowledge and sanction of France and England." If the Dominicans resisted this dictation, they were threatened with a Haytien invasion. Under the specious title of "the mediating powers," France and England always hold the negroes in readiness to be let slip like bloodhounds on the whites at the east end of Hayti, if they prove at any time refractory to European policy.

The pretext for this forcible and high-handed dictation in our inter-American negotiation was that the treaty contained some encouragement for the establishment of steam-lines, and provided for a suitable naval and coal depôt in the admirable Bay of Samana. This is the natural and invaluable point of intersection for our lines of trade with South America and Africa, as well as Central America and the West Indies. It is to the Caribbean Sea, and the outlets of our isthmus routes, what Cuba is to the Gulf of Mexico and the mouth of the Mississippi. These European powers would not permit this American state to enjoy the advantages which nature has lavished upon it, and, at their interference and command, Samana remains a closed port to our citizens.

So many other American interests were at stake, that it seemed advisable to waive the question of a coal depôt, in order to deprive France and England of every excuse for combining with Hayti to attack the Dominican territory. Besides, to confess the whole truth, I had in view the necessity of bringing out and obtaining conclusive proof of the character and extent of these European encroachments. Actuated by these considerations, and the critical position of the Dominican republic, the article respecting a depôt at Samana was omitted in the second convention.

The treaty, thus modified, was signed by all the plenipotentiaries October 5th, after every clause and article had received the full concurrence of the Dominican executive. It secured perfect liberty of conscience and worship to our citizens, and the most complete right to acquire, hold, and bequeath all kinds of property in the Dominican republic.

It reciprocally guaranteed all advantages of trade, travel, and residence by the most favored nations, and it particularly recognized and established the important principle—without which no American treaty ought to receive the seal of the United States—that the flag covers the goods, and prohibits arbitrary search on the high seas. Perhaps it was this last and truly American principle which provoked the displeasure of England, who seems to persist in her title of "mistress of the seas" even on our American coasts.

After the promulgation of the treaty with the United States the French and British consuls called an allied squadron for the second time before the Dominican capital to overawe that government and prevent its ratification. The unfortunate Dominicans had no alternative but obedience, and the convention with the United States was sacrificed in the mode dictated by the agents of France and England.

These agents even went farther, and demanded, as the price of their mediation with Hayti, that the Dominican government should stipulate, as a permanent bar to the establishment of American steam-lines and depôts, and the introduction of American settlers on Dominican soil—

"Not to permit any government to found or occupy any dépôts or factories of any kind on the Dominican territory; not to tolerate the landing on the said territory of parties of emigrants armed or unarmed," etc.

Such privileges had been previously conceded and secured to European companies by special grants, and these prohibitions were expressly aimed at Americans.

I can not severely blame the Dominican government for receding from its engagements with the United States, with the evidence I had before me that it was under stringent European duress. I have the evidence of this interference at command, and also of the protection afforded by the French and British consuls to the negro conspirators, who had planned the general massacre of the white authorities, and there is no doubt that the British consul was an active accomplice in the plot.

The Dominican journals which advocated the American treaty were suppressed, and the editors were obliged to leave the country at the direct instance of the European agents, who, in all their aggressions on American rights, publicly avowed they were carrying out the wishes of their respective governments.

For this whole class of encroachments there is but one available answer: suspend the neutrality laws until the encroaching powers shall give ample security for future non-interference, or so modify them as to allow our citizens the same advantages in defending that unfriendly powers have in attacking American interests. The people will be with you in your efforts to open a new and noble era in our foreign policy; and firmly trusting in your triumphant success, I have the honor to be, sir, very respectfully, your obedient servant, WILLIAM L. CAZNEAU.

I.

AN ADDRESS ON THE OCCASION OF THE SECOND ANNIVERSARY OF THE PALMETTO ASSOCIATION: DELIVERED IN COLUMBIA, S. C., TUESDAY, MAY 4TH, 1858, BY JOHN A. QUITMAN, OF MISSISSIPPI.

COMRADES,—Upon your cordial invitation I have come from the busy scenes of political action to participate with you in reviving the memory of other days. Notwithstanding the glorious recollections which crowd on my memory when standing among the remnant of the Palmetto Regiment, I can not at once divest myself of the gloomy reflections left on my mind by the political scenes in which I have so lately mingled; the result of which must end in the dishonor, degradation, and vassalage of the South, unless averted by her determined will and bold action.

Deeply as these reflections weigh upon my mind, I will endeavor for a time to forget them in the emotions to which this interesting occasion gives rise.

I assumed the general command of the Palmetto Regiment amid the bursting of bombs and the roar of artillery on the burning sands of Vera Cruz. Throughout its brilliant campaign in Mexico, I shared, to some extent, its dangers and its honors, and at the close of the campaign left it occupying the imperial palaces of the Montezumas, to the fall of which it had so conspicuously contributed. Thus associated with the regiment during one of the most brilliant campaigns recorded in military history, it will be expected, upon this reunion, that I should at least present a brief sketch of its operations. Could I have had an opportunity of preparing this address in my own library, surrounded by the reports, orders, and official papers connected with the regiment, I might have attempted the interesting task with better prospect of success; but, cut off from these more reliable data, I must throw myself on your indulgence for presenting merely some reminiscences, furnished from my unaided memory, of the honorable career of the Palmetto Regiment, trusting that yet some pious son of South Carolina may perform the task of adding to her history a glorious page which reflects upon her and her sons so much honor and credit.

The war with Mexico was distinguished from other wars in which we have been engaged. It was our first war of invasion. It is true that, in the war with Great Britain, there were several incursions made into the enemy's territory for temporary objects, but no regular invasion was contemplated or carried into execution. It was, again, the first war in which a volunteer force *was mainly relied on* for its prosecution. This peculiar description of military force may almost be said to have originated in the war with Mexico. Before it was planned by legislation or reduced into system, it spontaneously sprang into existence from the military spirit of our people, and presented itself to our astonished statesmen ready to be moulded into the most formidable material of war. Scarcely had it proclaimed that the government would receive into service a limited number of volunteers, than more than three hundred thousand men, organized into regiments, battalions, and companies, from all parts of the country, but especially from the Southern and Western States, eagerly pressed the tender of their services. This novel spectacle astonished Europe. Her statesmen had long before been compelled to acknowledge, in the rapid growth and development of our country, the adaptation of our free institutions to the peaceful pursuits of life ; but they still urged that they were not suited to a state of war, and that the weakness of our system would be manifested whenever we should be called on to prosecute an aggressive war. They had no idea that soldiers could be procured from any other motive than that of pay; and it was only when it became manifest in this case, from the class of men who volunteered, that the great mass of them could not have been influenced by mercenary motives, that they found they had overlooked entirely important elements in our system, and that it was as well adapted to a state of war as of peace. The aptitude with which these troops acquired drill and attained discipline, and especially their prowess in battle, are still the wonder and admiration of the military critics of other nations.

This element of military strength is peculiarly American. It exists among no other people, and may be regarded as a never-failing resource in all emergencies.

The State of South Carolina, although remote from the theatre of war, although not disturbed by the restless spirit of adventure which forms so distinguishing a trait of character in the pioneer population of new states, yet was as thoroughly imbued with the military spirit of a free and gallant people. Desirous of emulating the chivalry of their sires, her sons demanded a place in the volunteer line for their own Palmetto Flag. They were accepted and received into the service of the United States some time in the fall of 1846, under the then act of Congress authorizing the President to call for twelve-months volunteers ; but shortly afterward the government changed its policy, and determined not to receive volunteers for a shorter time than during the war.

Influenced by patriotism, and by a high sense of state and personal honor, the regiment, officers and men, consented to the change of engagement, and in December were regularly mustered into the service for "during the war."

In the mean time they had passed through the very important process of organization and the selection of their officers. The result, so essential to the efficiency, the character, and the fame of the regiment, was the election of Pierce M. Butler, colonel ; J. P. Dickinson, lieutenant colonel ; and A. H. Gladden, major. It was the good fortune of South Carolina, and especially of the Palmetto Regiment, that at this interesting period the services of such a man as Colonel Pierce Butler were available. He possessed every qualification required for this important charge. Having held the high position of governor, and fulfilled its duties to the satisfaction of the people, his reputation was coextensive with the state ; with much military experience, both in the regular and volunteer service, he was known and distinguished for his gallant and chivalrous spirit, and the winning graces of his personal manners. Never have I known a commander appear to possess more of the confidence and affection of his men. Firm, and sometimes even stern, he yet seemed to control those under his command more by the fear of incurring the loss of his respect than that of punishment. He could have commanded such a regiment even without a commission. In the excellent selections of the other field-officers, the regiment evinced their high appreciation of that first essential quality of an officer as well as soldier, that of unblenching courage. To the accomplishments of a gentleman, Lieutenant Colonel Dickinson added a daring, dashing gallantry, which called from his superiors more frequently for restraint than encouragement.

Major Gladden, upon whom the command of the regiment devolved after the battle of Churubusco, had not only the opportunity of proving his coolness and courage in battle, but also his capacity and fitness for command. He received from his noble regiment the highest credentials they could confer on him by electing him to fill the high place which had been made vacant by the fall of their talented and beloved colonel.

I have alluded briefly to the personal character of the field-officers. The limits of this address will not permit me to particularize farther. My object is to present the general character of the corps. That purpose will be better attained by grouping together the company, officers, non-commissioned officers, and men, as a distinctive corps, possessing a common history, a common fame, and an undivided glory.

It was one of the most remarkable features of the Mexican war, which I hope will ever constitute a fixed trait of our volunteer system, that the general personal material of this force was of high grade. It was not uncommon to meet in the rank and file men who had been classically educated, professional men, tradesmen of respectable standing, and even men of independent property or comfortable expectations; in fact, you found there men holding in society at home a rank equal to that of the officers who commanded them.

What but motives similar to those that prompted the soldier of republican Greece or Rome to rally round his country's standard and perform prodigies of valor could have stimulated such men to subject themselves voluntarily to the deprivations, discomforts, and toils of war, and to the perils and dangers of the battle-field!

Whatever may have been the motives, whether a patriotic desire to serve their country, the love of glory, or the ambition of personal distinction, they indicate an elementary material from which invincible armies are constituted. I would not be understood as claiming this superiority for all volunteer corps alike; I speak of it as a general trait. Such, at least, was the personal character of the Palmetto Regiment. It was a fair representation of the people of the gallant state from which it sprung.

I have presented this fine corps, officered, organized, and mustered into service. I will not, in this narrative, accompany it in its departure from the state, its marches by land, or its voyages by sea. I will meet it at Vera Cruz, amid the roar of artillery, on an enemy's shore. But I may be permitted to indulge in some reflections, which naturally arise upon contemplating the position of that regiment, about to be sent forth as the military representative of a proud state, jealous of her honor and her fame. The departing soldiers could, no doubt, read in the countenances of their countrymen and country-women the farewell of the Spartan mother to her son, when she delivered to him his shield, and said, "Return with this or on it."

With the state pride for which South Carolina has been distinguished, I doubt whether there could have been found a man or a woman who would not have preferred, had the melancholy alternative been presented, that every man of that corps should perish on the field of battle, than that it should return in full health, but stained with dishonor and disgrace! To that corps, the remnant of whom now stand before you as your chosen champions, you had intrusted the military reputation and honor of your state. Both were staked on their good conduct. You had intrusted to them your most valuable jewels. Had they failed, at any and every sacrifice, to maintain the honor and reputation of the state; had they shrunk from their duty in the deadly conflicts they had to encounter, the disgrace would also have fallen upon you. Years would not have wiped away the blot left upon the fair escutcheon of your commonwealth. The Romans, when they gazed upon the desperate conflict of the Horatii with the champions of the Samnites, could scarcely have felt a deeper interest than did you in watching the progress and conduct of your regiment in Mexico. Before the close of the memorable year 1847 your anxieties had all terminated. Your gallant volunteers had not only signally maintained the honor and reputation of the state, but had laid on the altar of her renown fresh and brilliant wreaths of fame.

While the regiment was awaiting orders in South Carolina I was at Monterey, commanding a field brigade of selected volunteers. In December, 1846, after the battle of Monterey, I was detailed by General Taylor, at the head of five volunteer regiments and a battery of light artillery, to advance upon Victoria, the capital of Tamaulipas, and take possession of the city, and of the passes of the mountains in its vicinity. Shortly after this duty had been performed, I received orders to join the forces then assembling at Tampico under General Scott for the purpose of invading Mexico through Vera Cruz. My first application, after reporting to the commander-in-chief at Tampico, was a request to assign the South Carolina regiment, then at the island of Lobos, to my brigade, and in reply had the very great satisfaction to learn from the general that Col. Butler had requested him to assign his regiment to my brigade, unless it could be attached to the regular brigade under General Worth. He remarked that he would not resist this concurrence of wishes, and accordingly the South Carolina, the Georgia, and Alabama regiments, were constituted into a brigade under my command. With the two latter regiments I sailed from Tampico, and arrived at Anton Lizardo in time, on the morning of the 9th of March, 1847, to take part in that splendid and successful military-nautical movement of the debarkation of General Scott's army of invasion at Vera Cruz. It was a skillfully-planned, highly-imposing, and entirely successful movement. The point selected for the descent was the beach west of the city, just without the range of the heavy guns of the Castle of San

Juan de Ulloa. In less than an hour after the debarkation commenced, ten thousand men, armed and ready for action, stood upon the beach.

It was here, during this exciting scene, that I observed an officer of noble mien and martial bearing approaching me, surrounded by a group of officers who seemed to be worthy followers of such a chieftain. He reported himself as Col. Butler, commanding the South Carolina regiment, ready to receive any orders I might convey to him. This was my first personal acquaintance with one for whose character, both as a soldier and a man, I soon acquired the highest respect and esteem.

The siege, bombardment, and final capture of the city of Vera Cruz and the strong fortress of San Juan de Ulloa, although not generally so regarded in popular estimation, perhaps from the trifling loss sustained by us, was, in my judgment, one of the most brilliant achievements of Gen. Scott's remarkable campaign. In establishing the lines of investment, my brigade was a part of the time very actively employed in skirmishing. At one time, the South Carolina and Georgia regiments being in advance, a serious attempt was made by a large body of Mexican cavalry and infantry, under cover of a heavy cannonade from the works of the city, to drive us back from the sand-hills which we occupied. A deep ravine, which commenced near to our position, and penetrated within the position occupied by the enemy, seemed to furnish a better route for assailing them than by a charge in front. Four companies—two from the Georgia regiment and two from South Carolina—were therefore detailed, under command of Lieut. Col. Dickinson, to attack the enemy by this route. The movement was successful, and the enemy soon retired. It was in these operations that Lieut. Col. Dickinson was seriously wounded, being, I believe, the first American wounded at the siege. He was certainly the officer highest in rank whose blood was shed on that memorable event.

It may be worthy of remark that, during the siege, the loss in killed and wounded of my brigade, though few, was greater than that of the whole balance of the army.

The siege of Vera Cruz afforded me an opportunity to become more familiar with the character of the new regiment which had fallen under my command. Immediately after we had landed a violent "norther" had interrupted our communication with the shipping, and we were thus, for some time, without the means of transportation; this was but of slight inconvenience to the troops posted on the flank of our line, and thus near the sea, but was a heavy burden on those more centrally situated. My brigade, though stationed immediately in rear of the city, and nearest to its walls, was between three and four miles from the point at which our commissary and other stores were landed. Until transportation could be gradually procured, all provisions, supplies, cooking utensils, etc., were packed on the backs of men, and carried that distance, over a rough path, over steep sand-hills and under a burning sun. This kind of toil and labor is felt most severely by the soldier, because such casualties are not anticipated; yet it was submitted to with patience, and no murmur reached my ear from the brave Palmetto Regiment.

When the "heroic city" had surrendered to the American arms, I was directed by General Scott to concert with Commodore Perry a joint naval and land expedition against the city of Alvarado and neighboring towns, the principal objects of which were to dismantle the fortifications which commanded the entrance into the harbor, and to open the country which lies adjacent to the Alvarado River for a supply of mules. The land-force was overwhelming, intentionally so constituted, to prevent resistance, and before it reached within eight miles of the city, the latter had surrendered to a small schooner of Commodore Perry's squadron. The objects of the expedition were thus attained without bloodshed; but the march for sixty miles along the sea-coast and back, under a tropical sun, and through the deep sands, with none but brackish, unhealthy water to slake our thirst, produced much disease in the regiments constituting the brigade, and especially in the South Carolina regiment, which had never before, since its arrival in Mexico, performed a full day's march.

When the Alvarado expedition was planned, it was not believed that Santa Anna would be enabled to rally his forces in sufficient strength to oppose the advance of our army at any point between Vera Cruz and Jalapa; and as our means of transportation were very slender, it was hoped that an abundant supply of mules could be procured from the valley of the Alvarado River, where they were reported to be abundant and cheap. The news, however, that Santa Anna was fortifying a position at Cerro Gordo induced General Scott to advance Twiggs's division, and afterward Patterson's, in that direction, Worth's being detained at Vera Cruz until further transportation could be procured.

When the Southern brigade returned to Vera Cruz, it was with the greatest difficulty that a few wagons could be added to our already light train; but such was the ardent desire of officers and men to move forward to the scene of the expected battle, that they proposed to carry forty rounds of ammunition and three days of provisions per man on the march. I have gone into these details to correct a common error, which existed even in my command, that the detail of the Southern brigade for the Alvarado expedition was an unfriendly act, intended to deprive them of participation in the battle of Cerro Gordo. On the contrary, the designation of a corps for separate and distinct active service is a compliment to them as well as to their commander. I know that in this case there were competitors for this service.

Pursuing the purpose before indicated, I shall not attempt even a hasty sketch of this glorious campaign, but confine myself to such events as are connected with, or illustrate the character of the Palmetto Regiment.

The last corps has now left the sea-shore, to take its place in that gallant army whose deeds and achievements form the wonder of history.

The battle of Cerro Gordo has been fought and won. The enemy have been beaten and dispersed. Those frowning fastnesses no longer obstruct the quiet movements of our troops into the interior.

While the army was encamped at Jalapa, an important modification of its elements took place, some of which affected the position of the Palmetto Regiment. In consequence of the near approach of the expiration of the term of service of the twelve-months volunteers, seven regiments in all, the general-in-chief determined then to order them home, under the command of Major General Patterson. Gen. Pillow also, being wounded, returned to the United States on leave. Gen. Shields being severely wounded and not on duty, I was left as the only general officer in command of the remaining volunteer regiments, consisting of the South Carolina, New York, and First and Second Pennsylvania Regiments.

Of these, the First Pennsylvania Regiment was detained in garrison at Perote and Puebla, and never crossed the mountain rim which surrounds the valley of Mexico, and, of course, did not take part in the last bloody battles of the valley. Thus the Palmetto Regiment constituted, in the great battles of the valley of Mexico, one of only three regiments of a distinct army corps, and that one numerically the weakest of the three.

While the army lay encamped at Jalapa, General Worth, with his division, about 2000 strong, was thrown forward to Perote, of which he took quiet possession. Soon afterward I received orders to join him with my brigade, then consisting of but three regiments—South Carolina, New York, and First Pennsylvania, the Second Pennsylvania having been detailed as the garrison of Jalapa. Although the superior in lineal rank of Gen. Worth, yet, as this might be regarded as " detached service," in which his senior brevet rank would prevail, I cheerfully submitted to his command, and, re-enforced by Wall's light battery, marched to Perote, and there, as directed by General Scott, was obliged still farther to reduce my command by leaving in garrison Col. Wynkoop's regiment of First Pennsylvania Volunteers. While on this march, ascending the snow-capped mountains of Perote, we encamped late in the evening in the open spaces of a small, wretched village. The evening was cold and frosty, and the men, generally, thinly clad. The quarter-master was ordered promptly to procure a supply of fuel. He had just reported to me that he had purchased it, cut and ready for use, when a Mexican, under great excitement, rushed into my quarters complaining that the soldiers were tearing down and burning the materials of his garden fence. Having directed a staff-officer to ascertain who were the trespassers, he soon reported to me that they were of the South Carolina regiment, but acting with the consent of one of their officers. Upon my message, Colonel Butler promptly proceeded to investigate the matter, and in less than ten minutes returned with the injured Mexican, his countenance now robed in smiles, acknowledging that he had received ample satisfaction for his damage.

Before we separated at Perote Gen. Worth and myself had a full conference on the subject of our march. His orders were to advance and occupy the city of Puebla, a city of about 80,000 inhabitants, in the most populous portion of Mexico, and ninety miles in advance of our main army. His division consisted of little more than two thousand men, and my command of about fourteen hundred, encumbered with a very heavy supply train. Regarding it as a bold movement on the part of the commander-in-chief, we determined to advance with every precaution. Accordingly, it was arranged that the several columns should move within supporting distance of one another; that there should be communication between us every day; that the two commands should form a junction at the village of Amozoque, eight miles from the city of Puebla, and there arrange the movement into the city in conjunction. It was distinctly understood that Amozoque was to be the point of junction, and that Gen. Worth would halt there until my command could come up. In the mean time, while on the march from Perote, I had received a commission as major general in the army of the United States, and of course ranked Gen. Worth; but, as the claim to command might occasion confusion at the interesting moment when the expedition was about to be brought to its conclusion, I did not urge it, especially as my intercourse with General Worth had been of the most satisfactory and agreeable character.

On the night of the 13th of May, my command encamped near the defile of El Pinal, where the road before us wound through the mountain by deep gorges, rendered more passable by artificial excavations. Anxious to surmount this dangerous pass at an early hour, reveille was ordered at three o'clock in the morning, and by the alacrity of the officers and the energy of our very efficient quarter-master, Capt. Samuel M'Gowan, whose services both in the line of his duty and as a staff-officer in action have not received the official notice they merited.

The troops, as well as the immense train of wagons, were put in motion from front to rear at the sound of the bugle. All had passed into the open plain, and had approached within three miles of Amozoque, the point of junction with General Worth. The morning was bright and lovely. On our right the plain gently ascended to the foot of the snow-capped Malinche, about four miles distant. Reports from the rear brought the information that the train was coming up in compact order, when suddenly a heavy gun was heard from the direction of Amozoque, and in a few moments the rapid discharges of Duncan's battery were heard, leaving no doubt that Worth's division was engaged with the enemy.

In the mean time orders had been sent back to bring up the train at full gallop; a suitable place was selected for the line of battle, and all precautions taken against surprise, when several dragoons, with foaming horses, brought Gen. Worth's message to me that a large force of the enemy, four or five thousand strong, were attempting to pass his position, as he supposed, with a view of attacking my command, assuring me that he would move up to our assistance as soon as possible. The position occupied by our line of battle, although hastily chosen, was a strong one. In front was a shallow ditch, fringed by a low straggling hedge, which, though constituting really no effective defense, yet presented an obstacle to the compact charge of cavalry, which Mexicans are not apt to break through, especially when they see behind it the unflinching eye of the American soldier. About the centre of the line was a slight elevation of the plateau from which our artillery could sweep the whole plain in front.

In a few minutes could be discovered in the distance the glitter of burnished steel, and soon on our left, moving toward our front, could be distinctly seen in the bright sun, and through the crystal medium

II.—Q*

of a Mexican atmosphere, squadron upon squadron of the enemy's lancers galloping toward our front.

Arrived within about a thousand yards of our line, they wheeled gracefully into line, while Santa Anna, who commanded in person, accompanied by his staff, advanced to the front to reconnoitre our position. I seized the opportunity of the pause to address the volunteer regiments a few words of caution, to direct them how to receive the expected charge. Confidence and determination marked every countenance, and when my remarks were concluded, three deafening cheers of defiance were wafted over the plain to the ears of the hesitating enemy.

Whether the strong position occupied by the volunteers or their defiant shouts produced the effect, it is impossible to say; but as soon as the reconnoitring party could resume their positions, their long line was again thrown into column, and they galloped toward the mountains, but not without suffering some loss from the canister of our artillery. These troops, as we afterward learned, were a body of cavalry about 3000 strong, commanded by Santa Anna in person. The object was no doubt to attack the detachment while encumbered in the narrow passage of Pinal; if possible, defeat it while at disadvantage —at least to cut off the large and valuable train of supplies by which it was accompanied. Had they found us in the defiles of Pinal, the plan might have succeeded of cutting off a large portion of our train, but a very early and prompt movement found us many miles in advance of the obstacles, and within supporting distance of Gen. Worth's column.

I have presented this incident more in detail than I intended, not because it is associated with the glory and reputation of the Palmetto Regiment, but because it has been almost wholly overlooked by the imperfect histories of the Mexican war, and sometimes misconstrued. I shall hereafter pass over all details which are not essential to present the character of your regiment, or to vindicate its reputation.

The junction with General Worth was effected, and the following day exhibited a remarkable scene : a corps of less than 4000 men ninety miles in advance of the main army, entering a hostile city containing within itself a population of 80,000 souls, surrounded by a populous country still occupied by numerous bodies of troops. When this small army corps marched into the main plaza, and stood there resting on their arms, surrounded by the dense crowd of scowling Mexicans, they seemed to be dwindled down in numbers to scarce a full regiment; yet they stood there, proud and confident, like superiors among inferiors—the Caucasian ruler and the hybrid subject. It was not until these detachments had peacefully occupied Puebla for more than a month that General Scott arrived with the remainder of the army.

The Palmetto Regiment, while in Puebla, was quartered in a spacious convent, where their good conduct secured even the respect of the Mexicans. Indeed, Col. Butler seemed to possess the confidence and respect of the priests. In my frequent calls on him, I, upon more than one occasion, found some of the more intelligent of them at his quarters, appearing to enjoy his society and conversation. Shortly after orders had been published to regulate the march of the army upon the capital of Mexico, I met at Col. Butler's board an intelligent priest, of very dignified appearance. It was in July, and in the midst of the rainy season. "Well," said he, "I learn that you are about to advance upon Mexico." I replied that we should move next week. "Then," said he, "the rains will be suspended." Upon being asked the reason of his prediction, he remarked, "Heaven has favored you from the beginning of the war, and Providence will continue her special interposition until you shall have fulfilled your mission of taking possession of the capital city."

During our stay at Puebla disease committed sad havoc in the army, and especially in the Palmetto Regiment. This tendency to sickness was no doubt increased by the thin and light clothing of the men. No state, as I was informed, had provided more amply for the clothing of her soldiers than had South Carolina; but, unfortunately, none of these supplies came to hand. They were lost by some accident on land or sea before they reached the regiment. This failure to obtain suitable clothing was a matter of deep concern to Col. Butler, and he ceased not his constant exertions to supply it until most of his men were furnished with such portions of dress as they most needed from the spare stores of the regular army.

Before the army left Puebla, Brigadier General Shields, who had just recovered from the dangerous wound received by him at Cerro Gordo, reported to me for duty. The South Carolina and New York regiments were constituted into a brigade under his immediate orders.

The volunteer division under my command was then formed of the South Carolina, New York, and Second Pennsylvania regiments, the marine battalion, and Steptoe's light battery. It commenced its march from Puebla on the 8th day of August, accompanied by Huger's train of heavy ordnance, General Twiggs's division preceding one day, and General Pillow's and Worth's commands following at intervals of one day's march respectively.

When, at an early hour of the morning, we reached the summit of the mountain rim that girdles the broad and extensive valley of Mexico, we were wrapped in a cloudy canopy through which the eye could not penetrate. As we began to descend the noble causeway which Spanish skill and labor had constructed, and had reached a point nearly half way down the long descent, suddenly and majestically the curtain of clouds rose, and there, beneath our feet, stretching off into the distance, burst upon our eager vision the wide and beautiful valley of Mexico. There it lay, with its silver lakes, its white villages, and highly-cultivated fields. In the distance, partly concealed by a conical hill, could be distinctly seen the battlements and spires of Mexico, the ultimate goal of our ambition and our hopes.

The atmosphere of these elevated plains is so pure and so transparent that it is difficult to measure distances with the eye. Now and then the sight would be arrested by the peculiar glitter of arms which marks the movement of bodies of armed men in the distance. Battalions of lancers were seen moving in different directions on the plain. Near the foot of the mountain, at a short distance in the plain, lay the first division of the invading army, and on the mountain slope was now descending a long column of the invaders. No wonder that excitement and commotion prevailed among the inhabitants of the valley!

I can not leave the scene which I have described without relating an incident which still remains vivid in my memory. The column was halted, the field-officers were invited to the front to partake with me of a morning lunch. Fourteen officers were seated on the grass-plot which skirted the road-side, enjoying their rude fare, and conversing with high hopes and bright anticipations about the stirring events in which they were soon to embark, when a serious voice from the company uttered the suggestion, "How many of us, gentlemen, will ever recross this mountain?" No answer was given; but what was then the future has now become the past. I am now enabled to make the response. Of the fourteen general and field officers present on that occasion, seven never left the valley living, and three others were so severely wounded as to be disabled from service to the end of the war. Your own gallant volunteers that were there resting on their arms scarcely suffered less proportionate loss.

We have now reached the eve of great military events. An American army of scarce 10,000 men, without an adequate siege-train, without any prospect of re-enforcements, and depending principally for their supplies upon the resources of a hostile country, had cut loose from their base of operations, abandoned all attempts to keep open a line of communication with the sea-ports, had now penetrated into the heart of the enemy's country, and were hovering about his capital, the approaches to which were protected by 500 guns, and defended by an army of forty thousand men. The boldness of this movement has no parallel in the history of modern warfare. It exhibits the bold genius and the self-confident and daring character of the great captain who designed it, and carried it out to a successful consummation. It was, however, a stake attended with some hazard. A failure to obtain possession of the city of Mexico would, in my opinion, have been fatal to the whole army. A single serious reverse, even, might have been followed by the most disastrous consequences. Notwithstanding that we were successful in every action, our loss in the five great battles of the valley was not short of 3000 men. When the American army descended into the valley, it mustered about 9000 effective fighting men. I doubt whether, the day after the city of Mexico was taken, we could have mustered 6000. One third of the number had fallen or been disabled in the severe conflicts of the valley.

In all these battles except that of Molino del Rey, your own regiment took a prominent part, and I but echo the universal sentiment of the army when I repeat that it covered itself with unfading laurels. There are historical monuments of its high claims to distinction which can never be disputed. The comparative losses sustained by different corps in the same action are at least a criterion of their exposure in the action at Churubusco: the loss of the South Carolina regiment was one hundred and thirty-seven, exceeding by more than thirty the loss of any other regiment engaged in the battle. At the battle of Chapultepec and the city their loss was more than one hundred exceeding that of any other corps engaged; and when at last the bloody causeway had been passed, and the head of the column, composed of the Rifles and the Palmettos, charged upon the formidable Gate of Belen, a scene was presented well described by the poet in the following lines:

> "The smoke has cover'd all things
>   In its darkest battle-shroud,
> Save where you living line of fire
>   Lights up the murky cloud.
> And there our gallant fellows
>   Are raging in the strife
> Before that stern and dangerous gate,
>   Whose toll is human life:
> They are chafing like the billows
>   Upon a midnight shore,
> With a tempest driving on behind,
>   And a wall of rock before!"

Before the smoke had ceased to curl over the heads of the brave victors, the Palmetto flag—the flag of your gallant regiment—was seen floating over the conquered walls—the first American flag within the city of Mexico. These facts alone furnish pages for comment. They stand as lasting monuments, which the future historian can not pass without pausing to meditate on, to admire and record. They entitle you to add to the palm which graces your banner the motto "*palmam ferat qui meruit!*"

I will not weaken the impression which this *coup d'œil* of facts must produce by detailing the prominent part taken by the Carolina regiment in the brilliant victories which conquered an empire. I can not, however, pass by some incidents which belong to the private history of the corps. I had been, prior to the battle of Contreras, much to my regret, placed in command of the reserve, including the dépôt of the whole army, and, notwithstanding my repeated applications to be allowed to take the field with the two regiments of my division ordered out, the privilege was sternly refused by Gen. Scott on pretense of the importance of my duties in command of the reserve, but really, as I believe, because my rank would have conflicted with his views as regarded other officers. I, however, on my own responsibility, detailed Brig. Gen. Shields to the command of the two regiments that were ordered out. On the afternoon of the 19th of August, while our troops were cannonading the position of Gen. Valencia at Contreras, it became known in my quarters that orders had been transmitted to me to designate two regiments of my division for the field, when Col. Butler, who for several days had been confined to his room by indisposition, was suddenly ushered into my quarters in full military costume, and expressed the most anxious desire that his regiment might be one of those detailed for the field. Upon my suggesting the objection that, with his indisposition, the exposure might be attended with the most serious consequences to his health, he replied, that, were I to overlook his regiment for that reason, he should ever be an unhappy man. At length, yielding to his entreaties, I designated the South Carolina and New York regiments, under Gen. Shields, with orders to move at once to the field of action. From that moment his manner was changed. He was cheerful, active, and full of energy.

In a short time the detail, ready to march, was formed in line on the public square. In taking leave of the officers and men, I still bear in mind the warm pressure with which my noble friend returned my grasp, with the remark, "Whatever may happen, we will maintain our honor." I never saw him afterward until "in his shroud the hero we buried." He fell the next day at the head of his regiment on the bloody but victorious field of Churubusco, where also the high-toned and brave Lieut. Col. Dickinson, who had assumed the command, shortly afterward received a severe wound, the effects of which also proved mortal.

The other field-officer, Major Gladden, though ever in the thickest of the fight, escaped unhurt. Of the conduct of the officers and men, Gen. Shields, in his official report to me, speaks as follows : "I selected the Palmetto Regiment as the base of my line, and this gallant regiment moved forward firmly and rapidly under a fire of musketry as terrible, perhaps, as any which soldiers ever faced."

The Castle of Chapultepec, after having withstood our bombardment for the whole of the 12th of September, 1847, was carried by storm on the morning of the 13th.

The South Carolina regiment, then under the command of Major Gladden, was, at the signal of the assault, ordered to advance by a low meadow to the foot of the hill, scale the first line of wall, and charge up the steep ascent. This was executed with steadiness under a severe fire of grape and musketry from the enemy. The wall was passed; and the regiment, led by their brave and cool commander, with bayonets fixed, and with the steady tread of veterans, charged up the steep ascent without firing a gun.

I had ordered the regiments of my division, so soon as the fortress of Chapultepec was carried, to assemble on the aqueduct, there to be organized into a column of attack on the city of Mexico. As an instance of the discipline and promptness, as well as bravery of the then commanding officer of the regiment and of his command, his was the first of the regiments engaged in the assault upon the fortress that was reported to me as ready for the new movement.

It was selected, with the gallant Rifle regiment, under immediate command of Major Loring, to head the column of attack upon the city by the Garita or Gate of Belen.

The description of this last bold and crowning exploit of the American arms in Mexico belongs to history: a full narrative would require more time and space than has already been devoted to this address; I shall, therefore, merely allude to an incident which occurred at the taking of the Gate. Anxious to give notice to the other divisions of the army that we were within the walls of the imperial city, I called for "colors," and soon Major Gladden rushed up and presented the Palmetto flag, which he had taken from the standard-bearer and brought up for that purpose. Lieut. Sellick, of your regiment, then also acting on my staff as ordnance officer, was detailed to plant it over the arch of the huge portal, a duty which, with the assistance of other officers, he performed, but not without receiving a severe wound. This occurred in the presence of more than five hundred witnesses, and leaves no doubt of the fact that the flag of the Palmetto Regiment is entitled to the honor of being the first American banner victoriously unfurled within the walls of the city of Mexico. For the purpose of dislodging bodies of Mexicans posted behind some low sand-bag batteries on the Paseo, and to be prepared to seize upon any favorable occasion which might arise to carry the citadel, Major Gladden was ordered to advance with his regiment fourteen arches, or about seventy yards within the Garita. In occupying this position he also was severely wounded and disabled. Thus, in the moment of victory, when the city was won, the regiment lost the services of its last field-officer, and thenceforth, to the end of its active services, it remained under command of Capt. Dunovant, its senior captain.

During the afternoon of the 13th, the enemy, finding that we had exhausted all our heavy ammunition, made several sallies from the citadel and adjacent parts of the city, with the purpose of driving us from the Gate by their superior numbers. Failing, however, in these efforts, and despairing of his ability longer to keep possession of the city, Santa Anna concluded, during the night, to evacuate the city. At the first dawn of day on the morning of the 14th, information reached us of this unexpected movement. I immediately put my command in motion. Leaving the South Carolina regiment in garrison at the Garita, and the Pennsylvania regiment at the citadel, I marched with the remaining troops into the Grand Plaza, and took possession of the National Palace. The first rays of the morning sun of that day that fell upon that proud seat of power were reflected back from the stars and stripes waving in triumph over its highest pinnacle.

At 8 o'clock the commander-in-chief, with his staff and escort, entered the Great Plaza, and was received with all appropriate honors by my command.

Our glorious task was now finished. Mexico was prostrate at our feet, ready to receive such terms as our country should dictate. Whether we acted wisely in giving back the conquered country to a race incapable of self-government may be regarded as very doubtful.

But this is not a proper occasion for political speculation, and my time admonishes me to bring this long address to a conclusion.

South Carolinians! You sent your noble band of champions to represent the chivalry of your state in the war with Mexico. They have not only maintained its reputation, but added fresh laurels to the fame of the state, and won for themselves a position among the bravest of the brave! The remnant of that brave band now stands before you. Permit their old commander, on leaving them his parting blessing, also to commend them to the fostering care and protection of the great state which they have served so well.

J.

QUITMAN AND CUBA.

Since this work has gone to press, a number of documents have fallen into my hands which I am compelled to insert here, with but little comment. As far back as 1823 the people of Cuba had contemplated their liberation from the iron rule of Spain. In that year they sent a secret committee to confer with Bolivar. That illustrious man was then in Peru, combating the royal forces; but General Santander, President *ad interim* of Colombia, warmly espoused the scheme. In 1826 Mexico and Colombia were organizing a joint expedition for the liberation of Cuba, but finally abandoned it, mainly in consequence of the policy announced by the United States at the Congress of Panama. In 1828 the assistance of Mexico was again invited, and an extensive combination, known as the "Black Eagle," was formed; but, before its plans matured, it was discovered and suppressed by the Spanish authorities. In 1836, the Cuban patriots, with the co-operation of a Spanish Liberalist, General Lorenzo, proclaimed the Spanish Constitution at St. Jago de Cuba, but were summarily crushed by Tacon, the captain general. In 1847 General Lopez made an effort at revolution, but his plans were discovered, and he was compelled to fly to the United States.

The Spanish authorities, becoming alarmed by these demonstrations, augmented their military and marine force, and distinctly threatened to proclaim the freedom of the blacks if these attempts were repeated. The captain general issued a circular to the several heads of departments in the island and other functionaries, inviting their opinion as to the best mode of introducing African and other free labor, in view of the probable abolition of slavery. He declared that the royal authorities had definitely determined on the introduction of the African apprenticeship in Cuba as a counter-revolutionary idea, and to harmonize with the policy of Great Britain and France; that Gen. Pezuela had been appointed to supreme authority in Cuba, specially with reference to this policy, and that Lord Clarendon, then the organ of the British ministry, had expressly stated in Parliament that his government would give its hearty co-operation and support. Even under these menacing influences, the patriots of Cuba continued their efforts, and at the peril of life maintained an active correspondence with Gen. Lopez, and other refugees in the United States.

In the winter of 1850 one of the most distinguished of these gentlemen waited on Gov. Quitman, and presented him the following communication in writing:

"Jackson, Miss., Dec. 13th, 1850.

"His Excellency J. A. Quitman: Sir,—As I have had the honor verbally to say to you, I have come to Mississippi to place in your hands a request, the contents of which are now in your possession. My object being especially to impress you with the high character of the source whence this message came, I felt a painful delicacy lest prejudices, which I was told had been excited against me in your mind, should be calculated to injure my present purpose. You have been pleased to deny having ever heard any thing of the kind, and to reassure me on the subject with a frankness that could not be mistaken, and in a manner flattering to myself, and certainly beyond my deserts.

"Don —— —— and myself have received the documents referred to above from two gentlemen of great influence, and known for their honorable character. One of them is very wealthy himself, and a member of one of the most wealthy and extensive families in the island, with whom he is on the most intimate terms. The other is an enterprising capitalist, a thorough business man, connected also with wealthy families, and he it is who assured me that one or two hundred countrymen could be rallied by him in the immediate vicinity of his estate. Such decision from men of his standing I had not heard of before. He mentioned several facts which I have repeated to you, showing the present excitement—the country people becoming more and more emboldened, and that the Cuban cockades had been sent to many Spaniards through the post-office, and one to the captain general. At the same time he added that it was his belief that Lopez, unprotected, would be fought against even by those who would advocate the cause under better guidance. He did not hesitate to say that the old Spaniards were irritated, and that an uncomfortable feeling, scarcely to be endured, existed between them and the Creoles—a state of things which required action of some kind or other. He stated that all confidence in Lopez was lost. Both these gentlemen are now probably in Havana, and none are better calculated to establish there a proper organization.

"If I understand rightly the nature of the proposal now tendered you, its chief object is to tie into one single action Southern interest and Cuban annexation; to create an intelligent American centre of action for the purpose of examining the subject, adopting a course, commanding and executing: a secret Southern committee for the annexation of Cuba I would venture to suggest as the first step, without attempting to resolve now all the complicated questions of necessity to be considered in this glorious undertaking.

"You have mentioned the present agitation on the slavery question, which you consider in a rising rather than a receding tide; and truly, if it is so, the opinion which Mr. Calhoun gave me, to wait for its final decision, might well deserve a serious consideration, like every thing emanating from that great man. But if an extraordinary excitement prevails in Cuba, it may not be in our power to calm the unsettled horizon of that island. However, could not the cause of Cuba be made the rallying banner of the South, and the honorable adjustment of the disquieting difficulties of the whole island? Were the extreme Southern men, possessing influence like yourself, to stretch forth a friendly hand to all the Southern Unionists on the *guaranteed condition* of striking together one great and bold blow for Cuban annexation, positive force and probable advantages would result to the South, instead of an indefinite and prolonged anxiety in a movement which has never had constant advocates. And once united in a common and popular cause, the union of the Southern States among themselves *would never be broken;* and commanding their unbounded respect in the North by the attitude assumed, and by the great object undertaken of liberating Cuba, concessions would be made before an exhibition of power which would forever be refused to the suppliant confederate, and the Union be preserved—that Union which has a charm for every American heart, in spite of injustice and humiliation. The accomplishment of a scheme so patriotic would be worthy of the gallant hand that unfurled the American flag on the capitol of Anahuac; and if, as I had occasion to observe to you yesterday, that was a proud day in your life, you may rest assured that, while saving the rights and honor of the South in the path herein proposed, the acclamations of twenty millions and upward of Americans would hail, and their children bless you as the preserver of the noblest structure of human freedom in existence, which, while perpetually threatening the monarchs of Europe, expands with hope the heart of the oppressed millions around them.

"The certainty among the influential men of Cuba of being under the guidance of a Southern association would awaken every energy of their soul, and those embarking in the enterprise could then feel that in risking their lives, which they have a right to do, they do not risk the success of their cause, which they have no right to expose.

"The noble ambition of your congenial and frank nature is certainly inspiring; but if I am enthusiastic in developing these views, I feel confident, bold as they may appear, that they will stand the test of a cold and close examination, and will prove to be safe and calculated for ultimate success."

From the same source the following letter was received:

"New York, February 24th, 1850.

"Gov. J. A. Quitman: Dear Sir,—When, some months ago, I obtained the inclosed introduction to you, I was informed that the election of governor then pending would preclude your acceptance of the proposition I contemplated. The embarrassments which we have experienced in the object of annexing Cuba by an expedition, and the certainty that they would disappear were you to aid us, the farther acquaintance with ennobling traits of your character, and the prospects of a speedy settlement of the slavery question, have now determined us to try our luck by boldly making our propositions.

"We are assured by a banker of high respectability and wealth, Mr. —— —— (I mention his name in strict confidence), that with your acceptance of the command-in-chief of an expedition which you would then organize, the loan could be secretly raised for one of four thousand men at least, to carry to the island of Cuba republican institutions, with a view to her annexation to the United States. My conversation with many other parties has led me to the conclusion that no less than one million could be raised at once, with your name privately given to one or two men of high character, on whose judgment others would rely. As the representative of the Havana Club, chiefly consisting of planters, I can assure you that, *with you*, the movement would be headed by respectable gentlemen of the island. I can add that among the lower classes there is also a very strong feeling in favor of the movement, which should be directed and controlled by the upper classes, so as to secure the blessings of annexation without the dangers of insurrection. I believe that any delay not warranted by the proper preparatory steps would be injurious, and perhaps place the enterprise in the hands of those not fully impressed with its requisites in a slave country.

"In boldly stretching your hand to aid Cuba in her struggle for liberty, you would manifest that happy appreciation of future events which marks a superior mind; petty considerations, or the fear of disapproval from your country's government, should not stand in the way of an act much easier to accomplish than is generally believed, and which will, perhaps, be in its mighty consequences the greatest of

.the age. The Senate and the press of the United States, who are the true representatives of your country's will, are too well known as friendly to this movement not to reconcile to it the most scrupulous patriotism. The practicability of starting the expedition from the South you are certainly too well acquainted with. .

"Gen. Lopez, who is now in the United States, and whose impetuous anxiety to go to Cuba may occasion the neglect of all the elements of success and order which we desire, would certainly join were he to know that such a person as you headed the expedition. In this union you would again have it in your power to serve Southern conservative interest, which I hold as dear as Cuban annexation.

"By liberal offers, to fall on the future resources of the island, the staff and officers of the several departments, which would be carried complete, could be made to consist of men of science and character from the American army.

"With decided encouragement from you, I would either send or go myself to meet you. It would be almost unnecessary to say that Cuba would lavish on you her wealth, as well as the honor and gratitude due to the achievement. You are too well aware of the influence—the unbounded political influence which, through the whole American Union, will be the reward of this act, which is destined to be a bond of union from the universal advantages it gives all the states.

"I hope, my dear sir, that I may find in you the enthusiastic support which becomes a high-minded military chief of your chivalrous disposition, and that it may be my duty at no distant day to hail you on the soil of my native isle as the liberator of my country, and the noble supporter of Southern institutions there."

Subsequently, as heretofore related in Chapter XV., Gen. Lopez and his aid, Gen. Gonzalez, visited the seat of government of Mississippi, and, after an interview with Gov. Quitman, submitted the following proposition :

"This shall attest, that we, General Narciso Lopez, chief of a meditated expedition for the assertion and establishment of Cuban independence, and Ambrosio José Gonzalez, member of the 'Patriotic Junta' organized in the United States of North America for promotion of the same object, do, on our own account and responsibility, and on behalf of our coadjutors in the United States, and of the people of Cuba in whose behalf all our proceedings are instituted, propose to the Hon. John A. Quitman, now Governor of the State of Mississippi, and late major general in the army of the United States operating in Mexico, to join and co-operate with us and all the good people of Cuba in their meditated struggle against the tyranny of Spain ; and as inducement for a frank and fraternal co-operation with us Cubans in that behalf, and to insure to us, by the consideration of his popular and highly distinguished military character, and his well-tried experience in civil and political council, the active sympathies and confidence of his countrymen, to whom, in this behalf, we also appeal as brethren for their cordial assistance, we do specially and distinctly propose that, upon engaging personally in such service, the said General John A. Quitman shall be invested with the office and powers of general-in-chief of the organization, movement, and operations of all the military and naval force which shall or may be employed in behalf of the contemplated revolution, and in behalf of which organization and movement I, the said General Lopez, who, in conjunction with other patriotic Cubans, have instigated said revolution, do cheerfully consent and propose to act as second in military command to the said General John A. Quitman.

"And we, the said General Lopez and the said A. J. Gonzalez, for ourselves and on behalf of the patriots of Cuba, and in the cause of Cuban independence, do promise to the said General Quitman the united and fraternal support of the people of Cuba in sustaining the authority of the said General Quitman with all respectful and prompt subordination to his military command.

"We also engage for the people of Cuba that the said General J. A. Quitman shall be liberally compensated in financial provision for his personal services, and that all officers and soldiers who shall join his standard from the United States or elsewhere shall also be liberally and fairly remunerated for their military services at rates and upon terms to be approved by the said General John A. Quitman.

"That in consummating these ends and objects we pledge, on our part, zeal, devotion, and fidelity, and submit in confidence to the well-established honor and integrity of the said General Quitman that he will so discharge the high and delicate trusts of his great commission as to maintain good-will and harmony among the various departments and interests subject to his command, and in such manner as shall best achieve the prosperity and glory of the common cause.

"To give better assurance to these propositions, it is intended that General Lopez shall repair to Cuba with all dispatch, and at once raise the standard of Cuban independence, and will, from the field of revolution, furnish General Quitman sufficient evidence that the people of Cuba approve these suggestions, and will welcome his presence to aid their cause as herein indicated.

"It is believed by General Lopez that General Quitman will concede that he, General Lopez, with the approval of the Cubans, shall be the recognized head of the civil administration, and that so much of civil authority as may be safely confided to the civilian during the conflict of arms about to be waged is reserved from this proposition, and is to be exercised and put in operation as emergencies and the most judicious policy of the parties interested may from time to time suggest and approve, having ever in view the ultimate triumph and establishment of free democratic republican government, and ultimate annexation to the great confederation of the United States of the North.

"If these propositions are favorably responded to by General Quitman, General Lopez, in proceeding to open the campaign, will point his proclamations and course of action with reference to such anticipated juncture, and will hope with greatest confidence, from such united action, for the glory and freedom of his country.

"Jackson, Miss., March 17th, 1850.

(Signed),

"NARCISO LOPEZ,
"AMBROSIO JOSÉ GONZALEZ.

"To Governor J. A. Quitman.

"ADDENDA.

"All the means and expenses for fitting out military expeditions, and furnishing supplies and munitions of war from the United States or elsewhere, shall be provided for by Cuba, and General Quitman will in no case be expected to incur personal responsibilities involving his private fortune. NARCISO LOPEZ,
AMBROSIO JOSÉ GONZALEZ."

Quitman's Reply.

"Jackson, March 18th, 1850.

"GENTLEMEN,—I received with profound gratitude the manifestation of your great confidence in my character and abilities contained in the proposals which you did me the honor to submit to me on yesterday.

"My devotion to the cause of civil liberty, and to the extension of the glorious republican principles of our government to the adjoining states of America, powerfully urge me to accept your proposals.

"Were I entirely free to act upon the impulses of my own inclinations, convinced as I am that civil liberty and human happiness would be promoted by the successful termination of your patriotic enterprise, I would at once embark in it, on one condition only : that the people of Cuba, by their own free act, should first erect the standard of independence. I am now, however, bound by official engagements to the people of my own state, which do not leave me at this time at liberty to contract obligations inconsistent with my assumed duties. It is possible, however, that, after a short period, these obligations, which my sense of duty now imposes on me, will cease to exist.

"In that event, should circumstances be favorable, I should be disposed to accept your proposals. Leaving myself, however, free to decline your propositions under any contingencies which might make it advisable in my estimation so to do, I can not ask that you should remain even conditionally committed to your propositions. On the contrary, I recognize your entire right in the mean time to adopt any measures you may deem proper for the promotion of your great enterprise, without reference to the proposals you have tendered to me.

"Under whatever circumstances they may be prosecuted, confident that your motives are purely patriotic, I hope that success may crown your efforts in behalf of your oppressed country.

"General Narciso Lopez, chief, etc., etc.
"Senr. Ambrosio José Gonzales, member, etc."

The Cuban Junta to Governor Quitman.

"New York, November 20, 1850.

"The freedom of Cuba and her annexation to the United States with the least possible effusion of blood have been resolved upon by several patriots and property-holders of Cuba now residing here. Having one common interest with the Southern States, we ask their protection and aid as the only effective means of accomplishing the object proposed ; and trusting to the great resources of those Southern States, and to the ability of their eminent men as statesmen and soldiers, we desire to form an organization that shall place the means of

VOL. II.—R

the patriots of Cuba and the complete direction of the revolution in the able hands alluded to above.

"General Quitman deserves fully our confidence; we address him in the first place, requesting him to adopt and patronize the cause of our freedom, taking on himself to be the centre and head of this great and generous movement, which commands the sympathies of half the American Union. Let him organize by himself, or through other persons deserving his confidence, what he may believe calculated to realize our object, either starting a secret and peaceful negotiation with the members of the Spanish administration in Cuba or Spain, or a respectable military expedition which should insure success and protect the country against anarchy, or, if it so strikes him, a combination of both measures, in order that they may aid and support one another; and, accepting the trust, let him say to us what action, what aid, what resources of a pecuniary nature are required from the Cuban patriots.

"If General Quitman should not be able or not desire to take for himself the prominent and glorious part to which we invite him, he will, we hope, in due regard to our unbounded confidence, deign to point out the person or persons he may consider better apt and disposed to take charge of the direction which we tender to him, and, in any.case, favor with his powerful influence the holy cause of the freedom and annexation of Cuba.

"As the interests of Cuba and those of the Union require that the former be liberated and annexed without being ruined, we request all true-hearted men, and especially General Quitman, to exercise their utmost influence to prevent that from the United States expeditions be started premature, insufficient, and badly organized or conducted, which, in their result, if not in the intention of those supporting such, may be more favorable to emancipation of the blacks than to the freedom of the whites.

"Lastly, the Cuban patriots who now address General Quitman engage to follow punctually his instructions in whatever he may think fit to ordain in order to realize the object of their ardent wishes herein expressed, and they farther engage to use all their energies and influence with their friends in Cuba to insure their efficient co-operation, which engagement they are ready to subscribe with their names, should it be judged necessary."

In the mean time, the disastrous expeditions of Gen. Lopez occurred, and the negotiations with Quitman were not resumed until 1853.

The Cuban Junta to Gen. Quitman.

"Natchez, April 29th, 1853.

"GENERAL JOHN A. QUITMAN: DEAR SIR,—The undersigned individuals, composing the Cuban Junta of New York, have the honor to address you for the purpose of exciting the noble sympathies of your heart in favor of the freedom of Cuba, which is our country.

"The tyranny which the Spanish government exercises in the island is a fact recognized by the whole civilized world, and the American people may say that it is a witness thereof. The Cubans have made efforts, though fruitless, on several occasions, to throw off the yoke that oppresses them.   Lately the revolutionary spirit has become general, and it would burst forth in a revolution if the military power were not an invincible obstacle to its manifestation.   The pronunciamentos which have taken place at Puerto Principe and Trinidad ; the liberating expeditions undertaken and directed by our unfortunate chief, Gen. Lopez ; the conspiracies subsequently discovered ; the printed documents which have circulated ; the blood that has flowed upon the scaffold, and the imprisonment and sentence of persons for political offenses ; and, no less than the repressive measures adopted by the Spanish government, are strong proofs of the general desire that animates the Cubans to substitute for the colonial government an independent, free, and just one.

"In this situation, the people of the island would have risen *en masse* to tear down the despotism if it were not impossible to do so under their anomalous circumstances.   Completely disarmed, without leaders to guide them, for the government has long since closed the military profession to the Cubans ; without the possibility of meeting together in any way, unless the government is present ; waylaid and watched even to the domestic hearth ; untrained and inexpert in revolutionary enterprises, they have not been able to concert or to carry out any great movement, nor to attain success in those which, up to the present time, they have undertaken.

"But Cuban freedom should not, for this reason, perish, the victim of Spanish despotism.   What may not be possible in Cuba becomes so on this classic soil of American independence, abundant in resources for the protection of the cause of liberty.   Therefore the clubs of the island, in connection with the Cuban exiles resident in this country, deliberated upon, and determined to form among them a public junta that should represent the interests of our revolution, with the purpose of uniting all the elements to initiate and carry it out upon the island, without bringing the federal government into any conflict in its international relations.   The junta was formed on the 19th of October last, and since then, the clubs and individuals that named its members, and all the towns, have addressed it, not only for the purpose of remitting funds to it, but also to open communications to concert and to mature the plans for the revolution.

"It has been one of the first duties committed to the junta that it should put in the hands of some experienced general of known probity the mission of liberating our country, and that general was yourself in first instance, marked by the public voice of all the Cubans within and without the island.   Your sympathy in our cause, your sufferings for it, the gifts which adorn you as an American general, and all the antecedents in your public life, have inspired the sons of Cuba with the unlimited confidence they have in you, the greatest proof of which is the sacred deposit which they come to place in your hands.   The time has arrived, and the junta deems itself competently authorized to approach you, in the name of the people of Cuba, with the declared object of supplicating that you be pleased to accept the nomination, which it now tenders you, of exclusive chief of our revolution, not only in its military, but also in its civil sense, until such time during the revolutionary epoch, or immediately after it shall have terminated, as in your judgment it shall be proper or possible to constitute the island a sovereign and independent nation, and as such, form such a government as shall best fulfill its wishes. From the moment you condescend to accept the call we make to you, the direction of affairs, the command-in-chief, the disposition of all the resources, of whatever kind, for our revolution, as well as the Cuban Junta itself, all shall remain subject to your orders.

"The afflicting situation of our country, the offers which are made to us, and the circumstances which surround us, move us to supplicate of you the most immediate decision. On the moment that you shall be pleased to honor us with a favorable answer, we are ready to make good our offers, and to enter upon covenants for our reciprocal security, and to establish such detailed stipulations as both parties may deem convenient.

"The liberty of an oppressed people, the immense gratitude which it will owe to you, the glory which awaits you, and the world, which is about to fix its eyes upon you, are motives that will excite your most generous sentiments to accept, and we hope you will accept this mission which we come to offer you.

"Your most attentive faithful servants, who kiss your hands."

Quitman's Reply.

"Monmouth, near Natchez, April 30th, 1853.

"GENTLEMEN,—I have the honor to acknowledge the receipt of your communication of yesterday. Profoundly impressed with the very great responsibilities which I should assume in becoming the chief of the revolutionary movement in Cuba, and distrustful of my abilities, in the great emergencies of the future, to realize the high expectations which you appear to entertain from my union with your sacred and patriotic cause, I still assure you that if the details can be placed upon such footing as to insure success, and not to compromit my own character and reputation, I shall feel myself called on by the great principles of action which have ever governed my conduct, by my hatred of despotism, by a high sense of duty to an oppressed people, and by my firm convictions that the prosperity of my own country would be promoted by the extension of civil liberty to Cuba, to engage in the glorious cause. I have not now time to specify fully the antecedents to my taking the high position to which you invite me, but from the result of our personal interview I believe you understand them. I hastily recapitulate some of them, asking liberty, at a period of more leisure, to explain them more fully.

"1st. A union in the enterprise of all the leading patriotic Cubans in this country who may be the representatives of portions of the people of Cuba.

"2d. The delegation of sufficient powers to the chief.

"3d. The providing of adequate means for the enterprise by the junta and their associates, under whose name and by whose authority the enterprise should be prepared.

"Upon the satisfactory arrangement of these antecedents, and the continued expression of confidence in me by the people of Cuba, I will assume the distinguished but very responsible position to which they, through you, have called me."

*Articles entered into between the Cuban Junta and General Quitman, and
signed by them respectively.*

"The Cuban Junta, established in the United States for the purpose of promoting and securing the independence of Cuba, hereby· transfers and delegates in the most ample manner, without any restriction or limitation, to General John Anthony Quitman, all the powers, rights and privileges which it exercises in the name and behalf of the people of Cuba, and in their name and authority invest the said General Quitman, as civil and military chief of the revolution, with all the powers and attributes of dictatorship as recognized by civilized nations, to be used and exercised by him for the purpose of overthrowing the Spanish government in the island of Cuba and its dependencies, and substituting in the place thereof a free and independent government, as may hereafter be selected by the people of Cuba by delegates freely·chosen. For these purposes he is to assume and have the absolute control and disposal of all the funds and means of every description now in the hands of the revolutionary party, as well as those which may hereafter be received. To have power and authority to direct the public treasury, to contract loans, issue bonds, or other evidences of debt, grant commissions, raise military or naval forces, purchase and charter vessels, establish the compensation of all persons engaged in civil and military service—in fine, to exercise all civil and military functions necessary and proper to effect the great ends in view, although they may not be herein expressly specified.

"*Second.* The aforesaid Cuban Junta, in behalf of themselves, their constituency, and the patriotic people of Cuba, solemnly pledge obedience and support to all the lawful commands of the said General Quitman, and with their lives and their fortunes will sustain and defend all the acts of the said General Quitman having in view the great result of overthrowing the Spanish power in Cuba, and establishing therein a free and liberal government which shall retain and preserve the domestic institutions of the country.

"*Third.* To obviate the dangers or disorder which might arise from want of a head in case of accident to the chief, the said General Quitman shall have power to name in his discretion a second and third in command, who shall alternately succeed in the powers herein conferred should he die or otherwise be unable to exercise them; which second and third may be deposed and others substituted in their places in his discretion while he exercises the command; and he shall also have power to fix the compensation they shall severally receive as such second and third.

"*Fourth.* In view of the powers herein delegated and the means surrendered to said General Quitman, it is confidently expected that he proceed to the exercise of these powers for the purposes intended at as early a time as is possible and practicable for the acquisition of the independence of Cuba.

"*Fifth.* It is distinctly understood that the extraordinary civil and military powers delegated in these articles to said General Quitman shall cease and expire so soon as a free and liberal government shall be established in Cuba, in the territory acquired by the revolutionary forces, *to wit:* The civil powers shall cease so soon as in his judgment the representatives of the free people of Cuba can be convoked and organized into a government; but the military powers shall not cease until the war of independence shall be ended with the final extinction or expulsion of the Spanish forces from the island, and until all imminent danger to the new government shall have disappeared.

"*Sixth.* For the purpose of preserving the necessary secrecy in regard to these arrangements, and to operate with more.effect, the said Cuban Junta will remain nominally organized, as it now is, but will be entirely and wholly subject to the direction and orders of said General Quitman, engaging to conform to them in all things, and to perform no material acts without his consent and approbation; and it will receive from him, from time to time, full instructions in regard to its duties.

"*Seventh.* If any unexpected event should occur to prevent said General John A. Quitman from fully assuming in his own hands the powers herein conferred, and from embarking in the contemplated enterprise, the aforesaid Cuban Junta will be reinvested with, and will so assume, the powers which they have herein delegated, in the same manner as if they had never been given.

"The above articles are now signed conditionally in duplicate, with the understanding that when the said General Quitman shall signify his readiness to assume the high powers and duties of chief of the revolution, these articles are to constitute the basis of his acceptance thereof.

"New York, August 18th, 1853."

Voluntary Proposition of the Cuban Junta to manifest their value of Quitman's influence to their cause. *

"The Cuban Junta in the United States, having made proposals to Gen. John Anthony Quitman to assume and control the direction of the Cuban revolution as the chief thereof, for themselves, and in behalf of their constituents and of the people of Cuba, hereby engage and promise that, if the island of Cuba shall become free and independent by the aid of his exertions as chief, for his services and sacrifices he shall be entitled to receive from the free government of the island, besides regular pay, the compensation of one million of dollars; or, if he shall fall in the struggle, the same shall be paid to his family.

"New York, August 18th, 1853."

He was now actively engaged in the great but complex and difficult work of collecting funds, recruiting and planning the expedition so as not to come in collision with the authorities of the United States. Such an enterprise required time, deliberation, and concert; but the Junta, operated on by constant appeals from Cuba, became impatient, and interfered with the powers they had confided to him. On the 16th of April he addressed them from New Orleans as follows:

* Gen. Quitman communicated this in confidence to the writer at the time, and declared that he never meant to accept any compensation above his actual expenses; but, if successful, and the Cuban authorities voted him the above sum, he would appropriate it to the establishment of a great military and naval college in or near Havana. He said that Cuba, once free from the Spanish yoke, ought either to ask annexation to the United States, or to establish a formidable navy for self-protection.

" New Orleans, April 16th, 1854.

"GENTLEMEN,—In reply to your esteemed note of yesterday, I state with pleasure, as an additional explanation of my last note, that I regard 3000 men as the minimum number required for a successful enterprise. It is my opinion, under present circumstances, that a smaller number would not inspire confidence, and would render the enterprise hazardous.

"I considered the statement in my note, that my acceptance was founded upon the existence of a fund of at least $220,000, as superseding all the conditions heretofore stipulated which were inconsistent with it, and, of course, that the condition requiring you to place in my hands all the means heretofore deemed necessary as abrogated.

" Nor have I any objections to say to you that I have at no time deemed more than one moderately-armed steamer, and sufficient transportation otherwise, essential. I have not expected that it would be in our power to procure transportation of the very first class. In this, economy as well as safety should be consulted. Of this, however, I must be the judge under professional advice.

"In relation to the time when the proposed assistance can be presented to the patriots of Cuba, as it is dependent upon contingencies which no human foresight can anticipate, I am unwilling to give any farther assurance than that all my energies shall be devoted to its consummation at as early a period as may be practicable.

." I have thus met all the questions contained in your note except that which refers to the changes in the character of the enterprise which may arise out of certain contingencies enumerated in your letter.

"Appreciating fully the motives which, at the moment of surrendering so important a charge, induces you to provide, as far as practicable, against future contingencies, I have given to this subject my most mature reflection, and, without time to present the operations of my own mind, I have come to the conclusion that to make any pledges in regard to the specific course of action I should pursue, in case of the occurrence of events which may asume every variety of phase and character, would not only be inoperative, but would most seriously trammel and embarrass my action, to the great detriment of the cause. Instead, therefore, of anticipating the intricate combinations of fortuitous events, I will content myself with giving you the general assurance that in all emergencies I will use my best judgment and skill to apply the powers conferred on me, and the means at my control, to promote the great cause of Cuban independence consistently with the Cuban honor.

"Believing you will, upon reflection, see that I can not, consistently with my character, take a different course, I remain," etc. etc.

I have no wish to pursue this matter into the field of controversy, or to assail the motives or the conduct of any of the parties concerned. There are many reasons why it is wise and humane to make no farther revelations. Precipitate measures originating in New York, without the consent or knowledge of General Quitman, provoked the interference of our government, and undoubtedly caused the failure of the great plan for the liberation of Cuba. Mortified and indignant at this interference with his well-digested plans, he dissolved his connection with the matter as follows:

"New Orleans, 30th April, 1855.

"Be it known to all whom it may concern, that I do hereby relinquish and surrender to the Cuban Junta, established in the United States for the promotion of Cuban independence, all the powers, rights, and faculties which were by them conferred on me by their contracts and agreements, made with me in New York on the 18th of August, 1853, and afterward ratified and concluded by the agreement made in Natchez in the month of May, 1854, reserving only such powers and rights as may be necessary to effect final settlement of any funds, effects, and claims which still remain in the hands of myself or my agents. All other effects and resources not now under my control are hereby relinquished to said junta, but without recourse on me.

"Witness my hand and seal, this day and year above written,

"J. A. QUITMAN [SEAL].

"J. S. Thrasher."

He never ceased, however, to feel the deepest interest for the Cubans, and to give his sympathy and confidence to those patriot members of the junta who knew the wisdom of his plans and the sincerity of his motives. His object in moving the repeal of the neutrality laws in Congress was mainly with reference to the liberation of Cuba, which, unaided, can never accomplish her independence. The configuration of the island, several hundred miles long, with an average width of only forty-five miles, enables the government, with its steam marine, to concentrate on short notice, into any insurgent district, an overwhelming force; while the scattered and unarmed population, the rigid espionage and severe police, prevent concert on the part of the Cubans.

In concluding this notice of Cuba and the Cubans, it is impossible to suppress the admiration which must be entertained for the fidelity with which her exiled sons (with very few exceptions) adhere to her desperate fortunes. Nor can I omit to refer to the many evidences contained in the papers of General Quitman of the zeal, ability, perils, and sacrifices exerted and endured for her by a noble-hearted American, J. S. Thrasher, Esq., formerly of the New Orleans Picayune, now of the New York press. A more distinguished instance of fearless and persevering efforts for an oppressed people may not be found in the annals of any country.

THE END.